Praise for

RAEPHEL

"In this third volume, Mary Elizabeth Ames has again told a compelling science-fiction story of romance, adventure, conflict, and the challenges of beginning new life and dying in a world altered by gamma radiation. Woven throughout this story is the science of genetics, the ideal of community cooperation and compassion, the search for ethics and justice, and the drive to understand newly altered life-forms that can transform into other species. The work is recommended for any one in middle school or above who is drawn to science fiction."

—Catharine A Kopac PhD, DMin, GNP-BC
Adjunct Associate Professor, George Washington University, Consultant and Ethicist

"I really enjoyed reading the book. The various adventures were so interesting and page-turning."

—Tacey Battley

Raephela

by Mary Elizabeth Ames

ISBN 978-1-64663-499-6

Cover design by Skyler Kratofil.

Published by

köehlerbooks™

3705 Shore Drive
Virginia Beach, VA 23455
800–435–4811
www.koehlerbooks.com

RAEPHELA

Mary Elizabeth Ames

VIRGINIA BEACH
CAPE CHARLES

TABLE OF CONTENTS

In Memoriam
Nancy Todd Renfro, MEd
1941–2020
Distinguished Educator

~~

Dr. George Crossman, PhD
1926–2020
Distinguished Historian and Scholar

PREFACE

The novel *Homo Transformans: The Origin and Nature of the Species* describes a new species of human whose members can transform into other species of animals—provided they have the genes to do so. The (imaginary) power of some humans to undergo metamorphosis is predicated on the science of genetics. The author blends genetics into the storyline to illustrate how genes work, how they are inherited, and how they interact. The novels *H'Ilgraith* and *Raephela* continue the saga while updating and introducing additional gene functions and features of genetic engineering. Supplemental notes augment the scientific information for those readers who want to delve deeper into the science.

The author has attempted to make the content regarding the genetics of *Homo sapiens* (*H. sapiens*) scientifically accurate as of the time *Raephela* was written. The reader is encouraged to consult the National Institutes of Health Genetics Home Reference website (https://ghr.nlm.nih.gov) for more information about genetics.

PROLOGUE

Approximately 750 years ago, life on Earth was shattered by a gamma ray burst when an unstable blue star exploded into a supernova. People barely had time to seek shelter deep underground, taking with them the animals, plants, and technology they could muster. When they finally resurfaced, human technology had been shocked back into the fifteenth century.

Metamorphosis

In the interim, some people developed the ability to undergo metamorphosis, reliably and at will, into another species of animal— primarily, mammals. These people were designated a separate species of human, *Homo transformans* (*H. transformans*). The ability of some people to transform wrought havoc upon human society. The Cassius Foundation, an especially malevolent organization, misused genetic engineering to modify further the genome of *H. transformans* and other species to create powerful human and animal hybrids. It subsequently used these hybrids to subjugate any society the foundation could reach.

People who could flee from the Cassius Foundation's persecution did so. They settled in new territories remote from the foundation, establishing three interrelated communities. The House of H'Aleth was the first, followed by the House of Erwina, and later the House of Gregor. Although at peace, the three sister houses remained alert for signs of the foundation or any other aggressor encroaching upon them. Eventually, rumors of communities that succored *H. transformans* spread, and the Cassius Foundation discovered H'Aleth.

A Battle Plan Gone Awry

None of the three sister houses had ever raised an army. They relied instead on the skill and expertise of their scouts to patrol and defend their respective territories. Rafe Cassius, then head of the Cassius Foundation, attacked H'Aleth, destroying the village and estate that had housed H'Aleth's government and research center. Subsequently, Rafe decided to conquer the House of Erwina and confiscate all of its resources—especially its population of *H. transformans*. Alerted, Erwina's scouts gathered quickly to create an armed force to slow the enemy's advance, a delaying action to give their people time to disappear into remote territory. When Rafe led the foundation's army to invade Erwina, it encountered resistance from a small force of defenders. Unbeknownst to the two combatants, the Biogenics Corporation—the foundation's chief rival—had sent its army to wait surreptitiously in the wings.

Rafe conscripted nonviolent, crippled hybrid humanoids to be his first wave in the battle with Erwina's forces. He had culled them from his villages to serve as cannon fodder. They would distract Erwina's defenders while his main force waited. Once the defenders were engaged, Rafe would launch his second wave of animal hybrids and trained fighters to crush his enemy's meager forces.

To Rafe's dismay, H'Ester, then mistress of the House of H'Aleth in exile, was on the battlefield. She realized that the initial attackers were hapless humanoids from Cassius villages and were compelled to attack. They were no match for Erwina's skilled scouts. So she called to Erwina's forces to hold their fire. Then she called to the humanoids to drop their weapons and come to her. The majority of the humanoids, desperate to escape the fight, did so and were saved from being slaughtered.

When Rafe saw his first wave dissolve and flee from the battlefield, he became enraged. He issued all of his remaining forces to crush Erwina's defenders. The tide of battle turned when a great gray dragon took command of the field (illustration 1). Dragon fire killed Rafe and the remaining animal hybrids, while the rest of the foundation's forces fled in disarray.

Illustration1: Great Grey Dragon

Neither Biogenics's nor Erwina's forces pursued Cassius's fleeing army. Upon the dragon's arrival, Biogenics quickly retreated from the battlefield to return to its own territory. Its commander had no desire whatsoever to engage with a great gray dragon. Thus, there was no pursuit of the enemy's forces and no attack on the foundation's fortress. Given future events, one could argue that this was an oversight (map 1).

Map 1: Territories

Part I
A Watchful Peace

Illustration 2: Cercopithursids

Illustration 3: Serojabovids

CHAPTER 1
A New Settlement

With the defeat of the Cassius Foundation, the restoration of H'Aleth began—starting with building an outpost to watch for resurgence of the foundation. H'Ester invited the hybrid humanoids who had fled from Cassius to stay in H'Aleth territory. They were not of an inherently violent disposition and were among the first inhabitants of the outpost. They included cercopithursids (illustration 2), who had baboon and bear characteristics, and serojabovids (illustration 3, with boar and bison features, among others (appendix A). Both had been laborers for the Cassius Foundation. Over time, the outpost succored many other genetically engineered hybrid humanoids of the foundation's creation. In return, the humanoids set watch on the border between H'Aleth territory and Cassius territory.

As one of the first actions toward restoring H'Aleth, scouts were reintroduced into the region. In turn, hybrid humanoids were introduced to the scouts. The former needed to recognize scouts as friends, both as humans and as their alternate species. The scouts taught the humanoids not to attack any wild animal and showed them how to find other sources of food. Once this hurdle was passed, a host of people from Erwina and Gregor descended upon the new outpost. These included geneticists, medical and veterinarian staff, and experts in animal husbandry. Their goal was threefold: tend to the bizarre disabilities of the many humanoids that settled there, reestablish renewable food sources, and teach the humanoids how to sustain these resources.

Initially, the fearsome visage of most hybrid humanoids gave many people pause. It took some time to become accustomed to their physical characteristics. Many of them lacked speech, so it took even longer to recognize that their vocalizations—often consisting of growls, grunts, and snarls—did not represent savagery. Some made no sounds at all. Still, all of them were *H. transformans*, genetically altered by the Cassius Foundation and ultimately trapped in a partial transformation that they could not reverse.

The conditions of the hybrid humanoids engendered a mix of anguish for their misfortune and a fierce desire to relieve as much of their suffering as possible. The medical staff from Erwina and Gregor set about treating the ones who settled in the outpost. They knew they could not restore the ability to transform, nor reverse physical characteristics. Staff could correct some of their physical deformities and ameliorate others. They also treated many of the illnesses and injuries that were present secondary to poor nutrition and abuse. In caring for the hybrid humanoids, the H'Aletheans and Erwinians realized something.

"Despite their appearance, they have retained most of their human characteristics," said Master Mikalov, the chief geneticist at Erwina.

"I agree," said Dr. Jozefa. "Those who suffered brain damage have lost some of their mental acuity, memory, ability to speak or comprehend speech, and other mental faculties. Nevertheless, they are still *H. transformans* and should be treated as such."

"Then we should no longer label them hybrid humanoids," H'Ester declared. "They are *H. transformans* who suffered a maltransformation."

"Clinically, we may need a way to distinguish them from others whose maltransformations were accidental and not coupled with genetic reengineering," suggested Master Mikalov.

"Not for long," remarked Dr. Jozefa. "Those who undergo an accidental maltransformation typically have a shortened lifespan. I suspect those altered by the Cassius Foundation will have an even shorter life due to bad genetic engineering and mistreatment."

"Then perhaps we should refer to them as altered *H. transformans*," H'Ester suggested. "In any case, we will cease referring to them as humanoids or hybrid humanoids. They are still people," she added emphatically.

Thus, the people of Erwina and Gregor made the lives of altered *H. transformans* more comfortable. Much new knowledge stemmed from these efforts and was incorporated into the curricula taught at Erwina and Gregor.

A New Home

It did not take long for some altered *H. transformans* to remember how they once lived. Yet many could not remember at all. Nevertheless, they soon recognized the significant improvement in their quality of life and had no wish to leave. The outpost became their new home, a haven for refugees from Cassius villages. Most of them had been used as laborers. With the aid of the H'Aletheans and Erwinians, those who were mentally and physically fit helped to build the outpost, including its shelters, gardens, and other amenities.

The combined efforts of H'Aletheans and Erwinians forged a strong bond with the altered *H. transformans*, even among those who no longer recognized who they once were. Although H'Alethean scouts were the first line of defense, many altered *H. transformans* were prepared to defend the outpost if necessary.

During this period, hundreds of animal hybrids were released by the Cassius Foundation (appendix B). Once freed, most of these solitary hybrids ranged throughout the territories. In captivity, they had become highly competitive for food and dominance. Having been starved most of their lives, they were eager to attack any potential food source, and as far as these hybrids were concerned, humans were just another prey species.

The Hunt

For animal hybrids such as a hungry lupuseroja (illustration 4), the outpost was a smorgasbord. As any predator would do, it crouched down in the grass and watched the herd, looking for the most vulnerable member. Ideally, its victim would be small enough for the lupuseroja to snatch and then quickly race away with its prize before the herd could react.

Illustration 4: Lupuseroja

Predators typically targeted an injured, disabled, or weak animal. The lupuseroja saw many lame members. They were much too large for the lupuseroja to carry or even drag away. A predator could get trampled in the attempt.

As the herd milled around, the lupuseroja spotted a smaller, slender individual squatting on the ground. One of the masons from Erwina, an *H. sapiens* man, was selecting dried grass stalks for use in making mortar. Compared to the other herd members, he appeared quite vulnerable—a perfect target.

To reach its prey, the hybrid had to traverse the herd. Slowly, stealthily, it crept closer, narrowing the distance between itself and its target.

At the expense of a shortened stride, the lupuseroja's short legs helped it hide in the grass. The herd seemed not to notice its approach. The altered *H. transformans* had lost most or all of the heightened senses that normally would have been available to them. So they were unaware that a predator was in their midst.

Suddenly, the lupuseroja streaked through the herd, launching its attack and alerting its members. The man spotted the lupuseroja lunging for him and jumped up in a desperate attempt to dodge the animal's attack. Suddenly, a serojabovid slammed into the attacker, grabbing it and pulling it to the ground.

The fight between the two adversaries was brutal yet brief. The serojabovid's tusks were not as formidable as those of the lupuseroja. The latter was better equipped to bite and gore its attacker. Fortunately, help was at hand. Several altered *H. transformans* weighed in on the contest, literally. Although they were too crippled to inflict much damage, they crowded around and on top of the two combatants in an attempt to break up the fight.

The lupuseroja quickly realized it would be crushed under a barrage of large clumsy bodies if it did not get free. It had already lost any chance of a meal. In the ensuing melee, the lupuseroja finally extricated itself and fled.

Although seriously wounded, the serojabovid recovered with treatment of his wounds. H'Aletheans and Erwinians alike hailed the serojabovid and his comrades as stalwart defenders. The outpost had become a village.

The Passing of Altered H. transformans

Dr. Jozefa had been correct in his assessment. During the early years of the outpost, most of the altered *H. transformans* that had found refuge there died within a few years. Their deformities extended to internal structures which had been distorted and misaligned by the foundation's genetic experiments. These changes dramatically shortened their lifespans, and most succumbed to organ failure. Once tissue and blood samples were taken, their bodies were cremated—as was done for all *H. transformans*—to keep their genes from being discovered and misused.

Over time, most of the violent animal hybrids that the Cassius Foundation had released were fought off and killed. Yet many remained alive by avoiding human contact.

CHAPTER 2
PREMONITIONS

Over the next few years, the House of H'Aleth was reestablished (appendix C, Restoration of H'Aleth). Many of the people of H'Aleth who had fled to Erwina and Gregor before its destruction returned to repopulate and rebuild their homeland. They reclaimed and resettled abandoned villages that had not been destroyed by war or fire and began tending fields of grasses embedded with grains that had continued to flourish. The H'Aletheans also expanded their territory into unoccupied land further west. New villages melded into the surrounding terrain. One of these became H'Aleth's new center of government and research. Wildlife habitats remained largely undisturbed, which added to the illusion that the area was still uninhabited by humans. Even after the defeat of the Cassius Foundation, people were careful to obscure the locations of their villages from anyone not of the three houses.

As mistress of the House of H'Aleth, H'Ester guided the restoration of H'Aleth as a sovereign territory. When she was a student at Erwina and known as Ruwena, H'Ester's studies included civics and governance. These courses, combined with the mentorship of Matron Trevora, served her well. Architecture and related studies, however, were not her strong suit. So she left the building of a new manor house and research facility in the capable hands of the master builders and architects of Erwina. Similarly, she turned over the care and treatment of the altered *H. transformans* to physicians and veterinarians from Gregor and Erwina.

On Patrol

During the initial resettlement of H'Aleth, both H'Ester and Evan, her husband, also served as scouts. They focused on the northwestern territory, H'Aleth's Caput Canis, which both of them knew well. Matron Kavarova had returned to H'Aleth to serve as its chief of security. Since she could not dissuade H'Ester or Evan from scouting, she tasked Warren, one of Erwina's most experienced scouts, to keep track of them.

"I want you to conduct surveillance in Caput Canis where H'Ester and Evan are also scouting," she told him.

"You want me to keep an eye on them," Warren stated. "That shouldn't be a problem."

Not so long ago, Warren had responded to H'Ester's desperate cries when Evan was severely wounded in a fight with a hybrid wolf. Warren had been a brown bear, Evan a gray wolf, and H'Ester a Cooper's hawk. Afterwards, Evan, H'Ester, and Warren became close friends and remained so. When Warren caught up with the couple in Caput Canis, the three of them decided to patrol the region together. This proved to be a wise decision.

Given the largely wooded and mountainous area the trio patrolled, H'Ester conducted aerial surveillance as a long-eared owl. Her exquisite vision allowed her to see other animals at long distances, even in the low light of a dense forest canopy. In mountainous areas, she would transform into a cougar, a powerful and agile predator. Evan patrolled the region as a gray mountain wolf, and Warren did so as a brown bear. Between the three of them, they could dispatch almost any animal hybrid they encountered—especially with an early warning from a sharp-eyed owl.

H'Ester, however, had to contend with any aerial predators alone. She kept a close eye on the canopy. Her mistress, H'Ilgraith, had warned her about the harpyacalgryph, an aerial hybrid raptor, and described the arboreal viperoperidactyl and moresistrurus—weaponized reptiles that hid within the canopy. Yet these hybrids were not the only arboreal predators.

Perilous Flight

As the trio moved through a forested area to the east of the River Lupus, a well-camouflaged and motionless creature watched their approach (illustration 5). It paid particular attention to the owl, which was in flight. Given the owl's trajectory, the bird would fly right past the tree where the creature lay in wait. A carefully timed attack would snare the unsuspecting bird.

Illustration 5: Hieractopera

Instead, the owl landed on a branch just to one side, well within striking distance—and well within the owl's visual field. The instant the creature launched itself, the bird saw its movement and flew out of its strike path, screeching a warning.

The creature could not follow. Neither could it stop its descent. It would have landed on the ground had it not been for a large, upright brown bear walking right into its glide path. The creature landed squarely on Warren's head, wrapped its wings around it, and began biting and tearing at it. Evan, as a wolf, could do nothing to help unless Warren came down on all fours. H'Ester abruptly turned and attacked the creature. Although she was much smaller, her beak and talons were still formidable. The creature had to release its grip on Warren to counter her attack. This was its undoing. When Warren shook the creature off, it fell to the ground. Seconds later, a gray mountain wolf ended its life. Warren escaped with only a few scratches and bite marks.

None of the three had ever seen such a creature, nor had they heard of one like it. The possibility of a new hybrid was concerning. It could be a sign that the Cassius Foundation was reemerging. The three scouts immediately sought out the nearest outpost, which was between the rivers Lupus and Panthera at the crown of the Capus Canis. Warren, still a brown bear, received treatment for the wounds to his scalp.

H'Ester and Evan transformed into human form, each donning one of the outpost's spare robes. H'Ester tasked a scout to take the creature's body directly to the schoolhouse at Erwina.

"They have the resources to perform an initial examination before sending it to Gregor," she said. "I will fly back to H'Aleth and notify Matron Kavarova of this new hybrid and describe it to her. Then she can send its description out to all the scouts and villagers." Turning to Evan and Warren, she said, "I will meet you back here in three days."

Evan had a different idea. "I'm going with you," he announced firmly. Although an owl could outfly a wolf in a direct line, dodging through the canopy would slow its speed. "I will pace you on the ground, and we will travel together." H'Ester knew better than to argue.

A Disturbing Sign

Erwina's analysis readily determined the physical composition of the creature. It was a mix of two different classes of animal—part raptor and part bat—and much larger than either species. It had the head and talons of an eagle, the body of a bat, and the wings of an eagle distorted by the fingers of a bat's wings. The bat-skin wings were covered with tufts of fur and feathers. The creature's body was too large and heavy to allow powered flight. Based on a description of the attack, it could barely glide.

Yelena, Gregor's chief geneticist, analyzed its genome and named the creature *Hieractopera* [*hī*-er-ac-*tŏp*-er-ah]. Her analysis led to even more questions.

H'Ester convened a meeting of her council with representatives from both Erwina and Gregor. She asked the members present, "Does this new hybrid herald a significant threat?"

"It could, given the right target," answered Matron Kavarova. "It could have killed an owl." She looked directly at H'Ester.

"This hybrid was genetically engineered using older techniques, so it may not be new," remarked Yelena. "It's possible that we simply have not seen it before."

"Then why is it still alive?" asked Edrew, H'Aleth's wildlife specialist.

"I've asked myself the same question," replied Yelena.

"Is it possible that the Cassius Foundation has not advanced any of its techniques?" asked Evan. "After all, it has kept itself isolated ever since its defeat."

"It's possible, but I wouldn't count on it," answered Yelena. "Their geneticists are just as savvy as we are. It could be a clone of a hybrid created long ago."

"Then why haven't we seen more of them?" asked Warren.

No one had an answer.

What are we missing? Yelena wondered. She was worried. *Was this creature released with all the others? If so, why have we not seen it before? Because of its habitat? Or is it a new product of the Cassius Foundation and a harbinger of its rise?*

A Turn of Events

Soon thereafter, H'Ester was obliged to assume more administrative— and maternal—activities. She became pregnant and gave birth to her first child, a daughter whom she named H'Ariel. H'Ariel was followed in due time by her brother, Edric, and her sister, H'Edwina. H'Ester and Evan had agreed to space their children three to four years apart. The years between pregnancies allowed both parents to focus on giving each offspring a good start before the next one arrived. Having children kept both parents within H'Aleth's borders—much to Matron Kavarova's relief.

H'Ester still traveled to the villages, and she took her children with her. This served multiple purposes. She would learn what the villagers needed, and the villagers and her children would become acquainted. Evan accompanied them as both scout and father. Both taught their children to recognize animal species and fruit-bearing plants native to an area. Evan also taught them how to look at the sun and the night sky to get their bearings. This knowledge was essential. It would be years before their children would come of age and be able to transform. Until then, they would not have the abilities an alternate species provided to avoid danger or escape from it. By the time each offspring was old enough to go to school at Erwina, they had the knowledge they needed to find their way home.

CHAPTER 3
A Wary Respite

The three houses had entered a period of cautious respite. During this time, they gradually and cautiously advanced their technology while keeping a low profile (appendix D). Such changes might bestir a monster—one they sensed would rise again. All maintained a close eye on their borders. Even Gregor kept watch on the mountain pass that led to its territory. Although its location in the far north had sheltered it from the foundation's advances so far, the pass offered a wide-open avenue during the summer season.

Meanwhile, several small settlements in the unincorporated open territories became permanent. Finally, the Biogenics Corporation, which had been and remained the foundation's archrival, entered into an alliance with the three houses.

For a while, the allies enjoyed a guarded peace undisturbed by direct threats from the Cassius Foundation. Yet they knew better than to be lulled into complacency. All members of the alliance cooperated in maintaining surveillance. They knew that the foundation had not been wholly defeated. Rather, it had withdrawn and become a secret society, preventing any knowledge of its activities. This was worrisome.

A Watchful Interlude

Those in governance and security remained alert to the possibility that the Cassius Foundation might try to reassert itself. They were concerned about what new creations the foundation might set against them someday, and remnants of the foundation's malevolence still roamed throughout the territories.

H'Aleth remained the first line of defense should the foundation resume hostilities. The majority of H'Aleth's scouts were lost during the defense of their house. Only those who escorted refugees fleeing to Erwina and Gregor survived; however, they were far too few to defend H'Aleth's restored territory—especially its borders. Fortunately, Master Titus, Erwina's chief of security, had accelerated the training of scouts in anticipation of Rafe Cassius's invasion of Erwina. He deployed many of these apprentice scouts to hone their skills with experienced scouts in H'Aleth, where they became seasoned scouts themselves.

Outposts were reinstated all across H'Aleth's borders (map 2). They provided apprentice scouts with opportunities to develop their expertise and skills in regions close to Cassius territory. Hidden foxholes were dispersed across areas where an invading force might try to advance, including the southeast coastline, in case another warship appeared.

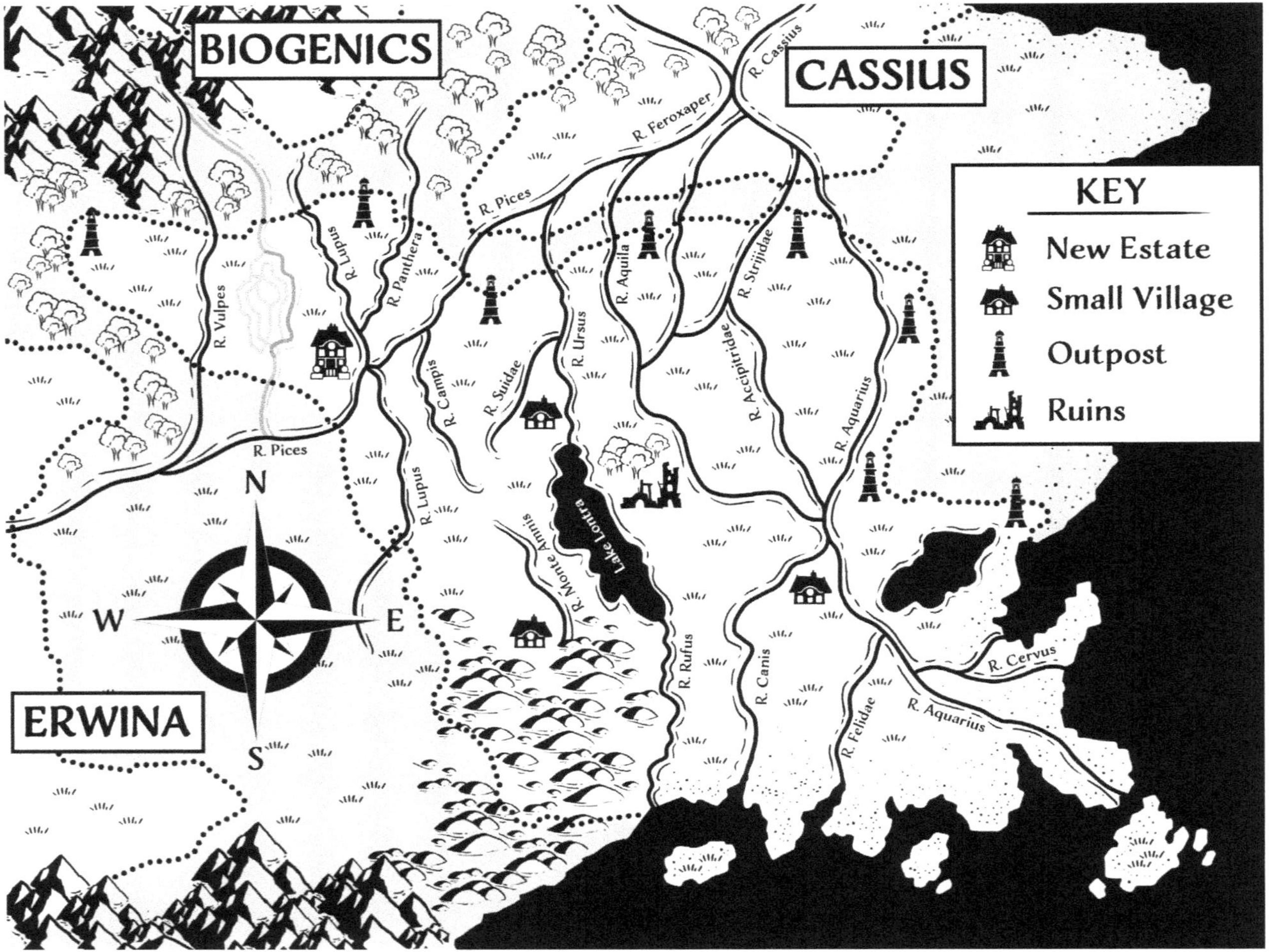

Map 2: H'Aleth's Borders

A Stark Reminder

Scouts stationed at these outposts could not whittle away their time. They had to remain alert to the sudden appearance of an intruder. Rafus Cassius had released most of the remaining hybrids to spread throughout the territories. H'Aleth took the brunt of the invasion. Except for aerial hybrids, most of the animal hybrids could not swim across the River Taurus to reach Biogenics territory directly.

Forced to rely on the heightened senses of their alternate species to detect hunters and hybrids, many scouts kept watch in these forms. Although this tactic provided a measure of advance warning, it also pitted them against animal hybrids genetically engineered with more weaponry. Battles were fierce, and lives were lost on both sides unless at least one scout remained in human form to serve as a skilled archer.

The ursuscro was the deadliest hybrid by far, followed by the cercopithursus. Both had the base genome of a male brown bear. The ursuscro was embellished with the genes of a boar, whereas the cercopithursus was augmented with the genes of a baboon. Both received the additional armaments associated with those species, along with the dispositions that accompanied them. The serojacuta, possessing the base genome of a hyena supplemented with the genes of a boar, ranked third. Although it was nowhere near as large as the ursuscro or cercopithursus, it was still a powerful animal with a bite force of 1,100 pounds per square inch. Early one morning, the serojacuta demonstrated all of its capabilities.

H'Aleth had established a remote outpost east of the River Strigidae, on the hump of the Canis Corpus. Here the borders of H'Aleth and Cassius were closest and not far from a Cassius village where a serojacuta had escaped. The hybrid traveled south and, detecting deer nearby, entered H'Aleth territory. Raised and used as a guard animal in a Cassius village, the serojacuta was not a creature of stealth. The buck was alerted. Instead of bolting away immediately, it watched the predator. When the serojacuta launched its attack, the race was on.

The deer sprang away, quickly reaching a speed of twenty miles per hour through the underbrush. Nevertheless, the serojacuta was outpacing its quarry, gaining on the deer, when they reached a tall earthen mound. The deer easily cleared it. The serojacuta had to scramble over it and lost ground as a result. Meanwhile, the deer called a succession of bleats to alert sensitive ears that it was in distress. Moments later, a gray wolf burst onto the scene to challenge the serojacuta. The ensuing fight between the enhanced hyena and the wolf was vicious and violent. The deer, also a scout, quickly turned and charged the serojacuta in an attempt to impale it (illustration 6, Predators and Prey).

The serojacuta's tusks gave it the advantage it needed. Before the deer could intervene, the wolf was overcome. Nevertheless, the deer attacked the hybrid, forcing it away from the wolf. Although the fight lasted only a few minutes, it was enough time for two scouts in human form to arrive. Their well-aimed arrows killed the serojacuta. Alas, it was too late for the wolf. A scout was lost that day.

A Puzzlement

Altered *H. transformans* had not been seen in decades; however, animal hybrids still persisted. This was puzzling. Both biologists and geneticists thought the animal hybrids would be as short lived. Apparently not. Still, most native wildlife and hybrid animals avoided human contact. There were exceptions, of course—particularly when an animal was driven by hunger.

Illustration 7: Cercopithursus

Late one evening, a cercopithursus (illustration 7) was hunting for prey in the forest when it spotted a ram grazing on grasses beyond a village, close to the forest's edge. As the hybrid approached stealthily, downwind of the ram, a *Homo sapiens* woman came into view. She had come to lead the ram back to its enclosure for the night. Lacking enhanced senses, she too was unaware of the danger.

Illustration 6: Predators and Prey

Intent upon both the ram and the woman, the cercopithursus failed to notice a large male boar creeping up to intercept it. The situation changed abruptly when the woman walked between the hybrid and its intended target. The cercopithursus immediately switched targets and launched an attack on the woman, a closer and more vulnerable prey species. The boar charged.

To all appearances, a 400-pound boar had no chance of overpowering an 800-pound bear-baboon mix. Yet the elements of surprise, formidable tusks almost a foot long, and a ramming speed of over twenty-five miles per hour gave the boar the advantage it needed. The boar slammed into the cercopithursus, its tusks goring the hybrid's flank. The crippled hybrid could not continue its attack or pivot to engage the boar.

The woman's screams aroused everyone in the village. It took hardly a moment for skilled scouts to appear and kill the cercopithursus. Although badly shaken, the woman was unharmed. The unscathed boar, Master Iranapolis, trotted off to continue his surveillance. The ram had bolted from the scene and was nowhere to be found. Soon, the wavering call of a great horned owl alerted other villagers to the ram's location.

As was customary, the scouts delivered the cercopithursus's carcass to H'Aleth's main village. The researchers there sent tissue samples to both Erwina and Gregor for study by their biologists, veterinarians, and geneticists.

The loss of a magnificent brown bear from the corruption of its genome by the Cassius Foundation brought a mix of sadness and resolve. Although such incidents had become less common, they were not rare. They served as a reminder to the people of H'Aleth and Erwina that danger was never far away.

Supplemental Notes and Citations
Genome

The genome is the total gene compliment (genetic profile) of an individual organism, including both coding and noncoding genes and mitochondrial DNA (Zahn, *et al.*, 2019).

Deoxyribonucleic acid (DNA)

DNA is genetic material that consists of an array of gene sequences (nucleotides) supported by a structure shaped like a spiral staircase (backbone) made of sugar and phosphate (Frixione & Ruiz-Zamarripa, 2019; Minchin & Lodge, 2019; Travers & Muskhelishvili, 2015). DNA effectively stores data needed for protein synthesis based on the arrangement of its nucleotides (adenine, thymine, guanine, cytosine). These sequences are clustered and bound together in strands called chromosomes (figure 1).

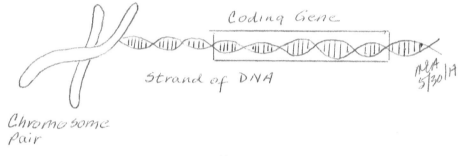

Figure 1: Chromosomes

Chromosomes

Chromosomes provide structure and organization for DNA sequences. The location of a particular DNA sequence on a chromosome affects how it will interact with other DNA sequences (Deakin, *et al.*, 2019).

Humans have a complement of twenty-three paired chromosomes for a total of forty-six (euploidy) (Chen, *et al.*, 2017). One of these pairs consists of the reproductive chromosomes: either two X chromosomes for a female (X, X) or an X and a Y chromosome (X, Y) for a male.

CHAPTER 4
A New Lineage

A Closely Guarded Secret

By convention, each of the three houses kept a copy of its peoples' genetic profiles (genome). H'Aleth and Erwina sent a copy of their profiles to Gregor for safekeeping. This was not the case for H'Ester, who had three transforming X chromosomes (trisomy, $3X^T$), or her descendants (pedigree 1, H'Ester's Descendants). Only Gregor housed their genomes. DNA analysis conducted at birth demonstrated that all H'Ester's descendants possessed a transforming X chromosome, including females who had two of them ($2X^T$). It also revealed that one of her granddaughters had three X^T chromosomes, and her son and one of her great-grandsons also possessed an extra X^T chromosome (trisomy, $2X^T/Y$) (appendix E). Thus, H'Ester was designated the genetic founder of male offspring who carried an extra X^T chromosome. She had engendered an even more powerful legacy than her great-great-grandmother, Ruth.

The only people apprised of these profiles were direct descendants of H'Ester and those with a need to know: the heads of each house, their chiefs of security, chief medical officers, chief veterinarians, the dean of the schoolhouse at Erwina, and select mentors. Each of them committed the knowledge to memory.

Secrecy was maintained not only to protect H'Ester and her family but also to avoid attracting unwanted hostile intentions. Bounty hunters did not disappear with the Cassius Foundation, and many were still in its employ. Consequently, the genetic profiles of H'Ester and her descendants—especially Edric, H'Amara, and Evander—were kept a closely guarded secret.

A New Generation

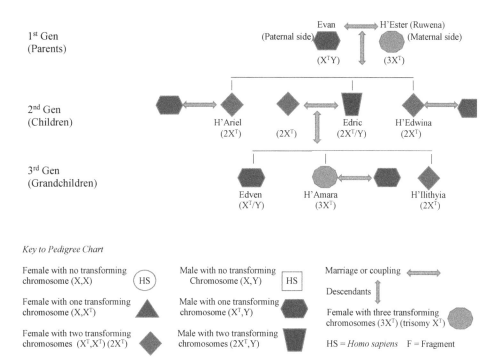

Pedigree 1: H'Ester's Descendants

Edric was the first known male offspring to have two transforming X chromosomes. No one knew what to expect, not even H'Ester, and no one would know until Edric came of age. In the meantime, there was much speculation regarding his capabilities. His genotype included the genes for gray wolf, gray fox, wild boar, cougar, and river otter—all mammalian—and genes for an avian species, the Cooper's hawk (appendix F). This was not unusual since his mother's genome supported transformation into a

Cooper's hawk as well as a woodland owl. It remained to be seen whether or not Edric would be able to transform across multiple families—*Canidae, Felidae,* and *Suidae*—and, possibly, even across classes—mammalian and avian. Unbeknownst to him or anyone else, Edric also inherited many of the physical characteristics (phenotype) of his maternal grandfather, an unknown male via in vitro fertilization.

As a youngster, H'Ester told Edric what alternate species his genome supported. Although he had the genes of a river otter, geneticists at Gregor identified that many of them were rendered inactive when he was little more than an embryo. Edric was very disappointed. H'Edwina would be able frolic in rivers and streams when she came of age, and he longed to have that capability as well.

"I could still try," he suggested. "Maybe they will turn on."

"Absolutely not!" H'Ester commanded. Her stark memories of the consequences of forced transformations had never faded. "You will die," she said grimly.

Edric saw the haunted look in his mother's eyes. Still, for a while, he held out hope. As he approached his coming of age, he realized that he would not be transforming into an otter. He felt no sense of kinship with the species. Indeed, those genes were turned off.

Top Gun

For males, the average age for transformation was thirteen to fourteen years old. For females, it was eleven to twelve. So, for a year or two, girls held sway over boys. For most girls, this would not last unless they had two X^T chromosomes.

Both H'Ariel and H'Edwina were $2X^T$ and confident that they would be a match for their brother. As Edric matured, he did not hesitate to point out that he would become stronger and more powerful than they.

"I have a Y chromosome," he bragged. "More muscle, more red blood cells, bigger bones."

"Thicker skull," his sisters added.

"In raptor species, females are larger than males," H'Ariel reminded him.

Whereupon Edric determined he would rely on the wolf and cougar to trump his sisters. In both species, the male was decidedly larger than the female. "I'll be able to best you," he claimed with confidence.

"You think so," H'Edwina remarked. "There are two of us."

Edric did have one consolation. Both of his sisters were slight of build, like their mother and the rest of their maternal lineage. In contrast, Edric would become tall, well built, muscular, and quite handsome—traits of his unknown grandfather.

To All Appearances

Before H'Ester's children were born, only $2X^T$ female *H. transformans* could metamorphose across families and across classes—much to the men's annoyance. Edric could have dispelled that notion had he not needed to keep his capabilities secret. *Homo transformans* males were supposed to have only one X^T chromosome. So, when Edric came of age, he could only assume those species expected of him—foxes and wolves—while he was among his friends and fellow classmates. These species, both within the *Canidae* family, were consistent with the capabilities of many other *H. transformans* males and with being a direct descendant of Edvar, his great-great-grandfather.

H'Ester's children received the same instruction on the rules of transformation and the same guidance developing their abilities as did all other *H. transformans* children. It was no surprise that H'Ariel and H'Edwina $(2X^T)$ could transform across classes. Any female $2X^T$ *H. transformans* could do so. As a direct descendant of Ruth, they could also transform directly from one species into another species. This level of capability was expected of them. It was not expected of Edric.

Faculty members initially coached Edric in the process of transformation along with his fellow classmates. While with classmates, his transformations were limited to a gray fox and a gray wolf. He accomplished these skills fairly easily and at an early age, when girls were developing their capabilities. He soon became confident of his ability to transform into both species at will.

"Wow!" one of the boys in his class exclaimed. "How come you can transform so soon?"

Edric was stumped. Although he knew why, he did not know what to say without revealing his capability. Matron Theodora, who taught the transformation classes, came to his rescue.

"His lineage gives him an advantage," she explained. "Don't forget that, as humans, we have a close genetic relationship with the *Canidae* family. What do we call that kind of relationship?"

The students immediately recognized a pop quiz question. "Genetic homology," they all answered, virtually in unison.

Thus, Edric's fellow students attributed his proficiency to his family heritage and to a genetic characteristic they all possessed. Although the boys in the class were impressed, the girls were not. They kept a close eye on this upstart.

A Secret Life

Edric could not practice transforming into a cougar or a wild boar among his classmates. He had to be coached in secret to develop these capabilities—not an easy task as it incurred greater risk of discovery. Given the vulnerability of younger students, the compound housing the schoolhouse was heavily patrolled by experienced scouts and faculty members, all of whom could transform into powerful animals. Upperclassmen often participated in these patrols as level one apprentice scouts. Even the youngest students were taught to be observant and report anything they thought was out of the ordinary. Thus, there were many eyes, ears, and noses to detect a potential threat.

When Edric was an upperclassman, his mentors took him beyond the perimeter of the compound to gain experience and hone his skills as a cougar and a wild boar. Edric's transformation into a cougar was not especially difficult due to the degree of genetic homology. Confident of his capabilities as a cougar, he decided to test them on his own.

Upon reaching his senior year in form IV, the final year of school, Edric served as an apprentice scout. This afforded him opportunities to practice scouting independently and gain additional experience as his alternate species without raising suspicion. One afternoon while on patrol as a cougar, Edric spotted a mule deer stag grazing nearby. He decided to practice his skills in stalking a prey species and targeted the deer. He had no intention of attacking it. He just wanted to see if he could get close enough to do so without being detected. Ever so carefully, he crept closer and closer. The stag continued to graze, seemingly unaware that an apex predator was closing in on him.

Edric was elated. He had come within range to launch a strike. Suddenly, the stag turned and attacked in a full charge, head down with antlers like spears aimed directly at him. Edric was taken completely by surprise. Instead of launching at the deer, he launched himself up the nearest tree and scrambled to a limb well above the stag's reach. When he finally turned around to look down, he saw the stag rearing up on the tree trunk—looking straight at him. Edric realized then that the stag was not a native species and had not been fooled. He was another *H. transformans*.

Later that day, he heard a faculty member tell the story of how, as a stag, he had turned the tables on cougar who attempted to stalk him.

"In all likelihood it was one of our students testing her skills," he said with a chuckle. It was a source of much amusement to his fellow faculty members, too. Edric was relieved that nobody knew who the cougar really was, largely because they assumed the cougar was a female student. Clearly, his ability to stalk prey left something to be desired.

Supplemental Notes and Citations

Genotype/Phenotype

Genotype is an individual's overall genetic composition, whether or not it is expressed as an observable characteristic—the individual's phenotype.

Genetic homology

Gene sequences may be conserved and reused among classes within the animal kingdom and a few even across kingdoms (Tschopp, *et al.*, 2017). This suggests a shared ancestry. The closer the degree of genetic homology between species, the more closely they are related.

Trisomy

Trisomy is a genetic condition in which cells have three copies of a chromosome instead of the customary two copies. In *H. sapiens*, there should be twenty-three pairs of chromosomes for a total of forty-six chromosomes. Any number of chromosomes above or below forty-six in humans is abnormal (aneuploidy).

Aneuploidy is an abnormal number of chromosomes for a given species (Badeau, *et al.*, 2017). It may be found in nonreproductive (somatic) chromosomes and in reproductive (X and Y) chromosomes.

CHAPTER 5
LESSONS LEARNED

In their alternate species form, all *H. transformans* students learned how to fight and escape an adversary, especially a predator. Experienced faculty and students would engage in stalking, sparring, and escaping as predator or prey. These sessions would begin with tutoring and gradually advance until training ended in a mock, nonlethal challenge. Such challenges often were repeated during the summer games, when former students and faculty faced off to see who would triumph.

A Learning Curve

Once Edric developed proficiency in transforming into a cougar, he tended to stay as a cougar for a while. He liked the agility, reflexes, speed, strength, and stealth of the cougar, which afforded him the freedom to range over a wide variety of terrains. He spent considerable time in the western woodlands and montane forests, honing his skills as a cougar and strengthening his power.

During one such excursion in the woodlands of Erwina, Edric suddenly heard the growl of a native cougar. Before he could react, the native cat was upon him in a furious attack. Edric was in trouble. As a cougar, he had only engaged in mock fights with a faculty member. His one advantage was his larger size. He managed to roll over and dislodge his adversary, then bolted away as fast as he could. He leaped up into a tree before it dawned on him that his attacker could do the same thing. Once he turned around, however, he would have the high ground and an advantage.

The native cougar, clearly a female, did not follow him. After hissing, growling, and spewing at him, she withdrew. From his vantage point in the tree, Edric saw the reason why she had risked attacking a much larger and more powerful—at least, theoretically—male cougar, without pursuing him. She had three cubs. Edric decided to stay exactly where he was until the female and her cubs left the area. In the meantime, he occupied himself with licking his wounds.

Later, after limping home, Edric asked his mentor, Master Erwen, "How do I learn to fight as a cougar? Really fight," he emphasized.

"Experience," replied Erwen.

"Great!" Edric responded with a hint of sarcasm, having just gained some experience.

"Calm down," Erwen admonished. "One of Erwina's faculty, Madam Merena, is very experienced. She is a powerful swimmer and an excellent fighter. You would not have escaped her. I will arrange for the two of you to engage in mock fights. Be advised," he added, "Madam Merena's alternate species is the jaguar. You will be tested."

The test would pit a 160-pound male cougar against a 95-pound female jaguar. *How tough can this be?* Edric thought. He found out.

Boar Propriety and Etiquette

For Edric, transformation into a wild boar proved to be his greatest challenge. As members of the *Suidae* family, boars were a more distant genetic relative. Although wild boar was not a common alternate species for *H. transformans*, neither was it considered unusual. Master Iranapolis, a faculty member at the schoolhouse, could transform into a formidable wild boar. He helped Edric develop the ability and master the animal's capabilities and behaviors.

When the time came to learn to fight as a boar, Edric had reservations. Master Iranapolis was an elderly gentleman. Even as a boar, he had graying hair around his muzzle,. and the tuft of hair atop his head was gray. He also had scars on his trunk and head from previous battles with hybrid animals and other predators.

"I want to learn all I can from Master Iranapolis," he assured Master Erwen. "But I'm worried about sparring with him as a boar. He is a much older man and therefore an old boar. If he is not quick enough to escape a blow, I might injure him by accident."

Master Erwen just smiled. "It is good of you to be concerned about Master Iranapolis's welfare. But you needn't worry. He is very experienced and continues to serve as a master scout in his alternate species. As a human, he is a master of martial arts and instructs students in boxing and wrestling. He remains a formidable opponent both as a human and as a boar. Native predators invariably underestimate him, and no animal hybrid has ever bested him."

Somewhat relieved by Master Erwen's reassurances, Edric sparred with Master Iranapolis under controlled conditions, which minimized the risk of injury. Initially, he and Master Iranapolis would engage in mock fights for practice. He learned the strategies and techniques a boar would employ to attack a threat, such as another male boar, and to defend itself from a predator. Later, as a boar, Master Iranapolis squared off with Master Erwen in gray wolf form to demonstrate battle tactics between a boar and an apex predator. Finally, Edric accompanied Master Iranapolis on a trip into the montane forest to observe native boars and their behaviors.

"Hopefully, we will encounter a sounder of boars," Master Iranapolis told him. "Mature boars are usually solitary; however, they may form small groups. We will see if you can join them. Stay alert for predators."

Wolves and cougars, thought Edric. The irony did not escape him. *Two of my alternate species prey on boars.* "Perhaps I should travel as a wolf or cougar as a measure of safety," he suggested. "There is no one to see a boar traveling with one of its apex predators."

"You need to experience living as a boar in the wild," Master Iranapolis insisted. "I am not without defenses," he added with a smile.

When they were well beyond the compound, both transformed into boars. After a while, they spotted a family of wild boar—a male, a female, and a bevy of piglets—foraging in a glade. Edric decided to stroll into the glade to do a little foraging himself. Two seconds later he was bolting away.

The family patriarch had taken umbrage at the presence of an unrelated male.

A Sudden Awakening

Edric managed to circle around and rejoin Master Iranapolis at the edge of the glade. They had started to move away when a massive, long-haired, boar-like creature burst into the clearing, attacking the boar family. The patriarch turned to face the attacker as the female and her piglets scattered. The lone male stood no chance against this enemy. In an instant, Master Iranapolis charged the creature and gored its flank. The hybrid immediately turned to engage its attacker, only to have it dodge his blow. Edric, in turn, rammed into the creature's side.

Edric's attack did little more than distract the hybrid temporarily; however, it gave Iranapolis the opportunity to launch another attack. This time, the hybrid was ready and slammed Iranapolis to the ground. It was about to tear into the old boar when Edric charged, dove under its belly, twisted his body around, and dug his tusks into the creature's soft underbelly, rending it open (illustration 8, Synergy). It was a mortal wound.

When Edric saw his mentor about to be killed, a fierceness arose that brought all the strength of his alternate species to bear. In that moment, his power and skills surged as one; the wolf's speed, the cougar's agility, and the boar's aggressiveness served him well. Afterwards, he realized what his alternate species could accomplish when human knowledge augmented this synergy.

One Fine Day

The encounter with the hybrid boar reawakened a waning vigilance among the territories. Analysis of the creature's genome revealed it was an augmented boar–wolf mix—a serojalupus—and a completely new animal hybrid. Erwina alerted its sister houses, Biogenics, and villages in the open territories. The Cassius Foundation was reviving.

Illustration 8: Synergy

Both H'Aleth and Erwina dispatched additional scouts to provide coverage across the northern borders of their territories from west to east. Security was especially tight near Cassius territory. H'Ariel and H'Edwina maintained aerial surveillance, while Edric patrolled across H'Aleth as a cougar or a wolf.

Several months passed with no new sightings; yet a sense of wariness persisted. One day, a young woman headed into H'Aleth's plains, far away from its borders with Cassius territory. It was sunny and warm with a brisk breeze stirring the grasses. She too was an *H. transformans*, who had recently completed her education, specializing in agriculture. She wanted to expand her knowledge of food crops and how they could be integrated into the environment. H'Aleth's plains were an agricultural gold mine, so she had accepted an internship with H'Aleth's agriculturalist.

The young woman was out in the middle of nowhere, amid the plain's different grasses, when she spotted a gray wolf. It stood still, staring at her. She also stood motionless, returning the wolf's gaze, uncertain of its species. Red wolves usually patrolled the plains. *Is this a native Canis lupus*, she wondered, *or a scout?* When the wolf sat down, she knew the answer. So she continued her examination of the different grasses and grains around her.

As a gray wolf, Edric had forayed into H'Aleth's plains where he spotted the young woman. He quickly realized that she had not been trained as a scout. This put her at hazard, even in H'Aleth territory. Edric kept watch as she moved through the mix of wild grasses and grains. When she finally saw him, he sat to indicate he was not a threat. Afterwards, he continued to tag along—at a proper distance. She was attractive, and Edric was intrigued.

After a while, the young woman finally turned and spoke to him. "Good afternoon. My name is Lilith," she said by way of introduction. Her lilting voice was music to Edric's ears. Suddenly, he was smitten. He did not know what to do or what to say—as if he could have said anything. So he just stood there on all four feet and stared at her like an idiot. Lilith smiled and beckoned to him. "Please join me," she said. They spent the rest of the day together.

Later, Edric learned that Lilith also preferred to be away from the hustle and bustle of a large village. They spent several weeks together, roaming around H'Aleth. Edric taught Lilith scouting skills. Lilith tried to teach Edric about different types of grains and their agricultural significance. Invariably, his eyes would glaze over. She finally abandoned the effort.

Both H'Ester and Evan blessed their marriage.

Supplemental Notes and Citations

Gene synergy

Synergy occurs when two or more genes interact with each other to produce an effect they would not otherwise have had if they had acted independently or were simply added together (Perez-Perez, *et al.*, 2009; Xing, *et al.*, 2017). For example, the interaction of two specific genes may cause changes that increase the risk of Alzheimer's disease, whereas either gene acting independently does not (Robson, *et al.*, 2004, Watkinson, *et al.*, 2008). These genes may be closely related as in two variants of the same gene paired together. Alternatively, they may be two or more interacting genes in the same pathway.

CHAPTER 6
Changing of the Guard

With her offspring fully grown and independent, H'Ester planned to relinquish her role as mistress to her eldest daughter, H'Ariel. H'Edwina had married and moved to Gregor with her husband. H'Ester was relieved that at least one of her offspring would be safe at Gregor. H'Ariel would be in relative safety at the well-fortified village and estate that housed H'Aleth's seat of government and research. Hopefully, Edric and Lilith would alight somewhere nearby.

Transitioning

Edric and Lilith had yet to settle down in any one place. They liked to explore regions in both H'Aleth and Erwina. When H'Ariel accepted the role of next mistress of the House of H'Aleth, Edric assumed he was off the hook.

"That is not the case," H'Ester remonstrated. "You still have duties and responsibilities to your house. You are expected to join H'Aleth's council, and you must be prepared to become its master in the event H'Ariel cannot."

"We must give Edric and Lilith time to settle down," Evan whispered to H'Ester. "The world they live in now is different from the one we once knew."

"The one we knew may yet return," H'Ester replied quietly.

On the Road Again

When H'Ariel assumed the duties of mistress of the House of H'Aleth, the change permitted H'Ester and Evan to roam throughout H'Aleth and sometimes beyond into Erwina and Biogenics territories. H'Ester had acquired some of H'Ilgraith's wanderlust. Schooling at Erwina and her former duties as mistress of H'Aleth had not lessened her former mistress's influence on her. On their forays, H'Ester and Evan stayed alert, relying on their respective alternate species to keep them safe. Invariably, they ended up scouting.

Scouting was in Evan's blood. Both of his parents were scouts for the northeast outpost and loved the territory. When Evan was sent to Erwina at age four, he already had learned the value of remaining alert and attentive to his surroundings. His parents tutored him in scouting techniques during his visits home. Once he could transform, he often accompanied his parents on routine surveillance rounds. Later, at Erwina, Evan was tasked to tutor H'Ester (then Ruwena) in scouting methods. After the two became a couple, they went on many scouting expeditions together.

H'Ariel gently scolded her parents for going so far afield. "Why can't you two be scouts for the schoolhouse at Erwina? You could be teaching the students how to conduct surveillance." Speaking to her mother, H'Ariel added, "You could teach them about the altered *H. transformans* and animal hybrids that you encountered and how to recognize them." H'Ariel had a point. The Cassius Foundation might resurrect these hybrids.

"We will consider it," her mother replied, looking at Evan.

Indeed, both of them did instruct and mentor students at the schoolhouse—during the winter term. Winters could be quite harsh in the northern regions. H'Ester especially was willing to stay by a dormitory fire. She remembered all too well the desperate winter she and her mistress had spent in a Cassius village. Evan was much more cold tolerant, having grown up where winter storms often prevailed.

With the first spring thaw, H'Ester and Evan were off to resume their travels. Headmaster Joseph, dual-hatted as governor of Erwina and dean of the schoolhouse, notified H'Ariel via avian courier the moment H'Ester and Evan left the school grounds. In turn, H'Ariel sent word to the scouts so they could keep a watchful yet distant eye on her parents. This was not always easy to do. From time to time, however, the scouts would spot a pair of red foxes—a male and a female—sitting side by side atop a grassy knoll, scanning the territory and sniffing the breeze. The scouts knew immediately who the two foxes were.

H'Ester and Evan periodically returned to the estate to share what they had seen and to receive reports. Everyone needed to be aware of any activity suggesting that the Cassius Foundation was becoming active.

A Deadly Encounter

Whenever H'Ester and Evan were away from human habitation, they transformed into a pair of red foxes or a pair of gray wolves. If they encountered a suspicious scent or sound, Evan tracked it on the ground, and H'Ester became a woodland owl to conduct aerial surveillance.

A narrow strip of land between H'Aleth's northern border and Cassius's southern border stretched from the neck of Caput Canis in the west across the dog's spine to the east. This was the most dangerous place for encountering Cassius's creatures. On one of their treks along this border, Evan snapped a low growl. The woodland owl's exquisite hearing picked up the warning. She immediately lifted off the branch where she was perched and glided silently to another tree in the direction Evan had indicated. She was stunned to see a lupuseroja—the same kind of hybrid that nearly killed Evan almost sixty years ago—feeding on the remains of a deer carcass.

H'Ester was terrified. Evan was no longer in his prime. If he encountered this lupuseroja, he would surely be killed. *If I try to lead the lupuseroja away, Evan will only follow*, she thought. *How can I lead Evan away without drawing the hybrid's attention? It might just continue to feed.*

H'Ester flew back to Evan and landed on the ground in front of him. She began walking away from the hybrid, hoping Evan would follow her lead.

Alas, H'Ester's flight had drawn the attention of the lupuseroja, although it had no interest in the bird. The hybrid's attention was on the wolf, for it might be another predator hoping to steal its meal. The hybrid rose to a crouched position, deciding to take the fight to the wolf. To H'Ester's horror, Evan launched a counterattack of his own.

Illustration 9: Theracapracanis

The two never engaged. Another hybrid predator was angling to seize the lupuseroja's dinner. A theracapracanis (illustration 9) had crept up from the side. When the lupuseroja's attention became focused elsewhere, the theracapracanis saw its chance and attacked the lupuseroja just as the latter charged Evan. The ensuing battle was fierce and bloody.

H'Ester shrieked at Evan. Evan knew that the only way to get her away was to get away himself. So he bolted from the scene with H'Ester flying above him. About five miles later, he stopped to listen for any pursuit. He heard none. A soft hoot from H'Ester confirmed that they were in the clear.

Neither of them would ever know the outcome of the fight between the two hybrids. Yet they had gained valuable information. Two species of hybrids, which should have disappeared long ago, still roamed the territories. They needed to report this as soon as possible.

The Waning of H'Ester and Evan

As H'Ester and Evan grew older, the couple's strength and endurance began to diminish. Their pace slowed, and the distances they could travel in a day became shorter. H'Ester knew that Evan did not have the long lifespan bestowed upon her lineage. His strength was failing when they reached the northeast outpost of Erwina. The first winter snow had already fallen. H'Ester sent a courier to H'Ariel and H'Edwina to tell them their father would not be returning home again. H'Ariel dispatched the same courier and message to Erwina and sent word to Edric. Then, as a great horned owl, she flew to the grotto where the northeast outpost was hidden. H'Edwina could not come. Winter came much earlier to Gregor, and a violent storm prevented her from flying back to H'Aleth. Edric, as a wolf, raced to arrive in time.

Not long after the family had gathered, Evan transformed for the last time into a gray wolf. H'Ester did the same and laid down next to him, as did Edric. As a red wolf, H'Ariel's coat was not as thick; nevertheless, she too transformed to lie down beside her father. H'Ester's and Edric's winter coats helped both H'Ariel and Evan to stay warm.

Nestled among his family, Evan passed away the next day. As was done for all *H. transformans*, Evan was cremated. Unlike other *H. transformans*, whose ashes were returned to the family, H'Ester scattered Evan's ashes over the northeast region beyond the outpost. *This is where he would want to be*, she thought. Then, as a long-eared woodland owl, she joined H'Ariel and Edric, still wolves, for the journey back to the estate. To cope with her grief, H'Ester provided aerial surveillance, as in times of old when she did so for Evan.

The Passing of H'Ester

H'Ester lived to see her grandchildren grow into young adults. Edven was named in honor and remembrance of his grandfather. At H'Ester's request, H'Ilithya was named in honor and memory of H'Ilgraith. When H'Ester's strength began to fail, she too traveled to Erwina's northeast outpost. H'Ariel accompanied her, knowing full well her mother's intent. It was an arduous trip for a 100-year-old owl. Not long after their arrival, H'Ester passed away. H'Ariel spread her mother's ashes over the same territory where H'Ester had spread Evan's. Perhaps in spirit they would be together again.

Part II
A Secret Society

CHAPTER 7
Palace Intrigue

After the Cassius Foundation's defeat on the battleground of Erwina and the death of its leader, Rafe Cassius, the remnants of the foundation withdrew into itself. Initially, everyone expected the foundation to resume its aggressive takeovers of other areas. Yet scouts observed little activity except for bounty hunters and a sudden influx of animal hybrids. The former continued to conduct raiding parties in an attempt to kidnap *H. transformans* and anyone else they could sell. The animal hybrids flooded into every territory to plague people and other animals alike. Scouts encountered no new hybrids of any kind, and there was no sign of the Cassius Foundation itself. It was almost as if the foundation had become dormant.

It had not.

Waiting in the Wings

Although the Cassius Foundation lost a major battle, its organization was not defeated. It needed to withdraw and regroup, especially after the loss of Rafe. Rafe had never taken a wife and, despite his participation in breeding programs, had no known offspring. His sex chromosome trisomy $(2X^T,Y)$ had rendered him powerful; however, unbeknownst to him or his family, he was unable to sire male offspring. Consequently, there was no heir apparent.

With Rafe's death, another battle raged inside the foundation for who would assume the reins of power and rule over all its territories. Rafe had dominated his younger brother, Rafus [*Rā*-fŭs], and ignored his older sister, Rhaphedra [rah-fĕd-rǎ] (pedigree 2, Raephela's Ancestry).

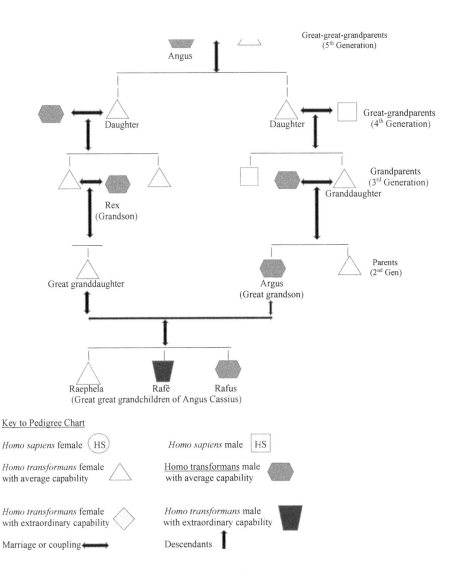

Pedigree 2: Raephela's Ancestry

Rhaphedra, an *H. transformans*, had defied her father, Argus Cassius, and married an *H. sapiens* man, by whom she had a daughter, Raephela [Rā-fĕl-ă], also an *H. transformans*. Rhaphedra and Raephela were reviled and ostracized. Rafus, ever in his brother's shadow, oppressed and tormented his sister, who he saw as a potential rival. He constantly threatened her life and that of her daughter. Ultimately, Rhaphedra had to sacrifice her husband in order to save her daughter.

As a child, Raephela watched her mother wither under her uncle's oppression. She was determined to outwit Rafus and avenge her mother. She spied on him and studied his weaknesses. These were most apparent when he encountered his older brother. Rafe was clearly in command, and his disdain for his brother was evident. So Raephela also watched Rafe from the wings. Staying in the shadows, she studied his operations and learned as much as she could about the strategies and tactics he used to keep control of the foundation and take control of other territories. As she grew older, she also kept abreast of the research his geneticists were undertaking.

A Fatal Decision

During the battle in which the foundation was defeated, Rafus had remained in the Cassius fortress. With the death of his brother, he assumed control of the foundation. He was ill-prepared to do so. Many years under Rafe's yoke had made him envious and jealous of his older brother. It had also made him weak.

Rafus immediately ordered the release of predatory animal hybrids close to H'Aleth and Erwina territories. "Send them all out," he commanded. "Let them sweep through their territories and attack anyone who remains there or tries to settle there."

The gamekeepers released most of the animal hybrids still remaining. Aerial hybrids—the aegyopteras, lyvulfon, and harpyacalgryph—would launch overhead attacks. Arboreal hybrids—the moresistruri (illustration 10) and viperoperidactyls (illustration 11)—

Illustration 10: Moresistruri

Illustration 11: Viperoperidactyls

would lie in wait in the trees. They were virtually invisible among the leaves and branches and ambushed anyone or anything that passed by them. Lupucercopiths, serojacutas, lupuserojas, and theracapracani would stalk their prey as would any carnivorous predator.

Rafus did not stop to think that this action would also put the foundation's army at risk. Furthermore, many of the hybrids had their own ideas about where to go. Once released, they scattered throughout all the territories. Raephela was appalled. The heedless loss of so many valuable animal hybrids depleted the foundation's resources for defending its own territory or mounting another attack.

Raephela saw her chance. She immediately rose up and crushed Rafus, taking control of the Cassius Foundation. As one of her first acts, she ensured that Rafus made no further decisions.

Taking Command

Raephela promptly consolidated the remnants of the foundation's army and redirected efforts to rebuild it. She called in bounty hunters to capture able-bodied males to be conscripted into her army. "Take by force any that resist," she ordered. "Capture their families as well. I will hold them hostage to ensure they serve me." *All will serve me if they want to survive*, she thought.

Then she turned to her remaining military lieutenants. "Rebuild my army and expand my armories," she commanded. "I want every conceivable weapon available, especially those that can inflict mass casualties. Build me a weapon that can throw fire the way dragons do."

The lieutenants promptly assured Raephela that they would begin immediately. There was one minor detail. They had no idea how to build a machine that could spew dragon fire.

Finally, Raephela turned to her chief geneticist, Mason, with a similar demand. "Recreate the hordes of hybrids we once had and develop new ones that will be even more deadly," she demanded. He assured her that his staff could clone many of the existing animal hybrids.

"Creating new ones that can survive and be effective can take much longer," Mason said.

Raephela leaned toward him, speaking in a clear and all too quiet voice. "I suggest you find efficiencies." Mason understood the implications.

Raephela did not bother with the logistics of her demands. *I will let my lieutenants worry about such matters*, she thought. *I will restore the foundation to its former glory and expand its dominion.*

Ascension

Raephela's great-great-grandfather had dreamed of establishing himself and his family as royalty. After being sidelined for years by her uncles, she was determined to achieve that status. She would anoint herself a queen and ascend to the throne her ancestor coveted. Although she too could transform across *Suidae* and *Bovidae* species, her preferred alternate species was the wild boar—a species greatly feared by those who surrounded her, thanks to her uncle Rafe.

Raephela also set about ensuring that her progeny would remain in power. She was just as ruthless as her uncles. She quickly took steps to ensure that she was the only surviving family member directly descended from Angus Cassius. After Rafus mysteriously disappeared, Raephela banished his family, who left willingly to save their lives—to no avail. Raephela sent assassins to murder any remaining maternal or paternal cousins.

Subsequently, she mated with an *H. transformans* male and bore an *H. sapiens* son, who vanished shortly after birth, along with the male who sired him. A second mating with another *H. transformans* male yielded the *H. transformans* daughter Raephela wanted. Encumbered and discomfited by pregnancy, Raephela wanted no other offspring. So the male who fathered her daughter also disappeared. There would be no other descendants of Angus Cassius to challenge her or her daughter—or so she thought (pedigree 3, Raephela's Descendants). She had no idea that she shared her lineage with an unknown cousin.

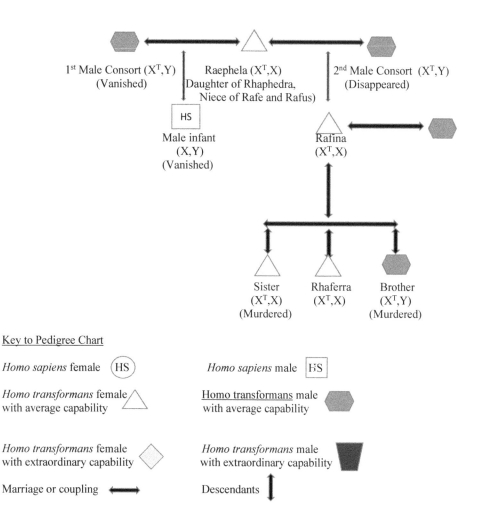

Key to Pedigree Chart

Homo sapiens female (HS)

Homo sapiens male [HS]

Homo transformans female with average capability

Homo transformans male with average capability

Homo transformans female with extraordinary capability

Homo transformans male with extraordinary capability

Marriage or coupling ◄──────►

Descendants ⬇

Pedigree 3: Raephela's Descendants

CHAPTER 8
BRANCHING OUT

Raephela was determined that the Cassius Foundation would regain its former standing by overpowering its enemies. She halted overt raids on villages and territories and ordered her lieutenants to rebuild in secret. She wanted to lull the neighboring territories into a false sense of security. Gradually, the foundation's absence led to a growing sense of safety and relative tranquility.

Although sightings of hybrid humans and animals gradually decreased after Cassius's defeat, they did not disappear completely. Rafe had not released all of his creatures to battle Erwina. He had kept many in reserve for a future assault on Gregor, only to have Rafus release most of them. Nevertheless, many animal hybrids remained, including those set aside to guard the fortress itself. The majority of them served as guard animals in Cassius villages. Moreover, the foundation still retained its capacity to genetically engineer bizarre hybrids.

A New Order

Although the Cassius Foundation had been defeated on the battlefield, its fortress with its research facilities remained intact and operational. During Rafe's reign, the foundation's research staff had quietly observed his long descent into madness. His irrationality and wild delusions of genetically engineering a dragon nearly drove them crazy. By the time Raephela took charge, the research division was floundering and in disarray. Countless projects had been started, yet few showed any progress—specifically those attempting to create ever more bizarre hybrid humanoids. Hence, the researchers breathed a sigh of relief when a rational, if ruthless, family member assumed control.

Once Raephela took the reins, genetic research and development resumed at an accelerated pace. "You are to cease work on any new hybrid humanoids," she decreed. She was outraged by the huge amount of resources devoted to developing them. Most failed to survive, resulting in little or no return on the investment. "Keep copying those that were successful," she added.

"Your first priority is creating weaponized animal hybrids that will be aggressive and deadly," Raephela ordered. "Animal hybrids are much easier and less expensive to develop, and they are more effective." Although there would still be many failures, she knew the costs would be much lower.

Raephela's researchers welcomed the order to abandon developing new hybrid humanoids. They had enough trouble trying to replicate the humanoids they already had. Differences in individual human genomes often precluded the successful transformation and survival of a hybridized *H. transformans*. Those altered transformans who maintained a predominantly humanoid appearance could be recreated with adequate fidelity. These included the serojabovids, cercopithursids, crocutalupoids (illustration 12), the papiopanoids (illustration 13), and the ursoxinoids. Of these, the papiopanoid was the most successful by far since both humans and chimpanzees are part of the *Hominidae* family.

Initially, the foundation's geneticists used the same technology readily available under Rafe's rule to create new animal hybrids. They copied the DNA associated with desirable characteristics and inserted it into the DNA of other animal species. They relied on genes from other living animals to create enhanced hybrid animals. Once the geneticists agreed on where to insert a gene, they usually relied on viral vectors to incorporate the foreign DNA into the host's genome. This process often resulted in breaking one or more of the recipient's native chromosomes. When native DNA repair mechanisms could not identify where to reattach DNA segments, both native and non-native DNA was lost. Thus, the foundation's cut-and-paste method of genetic engineering often resulted in disaster.

Illustration 12: Crocutalupoids

Illustration 13: Papiopanoid

Geneticists also continued to clone existing animal hybrids proven to be lethal. Most of these creatures were mammals whose base genome was that of an apex predator. The two highly successful avian hybrids were the harpyacalgryph and the lyvulfon. The most successful reptilian hybrid was the viperoperidactyl.

Having devoted considerable resources to recreating the lyvulseroptera—an especially deadly if clumsy animal hybrid—Raephela's scientists abandoned the effort. There were no surviving specimens. The few that Rafe Cassius had developed were destroyed by dragon fire during the battle with Erwina and Biogenics.

"Rafe held the only genetic recipe for this creature in his mind," Mason informed Raephela apologetically. "When he was killed by dragon fire, the recipe was lost with him."

Raephela was unsympathetic. "Stop wasting time and resources on such a ridiculous creature. Perhaps if you develop more advanced engineering techniques, you can design more powerful hybrids. I suggest you get to it," she snapped.

Branching Out

Spurred by Raephela's demands, the Cassius scientists and geneticists branched into the *Reptilia* class. Having nearly succeeded in engineering the varanhieracta, they decided to try again. The varanhieracta had been a failed experiment using the Komodo dragon for the base genome. The creature would have been terrifying had it survived.

Since then, their genetic engineering methods had improved and expanded considerably. Upon reexamining the original varanhieracta, the geneticists quickly discovered where their previous colleagues had erred. Using newer techniques, they were able to correct their mistakes.

Subsequently, the geneticists stripped out the avian genes which made the varanhieracta's bones hollow. Then they blunted the influence of genes associated with the animal's massive size and weight. Finally, they reintroduced modified muscle stem cells with genes that directed the development of large chest and shoulder muscles.

In lieu of avian genes for feathered wings, the geneticists introduced bat genes for the wings. Then they introduced genes for buffalo skin, which formed the hide for the modified varanhieracta's wings and torso. In making this last change, the researchers traded the tough skin and heavy scales of the native Komodo for the flexibility of mammalian hide. Still the creature could not fly and could barely crawl on the ground.

Finally, the geneticists took a more pragmatic approach. They used the base genome of the Komodo dragon and embellished it with genes that gave it additional armaments. This was the basis for the *Varanacrocactutus*—otherwise known as the varan (illustration 14)—which hosted the spiked horns of an antelope, the jaws and bite force of a crocodile, a double row of serrated teeth from the alligator gar, and the Komodo's own natural venom. The varan could rend and gore its prey. Like the native Komodo dragon, it could achieve bursts of speed up to twelve miles per hour—fast enough to catch a human. They were also very good swimmers. Thus, it seemed highly likely that the varan would be effective against the foundation's adversaries.

Illustration 14: Varan

The geneticists presented their new hybrid to Raephela. To their relief, she was pleased. "A splendid beast," Raephela declared. "Now test it."

Supplemental Notes and Citations

Hominidae

Hominidae is the biologic family that includes humans and the great apes (gorillas, chimpanzees, orangutans). Humans and chimpanzees share approximately 96% of their DNA (Varki and Altheide, 2005).

Gene editing

Numerous enzymes (nucleases) are available to copy a desired DNA sequence, excise a damaged sequence, and insert the desired sequence (Khadempar, *et al.*, 2019; Kim, *et al.*, 2019; Swartjes, *et al.*, 2020). Clustered regularly interspaced short palindromic repeats/CRISPR-associated protein 9 (CRISPR/Cas9) and other nuclease agents can target and cleave DNA at a specific location; however, they have some shortcomings. CRISPR/Cas9 creates double-stranded DNA breaks to edit the DNA, which requires cellular mechanisms to mend the breaks. It is not always precise and can be off target.

More recently, base editors can target changes to a specific base (e.g., changing adenine to guanine) and convert base pairs (e.g., cytosine–guanine to thymine–adenine) (Eid, *et al.*, 2018; Kim, *et al.*, 2019; Swartjes, *et al.*, 2020). They can effect change without requiring double-stranded DNA breaks.

Prime editing is another method that avoids double-stranded DNA breaks (Fu, *et al.*, 2019; Swartjes, *et al.*, 2020). It uses CRISPR nickases—modifications of CRISPR nucleases—to break a single DNA strand. Prime editing supports replacing, inserting, or deleting small segments of DNA. Nickases can decrease off-target effects.

Viral vectors

Viruses that have been stripped of their pathogenicity are being used to transport normal genes into cells and upload specific gene sequences into cellular DNA (Kotterman, *et al.*, 2015; Lundstrom, 2018). The normal genes provide the functionality that the abnormal genes disrupted (e.g., the CFTR gene for cystic fibrosis, the DMD gene for muscular dystrophy, and the factor VIII and factor IX genes for hemophilia) (Barthelemy & Wein, 2018; Maiuri, *et al.*, 2017; Nienhuis, *et al.*, 2017). Adenoviruses and lentivirus are commonly used as viral vectors (Kotterman, *et al.*, 2015; VandenDriessche & Chuah, 2017).

Komodo dragon bites

The bite of a Komodo dragon can inflict serious wounds leading to significant blood loss. It also injects venom, which may act as both an anticoagulant—which potentiates bleeding—and as a shock-inducing agent (Fry, *et al.*, 2009; Lind, *et al.*, (2019). Their bites are also highly infectious and may be the primary cause of death (Ducey, *et al.*, 2016). Almost all animal bites, including human bites, are infectious (Maniscalco & Edens, 2020). Mouths harbor bacteria, and canines cause penetrating wounds that embed pathogenic bacteria into the wound. If not treated promptly and effectively, sepsis—a blood-borne infection—can occur.

CHAPTER 9
TRIALS AND TRIBULATIONS

It was customary practice to pilot test all surviving newly developed animal hybrids. Raephela tasked foundation guards to evaluate the varan's capabilities and effectiveness on unsuspecting people. Typically, the foundation conducted these trials on villages in open, unincorporated territories. Many of them were relatively isolated and lacked the security and surveillance capabilities of H'Aleth, Erwina, and Biogenics. This tactic also minimized the chance that someone from the other territories would discover the foundation's new hybrid before it was used in an attack. This strategy did not always work as planned.

Best-Laid Plans

Just north of the Cassius fortress, the River Taurus slowed as it made a wide turn to the west. Several guards from the fortress transported the caged varan across the river on a small barge, which also carried a cart. Once across the river, the guards lifted the cage onto the cart and proceeded into the montane forest to the west of the river. They had to transport the hybrid far away from the river. Since its base genome was a Komodo dragon, it was a good swimmer. If the hybrid escaped from the guards, it might find its way unsupervised back across the river to wreak havoc in Cassius territory.

The area hosted many unincorporated villages, which could be found if one knew where to look for them. The Cassius Foundation had tried to claim this territory for itself, so the guards knew it well. Finn, Raephela's lead guard, had already picked out a village that met their requirements. It was located far away from the scouts of H'Aleth and Erwina and to the east of Biogenics territory. *Perfect*, he thought.

The Biogenics Corporation had a long border with the Cassius Foundation. Long ago, it had been obliged to expand its army to defend its border. Rex Cassius had attempted to invade Biogenics across the northeast border and attack its marketing-and-sales headquarters. During that period, Biogenics established multiple outposts along its border. It stationed soldiers in each outpost to detect and engage enemy forces that tried to encroach upon its territory. These outposts were well concealed, and one was not far from the village the guards were targeting.

The Proof Is in the Pudding

The village consisted primarily of an open marketplace where people brought their wares to sell and services for hire. They included farmers, a bowyer, a machinist and an armorer for farm tools, a goatherd, weavers, seamstresses and tailors, and any other occupations the region would support. Two guards dressed as villagers entered the marketplace to survey the village and identify where the market was the busiest.

The villagers were immediately alert to the presence of strangers. The newcomers could be hunters. Although the strangers seemed aloof, they did not act hostile and eventually passed through the marketplace and left.

After scouting out the market area, Finn identified the place where his guards would release the hybrid for maximum effect. "All the booths and tables face the open center of the market," he noted. "The food market has the highest number of people gathered around it, and the tables are lined up in a row. Once the market is busy, release the hybrid adjacent to the food market and watch what happens. After you have observed its effect, burst upon the scene as the villagers' saviors and recapture the hybrid. When you return to the fortress, report back to me." Shortly thereafter, Finn departed. Many years of experience had taught him to remove himself from the pilot tests of new hybrids.

Later that evening, when the marketplace was deserted, the guards lugged the caged varan to a secluded spot behind the food court. There they waited until early morning when the marketers began to set out their wares. Soon, scores of villagers descended upon the marketplace.

The hybrid had not been fed in a month. When a guard unlocked the cage and let the door swing ajar, the guards quickly retreated to a safe distance. They watched as the hybrid flickered its forked tongue, smelling scents in the air, as it crawled out of the cage. It began to stalk the first prey it saw—a woman looking through the vegetables at the last booth in the row.

The varan came within a foot of the woman's right leg. Its mouth open, it reached to bite her.

"Look out!" someone shouted at the top of his voice. When everyone, including the hybrid, looked up, the shouter pointed at the creature. The woman screamed and stumbled backward, drawing the hybrid's attention back to her. A sharp-witted villager picked up a rock and heaved it at the hybrid, hitting its body and distracting it momentarily. The blow had no other effect; however, it was enough to allow the woman to run away. When the villagers began to flee, the varan charged, seeking the nearest prey it could reach. In the excitement, a flock of chickens had been flushed into the market center. The hybrid snapped at a hen and then had to divest itself of a mouthful of feathers.

The bowyer, a skilled archer, loosed three arrows, one after the other, striking the hybrid's torso. Two bounced off, while the third seemed to stick. The third arrow irritated the varan, which reached back and managed to dislodge it. Unimpeded by the arrow's slight wound, the hybrid resumed its charge. In the crowd, none of the villagers were able to outpace the creature. One finally fell victim to the hybrid's powerful jaws.

The villagers' cries and shouts had not gone unheard. The guards quickly crept back to watch the fray. They would need to report the results of releasing the varan. With their attention focused on the action in the village, they remained unaware that they were not the only ones who heard the cries.

The Element of Surprise

At an outpost not far away, Biogenics soldiers also heard the commotion. The post's captain immediately deployed a cadre of six soldiers to intercede.

"It may be a raid by bounty hunters, seeking out *H. transformans* to kidnap," he advised. "In that case, they will be well armed." If true, it also meant that the Cassius Foundation had ventured deep into the contested regions and all too close to Biogenics's border.

The soldiers set out at a brisk pace while maintaining a low profile. Their goal was to intervene as quickly as possible without giving up the element of surprise. They encountered no difficulty creeping up behind the guards; the latter were focused solely on the mayhem created by the varan. When the soldiers ambushed the guards, the ensuing skirmish was violent and brief. Three of the four guards were killed. This convinced the fourth guard to drop his weapons and be captured.

Meanwhile, the villagers pelted the varan with anything they could find. Although it had not suffered significant injury, the hybrid was not getting a decent meal out of the exercise. Hearing the clash between armed opponents nearby, the hybrid decided to try its luck there.

Fortunately for the soldiers, the first combatants the hybrid encountered were the downed guards. Knowing no allegiance to anyone, the varan promptly began scavenging on the first fallen guard it reached, drawing the horrified soldiers' attention. They were sickened to see it chewing on the dead guard.

The captured guard suddenly broke away. Four soldiers promptly reengaged with him while the other two kept an eye on the varan. Once again, the fighting drew the varan's attention. Having been deprived of food for so long, it decided a second entrée was in order and charged one of the soldiers watching it. Both soldiers jumped aside and ran to get away from it. They had to decide quickly what action had their highest priority: fighting the remaining guard or battling the hybrid. The varan decided for them. It suddenly turned and ran at them again. Everyone jumped aside, allowing the remaining guard to break away.

The hybrid must have felt threatened. It disappeared into the forest where it climbed a large tree and blended in with the trunk. When the soldiers tried to hunt it down, they could not find it.

Thus, only one guard escaped to report the varan's successful attack to Raephela. Although Raephela was irritated that the hybrid had been left behind, she was not beside herself. The varan had already been cloned.

Biogenics soldiers also reported the creature to their superiors, providing a thorough description of the varan's features. Biogenics quickly apprised the chiefs of security at H'Aleth and Erwina, describing the hybrid and in whose company it was found. This information immediately informed the allies that the Cassius Foundation was resurging.

As for the varan, it decided that the area where it was released held a bountiful buffet of prey species. It was not long before it rediscovered the river and expanded its range to the other side—into Cassius territory.

CHAPTER 10
A New Direction

Over the previous generations, Cassius geneticists had exhausted the most desirable genetic modifications that would create a formidable array of animal and human hybrids. They had exploited the available armaments provided by reptiles, mammals, and birds. Yet they had no dragon DNA. It finally dawned to them to look at the fossil record, to a more ancient branch of the animal kingdom—the dinosaurs.

Paleontologic Pursuits

Raephela granted Mason an audience to propose another potential source of animal weaponry.

"Some dinosaurs have unique armaments not found in modern animals," he told her. "Incorporating their armaments into modern animal hybrids would be a surprise to our enemies."

Raephela found this possibility intriguing. She directed the foundation's geneticists to obtain fossils of apex predator dinosaurs. "Search for large carnivorous dinosaurs and retrieve their DNA," she ordered. "These species may compete favorably with the gray dragons of the northern mountains."

I doubt that any dinosaur would compete successfully with a fire dragon, Mason mused. A prudent man, he did not voice this opinion. He had no intention of resurrecting any dinosaurs. He just wanted to harness the DNA that had made them effective, successful predators.

"Some of the herbivore species also have striking weapons for defense, including some impressive horns," Mason added and held his breath.

Raephela stared at him icily and then replied, "Those too," and walked away.

There was one minor problem. The Cassius Foundation had never invested in a paleontologist. Fortunately, a few Cassius scientists possessed a broad scientific background, including Ryker, a geologist.

When consulted, Ryker advised Raephela, "The Cretaceous period produced many suitable candidates. I suggest looking for the therapod group. They were large, carnivorous predators with impressive razor-sharp teeth." He then proceeded to describe some of the individual species in the *Tyrannosauridae* and the *Allosauridae* groups (appendix G).

Raephela immediately settled on two of them: the tyrannosaurus and the allosaurus. "These two species should be a match for a great gray dragon," she asserted.

Perhaps in size, thought Mason, *but not in firepower*.

Later, Mason asked Ryker, "Where do we find fossils of these dinosaurs and how do we recognize them?"

"They are usually found in layers of sandstone and occasionally in limestone," Ryker replied. "As for identifying the fossils, you will need to consult with a paleontologist."

Mason greeted this information with silence. After a moment, he said, "We don't have a paleontologist."

"I know," responded Ryker.

Already daunting, the project now appeared virtually impossible. Most of the fossil-rich sandstone lay within the boundaries of H'Aleth and Erwina. Given the sustained surveillance by both of their populations, an incursion into these territories would not go unnoticed. Limestone caverns could be found throughout every territory. Some could even be found in the northern mountains—territory of the great gray dragons. When Mason presented these issues to Raephela, she became angry.

"Find the fossils of well-armed prehistoric animals and extract their DNA!" she shouted.

Terrified as he was, Mason was equally appalled by the idea of digging up fossils. "If we go ourselves, it will take us away from our current projects. Perhaps bounty hunters can dig up the fossils," he suggested gingerly.

Raephela considered this notion. Mason had a point. "They won't be happy about it," she said, mostly to herself. "They are paid to do what I tell them to do," she announced forcefully. "It is simple enough to dig up old bones." Then she turned to Ryker. "You will go with the hunters and direct where they should excavate for fossils." She chose to dismiss the dangers associated with trespassing in other territories, including the mountains.

Raephela directed that teams be sent into both the southwest and the northeast mountain ranges to search for fossils of apex predators from the Cretaceous period. Hopefully, the sandstone of the southwest and the limestone of the northeast would reveal the remains of carnivorous dinosaurs.

Bounty hunters were unenthusiastic about digging up old bones. They were even less enthused about venturing into mountains where dragons kept their aeries (appendix H). Any hunter who reached the foothills of the southwest mountains was in danger of encountering a red dragon. The great gray dragons flew from their northern aeries to seek prey in the montane forests below. Nevertheless, an icy stare from Raephela convinced the hunters they were going anyway. They had a better chance of surviving an encounter with a dragon.

A Case in Point

A band of hunters seeking fossil remains were traveling through a montane forest that spread out below the northern mountains when they came upon a large granite outcrop that barred their way. It stood nearly thirty feet tall.

"Should we scale it or go around?" asked Dawson, a member of the party. They were equipped to scale the rock faces they would encounter in the mountains.

"Scale it. It's not that high," said Cole, the lead hunter.

"We'll have plenty of climbing to do when we get to the mountains," retorted Dawson. "Let's just walk around it."

"It will be quicker to scale it," Cole insisted.

"No, it won't," argued Dawson. "Not after we have unpacked and repacked all our gear."

The debate continued, providing a brief respite from the hunters' trek. It did not last. All six of them jumped up when they heard an animal crashing through the underbrush. A native white-tailed deer raced right past them. Close behind it, a native brown bear followed. The bear immediately noticed the six hunters gathered in front of the outcrop. In seconds, the bear decided that easier prey was at hand and would require far less effort to acquire.

Before the hunters could draw their weapons, the bear cut down the closest one. The remaining hunters dispersed quickly while the bear was engaged, abandoning their gear. Yet this only spurred the animal to give chase. As it charged after another hunter, an airborne mammal suddenly appeared. It streaked through the canopy, diving toward the scene and shooting past the hunters to snatch the bear in its jaws while in flight. Continuing its flight out through the canopy, its speed created enough wind to pin two of the hunters against the granite outcrop and knock the others to the ground. For a moment, the hunters were rendered helpless.

A juvenile great gray dragon was honing its flying and targeting skills on a practice run. His goal was to traverse the forest in flight, acquire his target with precision, and leave all else undisturbed. Dragons acquired these skills as juveniles while they were still small enough to fly through a forested area. Fully grown adults could fly only through a thinly wooded region without crashing into trees.

After the young dragon flew away with his prize, the hunters rose to their feet. Relieved, they thought to take a moment and catch their breath. Just then, the juvenile's sire reared up from behind the outcrop and climbed atop it. To the hunters' horror, the dragon looked down directly on them (illustration 15).

The adult had been monitoring his offspring's effort. After a brief look

Illustration 15: A Watchful Parent

at the hunters, he launched into the air. The force of his wingbeat created a wind gust that knocked the hunters down again and pinned them to the ground. The adult quickly departed to follow his offspring.

Once the hunters recovered, they reacquired their gear and turned back, carrying their dead comrade with them. They did not say a word. Their glances to one another revealed a tacit understanding. They would not be coming back—ever. Or so they thought.

CHAPTER 11
AN ALTERNATE STRATEGY

Fossil-hunting excursions in the southwest mountains were even less successful than those into the northern mountains. A direct incursion across the northern border of H'Aleth invariably provoked an altercation with H'Aleth's scouts. The peal of an eagle or the screech of an owl alerted the hunters that they had been spotted. H'Aleth's scouts would soon be upon them. Although some hunters were skilled archers, few could match the skill of a scout. A quick retreat was the only way hunters could avoid a confrontation. Most withdrew shortly after crossing the border.

Rarely, a lone, skilled bounty hunter would slip past a scout. Yet a single hunter could not excavate and transport the bones of carnivorous dinosaurs like the tyrannosaurus. Raephela's demands required a party of hunters, which could never reach the interior of H'Aleth.

"No amount of money is worth this," grumbled a frustrated hunter. Still, hunters feared returning without bones of some kind.

A Curious Situation

Initially, the H'Aletheans presumed—with justification—that the hunters sought to capture *H. transformans*. In the past, hunters had targeted them specifically, especially women. Of late, however, hunters had been avoiding villages; the scouts were puzzled by the hunters' lack of interest in kidnapping anyone. Instead, their dogged determination to try to reach the southwest region suggested they were focused on acquiring dragon chicks and eggs.

H'Ariel called a council meeting with Evard, her chief of security; Edrew, her wildlife specialist; and her lead scouts. Edric also attended.

"They must be after dragon eggs," surmised Edrew. "The Cassius Foundation has always wanted dragon DNA and have yet to acquire any, although it is not for want of trying. Any hunter who tries to steal a dragon egg is taking a terrible risk," he said grimly.

"For decades now, we have had a tacit understanding with the red dragons to live and let live," said H'Ariel. "We don't attack them, and they don't attack our scouts. Hunters could easily jeopardize this arrangement. We must keep them out of the southwest mountain," she added with a tone of urgency.

"We have so far," Edric remarked, "with few exceptions."

"I suspect that the majority of hunters must be under some kind of duress by the Cassius Foundation," offered Evard. "Otherwise, it makes no sense for them to risk their lives. And dragons aren't the only threat. When hunters have attacked our scouts, our people have been obliged to return fire—sometimes with lethal consequences."

Although the council's assessment of the hunters' quarry was incorrect, the urgency of the situation remained. They needed more scouts to cover the southwest region, especially the foothills.

"Scouts covering the northeast border will intercept any hunters attempting to cross in that area," Evard remarked. "So far, the southeast region of H'Aleth has not reported any incursions. So, I suggest we reassign two of those scouts to the southwestern foothills."

H'Ariel authorized the transfer; however, she was concerned about leaving too few scouts to watch over the southeastern border.

"I think I may have a solution to that problem," said Evard. "I will contact Erwina and let them know we have two openings for apprentice scouts."

The Boondoggle

As Raephela's hunters straggled back from the southwest mountains, their numbers were much reduced. Skirmishes with H'Aleth's scouts had resulted in many casualties.

"It's no use," reported one of the remaining hunters. "We cannot get past H'Aleth's defenses. We need more men and arms."

"No," replied Raephela decisively. "A large contingent of armed hunters will arouse suspicion that we are capable of mounting an invasion." She wanted the foundation's enemies to remain complacent.

Then Raephela remembered the boondoggle her grandfather, Rex Cassius, had undertaken. He wanted to build an armada to invade H'Aleth by sea. He expended a fortune on building a warship and constructing a canal to transport it. The canal spanned hundreds of miles, creating a water route from the fortress in the west to the ocean in the east.

Raephela dismissed any notion of building a fleet of warships. She was fully aware that her grandfather's sole warship had set sail and was never seen again. She considered the notion of an armada pure folly and a waste of resources. Her uncle Rafe did find one use for the canal. Whenever the River Aguila reached flood stage, he would order the northern gate to the moat be opened along with the locks in the canal. This allowed the floodwaters to drain away.

Perhaps there is another use for the canal, Raephela mused. *It may provide a way to reach the southwest mountains without crossing H'Aleth's territory.* So she dispatched a small contingent of lieutenants, surveyors, and a civil engineer to investigate the canal and determine its condition. "Find out if it can be used to transport men and supplies as well as ships," she ordered.

An Educational Outing

The canal was immense. It had to be wide and deep enough to sail or row a battleship fully loaded with crew and matériel. The survey party inspected the canal, beginning with its locks, which allowed water to flow out of the moat surrounding the fortress and into the canal. As expected, the locks closest to the fortress and those that followed were in good condition, as was the canal itself, up to its juncture with the River Cassius.

At the canal's junction with the river, four locks governed the flow of river water into and out of the canal. Two canal locks were positioned on either side of the river where the canal opened into the river—one on the near side and one on the far side. They governed the flow of water through the canal. Two river locks were positioned on either side of the canal—one upstream and one downstream. The upstream river lock controlled the river's flow downstream. The downstream river lock was positioned just below the canal locks. When the canal locks were closed and the river locks were open, river water flowed downstream as it would normally. To divert river water into the canal, the lower canal lock was opened and the lower river lock was closed. The upper river lock was then opened, allowing river water to flow into the canal. Of necessity, the upper river lock was huge and functioned like a dam so that water flowing through it could be regulated. It also served as a bridge across the river.

When the survey party reached the River Cassius, the canal locks were closed and the river locks open. An examination of the gears revealed that they had not been maintained. Nevertheless, the locks were holding. Not long after crossing the upper river lock, the survey party noted increasing undergrowth invading the canal. As they traveled eastward toward the ocean, they spotted secondary growth, including saplings, growing near the canal and its embankments. Then they came upon the turrets built along each side of the canal.

"What a massive construction project," exclaimed the civil engineer who accompanied the survey party. He knew the history of the canal from records and schematics he had found. Yet he had not envisioned the scale of the project until he saw it.

Notably, wildlife was abundant inside the woodlands beyond the clearings on both sides of the canal, yet few species were seen in the clearings. *It's almost as if they are avoiding this space*, thought Tyler, the surveyor. The next day, he and the rest of the survey party discovered the reason why. A section of the canal had been ripped apart and torched. All of them immediately looked skyward and hastened their pace. Once the survey was finished, the survey party chose to bypass that section on their way back to the fortress.

Another Avenue

Weeks later, when the survey party returned to the fortress, they reported their findings to Raephela. "Most of the canal is intact. Though it has become overgrown with vegetation, the shrubs and saplings growing there can be removed," Tyler explained. "The canal's terminus is underwater. The depth of the water depends upon the tide."

"What do you mean by most of the canal?" asked Raephela with a frown.

"One segment is completely destroyed and in ruins," Tyler replied.

"Earthquake?" Raephela asked.

"Dragon fire," Tyler answered. "The turrets are collapsed, and the stones that fell into the canal are fused. Everything is charred."

Raephela thought for a moment. "Did you detect any sign of recent dragon activity?"

"No," Tyler replied. "Quite the contrary. This segment is also overgrown with shrubs and a few skinny saplings growing among the debris."

I wonder what provoked the dragon's wrath, Raephela thought. Then she dismissed the question. *That was a long time ago.* She summoned the bounty hunters she had tasked with finding fossils in the southwest mountains. She now had an alternate route for them to take.

CHAPTER 12
SOUTHERN INCURSION

Raephela summoned her hunters. She promptly gave the lead hunter, Barret, his marching orders.

"You and your men will follow the canal eastward until you cross the River Cassius," she commanded. "Then turn south and head for the Cassius village which lies just inside the southeast border of my territory. Continue southward along the coastline, skirting H'Aleth territory. Eventually, the coastline will curve west, as will you.

"You will continue following the coastline until you reach the coastal plains of H'Aleth. Cross them until you reach the desert and the southwest mountains beyond. Our intelligence has revealed that the coastal plains are completely uninhabited except for native wildlife. You should encounter few, if any, scouts. Nearly all of H'Aleth's scouts are deployed across its northern border."

Raephela's report that the coastline was unoccupied by humans was technically correct. H'Aletheans had deliberately left these areas undisturbed. Even so, scouts whose alternate species were native to the region still patrolled it. It proved to be a moot point.

An End Run

The hunters traversed the canal—sometimes walking inside it for cover, other times walking alongside it for ease and greater speed of travel. Raephela had ordered the canal to be cleared of vegetation for as far as the hunters would need to follow it. Although they kept a sharp eye on the sky, they saw no dragons nor signs that any had passed through the area.

Unclaimed territory abutted the southern Cassius border. Once the hunters crossed the border, they headed south, following the coastline far to their left. Before long, they reached the region that lay outside H'Aleth's eastern border.

Most of the territory between H'Aleth's eastern border and the coastline was swamp. It lay well beyond H'Aleth's established borders and was largely unmapped. The hunters would have to traverse a wild and largely unknown region to reach H'Aleth's southeast border near the coastline.

Barrett dismissed the swamp as a significant impediment as long as his party did not encounter any H'Aletheans. "By traveling through the swamp, our tracks will disappear," he told his comrades. "We will turn west as soon as we reach H'Aleth's southern coast. That way, we should avoid any H'Alethean scouts when we cross the coastal plains. We should be well south of the areas where their scouts are deployed. Few scouts patrol the southwest mountain range," he added. Thinking that the coast was clear, the hunters entered the swamp.

Another's Domain

Oddly, H'Aleth scouts never encountered hybrids along the southeast coast of H'Aleth, even though the region beyond bordered Cassius territory to the north. H'Aletheans suspected that any hybrids that wandered into the area became trapped in the bogs or fell prey to alligators that lurked in the waters. An occasional cougar also hunted the native prey species that lived there. Even in broad daylight, the swamp was dark and remote.

From time to time, scouts conducted surveillance in the swamplands. They mapped much of the region, taking care to note pitfalls in the terrain. They recorded the most common species of flora and fauna, major waterways, and an enormous brackish lake near the coastline. At one time, it may have been a bay that since had become enclosed. Due to its mild salinity, the scouts suspected it still had access to the sea.

Scouts watched for any undiscovered species within the region. Since they rarely glimpsed a major predator, the scouts wondered if another apex predator inhabited the swamp. In fact, unbeknownst to them, the lake harbored an *Odontus pristis* (illustration 16), an aquatic species of dragon. As the region's apex predator, it preyed on both swamp and marine wildlife—and any other species that wandered into its domain. A large cavern underlay the lake. A channel leading from the cavern opened onto the ocean shelf that extended beyond the shore, giving the pristis access to the bay.

Illustration 16: Odontis Pristis

Like most dragons, the pristis did not use fire to hunt its prey. Fire served as a beacon to any prey species and could destroy its habitat. The pristis relied on stealth. Since the dragon could not fly in the swamp, it would rise up from the lake, push into dense vegetation for camouflage, and lie in wait for unsuspecting prey. Its scales lent the impression of a rock mound, while its scent was that of brackish water and mud. Since a dragon's eyes reflect light, the pristis kept them closed at night lest they reveal its location. Infrared sensors below each eye detected and targeted warm-bodied animals, including humans.

The Hunt

Raephela's hunters could not pass through the dense swamp in a single day. They had no map, and there were many perils to avoid: bogs, sinkholes, and quicksand; alligators, poisonous water moccasins, and wolf spiders; and last but not least, getting lost. The canopy was so dense they could not navigate by the stars and were obliged to stop at night. They had to await sunrise to continue on their journey. This proved to be their undoing.

Each evening, when virtually all light was lost, Barrett brought the expedition to a stop. The hunters set up a cold camp to avoid risking discovery or a conflagration. Two hunters at a time kept watch until daylight began to stream through the canopy. Then they broke camp and continued on their trek. They followed this routine for two consecutive nights.

On the third night, the hunters stopped in an area they thought must be near the coastline. They could hear the soothing, soft lapping of water. Over the previous two nights, the hunters had recognized sounds of raccoons, minks, and other nocturnal animals that moved through the swamp. On this night, however, the sentries heard the sound of a large animal sliding its body over the ground.

"Crocodile," hissed the first sentry.

"Or alligator," whispered the second sentry.

The sentries quickly roused their comrades with a quiet warning that a dangerous predator might be at hand. They made their weapons ready and lit two flares. The hunters' actions were met with silence, and they saw no wildlife at all. Thinking their flares had chased the animal away, they relaxed.

That would have been a logical conclusion had the wildlife not already fled the area. Little did the hunters know that a predator had zeroed in on their body heat signatures, and the flares acted like a beacon.

Suddenly, a dragon crashed through the vegetation and set upon them. One forelimb caught a hunter in its talon. Another hunter was crushed under a hind leg. A third hunter was snatched up by jaws with serrated teeth. The fourth hunter threw his flare at the dragon as he tried to run away. The dragon tracked the flare until it extinguished and then targeted the last hunter. It dropped the third hunter and lunged forward to snatch the fourth in its powerful jaws.

Missing in Action

Raephela never heard from the hunters she had sent into H'Aleth. Nor did they ever return. To suggest that Raephela was frustrated would be a masterpiece of understatement. She blamed the H'Aletheans for the loss of her hunting party.

"They will pay for sabotaging my hunters," she raged, conveniently ignoring the fact that she had sent them to invade H'Aleth. Ironically, the H'Aletheans were blissfully unaware that hunters were encroaching on their coastal territory.

Ignorance cost Raephela more than manpower. Her hunters might have discovered dinosaur remains in the swamp had they known where to look for them. Bogs can preserve fossils, and the swamp hosted many bogs.

Supplemental Notes and Citations

Infrared sensory perception

This capability is found predominantly in insects, reptiles such as snakes, and vampire bats (Roper & Grace, 2012). Their infrared receptive sensors can detect and project the image of a prey species and allow these animals to target their prey accurately in the dark.

Bog conditions

The anaerobic conditions in bogs provide an environment in which bone and soft tissues can be preserved (Lynnerup, 2015). The lack of oxygen inhibits the growth of bacteria and fungi which degrade soft tissues and DNA.

Brackish water

Brackish water is a mix of fresh water and seawater, resulting in reduced salinity. A wide variety of animals may inhabit brackish water, including reptiles (e.g., alligators, saltwater crocodiles), fish (e.g., catfish, tilapia, bull shark), and amphibians (e.g., frogs).

CHAPTER 13
ARCHOSAURIA

Meanwhile, Raephela's geneticists were engaged in their own exercise in futility, scrambling to find any samples of dinosaur DNA that had not degraded. First, they tried to distinguish avian from non-avian dinosaur DNA. This proved to be problematic. For avian DNA, they had only the DNA from extant species. Without a paleontologist or paleobiologist, the geneticists could not differentiate between herbivorous (saurischian) dinosaurs and carnivorous (ornithischian) dinosaurs. In the end, they succeeded in retrieving only a scant amount of DNA from the bones of a triceratops.

A Mad Scramble

Mason informed Raephela that there was no point in trying to recreate a dinosaur. "We don't have the DNA. Even if we could resurrect a triceratops, the beast is an herbivore. We can use the scant DNA we extracted to augment the bone structure of existing species. Especially those that are very large, such as rhinoceroses and elephants," he added.

"And where, exactly, do you expect to get those species?" quizzed Raephela sarcastically.

"We might be able to use bison. They are roughly comparable in size to a black rhinoceros," he replied. *At 1,800 pounds, so is the moose,* he thought, *but the rhino may have greater appeal. It already has an impressive horn.* One must be careful to stay in Raephela's good standing.

The geneticists preserved the original snippet of triceratops DNA by making copies of it to use experimentally. In an effort to determine which features and functions the DNA supported, they relied on their customary trial-and-error method of experimentation. After implanting different triceratops DNA segments into fertilized bison ova, they observed their development. As expected, most did not develop past the blastocyst (second) stage. A few developed into embryos and revealed some desirable features before the embryo failed.

The geneticists finally stumbled upon the genes that coded for the horns and frill of the triceratops. To create a mammalian equivalent of a triceratops, the geneticists spliced those specific gene segments into a bison ova. Since the bison has horns of its own, they hoped its augmented genome would express the triceratops horns.

When an embryo developed into a fetus and a live calf was born, the geneticists were elated. As the calf developed, the large front horn and frill of the triceratops also developed. Unfortunately, they were much too heavy. The hybrid calf was unable to raise its head. Repeated efforts to do so eventually broke its neck.

There was one consolation. The geneticists found thickened horny plates covering the calf's head, neck, and body. They were similar to the scutes found on a triceratops. Long ago, Rafe Cassius had given his lyvulseroptera a coat of armor—plates of thick keratin suffused with calcium phosphate. Although the lyvulseroptera's genome was lost, Rafe's geneticists had engineered the plates and documented their work. Mason immediately latched onto it.

Back to the Drawing Board

"If we engineer the uptake of calcium phosphate into the calf's plates, we could make them and the calf resistant to fire," Mason hypothesized. Unbeknownst to him, the lyvulseroptera's plates had resisted the transient fire of a red dragon, but not the firestorm unleashed by a great gray dragon.

One creative geneticist suggested, "We could add growth hormones to increase the size and weight of the bison and enlarge its bony structure."

"It doesn't really need a full size frill," said a third geneticist. "If we strip out those genes, it should reduce the weight on the neck considerably."

So began the redesign of the bison hybrid. After several more trials, the geneticists were successful in creating a massive hybrid with the horns of a triceratops and fire-resistant scutes—at least, theoretically. The beast stood nearly twelve feet tall at the shoulder and weighed an estimated 12,000 pounds. It was almost as large as a triceratops. The geneticists dubbed it the bovi—short for bovicerahorridus (illustration 17).

Illustration 17: Bovicerahorridus

Mason was ecstatic. He could hardly wait to report these findings to Raephela.

"Our new triceratops–bison hybrid may be comparable to a real triceratops. It could compete successfully with a dragon," he boasted.

This remark revealed how little the Cassius Foundation knew about dragons. Red dragons stood twelve to seventeen feet tall at the shoulders. The head and neck added an additional six to eight feet. With a body length of fourteen to twenty feet (not including head and neck), the tail added another twelve to sixteen feet. Great gray dragons were far larger.

Raephela was skeptical. "Have you tested its power?" she asked.

It's a gigantic bison! thought Mason, who was careful hide his exasperation. "We will make arrangements with the guards to put the hybrid through its paces," he replied.

Paces

Given the hybrid's huge size, the guards did not have a cage large enough to hold it. The bovi was allowed to graze on the scrub vegetation outside the fortress. Five guards were assigned to prod the bovi with spears to make it react. When that didn't work, they loosed arrows upon it, which was equally ineffective. The shutes were impenetrable, so the arrows ricocheted off the hybrid's artificial armor. The guards tried pushing and pulling on the animal to no avail. Its six tons remained immovable until the hybrid decided to graze elsewhere. Then, it simply hauled the guards along with it. In the end, the guards were the only ones being put through their paces.

Finally, Finn, Raephela's lead guard, decided to release a mix of serojacutas, theracapracani, and lupucercopiths. He assumed that these hybrid predators would attack the bovi as if it were prey. They did not. As rivals for food and dominance, the hybrids immediately attacked each other. Minutes later, those who survived did espy a prey species—humans. Two of the horrified guards failed to react quickly enough and were cut down. The other three were forced to kill the hybrids in self-defense—except for one.

An adventurous theracapricanus decided to tackle the bovi. It jumped onto the massive beast and grasped its snout in powerful jaws. This maneuver would suffocate any ordinary prey. Taken by surprise, the bovi shook its head violently in an attempt to dislodge its attacker. The theracapricanus clung to the massive hybrid by digging its front claws into the bovi's jaws while its back claws gripped its throat. Finally, the bovi slammed its attacker into the ground. Stunned by the blow, the theracapricanus released its grip, and the bovi promptly trampled it.

The bovi bolted, running out of control and thrusting its head in the air. It was unstoppable. The remaining guards could do nothing except get out of its way and watch the beast as it ran off across the open field. Once it came to a stop and began grazing again, they attempted to approach it. Easily spooked, it charged them and then stopped as the guards fled. It became clear that humans would be unable to control this hybrid's behavior. Cannon fire would be needed to bring it down—not unlike a great gray dragon.

Supplemental Notes and Citations

Avian and non-avian dinosaurs

Archosauria is the oldest crown group of reptiles, including dinosaurs (Bailleul, *et al.*, 2019). Dinosaurs subsequently branched into avian (bird) and non-avian (reptile) lineages (Griffin, *et al.*, 2020; O'Connor, *et al*, 2018; Organ, *et al.*, 2007). The general consensus is that birds diverged from dinosaurs during the Mesozoic era.

Ancestral diapsid → Archosaur → Therapod dinosaur → Birds and Reptiles

Using molecular cytogenetics, researchers recreated the genome (karyotype) of a potential ancestor for birds and dinosaurs, which shows their divergence. Birds have a much smaller karyotype than do reptiles.

Research into the constituents of eggshells shows little difference between dinosaur eggshells and those of modern reptiles and birds (Montanari, 2018). All dinosaurs, birds, and reptiles have hard shells consisting mainly of calcite (a hard form of calcium carbonate).

Non-avian dinosaur fossils are usually found in sedimentary soils—such as clay, mud, silt, and sand—most commonly in the deserts and badlands of western North America (Utah, New Mexico, Arizona, Montana) and in Alberta, Canada.

Ancestral DNA

It is highly unlikely that ancestral DNA over one million years old will be found (Pääbo, *et al.*, 2004). Even then, only short fragments are available. Degradation by enzymes, damage by bacteria and other microorganisms, and oxidation break up DNA. Even the process of preservation can damage it. Preserved DNA may be found embedded in bone crystals where they were protected from degradation (Salamon, *et al.*, 2005). For fragments that are found, polymerase chain reaction (PCR) can reproduce the DNA.

Polymerase chain reaction (PCR)

Polymerase chain reaction is a laboratory procedure that amplifies target segments or fragments of molecular DNA (Ghannam & Varacallo, 2020; Li, *et al*, 2018). It is highly sensitive in identifying specific gene sequences and can replicate millions of copies for study.

Conventional PCR has its limitations. Hence advancements in PCR technology have improved PCR processing significantly (Yu, *et al.*, 2017). Shortened reaction times (ultrafast photonic PCR), improved sensitivity and specificity (nanoPCR), and amplification when only a few nucleic acids are available (droplet digital PCR) have expanded the PCR's capabilities (Li, *et al.*, 2018; Sang, *et al.*, 2017; You, *et al.*, 2020).

Molecular cytogenetics

Cytogenetics is the study of the structure and function of chromosomes and their influence on cell function (Palumbo & Russo, 2016.) Chromosomal rearrangements can lead to mutations and genetic instability. Molecular cytogenetics can identify complex chromosomal rearrangements in greater detail.

Replicating DNA

Helicase is an enzyme that unwinds the DNA double helix. DNA polymerase is an enzyme that can make multiple copies of the desired DNA sequence. Polymerase chain reaction provides the identity and location of specific genes and can be used to make copies of a specific DNA sequence.

Part III
Cloak and Dagger

CHAPTER 14
Whither a Paleontologist

Without the benefit of a paleontologist or an archeologist, the Cassius bounty hunters ultimately brought back many useless bones. The vast array of skeletal remains proved to be mostly modern animal species native to the territories where the bones were collected.

Cassius's scientists readily identified the bones of modern animals; however, the process of sorting which bones belonged to what animal took considerable time.

A Modicum of Success

The hunters had fared poorly in their search for fossils. Raephela was less than pleased with the outcome. Hunters began quietly disappearing to their respective haunts before she could exact any punishments. They did not seek payment for time and materials.

A few years later, actual dinosaur fossils were accidentally discovered in a limestone cavern. Two hunters had fallen into a cave serving as the entrance to the cavern. There they found massive bones that had been preserved when the ground collapsed and closed off the cave to ambient air.

"What kind of animals bones are these?" asked one hunter.

"I don't know, and I don't care," replied Cole, the lead hunter. "Given their size, they may be just what we're looking for." *These bones might save us from Raephela's wrath*, he thought, *and we might even get paid*. He ordered the excavation of several bones, which his crew hoisted out of the cavern.

Ryker, the foundation's geologist, recognized the fossils as belonging to the Cretaceous period based on the fossils of flowering plants embedded in the rock layers. Yet he was at a loss to identify the type of animal from the bones alone. He simply lacked the expertise. An enormous bone could be a dinosaur, or a mammoth, or a prehistoric rhinoceros. It could be a carnivorous predator or an herbivore. Jaws with serrated teeth were readily identified and presumed to be some kind of carnivorous dinosaur. Horns proved more difficult to identify since they could belong to carnivores or herbivores. Most horns were too large to be supported by modern animals. Ryker did find an intriguing set of two slightly curved horns with very sharp ends that were small enough for a large mammal to support.

"I wonder if any of these bones belong to a dragon," one of the hunters asked.

"I don't know," Ryker replied. He had no knowledge of dragon lore and therefore did not know there would be no dragon bones. (Upon the death of a dragon, a clan member destroyed the remains with fire, leaving no trace.) "The geneticists will have to figure out what's what," Ryker added.

Easier Said Than Done

Cassius's geneticists immediately latched upon the fossils as potential DNA sources for new animal armaments. Yet their examinations yielded little DNA. Furthermore, without knowing the animals' species, they could not determine if it would be useful.

"It would be nice to know what species of dinosaurs these bones are from," murmured Mason.

Mason approached Raephela with trepidation. "We have many dinosaur bones, and we have extracted genetic material from a few of them," he said, deliberately omitting how little DNA his staff had actually retrieved. "Except for the horn of a triceratops, we do not know to which species of dinosaurs the bones belong. The geologist has been useless," he remarked, attempting to shift any wrath from himself onto Ryker.

"He found the bones," Raephela remarked flatly. "We need a paleontologist." *But where to get one*, she wondered. Erwina came to mind.

Raephela immediately summoned Cole and his bounty hunters. "Infiltrate Erwina," she ordered. "Focus on the village where they have a schoolhouse. There are a plethora of faculty there. Search among them. It is entirely possible that one of them will be a paleontologist. Kidnap that person and bring him or her to me . . . alive."

In fact, there was a paleontologist, Khristina; however, she resided in Gregor. Each summer, she traveled from Gregor to Erwina where she proctored students in their search for fossils on natural-history field trips. The bounty hunters knew naught of these arrangements. It was late fall by the time a party of four hunters set out to kidnap a paleontologist from Erwina's schoolhouse. The exercise would be futile. By this time, Khristina had already left Erwina to return home before the arctic winter closed the mountain pass south of Gregor.

To complicate matters further, the hunters knew little about Erwina's territory or the location of the schoolhouse. Erwina had never been considered a significant source of resources, so Cassius's raiders had not explored it.

"Do we know who we are looking for?" asked Dawson, Cole's second in command.

"No," Cole replied.

"Some old fossil who looks for fossils," laughed Logan, another hunter.

"What do we know about this schoolhouse?" Dawson persisted.

"Nothing," replied Cole.

"Do we know where it is?" queried O'Connor, the third hunter.

"Vaguely," answered Cole.

"Swell," muttered O'Connor under his breath.

"How big is it?" asked Cooper, the fourth hunter.

"No idea," replied Cole.

"Do they have armed guards?" asked Dawson, trying desperately to get any useful information about their target.

"Maybe," answered Cole.

"It's a schoolhouse," remarked O'Connor dryly. "They probably lock their doors at night. This ought to be a walk in the park."

"If we can find it," said Cooper, sarcastically.

"Do we know anything at all about this place?" asked Dawson, in a last-ditch effort to glean any intelligence.

"Nope," replied Cole.

"This is crazy," muttered Cooper.

"So what else is new?" replied Cole, who prudently decided not to tell his comrades how far they would have to travel.

A Walk in the Park

After boarding a barge loaded with the supplies, the hunters headed south via the River Taurus (appendix I). They were obliged to portage around the confluence of the Taurus and the River Cassius to avoid dangerous category IV whitewater rapids that led to the River Feroxaper (map 1, The Territories). Upon accessing the Feroxaper, the hunters ran its less difficult but still dangerous category III rapids. The hunters then took a right fork off the Feroxaper to flow into the River Pices, which cut across the neck of Caput Canis. At this point, the Pices flowed swiftly; however, there were no rapids as it descended through H'Aleth territory. Although H'Aleth's scouts patrolled this area, H'Aleth had built no outposts along the Pices. With any luck, the hunters would slip through without being spotted. They did and entered open territory. They had to portage again around the confluence of the Pices with the River Admare, which was named the River Vulpes by the H'Aletheans.

Afterwards, the Pices flowed due west through an expanse of forest. It posed little trouble for the barge or its passengers until the Pices met the River Ferveo. The hunters could not portage around this crossing. They had no option but to battle the confluence. The fierce turbulence and shear stresses between two discordant rivers created an enormous upwelling of water that tossed the barge as if it were a buoy. The hunters had to battle

Map 1: Territories

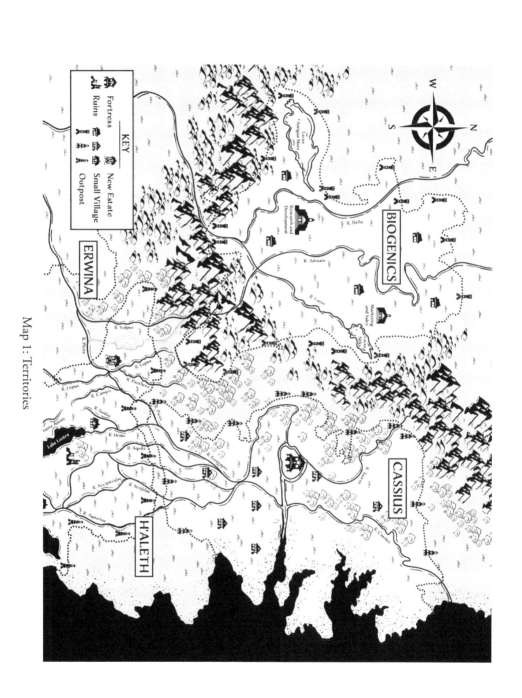

the water to keep to the right and stay on the Pices. Unbeknownst to them, they were aided by a playful river dragon, the sitka (illustration 18). It was having a rollicking good time testing its own strength and agility against the forces of the Ferveo. The dragon pushed the barge out of its way and into the channel that flowed into the Pices.

Illustration 18: Sitka

Once past the rivers' confluence, the Pices settled into a leisurely flow. Shortly thereafter, the hunters disembarked on a sandbar, on the south side of the Pices. They camouflaged their barge among some trees and brush alongside the river. Then, four of the five hunters collapsed. Only Cole was still standing.

"Are we there yet?" asked Logan with a groan.

"No," replied Cole.

"Can we take a break anyway?" asked O'Connor.

"No," replied Cole.

"You're killing us," complained Cooper.

"How much farther is it?" sighed Dawson.

"Not far," Cole answered quietly.

An Awkward Encounter

After retrieving their food, water, and weapons from the barge, the hunters headed due south on foot. From this point on, they had to take care. Erwina had scouts, too.

After a while, the hunters encountered a rocky ridge about twelve feet high. The height seemed to vary with the terrain. The structure was in fact a man-made mound of rocks, dirt, and debris built to look like a natural ridge. It steered any unannounced and unexpected visitors away from the compound housing the schoolhouse. Finally, the hunters found a place where the ridge was only eight feet high and scrambled over it. Their effort loosed several rocks in the process, which tumbled down and scattered. Sensitive ears easily targeted the sound.

Barely a moment later, a woodland owl landed unseen and unheard in the canopy above the hunters. It watched the invaders briefly and then silently flew away. Soon afterward, a gray wolf crept up toward the ridge from the south, as did a tawny cougar from the north. Both were tracking the intruders, not each other. Suddenly, Erwina's scouts, bows drawn, surrounded the hunters.

"Stand fast!" ordered Eowen, one of Erwina's lead scouts. The hunters' weaponry clearly identified what, if not who, they were. Still, Eowen gave no indication he recognized the four strangers' occupation. He needed to know what kind of hunters they were—sport or bounty. He suspected the latter. They were too well armed to be villagers hunting for food and too leanly supplied to be hunting for sport.

The hunters didn't move. There were too many arrows pointed in their direction. They remained unaware of the two apex predators close at hand.

"Put down your weapons," Eowen directed.

The hunters carefully laid their bows and quivers of arrows on the ground. They kept their knives hidden in their jackets.

"State your business," Eowen demanded.

"We're looking for a paleontologist," blurted out Logan. "We don't want to harm anybody. We just want to talk to him . . . or her," he stammered. His eyes belied that last statement.

Eowen, momentarily speechless, just stared at Logan. After twenty years of scouting, he thought he had heard every excuse that hunters of all stripes had to offer. Apparently not. Meanwhile, Cole entertained thoughts of strangling Logan.

Finally, Eowen announced, "We don't have any paleontologists." *I can't wait to tell Headmaster Joseph and Rulinda about these guys.*

"Oh, well then, we'll be on our way," offered Logan in return.

"Yes, you will," stated Eowen firmly. "Bind their wrists and then search them for other weapons," he ordered his fellow scouts. As the scouts removed an array of carving knives, stilettos, and short swords hidden under the hunters' apparel, there was no doubt that they had encountered bounty hunters.

"We will escort you out of our territory the same way you came," Eowen announced bluntly. The hunters had not troubled to cover their tracks.

Once the hunters and their escorts reached the River Pices, the scouts located the barge and unloaded it, leaving only the supplies of food and water. The scouts then ferried the hunters to the far banks of the Pices. After depositing the hunters on the bank along with their food, water, and a single knife, the scouts ferried themselves back across the Pices. After debating whether to destroy the well-built barge or keep it, they opted for the latter despite its size and weight. There was a bear and moose in their ranks to help haul it back to the compound, taking the hunters' weapons, traps, nets, camping, and camouflage materials with it.

Supplemental Notes and Citations

River dynamics

Differences in the rate and momentum of water, the structure of riverbeds, and the junction where rivers meet determine flow dynamics (Boyer, *et al.*, 2006). These differences create areas of intense turbulence (shear layers). The greater the difference, the greater the intensity.

CHAPTER 15
A Chance Encounter

Upon his return to the Cassius fortress, Cole decided to say nothing about his failed mission to kidnap a paleontologist. He also omitted the encounter with Erwina's scouts in his report and embellished it to imply that they had reached the schoolhouse. "They didn't have a paleontologist," he reported truthfully.

Specter

Ironically, Erwina's schoolhouse included a full-time geologist, Wyatt, who often partnered with Khristina on student field trips. In doing so, he had learned to identify many species of dinosaurs from their fossil remains. When Erwina's scouts informed him of their encounter with the band of hunters, he was concerned.

"Given the Cassius Foundation's predilection for conjuring up violent animal hybrids, I wonder if their geneticists are trying to resurrect predatory dinosaurs," he said, frowning.

"Can this be done?" asked Eowen.

"Not to my knowledge," replied Wyatt. "Ancient DNA is rarely discovered. When it is found, it is usually too degraded to use. You really need to ask Khristina." Nevertheless, he sent a courier to Gregor to inform his fellow geologist, Karel, that hunters had come to Erwina seeking a paleontologist.

Erwina also sent couriers to H'Aleth and Biogenics, informing them of the incident. In what had been a quiescent period, this thwarted attempt to kidnap a faculty member raised the specter that the Cassius Foundation had resumed its raids.

Before the war, the foundation had hired bounty hunters to kidnap scientists—especially geneticists—and capture *H. transformans*. Hunters decimated many encampments, sweeping up both *H. transformans* and *H. sapiens* indiscriminately. After the death of Rafe Cassius, the raids had largely subsided—except for in H'Aleth. Its scouts continued to encounter bounty hunters. The unsuccessful foray into Erwina territory put all three houses and Biogenics on alert.

Theropoda

Meanwhile, the foundation's search for fossil DNA had still yielded only a smattering of genes from the triceratops. *An herbivore*, Raephela fumed. Without the DNA of at least one therapod species, the geneticists could not imbue any extant animal with the characteristics of a large carnivorous dinosaur.

In an effort to placate Raephela, Mason explained, "There are many species that can supply large sharp teeth. The crocodile is a modern dinosaur with teeth nearly four inches long. The alligator gar, an enormous fish, has a double row of very sharp, fang-like teeth. Tigers and other big cats grow fangs that can be three inches long."

Raephela glared at him. In a low, menacing voice, she snarled, "The saber-toothed tiger had canines eleven inches long. I suggest you develop the equivalent." Mason knew she was not merely suggesting.

"Of course. Right away," Mason replied, bowing and backing away. *Thank goodness toothed species develop teeth the same way*, he thought with a sigh. He returned to his lab to inform his staff that they had yet another new project.

"Her Highness demands a saber-toothed tiger," Mason announced sarcastically. Subsequently he sent for hunters.

"Capture the largest female tiger you can find," he instructed. "And bring it back alive." He needed ova to develop a hybrid.

At first, Cole stared at Mason. Then he said, "I don't have enough manpower to capture a tigress alive. Tigers are too large, too powerful, and extremely rare. I might be able to bring back a female mountain lion."

"Then a mountain lion will have to do," sighed Mason. *Thank goodness for somatotropin.*

A Tacit Understanding

For the hunters, it was back to the northern mountains—despite their vow never to return. Fortunately, it was summer. The forest canopy was thick with leaves, which provided cover. Cole and his crew were less likely to be spotted by a dragon. Even so, everyone was worried.

"Neither the adult nor the youngster attacked us," Cole reminded his compatriots. "If we keep a low profile and don't act aggressively, perhaps they will not see us as competitors or threats."

"We're neither one," said Dawson emphatically. "We might be its prey."

"I don't think we are," Cole said thoughtfully, remembering how the adult simply looked at them before lifting off. "Otherwise, we wouldn't be here." *It was almost as if the dragon knew not to attack us. But how can that be?* he wondered and then dismissed the notion.

Raephela's hunters had no way of knowing that the three houses had reached an accord with several related clans of great gray dragons. All parties had agreed to be vigilant and warn the others of any sign of Cassius incursion or aggression. They also agreed to protect a lost member of another clan or house until that member could be returned to his or her own kind. Since the hunters had not threatened the dragon or his offspring, the dragon had reciprocated in kind.

A Fortuitous Event

When Raephela's hunters reached the montane forest below the northern mountains, they knew they had entered gray dragon territory. They fell silent. There was no idle chatter—not even whispers. They walked carefully in soft leather moccasins, following Cole's footsteps as he picked his way through the detritus on the forest floor. Cole carefully avoided stepping on dried leaves, twigs, and branches that would crackle and snap under human footsteps. As he did so, he looked for signs that a puma had been in the area—large paw marks of a cat in the dirt, claw marks on trees, or remains of a kill. Periodically, they would stop and listen for any sounds breaking the woodland silence. All of them kept a sharp eye on their surroundings, including the sky, and kept their knives at hand.

The hunters stopped abruptly when they heard trampling sounds. They recognized the footfalls made by humans along with the sound of something being dragged. Apparently, these humans had no regard for stealth, and they were on course to intersect the hunters.

Cole was certain that he and his men were the only hunters Raephela had dispatched to the northern mountains. He silently signaled his companions to disperse and remain hidden with bows drawn and ready. Cole did the same, and all waited to see who would pass by.

Soon a half dozen villagers came into view. They had killed a white-tailed deer and were headed back to their encampment, dragging it behind them. The deer had been killed for food, clothing, and tools. No part of the animal would go to waste. Unseen, the hunters waited for them to move on. When the villagers were well away, the hunters resumed their search.

Suddenly, they heard shouts, sounds of turmoil, and the screams of a mountain lion. The villagers were being attacked by a puma. When Cole looked at his comrades, they all nodded and raced to the scene. They found a few villagers attempting to fend off a puma trying to steal their deer. The puma clearly had the upper hand. Some of villagers were injured from swipes of the animal's powerful forelimbs and claws. Others were taking aim with their arrows to kill it.

Cole shouted at the villagers, "Don't shoot! Back off! We'll handle it!" Then he turned to his men. "Get the net. This is a female." His comrades were already scrambling to ready the netting.

The amazed villagers did indeed back away. The puma promptly began dragging the deer's carcass away. This proved to be her undoing.

From a safe distance, the villagers watched the hunters envelope the lion in netting. As the enraged animal attempted to strike its captors, she only became more entangled. Eventually, the hunters twisted the corners, two on each end, entrapping the lion. Yet even with two hunters holding each end, the puma's violent wrestling pulled the hunters toward her. They too were in danger of being clawed.

Pointing to two of the villagers, Cole shouted, "Get over here! Each of you grab one end and help keep tension on the net." The two villagers did as they were told. Cole took out a dart with a tranquilizing agent and loosed it at close range, striking the puma. The animal fought her captors for a few more minutes, aiding the spread of the drug. Once she was quiet, the hunters secured the netting.

Meanwhile, the villagers waited to see what would happen next. Would these hunters try to take them captive as well? Would they take the deer for themselves? The villagers who had drawn their bows had lowered them, yet kept them drawn in case they were needed for self- defense.

Cole recognized what the villagers were thinking. "Be on your way," he told them. "And take the deer with you." The villagers quickly regrouped, took up the deer, and began to leave in haste. A woman paused long enough to say, "Thank you" before turning away.

The hunters could hardly believe their good fortune. "Our quarry is in the bag," bragged Cooper.

"You can celebrate when we have delivered it," said Cole. "We still have to get it back to the fortress."

They learned later that the female mountain lion was a prize find. She was pregnant, which explained her desperate attempt to secure the deer.

Supplemental Notes and Citations

Theropoda

This early clade of carnivorous dinosaurs and their descendants included non-avian, avian, and herbivorous species (Hendrickx & Mateus, 2015; Zanno, *et al.*, 2009).

Tooth development

Tooth development across multiples classes of animals—mammals (including humans), fish, and reptiles—has been fairly consistent throughout evolution (Thesleff, 2014). For the most part, the genes that promote the development of teeth have been conserved and reused for nearly all species that have teeth.

Some of the differences in the shape of an animal's teeth evolved as species evolved (Koussoulakou, *et al.*, 2009). Carnivores have canines and claws to grasp and hold prey. Herbivores have molars for grinding vegetation. Thus, there is a strong correlation between diet and tooth morphology.

Somatotropin (growth hormone)

Growth hormone has a wide range of effects on almost all tissues throughout all stages of development, from embryo to adulthood (Devesa, *et al.*, 2016; Lu, *et al.*, 2019). It stimulates the growth of muscles, bones, and internal organs. It also influences the metabolism of proteins, fats, and carbohydrates. Excess production of this hormone causes excessive enlargement of tissues and bones—gigantism in children, acromegaly in adults (Lu, *et al.*, 2019).

CHAPTER 16
The Elusive X^T

Before the house of Gregor was established, the Biogenetics Company had begun searching for the genes that enabled some people to transform into another species of animal. Their scientists had already discovered that those people had many chromosomes that were larger than normal. These chromosomes carried the additional genes of another animal species. Further study revealed that an individual with only a partial set of another animal's genes could not transform into that animal.

After Biogenetics merged with the Eugenics Corporation, the newly formed Biogenics Corporation discovered that the ability to undergo transformation was tied to changes in the X chromosome, dubbed the X^T chromosome. Provided an individual had the complete genotype of another species of animal—usually a mammal—and an X^T chromosome, he or she could transform into that animal. So Biogenics scientists set their sights on discovering how the X^T chromosome functioned. They found themselves in a quagmire of genetic code.

Meanwhile, the Cassius Foundation also wanted to know which genes supported transformation and how they operated. Yet its founder, Angus Cassius, was not about to expend his resources to discover it. He directed his geneticists to continue creating powerful and terrifying human and animal hybrids that could bring other territories under his control. Meanwhile, he sent spies to infiltrate Biogenics and steal its research for his use. He would have sent spies to Gregor as well, had its location not been so far away and isolated.

Allies

Biogenics was not alone. Gregor's scientists were tackling the same question and had encountered the same problems. Once the treaty between Biogenics and the three houses had settled, a collegial relationship developed among the parties. Trade and common interests, including a common enemy, strengthened their ties. Once Biogenics disavowed any further experimentation with genetic hybrids, Gregor extended its services to the people of Biogenics and began to collaborate with Biogenics geneticists.

Over time, Biogenics acknowledged Gregor as foremost in the field of genetics and genetic engineering. Subsequently, Biogenics transferred most of its genetic engineering resources to Gregor. It also joined the H'Aletheans and Erwinians in providing tissue samples from the remains of any animal hybrids it encountered. Biogenics continued to maintain its own laboratories, as did H'Aleth and Erwina, to provide genetic analyses for its own population.

Gregor geneticists' goals were distinctly different from those of the Cassius Foundation. Gregor wanted to discover the intricacies of gene functions—especially what caused some genes to go astray—and how to rectify genetic disorders. Hence, Gregor's scientists focused much of their research on the genomes of altered *H. transformans* and animal hybrids. In these genomes they found misaligned and missing genes, broken chromosomes, and gene mutations—all of which triggered unintended changes in other genes. In working with these disruptions, they hoped to remedy at least some of the deformities wrought by the Cassius Foundation.

An Ancestral Fear

The mystery of the X^T chromosome was not lost on Raephela. As a direct descendant of Angus Cassius, she was an *H. transformans*. She and all of her female ancestors were born with a single transforming

X chromosome. Her family had yet to conceive a female with two X^T chromosomes. Despite their power and position, this shortcoming threatened to weaken their standing. When she assumed control of the Cassius Foundation, she also inherited the fear that her family would be perceived as weak.

Raephela's geneticists were confounded by the myriad additional genes on both somatic chromosomes and the X^T chromosome. They struggled to pinpoint which ones were active and became frustrated in their attempts to identify the functions of those that were.

"How many extra genes are there in this one?" asked Mason, referring to the genome of yet another *H. transformans*.

"I've lost count," sighed his colleague. "Every somatic chromosome has thousands of extra genes. The X^T has even more. The good news is that a large number of them appear to be inactive. The bad news is that many of the genes that appeared identical at first glance are actually polymorphic. They vary by one single nucleotide," she added.

"Perhaps these polymorphic genes all have the same function," Mason suggested.

"I can't tell," his colleague replied. "Their functions appear to depend on where they are located. Sometimes, the exact same gene situated in a different gene sequence has a different function."

"Of course it does," Mason said with resignation. *This is going to be another long day.*

An Old Strategy

Raephela finally recognized that the foundation's isolation had kept her geneticists in the dark. From the foundation's long rivalry with Biogenics, she knew the latter had been trying to discover how the X^T functioned. Her great-great-grandfather had tried to steal its research. *That was a long time ago*, she thought. *Perhaps Biogenics has become complacent since our defeat.*

Raephela dispatched one of her lieutenants, a female *H. transformans* who could become a shepherd dog, to infiltrate Biogenics. "Integrate yourself as a pet into a Biogenics family. Learn as much as you can about Biogenics's research on the X^T chromosome. Then report back to me."

Raephela assumed this would be a long-term assignment—worth the wait if her spy could pilfer the discoveries that Biogenics had made. Instead, her spy returned much sooner than expected.

"Biogenics is no longer doing research on the X^T chromosome at its facility," the spy reported. "They moved it to Gregor and are collaborating with their researchers."

This was not what Raephela wanted to hear. A moment later, however, she had a change of heart. *They have put all of their eggs in one basket*, she mused, with the slightest hint of a smile.

Long ago, Cassius geneticists had learned that the House of Gregor kept a vast collection of DNA specimens. It housed the genomes of *H. sapiens*, *H. transformans*, and most animal species, including dragons.

Raephela also suspected that Gregor stored DNA from fossils of species long extinct, including dinosaurs that once roamed a more tropical arctic. She was right. With the help of Gregor's geologists, Khristina found many preserved specimens in the arctic permafrost. Gregor's geneticists had the capability of preserving ancient DNA without damaging it in the process. They also knew how to extract DNA preserved in crystalized bone. Hence, Gregor held the only repositories of both dinosaur and dragon DNA.

Unfortunately, Gregor was the least accessible. *Except during summer*, thought Raephela as she began plotting her infiltration of Gregor.

Supplemental Notes and Citations

X chromosome

In *H. sapiens*, only one of the two X chromosomes in human females is active (Balaton, *et al.*, 2018; Disteche & Berletch, 2015; Shvetsova, *et al.*, 2019). The second X chromosome is largely inactive so that males, who have only one X chromosome, can be on a genetic par with females (Engel, 2015; Harris, *et al.*, 2019). Yet not all of the genes on the silenced

X chromosome are inactive. Approximately 15% to 20% of them are active or have cycles of activation and inactivation (Balaton, *et al.*, 2018; Shvetsova, *et al.*, 2019).

Polymorphism

Polymorphism is a variation in the structure of a gene—genetic variants—that may or may not affect its functions (Jarrar & Lee, 2019). Single nucleotide polymorphisms (SNPs) are the most common type of genetic variation. They represent a change in a single nucleotide (e.g., swapping a C for a T).

Although usually the result of mutations, most are benign and provide the basis of genetic diversity both within groups and across populations. The BRCA genes (tumor suppressor genes) provide an example of a polymorphism in two of these genes, which leads to a loss of function and an increased risk of breast cancer.

Pleiotropy

The same gene can have a totally different function in different locations. It can affect multiple phenotypes in very different ways. In contrast to polymorphism, a pleiotropic gene remains unaltered. Yet it can affect many unrelated physical traits and have multiple variable effects on different traits throughout the genome (Gratten & Visscher, 2016; Jordan, *et al.*, 2018). Thus, should a pleiotropic gene become mutated, the results can have a wide range of effects downstream on different tissues and organ systems.

Epigenetic influences

Epigenetic influences are nongenetic external or internal factors that, when attached to a gene, affect the function (expression) of the gene without changing the gene itself (Lacal & Ventura, 2018; Moosavi & Motevalizadeh Ardekani, 2016). These factors may be environmental (e.g., nutrition) and internal. One common biochemical factor in particular (DNA methylation) can turn a gene off. When epigenetic changes occur in reproductive cells, they can be inherited (imprinting).

CHAPTER 17
HERE, THERE, AND WHO KNOWS WHERE

In *H. transformans* females with one X^T and one X, the former would be dominant regardless of the parent of origin, and the latter would become silent (genetic imprinting). In an *H. transformans* female with two X^T chromosomes, the genes supporting transformation would remain active in both chromosomes, enhancing an individual's capability to transform. Thus, an *H. transformans* female with two X^T chromosomes would have greater capability than any male or female with only one X^T. Similarly, the rare *H. transformans* male with two X^T chromosomes (trisomy) would enjoy the same advantage.

Although this knowledge was well documented, unfortunately it did not explain the mechanisms by which the X^T conferred the capability to transform.

"How does the blasted thing work?" muttered more than one frustrated geneticist.

A Genetic Wrinkle

"Whoa!" exclaimed Viktor, a Gregor geneticist, one fine morning. "It's gone!"

"What's gone?" asked Yana, another geneticist working beside him.

"Part of the gene sequence I spliced into this DNA segment earlier this morning," Viktor replied.

Thus began the search for the missing sequence. Initially, both geneticists thought that DNA-repair mechanisms had removed the inserted DNA and then reconnected the original ends (a homologous recombination). They began looking for the missing sequence or evidence that it had been degraded. Hours later, they found it. It was not missing after all. Instead, it had reappeared in another DNA segment on a different chromosome.

Late that afternoon, all the geneticists working on the same project gathered to summarize their findings for the day and their plans for the next day. Viktor reported that a DNA sequence had relocated from one chromosome to another. This announcement was met with surprise.

"You've got to be kidding," voiced another geneticist.

"That can't be," asserted another. "Do you really think that gene sequence hopped from one chromosome to the other?"

"That can happen with chromosome breaks that result in the loss or transfer of DNA segments," remarked Yana. "But we didn't see any breaks, inversions, or transpositions in either chromosome. The sequence just seems to have moved of its own accord."

Genes on the Move

Previous study of the *H. transformans* genome had revealed the presence of large numbers of genes that had expanded the *H. transformans* genome. Geneticists theorized that a gamma ray burst (ionizing radiation) probably had induced this expansion of the gene pool. In doing so, the radiation altered the arrangements of genes and reconfigured chromosomes, especially the X chromosome.

At first, these masses of genes just seemed to be taking up space. Subsequently, Gregor's geneticists discovered that the genes in the expanded gene pool were not inert after all. This complicated matters considerably. Trying to decipher which genes did what and where in an *H. transformans* genome was already problematic. Matters got worse with the realization that many genes once thought inert could move to a different location within the genome (transposons). Afterward, they might or might not return to their original locations. The potential pleiotropic permutations seemed infinite.

"This is a nightmare," groaned one weary geneticist.

"This is exciting," chirped another.

Yet this discovery provided the very lead that geneticists needed in order to unveil which genes ultimately governed the ability to transform. Transposons abounded in an X^T chromosome. In an *H. transformans* with two X^T chromosomes, transposons in the second one were not silenced. Gregor's geneticists suspected it was these transposons that generated the females' enhanced capability to transform.

So, using viral vectors tagged with a fluorescent agent, geneticists flagged individual transposons—one at a time—on the X^T chromosome and then tracked each transposon to its destination. This effort took a year to accomplish. When it was finished, the geneticists had compiled a map that showed where each transposon relocated in the genome. Unfortunately, this information did not reveal how the transposon functioned at that location. The researchers could generate a reasonable hypothesis regarding its purpose based on the neighboring genes. Specifically, transposons in somatic chromosomes promoted and enhanced transcription of genes supporting the phenotype of an alternate species.

The geneticists called for volunteers, both *H. sapiens* and *H. transformans*, to enroll in a research study designed to determine when and in what order transposons were activated. *Homo sapiens* would serve as the control group. This study identified specific transposons on the X^T chromosome that relocated to other regions of the chromosome. This reshuffling of genes triggered a cascade of other transposons to relocate to transcription sites on nearly every other chromosome. Although most of these locations were common to all *H. transformans*, some varied depending upon an individual's gender and alternate species. These sites remained active throughout the period of transformation. As an individual resumed human form, most of the transposons transferred back to their original location.

A Mystery Solved

The researchers' hypothesis was confirmed. Genes in the X^T chromosome directed when and where transposons relocated and how they reordered genes in target chromosomes. In turn, this led to the activation of genes supporting transformation.

"This explains why the genes of an alternate species are expressed faithfully in an uninterrupted, noncorrupted transformation," summarized Greyson, one of Gregor's lead geneticists.

The researchers also found that a single X^T chromosome supported transformation into one or two alternate species. Those with two X^T chromosomes had a much higher density of transposons and thus a much wider range of alternate species.

There was one singular exception. Most of the somatic transposons in females with two X^T chromosomes were duplicated. One set remained permanently positioned at their transcription sites, and no longer shifted back and forth.

"This would account for the ability of females with two X^T chromosomes to transform quickly," suggested one researcher. "It may also explain why some two X^T females can transform from one species directly into another species without first resuming human form again."

"Only those who are direct descendants of Ruth can do that," Greyson reminded them. "Perhaps that is one mystery we should not solve."

As for the *H. sapiens* control group, researchers found that few harbored any transforming transposons on their X chromosome. Without these transposons, *H. sapiens* could not transform even if their genome included a full complement of genes for another species.

All test subjects experienced one minor side effect. To the volunteers' dismay, their skin, mucous membranes, and the white of their eyes were tinted green. Invariably, they were greeted with trite quips from bemused family and friends.

"What planet are you from?"

"An alien invader from Mars!"

"Take me to your leader."

To avoid undue attention, those who were *H. transformans* quickly learned to become their alternate species, provided it had a heavy coat of hair, thick fur, or dark skin—preferably all three. Those who were *H. sapiens* were stuck. Fortunately, the otherworldly hue disappeared within a week.

Supplemental Notes and Citations

Genetic imprinting

Genetic imprinting is a genetic process that silences one gene in a gene pair, allowing the other gene to be expressed. Normally, both genes in a gene pair are active. Imprinting is a genetic stamp that silences one of the two genes, effectively making the stamped gene inactive (Ferguson-Smith & Bourc'his, 2018; Yuanyuan & Jinson, 2019). Genetic imprinting is often set in the embryo. Consequently, imprinting has a significant effect on phenotype without affecting the genotype.

In general, the imprinted genes may be either the maternal gene or the paternal gene. Thus, the trait that is ultimately expressed will be that of the mother or the father (the parent of origin), not both (Monk, *et al.*, 2019). The X chromosome is an exception. The paternal X chromosome is imprinted and therefore silenced (Harris, *et al.*, 2019).

Imprinting is not caused by a gene mutation. This type of inheritance follows a non-Mendelian pattern of inheritance because imprinting causes an offspring to differentiate between maternal and paternal inherited genes (Monk, *et al.*, 2019).

Ionizing radiation (IR)

High-energy ionizing radiation (e.g., gamma rays) can penetrate to the cellular level, damaging tissues and disrupting DNA (Blanco, *et al.*, 2018; Mavragani, *et al.*, 2019; Reisz, *et al.*, 2014). There are two main processes by which IR can damage or destroy cells. It generates the production of reactive oxygen molecules, which causes oxidative damage to the cell. It also damages nucleosides and other DNA constituents, causing multiple breaks in DNA strands and triggering mutations. The damage may be too extensive for DNA repair mechanisms to correct. The extent of the damage depends upon the type of radiation, proximity to the source, and duration of the exposure.

Homologous recombination (HR)

Homologous recombination is an intrinsic genetic mechanism in vertebrates whereby damaged or missing parts of DNA (e.g., nucleotides) are repaired and rejoined (Wright, *et al.*, 2018; Saito, *et al.*, 2020). If only one of the two strands is broken, HR copies the corresponding gene sequence in the intact strand and integrates it into the damaged strand.

Ironically, ionizing radiation inhibits HR. Fortunately, an alternate repair pathway—nonhomologous end joining (NHEJ)—is unaffected (Saito, *et al.*, 2020).

Transcription

Transcription is the process by which genes initiate the building of physical components of the body. The desired sequence of DNA is copied (to preserve the original sequence) and subsequently adapted so that it can direct the production of a protein.

Transposons

Transposons, also known as transposable elements, are sequences of DNA that can change their location in a genome (Bourque, *et al.*, 2018; Carducci, *et al.*, 2019; Garcia-Perez, *et al.*, 2016; Platt, *et al.*, 2018). They comprise a significant portion of the genome and can even increase its size. At one time, they were considered junk genes with no particular purpose. Yet transposons can modify the function of a gene and trigger the expression of both coding and regulatory genes.

Transposons also are also capable of moving from one chromosome to another. They can rearrange chromosomes, which could lead to changes in karyotype (Garcia-Perez, *et al.*, 2016; Klein & O'Neil, 2018). They can trigger genetic changes in both embryonic and fully developed tissues. They can even engender the development and diversification of new species (Carducci, *et al.*, 2019).

Unfortunately, a transposon's ability to insert itself into a segment of DNA can cause considerable damage (Bourque, *et al*, 2018). They can disrupt DNA sequences, causing mutations and chromosome breaks.

Somatic (autosomal) chromosomes

Somatic chromosomes are nonreproductive chromosomes that determine the majority of physical characteristics except for gender.

Tracing viral vectors

Viral vectors can be tagged with a fluorescent agent. Once tagged, researchers can track the movement of the vector within a cell, the transfer of the gene within the nucleus, and the expression of the gene (Leopold, *et al.*, 2008; O'Hara, *et al.*, 2017).

CHAPTER 18
A New Target

Raephela considered the possibility of simply raiding Gregor's store of DNA—all of it. "Other than logistics, this should not be a problem," she told her lieutenants. "Gregor has no army. They have never come under attack, and they think their location makes them impregnable. Yet people from other regions travel there during the summer thaw. If they can, so can we," she asserted.

"Send two spies," she ordered. "One must be a geneticist. The other can be one of our bounty hunters. Outfit the hunter as a fellow scientist, a biologist. The geneticist will gain access to Gregor's labs. The bounty hunter will scout out Gregor's layout, resources, and security. Identify any weaknesses Gregor has that will facilitate an invasion. The people of Gregor are so accustomed to travelers during the arctic summer, they won't suspect a thing," she said dismissively.

The House of Gregor

Gregor was the third of three interrelated houses. Gregor's scientists immersed themselves in the study of genetics, medicine, and all aspects of biology. Biologists and botanists focused on the biology of all the animal and plant species, respectively, that they and their sister houses had encountered. Practitioners of human and animal medicine could focus on the cause, diagnosis, and treatment of disease in their patients. Geneticists focused on the genomes of different species—including genetically engineered animal and humanoid hybrids—to determine how genes functioned, factors affecting them, and methods for treating genetic disorders.

Nearly everyone at Gregor participated in some form of research underway in those specialties. They subsequently shared their research and discoveries with their sister houses. After the treaty with the Biogenics Corporation was signed, Gregor included them as well.

Gregor also provided advanced education and training in medicine, including veterinary medicine, and genetics, including genetic engineering. Thus, anyone from H'Aleth or Erwina interested in pursuing any of these disciplines traveled to Gregor for advanced studies.

To gain entry into Gregor, Raephela assumed that all her spies would need was a sample of DNA and the hint that it was very unusual or extremely rare. "This should be enough to intrigue the Gregorian geneticists and get you inside," she told her spies.

Not quite.

As a rule, people usually sought help first from H'Aleth or Erwina, which could be reached far more readily than Gregor (appendix J-1). Thus, either Erwina or H'Aleth vetted any visitors, including tradesmen, going to Gregor before they traveled there. Biogenics established a similar arrangement, typically clearing their people through Erwina. A courier would apprise Gregor's staff of the visitors to expect. Thus, unknown persons arriving unannounced at Gregor automatically raised suspicions.

A Passing Glimpse

Raephela's spies watched for a caravan of travelers bound for Gregor. When they spotted one, they melded into the back of the group. In contrast to most of the travelers, they wore their hoods over their heads even though the weather was mild and the sun shone brightly in a clear sky. Most of the travelers were convivial and often chatted with fellow travelers. To avoid drawing any attention, the two people at the back of the caravan kept their heads down and rarely spoke more than a few words. Had they not been bringing up the rear, such behavior would have been noted and thought unusual.

Vasgyl, one of Gregor's scouts, guided the caravan. The travelers had crossed through the pass and reached the tundra. It was in full flower. Those who had not traveled to Gregor in the past were amazed at the splashes of color everywhere. "How beautiful," they remarked among themselves.

Suddenly, Vasgyl shouted, "Look! Up in the sky!" He was pointing toward the west and slightly behind the group. The caravan halted abruptly as everyone—except two—stopped and looked skyward. Raephela's two spies walked right into the people in front of them.

"So sorry, our apologies," they murmured without looking up.

Where Vasgyl was pointing, an arctic dragoness was in flight with two fledgling chicks trailing just behind her. Given their heading, Vasgyl was fairly certain he knew where they were going.

"They are probably headed toward the River Tesca," Vasgyl shouted, so everyone could hear. "The river supports a wide variety of fish. The dragoness may be taking her chicks to the river for fishing lessons."

"Can we detour to the river and watch them for a while?" asked one intrepid traveler. Several others voiced their desire to go as well.

"As much as I would like to watch them too, it would be unwise to do so," Vasgyl replied. "With two chicks in tow, the dragoness will be intolerant of anyone or anything approaching them. We could draw her fire."

With that assessment and one last glimpse of the dragons, the caravan was eager to be on its way. Nobody wanted to be on the dragon's dinner menu.

Protocol and Propriety

When the travelers arrived at Gregor's research facility (illustration 19, appendix J-2), they were ushered into the reception area and greeted by Gregor's security staff. Security allowed those persons already well known to go forward. All newcomers were screened, including Raephela's spies. Rorik, a seasoned security agent, interviewed the two spies.

"Please identify yourself and state your business in Gregor," said Rorik matter-of-factly.

"I am Dr. Paulson, a geneticist," Paulson replied. "And this is my colleague Dr. Claren, a biologist. I need to conduct analyses on a unique specimen of DNA."

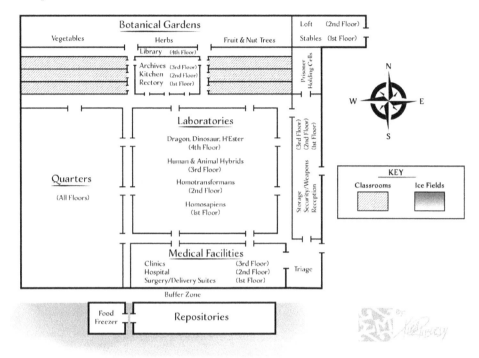

Illustration 19: Gregor's Research Facility

"What is your origin?" requested Rorik.

"We are from the Biogenics Corporation," Paulson ad-libbed. He knew better than to claim he was from H'Aleth or Erwina. Unfortunately for the two spies, the foundation was still unaware of the treaty between the three houses and Biogenics.

Rorik knew full well that no one from Biogenics had notified Gregor's security that they were sending one of their geneticists to Gregor. Even so, he did not skip a beat. "How long will you be staying here?" he asked.

"Only until we complete our analyses," Paulson replied.

"What type of analyses do you require?" Rorik asked.

"DNA analysis," Paulson answered.

"Any particular type?" Rorik queried.

"Polymerase chain reaction, mitochondrial DNA analysis, DNA sequencing, microarrays for single nucleotide polymorphisms, and others," Paulson answered, hoping that the litany of tests would be way over the security guard's head and would dispel any suspicions.

A Fly in the Ointment

The visitors' claim that they came from Biogenics did not go unnoted. When combined with their unannounced arrival and request for access to Gregor's laboratories, red flags soared overhead. Treaty members were well aware of the Cassius Foundation's history of espionage. All of them were certain that the foundation's spies continued to operate, even though the foundation had withdrawn from the public eye.

At first, Ivana, Gregor's chief of security, was concerned that Cassius had sent bounty hunters to kidnap their paleontologist. Khristina had conveyed to Ivana the warning Wyatt sent earlier. Alternatively, the strangers could be mercenaries hoping to steal classified information and materials, including DNA samples. These could be sold for a high price on the black market.

Ivana immediately notified Andrei, Khristina, and Yelena. "I suspect that these people are from the Cassius Foundation and are attempting to infiltrate us," she said. "I suggest we play along until we learn with certainty where they are from and what they want."

"I suspect you are correct," responded Andrei. "It is also possible that they have found some very unusual DNA and need our resources to analyze it. It may require more sophisticated techniques than they have available."

"I doubt seriously that they have our capabilities," Yelena asserted. "The Cassius Foundation has kept itself so isolated, it's unlikely that their scientists have the capabilities that we do."

Andrei turned to Ivana. "Assign additional security to the labs and to the staff quarters. Increase the security for Khristina's family in case someone attempts to kidnap them to hold as hostages." Then Andrei turned to Yelena. "Tell our visitors that we will conduct the analysis as soon as arrangements can be made. Since their visit was not prearranged, it will take a while for us to fit them into our current schedule. In the meantime, we will meet with them to discuss their requirements. This should buy us enough time to investigate them."

Andrei immediately sent couriers to Erwina, H'Aleth, and Biogenics. H'Edwina volunteered to serve as the courier to H'Aleth. She knew the most direct route to the main village. As a golden eagle, she could achieve a flight speed of 30 miles per hour and soar at 120 miles per hour. She could reach the estate in a few days. A security member whose alternate species was an arctic wolf raced to Erwina's northeast outpost where he relayed Gregor's message. A scout who could transform into a woodland owl carried the message to the compound while another scout carried the message to the Biogenics research-and-development headquarters.

Meanwhile, an escort showed Gregor's new visitors to their assigned quarters. "I am your escort for today," he announced. "The dining room will be open for dinner in an hour. That will give you and the other arrivals time to freshen up. If you have any questions or need any assistance, please feel free to ask me or any future escort to assist you."

Inside, Claren turned to Paulson. "We will have to follow their rules for a few days to dispel any suspicions they may have," she advised. "In the meantime, we can learn our way around the facility and be amicable."

Supplemental Notes and Citations

Mitochondrial DNA (mtDNA)

Mitochondrial DNA is found in subcellular organelles that produce biochemical cellular energy. This source of DNA is separate and distinct from the familiar nuclear DNA genome that directs an organism's phenotype. Where nuclear DNA is badly degraded or not available at all, mtDNA may be analyzed in lieu of nuclear DNA (Amorim, *et al.*, 2019).

Mitochondrial DNA is inherited almost exclusively via the maternal line (Bettinger & Wayne, 2016). In contrast, nuclear DNA is inherited from both maternal and paternal lines. In the absence of mutation, mtDNA sequences in all maternal relatives are identical (Amorim, *et al.*, 2019). Hence, they are not unique to a particular individual. Rather, they reveal the relationship among individuals of the same maternal lineage.

Microarrays for single nucleotide polymorphisms (SNPs)

Single nucleotide polymorphisms are a type of gene variation in which one nucleotide—adenine, guanine, cytosine, thymine, or uracil—in a DNA sequence has been changed (polymorphism). They are very common and reflect genetic variability. Microarrays are molecular biology methods of detecting and measuring SNPs (Gao, *et al.*, 2016), with an emphasis on evaluating their role in cancer (Berry, *et al.*, 2019).

CHAPTER 19
The Game's Afoot

For Raephela's spies, efforts to behave like gracious guests lasted less than twenty-four hours. On their way to the dining room, a most pleasant escort gave them an introductory tour of the first floor of the research facility.

"Since you are new to Gregor, we have arranged for you to have your own personal escort during your stay," the escort beamed. "Your escort will be immediately available to you whenever you leave your quarters and will take you wherever you need to go—the rectory, the restroom, the conference room."

"We can find our way," said Paulson curtly. Both he and Claren were eager to complete their respective tasks and depart as soon as possible. Paulson would focus on gaining access to the laboratories and the DNA storage facilities—especially the DNA repositories. Claren would concentrate on security measures, potential weaknesses in the facility's infrastructure, and avenues of approach that would support a surprise attack.

"It's no trouble at all," responded their escort sweetly. "Be sure to ask an escort to take you to the botanical gardens. It's very serene there."

Indeed, an escort was immediately available to them—stationed right outside their quarters. Already impatient, this restraint soured the spies' dispositions.

Setting the Stage

Over the next few days, all couriers returned with the same message.

Neither the other two houses nor Biogenics had sent anyone with such a request. This news only increased Ivana's suspicion that the two visitors were Cassius spies.

While couriers were accomplishing their missions, the spies met in a conference room with administrators, geneticists, research assistants, statisticians, and laboratory technicians for multiple sessions. The discussions centered on their needs for administrative support, their research design, their choices of DNA analysis methods, and the equipment they would require. The hidden agenda behind these sessions was to keep the two spies occupied and contained while Gregor investigated them. It afforded Ivana time to establish a system to track the two intruders. Last but not least, Gregor's staff could evaluate what the two knew about conducting DNA analyses, which might provide some insight into their visitors' intentions.

Although very impatient, Paulson handled all the discussions appropriately. After all, he was a geneticist and researcher in his own right. Meanwhile, Claren was going out of her mind. If she heard one more discussion about dependent and independent variables, multiple regression and factor analyses, or the sensitivities and specificities of testing methods, et cetera, et cetera, ad nauseum, she was going to strangle somebody—possibly all of them.

Finally, the stage was set. From the moment the intruders left their assigned quarters, designated staff members observed their activities wherever they went. Most of the time, Ivana assigned people who already worked in an area, such as laboratory technicians, gardeners, housekeepers, librarians, administrative secretaries—all of whom had been trained in surveillance at Erwina. Ivana also deployed some of her own staff to bolster security for the engine room, which housed the generators that supported the entire facility. She provided additional security for the laboratories, which everyone knew was the intruders' likely target, and for all exits and entrances to the facility. There was always the possibility that more intruders were waiting in the wings.

A Fox in the Hen House

The next morning, an escort led the two intruders to a laboratory workstation on the first floor. Unlike the laboratories on the upper floors, the first floor labs were open to students, teachers, visiting researchers, and curious onlookers. Amiable staff willingly answered questions and demonstrated selected procedures.

"Our geneticists and researchers study the genetics of *H. sapiens* in this lab," remarked their escort cheerfully as they entered the area.

It was not where the two intruders wanted to be. Both suspected that the labs on the upper floors held the DNA they coveted. Nevertheless, the first floor lab was a step in the right direction. *Hopefully, this means we have finally been accepted*, Paulson speculated.

Dr. Greyson, the first-floor laboratory's lead geneticist, greeted them warmly. "I understand you have some unusual DNA you wish to analyze," she said. "Dr. Dimas, one of our geneticists, and his lab technician, Kaden, will provide you with any assistance you need."

"I don't need a geneticist," snapped Paulson with a cursory nod toward Dr. Dimas. "I only need the technician." All three Gregorians had been apprised that Paulson was a potential spy. Kaden had been tasked to observe and assist Paulson with standard genetic analyses commonly conducted in a laboratory setting.

Dr. Greyson and Dr. Dimas withdrew as Paulson and the Kaden began to work. As the latter became engrossed in following Paulson's directions, Claren gradually stepped back, as if to get out of their way. A scan of the room revealed that everyone was busy working on a project. Claren quietly wove around the cubicles, taking care not to disturb anyone. As she moved through the lab and scanned the area beyond it, she saw no guards or security of any kind.

Unbelievable! Claren thought as she slipped out of the lab, whereupon she decided to take a self-guided tour of the facility and surrounding territory. She immediately ascended the stairs to investigate the upper floors. There were no guards; however, access to both the second and third floors was barred. Whereas the doors to the first-floor labs were wide open, these doors were closed and locked. A quick inspection of the locks revealed they required a code to gain entry. *This must be where they work on all the rest of their DNA samples*, she inferred correctly. She would test her skills at breaking codes later.

Claren quickly descended the stairs. When she reached the first floor, she scanned the hallway and found no one there. All was quiet except for the low murmurs of people speaking as they worked. She checked each doorway as she passed by the rectory and classrooms and slipped past the east hallway. Everyone was busy performing his or her assigned tasks. The reception area was prepared to receive new visitors later that day. For the present, it was empty.

A Change in Element

As Claren slipped outside, she gave a soft laugh and shook her head slightly. *How lax their security is. They must truly think their location makes them impregnable.* She failed to detect the staff members who had been watching her as she moved through the first floor. Nor did she see the snowy owl, in its summer plumage, perched in a nearby copse of Norway spruce which Gregor's founders had planted long ago (illustration 20, Hidden Sentinels).

It was a beautiful day to go for a walk. The sun was shining in a clear sky, and the temperature was about fifty degrees Fahrenheit. A light breeze made the ambient air feel a bit chilly. The tundra was in full bloom. There were bright yellow and red poppies, blue arctic lupine, white Labrador tea, violet parrya, and lavender pasque flowers everywhere. Claren took little note of them except to scan the wide-open space surrounding the facility. She saw no barriers or other defenses that would bar an assault on the complex. She did notice that the south end of the facility abutted a large mass of glacial ice.

Claren soon discovered the only unattached exterior building. The soft humming that emitted from the structure revealed the generators

Illustration 20: Hidden Sentinels

inside it. *Even their power source is unguarded*, she thought mockingly. She did not notice the arctic fox, in its summer coat, hidden among the burst of flowers. She did spot a magnificent caribou stag grazing not too far away. *If only I had my bow and a quiver of arrows.* Since she had no such weapons, she dismissed the deer.

Unbeknownst to Claren, all three—owl, fox, and deer—were scouts, keeping watch over her and marking where she went. They were perfectly camouflaged in the arctic terrain. Gregor's territory was foreign to Claren, as was its wildlife and vegetation. This huntress was out of her element. Soon thereafter, Claren returned to the lab to resume her place with Paulson.

"Oh, you're back," remarked the technician, who thought he should acknowledge the hunter's absence. It would have become obvious eventually.

"Yes. I missed breakfast, so I went to the rectory for something to eat," she lied smoothly.

CHAPTER 20
UNMASKED

From time to time, Claren slipped away from her escort when the latter became distracted, or so she thought. One of Gregor's security teams, headed by Rorik, had designed these distractions to allow Claren to move around while keeping her under surveillance. By watching where she went, security hoped to discern what she wanted to discover. Someone would often meet her during her travels, even in the stairwells. The individual would inquire, quite innocently, if she needed help finding her way. Except for the escort assigned to accompany the two spies, the person she encountered was always someone different. Gregor's staff members took care not to confront her. They wanted her to remain unaware that they too were spying.

Intentions

After several not-so-random encounters in the stairwells, Gregor's security team recognized one of Claren's intentions. This prompted Rorik to meet with Headmaster Andrei, Dr. Greyson, Ivana, and Yelena.

"She is trying to decode our locks," noted Rorik. "Most evenings during the dinner hour, she goes to the second and third floors in an attempt to crack the codes and get inside the labs. Several of us have seen her trying different combinations."

"Have you seen her carry any explosives?" asked Dr. Greyson anxiously.

"No, nor have any of us seen a weapon, although I think it likely that she carries one," Rorik replied.

"If we do not let her inside at least once, we will not learn what she is after," said Andrei.

"I do not want to invite her or her co-conspirator into the second or third-floor labs," Yelena remarked. "They might expect access afterward. We can engineer an opportunity for her to break the code on the second floor to gain access to that lab."

"Rather than letting her think she has been successful, I suggest we allow her to overhear that the door will be open at a particular time to receive some supplies and specimens," Ivana offered. "That should give her the opportunity to slip inside. We will need to recruit some people she hasn't already seen to be our suppliers."

"Erwina's northeast outpost can probably outfit a small caravan," suggested Andrei.

"How do we get her out again?" asked Dr. Greyson.

"Since she will be coming in with the supplies, we will make sure that she is ushered out with the people who brought the supplies. This should not raise any suspicions since she should anticipate leaving with them," Ivana answered.

"What if she takes something?" asked Dr. Greyson.

"Let her take it. Just make a note of what she takes. We will get it back later. Her choices of what to pilfer may give us valuable clues as to their purpose here," replied Ivana.

With Andrei's and Yelena's approval, Gregor's counterplot moved forward.

Dangling the Lure

Surveillance had become lax, or so it appeared. Everyone seemed accustomed to the two spies.

By chance, the next day Paulson asked for several hormones—somatotropin, thyroid, parathyroid, and testosterone. His request created a golden opportunity to lure the two spies into a trap.

"We are so sorry," exclaimed Dr. Greyson. "We don't keep those items here. We order them when we need them. We are, however, expecting a shipment of supplies very soon."

"They can't possibly do research here without these agents," Paulson fumed quietly to Claren. "Find out when those supplies are expected to arrive. When they unload the supplies, look for an opportunity to get some of them and any other items of interest."

Sensitive ears nearby overheard this hushed conversation. The owner of the sensitive ears reported the conversation to Dr. Greyson, who in turn notified Andrei and Ivana. "I think this is a good time for those supplies to arrive," Dr. Greyson suggested, "including the hormones Paulson has requested."

Staff quickly pulled a variety of supplies from storage, including the aforementioned hormones, and sent them to the northeast outpost with a request to outfit a caravan that would include the supplies Gregor had just delivered. They added one other item as well.

Once all the arrangements were made, Dr. Greyson informed the two spies. "We will receive a shipment of supplies when the next caravan arrives in a few days. It will include a limited supply of the hormones you requested. We will dispense a small amount for your use."

When the caravan arrived and began unloading supplies in a storage room, Claren slipped in among the suppliers and assisted them as if she were a member of Gregor's staff. In doing so, she spotted a very large egg carefully packaged in a bed of straw. The shell had a speckled gray color. *The better to hide it among mountain crags*, thought Claren excitedly. *Never mind the hormones. This is the real prize!* She packaged it up, hidden in some of the packing material, and walked out.

"Take the packing material to the rectory. The staff will reuse it," said the storeroom clerk helpfully, knowing full well who Claren was and what she carried with her.

Claren did no such thing. Instead, she went straight to her assigned quarters where she hid the egg. Then she sought out Paulson. Claren had taken the bait.

A Foiled Getaway

"Did you get the hormones?" Paulson asked impatiently.

"Forget the hormones," Claren said abruptly. "We need to leave as soon as possible."

"We can't leave yet," Paulson countered. "We have yet to procure any of the DNA specimens Raephela wants. If we come back empty-handed, she will be furious."

"We won't need them. We have something far more valuable than a smattering of DNA from extinct dinosaurs," Claren replied. "A dragon egg was among the supplies, and I have it!"

Paulson could hardly believe his ears. "How soon can we leave?"

"Now would be good, but it is not feasible. Too many people will notice that you are missing from your customary place in the genetics lab. We must continue to follow our usual routine for the rest of the day," replied Claren. "We can't leave during the night either, thanks to our escort."

"When then?" asked Paulson.

"I should be able to slip away," she said confidently. "The staff are accustomed to my running errands and fetching things for you. I will pack up our belongings. You will work late and miss the luncheon hour. During that time, you can slip out and meet me at the stables. I will have two horses ready."

"Are the stables not guarded?" pressed Paulson.

"No," Claren said, laughing. "They don't have anyone guarding this place." Claren had dismissed the friendly mastiff that also resided in the stables. Later that afternoon, she tucked the egg in her bodice. *It makes me look pregnant*, she noted with some annoyance, and threw a cape over her shoulders. Then she walked to the stables where she met Paulson.

"That's far enough!" Rorik declared when he saw them. Several of his security officers, with bows drawn, reinforced his command. Two arctic wolves also appeared to back up the mastiff Claren had disregarded earlier.

"We are aware you are here under false pretenses. You presented without any references, and we have been unable to confirm your origin. You will not be allowed to reenter our laboratories," he announced. He made no mention of the Cassius Foundation nor of the stolen egg. "Even so, Headmaster Andrei has agreed to complete the analysis of the DNA you have brought and provide you with the results."

"That will not be necessary," Paulson replied. He already knew that the DNA was from a hybrid animal.

"Then you will remain confined to your quarters until we arrange for your departure," ordered Rorik. "Your meals will be brought to you."

CHAPTER 21
A GRAVE DISAPPOINTMENT

Rorik already knew when the visitors would be departing. Summer in the tundra had begun to wane. Soon, it would be covered in snow. Ice packs would reform, and the ice field would extend further south. When signs of an impending winter storm appeared above the mountains, he hustled Raephela's spies on their way.

To speed their departure, the two spies and their guards rode on horseback until they were just beyond the southern pass. At that point, the guards provided them with supplies of food and water—no weapons—to continue their journey on foot. While guards watched the two spies disappear from sight, the two arctic wolves continued to follow them. The spies' heading confirmed that their origin was indeed the Cassius Foundation.

A Deadly Encounter

On foot, the spies could not return to Gregor. Heavy snow was already falling in the pass when they reached it. So they continued south to avoid the snowstorm, heading toward the River Taurus. There they retrieved the two-man kayak they had stowed to facilitate their return trip. The Taurus coursed along the western border of Cassius territory. With its origin in the northern mountains, its flow was rapid. The travelers would have to traverse its category II and III rapids. Claren, an experienced kayaker, shed her cape. Afterward, the river slowed as it neared the fortress. The two spies would disembark at the loading dock.

Before reaching the fortress, the river's waters were clear. It hosted a wide variety of fish and wildlife that fed on the fish, including the varan that disappeared after its successful debut in an unincorporated village. Its territory included both sides of the Taurus.

Unbeknownst to the two spies, the varan was submerged in the river, intending to acquire a meal. As the travelers neared the fortress, both were focused on their approach to the dock. Neither one saw the hybrid until their kayak slammed into it. Sensing an attack, the hybrid immediately lunged at its presumed adversary. The first snap of its massive jaws broke the kayak in two, taking the back half and Paulson with it. The second snap swallowed Paulson's head and thorax.

While the varan was occupied, the horrified Claren swam downriver as fast as she could. The egg in her bodice hampered her stroke; however, she was able to swim with it in place. Even if it broke, it would still be valuable. Her triumphant return was assured if she could reach the dock. Thankfully, it was not far away.

After reaching safety, she ran into the fortress, demanding to see Raephela immediately.

"I have a great treasure to present to her," Claren declared. She gave no further thought to Paulson. He had been a constant source of irritation and very demanding, ordering her to do this and get that. *Good riddance*, she sniffed with contempt.

A Fabulous Treasure

Pleased by Claren's return, Raephela assumed that her spies had retrieved the DNA she wanted. When she learned otherwise, her face darkened visibly until Claren presented the egg. Raephela was ecstatic. She almost glowed.

"This is indeed a fabulous treasure," she gloated. Immediately, she called for Mason. "You know what to do with it," she told him.

Mason stared in awe at the egg. As he grasped it tenderly, he replied, "Yes, Your Majesty."

Shortly thereafter, Mason was beside himself. He had discovered that the egg contained only gelatin. Not even the shell was of any use. It was comprised of the same elements that all eggshells had. Terrified and shaking, he presented the egg and its contents to Raephela.

"It's a fake," Mason said, his voice breaking. "Only the shell is real, and it's of no use."

Raephela erupted. "Find that hunter and bring her before me!"

Guards brought the terrified Claren to face Raephela. "The egg was brought to Gregor in a caravan," she cried. "I was present when the caravan arrived and took the egg as soon as it was unloaded. Paulson was sure it was a dragon egg," she added, placing the blame on the dead man. "We took great pains to avoid any damage to it."

Raephela studied Claren. It was undoubtedly a dragon's eggshell. Its size and pliability alone precluded any other species. *Something must have made the Gregorians suspicious*, she mused. *Paulson would have had the closest contact with Gregor's staff. Perhaps he revealed himself.*

For Claren, the wait was agonizing. Raephela was deciding her fate. Possible means of escape streamed through her mind; then she suddenly remembered what she had surveyed.

In a desperate move, she asked, "Shall I report on Gregor's security? I found many weaknesses which make it vulnerable to attack."

Raephela's demeanor changed abruptly. "Report," she commanded.

Relieved, Claren described the terrain, Gregor's near total lack of security around their complex, and the lax security within it. "They assigned an escort to us who stayed outside our quarters and accompanied us to the lab and back again. Once we were in our assigned place in the lab, the escort would eventually leave. At the end of the day, another escort arrived at the lab to take us back to our quarters." Claren could not help chuckling. "In the meantime, I was left almost exclusively to my own devices." She did not reveal that she had been unable to break the codes on the laboratory locks. "I can sketch a floor plan of the complex, if you want one," she added. In her sense of relief, she forgot to mention the arctic dragoness.

"Do it," Raephela ordered.

Claren was off the hook. With the intelligence that she provided, Raephela began to formulate a plan of action.

Supplemental Notes and Citations

Eggshells

Dinosaurs, modern reptiles, and birds have hard calcareous eggshells consisting of crystalized calcium carbonate (Montanari, 2018; Stein, *et al.*, 2019). Non-avian dinosaurs developed hard eggshells during the Late Jurassic and Cretaceous periods. In contrast, monotremes such as the duck-billed platypus have relatively soft, leathery eggshells (Sharp, *et al.*, 2011).

Part IV
Omens

CHAPTER 22
Harbinger

After the Cassius Foundation's attempt to infiltrate Gregor and steal a dragon egg, Gregor sent couriers to its sister houses and to Biogenics, alerting them that the foundation had sent two spies. Clearly, it had regrouped sufficiently to resume exerting itself outside its own walls—a concerning turn of events. Raephela's actions indicated either a desperate attempt to obtain resources or a return to the foundation's malevolent activities.

Preparedness

Fortunately, Erwina and H'Aleth had never ceased training scouts. Supervised excursions into nearby open territories reinforced classroom instruction. Subsequently, newly minted scouts interned at H'Aleth, which included reconnaissance inside Cassius territory. Surveillance of a Cassius village proved to be sobering. Scouts saw firsthand the suffering of hybrid humanoids while observing the capabilities of hybrid animals.

Scouts had to master many skills, including how to navigate H'Aleth's and Erwina's numerous lakes and rivers. They had to be expert kayakers and strong swimmers.

One day during the spring runoff, form III students at Erwina who were prospective scouts were honing their kayaking skills. Those who had demonstrated mastery of category II rapids advanced to training for category III rapids. Once they mastered category III, they would progress to category IV and possibly category V rapids in their senior year.

During one of these training sessions, Master Morloff—a master kayaker—proctored students' skills as they approached category III rapids on the River Ferveo. They were unaware that another entity could also navigate those rapids. While the kayakers headed downstream, a large reptile downriver from them sunned itself on one of many boulders along the river's route. When it spotted the kayakers, it slipped into a pool of water on the downstream side of a large boulder jutting out into the river. As it submerged, only the top of its head, eyes, and snout remained above the waterline. The swirling eddies camouflaged its head.

The kayakers were obliged to navigate many boulders, surfing the waves around pools of water on the far side. Failure to do so meant the kayaker could be trapped by the backwash of river water filling a pool. Once trapped, they faced a struggle to get out, and the danger of becoming an unwitting meal for a predator lying in wait.

Focused on navigating the turbulent waters of the river, the kayakers were completely unaware that they were rapidly approaching an ambush. The creature watched and calculated its strike. Without warning, it lunged and grasped the last of the kayaks in its powerful jaws. The effort crushed the kayak's bow and tossed the kayaker out into the water. The huge animal shook off the kayak's debris. Then it turned and chased after the kayaker, who was trying to stay afloat, avoid slamming into boulders, and dodge the creature that had attacked him. His comrades were already downstream when they heard the commotion. They promptly coerced their kayaks into position to catch their comrade as the river propelled him toward them.

At first, the other kayakers assumed the kayak had struck a submerged rock and careened out of control, breaking up in the process. Their floundering comrade, however, knew exactly what happened. He clearly saw the gaping mouth, the large serrated teeth, and the tongue of a viper just as the jaws closed down on his kayak. Without question, the creature was a hybrid—and a terrifying one. It was nearly impossible to track as most of its body was submerged in the turbulent waters. Aided and abetted by a powerful tail, it gained on the distressed kayaker. The only thing keeping them apart was the force of the river's flow.

Suddenly, another unknown aquatic species lunged alongside the kayaker, tossing him out of the way. An aquatic dragon romping in the river's rapids was returning to its home waters when it spotted an unwary meal that would prove quite satisfying. It snatched the hybrid in its own jaws and headed upstream with its prize (illustration 21, Serendipity). A powerful animal, the dragon easily traversed the Ferveo's tremendous current.

Fellow kayakers snagged their companion from the water and quickly navigated toward a pool where everyone could climb out of the river with their kayaks.

"So, they are real!" exclaimed one kayaker.

"People have not been imagining them all these years," said another in awe.

"Are you alright?" Master Morloff asked Edwin, the kayaker who had been attacked.

"Yes," Edwin replied, shaken and a bit bruised, yet otherwise unharmed.

"How did you escape from the dragon?" Master Morloff asked.

"I didn't," replied Edwin. "My boat was attacked by a creature with huge jaws like those of a crocodile, full of serrated teeth and long fangs on either side of its jaw." He paused and took a breath. "It had to be a hybrid of some kind. It was almost on top of me when the dragon rushed past me and grabbed it. I didn't know it was a dragon until I saw it swim away upstream with the dead hybrid dangling from its mouth."

A grim Master Morloff abruptly ordered his pupils to head back to the compound. "We have to get back to the schoolhouse now." The appearance of new hybrid that far south and so close to the schoolhouse represented a significant threat.

Forewarned Is Forearmed

When apprised of the incident, Headmaster Joseph suspended all boating activities on the river and mandated that only essential river

Illustration 21: Serendipity

transports take place. Given the hybrid's crocodilian appearance, the creature might be able to come on land. A watch was set on the river and its banks—for the hybrid, not the river dragon.

Typically, faculty at the schoolhouse integrated into the curriculum descriptions of the various hybrids created by the Cassius Foundation. The content was updated as new hybrids were discovered. Headmaster Joseph promptly advised faculty to incorporate a description of the newest hybrid into the appropriate courses.

Erwina's wildlife specialist was delighted to learn of the close encounter with a river dragon. "No doubt they have been cruising through the Ferveo's waters for centuries," he declared.

Meanwhile, Master Morloff had retrieved a small piece of tissue from the wrecked kayak. He suspected it was from the hybrid—torn off when the kayak splintered in the creature's jaws. He sent the tissue to Gregor for examination. Gregor's analysis revealed the base genome of a crocodile augmented with rattlesnake genes—specifically, those for the snake's fangs and poison. Based on the creature's genome, Gregor's chief geneticist named it *Crocodylatalus* [*Crŏ*-cō-dĭl-ă-*tăl*-ŭs]. Everyone else called it the croco.

Biogenics had previously reported an unknown reptilian hybrid, the varanacrocactutus, which had attacked a village woman in open territory. With the appearance of the crocodylatalus, both hybrids foretold the rise of the Cassius Foundation. Although still furtive and isolated, it had not been idle, and its shadow was spreading.

CHAPTER 23
An Unexpected Threat

R aephela had given no further thought to the hybrids her uncle released after the foundation's defeat. Given that they were released in enemy territory, she made no attempt to recapture them. She mistakenly assumed that they probably had been killed and therefore were lost to her. This was not the case.

Homeward Bound

To maintain the appearance of typical *H. transformans*, H'Ariel's children were educated at Erwina with the other children. H'Adrianna, H'Ariel's oldest child, had just completed her sophomore year as a form II student. This included two courses in caring for infants and young children (toddlers) and two years of martial arts training. She was growing up fast, a necessity for all children. At eleven years old, H'Adrianna was approaching the time when she would come of age. Already, she was developing enhanced senses of hearing, smell, and visual acuity. She sensed a growing kinship with certain animals. These changes foretold the alternate species into which she would transform.

H'Adrianna and Eldar, her seven-year-old brother, were traveling home from school with other youngsters returning to their villages for spring break. Three covered wagons departed from Erwina's schoolhouse in a caravan. Each wagon had a driver and four horses, carrying children who lived in neighboring villages. Nine mounted scouts escorted the caravan. All were very experienced, for they were guarding precious cargo.

At some point along the way, a wagon would break away with three scouts—one on either side of the wagon and one in front—and head toward the region of H'Aleth where the children's villages lay. One headed into the southwestern region of H'Aleth. Another continued due east into the grasslands. The third wagon, carrying H'Adrianna, Eldar, and five other children, headed north by northeast into the neck of Caput Canis. The company would follow the River Pices until it reached the main village and estate. Out of an abundance of caution, no other villages occupied that region of H'Aleth. There were, however, many hidden outposts.

As the eldest student in her wagon, H'Adrianna had been charged to shepherd the other children. All except the two youngest—one four and one five years old—had traveled by wagon many times. Sometimes, the montane terrain became very rough, causing considerable jostling and tilting of the wagon. H'Adrianna paired each of the two youngest children with a more experienced traveler.

Ambush!

Illustration 22: Lupucercopiths

The wagon was in the middle of nowhere when a pack of lupucercopiths (illustration 22), wolf–baboon hybrids, burst from the forest. The hybrids attacked the nearest scout's mount and the horses pulling the wagon. The scouts had barely loosed an arrow when the closest mount quickly went down under three hybrids. Their combined weight and power overwhelmed the horse, trapping its rider beneath it. One of the hybrids sank an elongated fang into the rider's thigh as it attacked the downed horse.

More hybrids attacked the wagon horses. The scout on the far side of the wagon immediately leaped from her horse onto the wagon to get a vantage point from which to attack the hybrids. She promptly targeted the ones assaulting the downed horse and fellow scout. The lead scout quickly turned to kill the hybrids attacking the wagon horses. Simultaneously, three more hybrids clamored to jump onto the driver's seat of the wagon. The driver, also a scout, loosed an arrow, promptly dispatching the closest one. The other two dropped away. Lured by the cries of the youngsters within the wagon, they searched for a way to get inside.

When the attack first started, the children could hear the horses' shrill neighing, the hybrids' snarls and growls, and the adults rallying to defend the wagon. Without knowing who or what was attacking them, H'Adrianna immediately closed the back opening of the wagon's canvas cover. None of the children were old enough to transform into an alternate species. So H'Adrianna searched for a means of defense. Upon finding bows and sheaths with arrows, she shouted at Eldar, "Get these to the driver!" Neither she nor the other children were trained in archery.

What can I do? she thought desperately. *Luggage!* She began piling cases, laundry bags, trunks, crates, and anything else she could move against the back of the wagon. Two other children and Eldar jumped in to help her.

Her mind raced with possibilities. *What if the animals attacking us claw their way through the cover? What if they get in from the front of the wagon? We will have no means of escape!* Then she remembered that every wagon carried a spare wheel, a wagon jack, and other tools in the event a wagon broke down. She searched through the toolbox and found a heavy wheel jack, wrenches, a sledgehammer with a long oak handle and a granite head, and other tools.

H'Adrianna selected the sledgehammer for herself and gave wrenches to Evan and the two older children. They formed a circle around the three youngest. "If the hybrids break through, aim for their muzzles," she told them. "I will hit them on the head." She knew their blows would not disable the hybrids, yet they might be painful enough to discourage them. She also knew that if the adults did not prevail, none of them would survive the onslaught.

Suddenly the wagon lurched, tossing the children and the luggage around and throwing both the second rider and driver against the canvas cover. The horses pulling the wagon had bolted, dragging one of the lupucercopiths with them. The driver had dropped the reins to battle the hybrids. As he scrambled to reach the reins and regain control of the horses, the lupucercopith let go to avoid being trampled. When the lead scout came alongside the lead horses, he brought them and the wagon to a stop. Meanwhile, the lupucercopith ran back to join its pack and the feast.

The second rider regained her footing and her arrows. Her horse had escaped harm, yet it had not abandoned its rider. It returned to her when she called it. Desperate to save their fallen comrade, the two remaining riders raced back to the place where the attack had occurred.

Wary Travelers

The wagon's driver, Wes, was the sole scout remaining with the children. He promptly checked on his charges. Other than a few bumps and bruises from being tossed around with the luggage, all were safe—if scared to death. After treating the wounded horse, he pulled it out of the line and hitched it to the rear of the wagon. Then, he realigned the remaining three horses to pull the wagon the rest of the way to the main village.

Wes knew he had to get the children home as soon as possible and report the incident to Matron Kavarova, H'Ariel, and the lead scouts for each region. Somehow, these lupucercopiths had formed a pack. This was unprecedented. With a sinking feeling, he realized that the lupucercopiths might not be the only hybrids to have survived this way. Worse yet, the boldness of their attack suggested little fear of humans.

Meanwhile, Eldar declared, "I will walk beside the lead horse and guide it to the village. I know the way, and this will free the driver to function as a scout."

H'Adrianna refuted her brother. "I was left in charge. I am older and more experienced than you. I will lead the horses."

"You were assigned to look after the other children," Eldar retorted.

"You are one of the 'other' children," H'Adrianna reminded him. "Besides, there are two others older than you are. I will delegate the eldest to take my place inside the wagon." As the two siblings argued, Wes—the one really in charge—made the decision.

"You are my apprentice scout," he told H'Adrianna. "Not only must you supervise the other children, as you were charged to do, but now you must also keep watch on our rear." Wes then designated Eldar as his assistant scout. "You will keep watch going forward," he told Eldar. It would be good practice for both youngsters, who might someday lead the House of H'Aleth.

"If we are attacked again, both of you must jump inside the wagon immediately and close the opening," Wes admonished. "Everyone must remain perfectly still and quiet."

H'Adrianna knew she could see farther and hear better than any of the other children. So she reopened the wagon's back entrance and positioned herself there. From that vantage point, she could keep an eye on the rest of the children, as well as any threat that might creep up on them from the rear.

Wes was deeply concerned about the fate of his fallen comrade as well as the two who had raced back to save him. He was just as concerned about what might lie ahead and whether or not he could get the children home. If anything happened to him, none of the children could take the reins. Still, there were four horses, including the injured one, to carry seven children. All but the youngest child had been taught how to ride a horse, and the youngest one could ride with another, more experienced rider. At least he did not have to worry about the children becoming lost. Both H'Adrianna and Eldar knew the way home.

CHAPTER 24
A New Wrinkle

Wes and the children arrived safely at H'Aleth's village and estate, as did the two scouts who had tried to save their comrade. When the scouts reached him, the hybrids feeding on the dead horse quickly fled into the forest. Alas, their comrade was already dead—crushed under the weight of his mount. Internal injuries and hemorrhage from the deep gash on his leg had sped his death. Aided by their mounts, the two scouts shifted the dead horse off his body and brought their fallen comrade home.

When apprised of the incident, H'Ariel quickly checked on her two children. Other than a few bruises, H'Adrianna and Eldar were unharmed, though quite shaken. While their memory of the attack was still fresh and sharp, H'Ariel took them to Evard to recount what they knew.

"We really didn't see what was happening outside the wagon," H'Adrianna told him. "We heard growls and snarls, the scouts shouting, the horses neighing frantically, and arrows being loosed. We saw claws as whatever was attacking us tried to get inside the wagon."

"You didn't see the creatures that attacked the wagon?" H'Ariel asked.

Both children shook their heads no. H'Ariel was relieved that her two offspring had not witnessed the attack and had not seen the scout being killed. Although death was not unknown to them, they had yet to encounter a violent one.

Origins

Lupucercopiths were not the only animal hybrids to be sighted in the open territories. Glimpses of what looked like a lupuseroja had been seen, albeit rarely. Hints of the cercopithursus also persisted. Since this hybrid looked like a normal brown bear from behind, its prevalence could not be determined. Sightings of the moresistrurus and the viperoperidactyl were difficult to verify due to their ability to blend into their environments. All of these were worrisome reports.

H'Ariel called her council together to discuss the implications of hybrid packs forming. She dispatched messengers to Erwina and Gregor, requesting the presence of their lead biologists, wildlife specialists, and geneticists to join their counterparts in H'Aleth.

No one had any idea that lupucercopiths or any other animal hybrid would form a pack and work cooperatively to bring down prey.

"Our scouts conduct surveillance all across H'Aleth and the neighboring open territories," Edric remarked. "We encountered only lone hybrids, most of which fled when they spotted us."

Edrew postulated, "Baboons live in troops, and wolves work in packs. Perhaps the hybrid species are genetically inclined to form a social group."

"I thought most native pack animals were related," countered Bowen, Erwina's chief of animal husbandry. "Strangers are rarely allowed to join. They are usually run off or killed."

"Perhaps the hybrids are related," mused Dr. Grayson quietly.

"What do you mean?" Edrew asked. "Hybrids can't breed."

"Can't they?" queried Grayson. "How do we know that?"

This question met with silence.

"Perhaps they are clones and reared together so that they will form a pack," opined Miriam.

"That is a possibility," Edrew acknowledged. "Yet, to my knowledge, packs of hybrids have not been seen before. At least, it has not been reported."

A Different Direction

Long ago, the three houses had disavowed cloning, even in animal species—although not because cloning was innately harmful. Rather, cloning countered the purpose of genetic variability. It also raised the specter of cloning for the purpose of harvesting organs—human and nonhuman—for transplantation

By contrast, when Angus Cassius ruled the Cassius Foundation, his geneticists attempted to clone hybrids without success. When Rex Cassius took up the reins, the foundation's geneticists finally succeeded in cloning a few animal hybrids with only nominal changes to their genomes. Much to his genetic engineers' torment, Rex ordered them to create and clone the deadliest and therefore most complex hybrids.

Years later, a H'Alethean band of scouts disguised as a wolf pack engaged in a daring mission deep within Cassius territory. During that incursion, they observed many hybrid laborers and animals—several of which looked identical. They had no individual variations in their appearance or markings. The scouts suspected that Rex Cassius had succeeded in cloning some of his hybrids. They were correct. Rex subsequently used the clones to terrorize the inhabitants of territories he wanted to conquer and to quell any resistance. Conversely, efforts to clone humanoid hybrids proved disastrous. Corrupted transformations had resulted in rampant errors in cellular division, resulting in genetic variations (mosaicism) in most of them.

An Unproven Supposition

The lupucercopiths' recent attack appeared to confirm that animal hybrids were being cloned. Unfortunately, the two scouts who returned to the attack site had only enough time to retrieve their comrade's body. Although the hybrids had fled, they awaited another opportunity to attack and resume feeding. The scouts dared not linger to gather up the dead lupucercopiths as well.

After the council meeting had ended, H'Ariel dispatched well-armed scouts to the site of the attack to retrieve any tissue or blood left behind. Edrew forwarded the specimens to Gregor. An analysis of their genomes would reveal any significant genetic variability among them. If none were found, then the hybrids were clones.

Probably, thought Yelena, Gregor's chief geneticist. Yet she had a nagging thought. *Have some hybrids developed the ability to breed?*

The persistence of animal hybrids mystified biologists and geneticists. For one, nearly all of the Cassius human and animal hybrids were males. The foundation specifically chose males for the physical differences between male and female genders; by virtue of testosterone, males generally were larger and more powerful. In addition, the animal hybrids were being bred to be more violent. Hence, they were likely to kill any other animal they encountered—hybrid or otherwise—if only for food.

It was well known that an *H. transformans* could not breed while in a transformed state. Hybrid humanoids were *H. transformans*, genetically altered and then forced into a transformation that they could not reverse. Given that hybrid humanoids were invariably sterile, Cassius assumed that animal hybrids also were sterile. The foundation expended no resources to test this assumption—a critical error in reasoning.

Crossbreeding

In contrast to *H. transformans*, animal hybrids were developed de novo with additional genes. They never underwent metamorphosis. Most of the changes involved nonreproductive (somatic) genes. Thus, genetic alterations would not necessarily interfere with their reproductive capacity. In truth, many of them did retain that capability. Once freed, most animal hybrids mated with females of their native species, if the latter could be overpowered.

Depending upon the hybrid's genetic alteration, the parent's hybrid features might or might not be expressed in the offspring. Since there would be no match for the hybrid gene in the native species, that hybrid gene would not likely be expressed unless it was dominant. Nevertheless, the gene could still be passed on to offspring (figure 2). Expression of the hybrid characteristic in subsequent generations depended upon whether the hybrid gene or genes had been inherited by subsequent generations.

Female

A   a

	A	A A female	A a female
Male	a	a A male	a a male

Key
 A = native (wildtype) gene, dominant
 a = hybrid gene, recessive

This pattern shows four possible combinations of hybrid and native genes. Each pregnancy has a 1 in 4 chance—or a 25% probability—of inheriting one of the four combinations. The table also shows that each pregnancy has a 50% probability of an offspring carrying a recessive gene (without expressing it) and a 25% probability of inheriting both recessive genes and expressing the characteristic.

Figure 2: Probability of a Hybrid Offspring in Subsequent Generations

If an animal hybrid mated with a species that had the same base genome and the pairing produced offspring, the presence of non-native genes would become diluted over time. Even so, the mating of hybrid offspring with other hybrid offspring could result in non-native genes being reunited, essentially recreating the original hybrid traits. Many mammals had short gestation periods (e.g., foxes fifty to sixty days, wolves sixty to seventy-five days, wild boar one hundred fifteen days, etc.), and many species produced several offspring per gestation (e.g., four fox kits, four to six wolf cubs, six boar piglets, etc.). Hence, many generations of hybrid offspring were produced within a single human generation. Thus, the Cassius Foundation's animal hybrids continued to persist, not because of long life, but instead because they were able to breed.

A group of biologists, wildlife specialists, and geneticists collaborated to observe and record sightings of two or more identical or very similar hybrids staying together. Although sightings were rare, over time the researchers' surveillance revealed that hybrids could breed with native species. They had seen the offspring.

Supplemental Notes and Citations

Mosaicism

As a rule, all of an individual's cells have the same genotype. In cellular mosaicism, there are groups of cells within an individual that have a different genotype. These changes from the original blueprint are often due to mutations (Campbell, *et al.*, 2015). Both somatic and reproductive cells can be affected. These changes are not uncommon in *H. sapiens* and most are benign; however, some of these mutations can lead to disease and genetic disorders (Campbell, *et al.*, 2015; Iourov, *et al.*, 2019; Qui, *et al.*, 2020).

Mitosis (somatic cell division)

Mitosis is the process of cell division in which the cell replicates, effectively cloning itself (Ohkura, 2015). The cell makes a copy of its twenty-three paired chromosomes so that when the body of the cell divides, one copy of the twenty-three paired chromosomes remains with the parent cell and the other copy migrates to the daughter cell.

Several types of cells can reproduce themselves in this manner. Cells that have a rapid rate of turnover, such as skin cells, are a classic example. This is an everyday affair.

Meiosis (reproductive cell division)

Meiosis is a specialized form of cell division that occurs only in reproductive cells (Ohkura, 2015; Zickler & Kleckner, 2015). This is a complicated process of cell division in which the parent cell divides twice, leaving its daughter cells with only a single (unpaired) set of twenty-three chromosomes (a haploid cell) (Alleva & Smolikove, 2017). Failure of a chromosome to separate in meiosis leads to an extra chromosome in one daughter cell and a missing chromosome in the other one (aneuploidy). This occurs more often in female reproductive cells that in male reproductive cells (Wang, *et al.*, 2019).

During fertilization when an egg and sperm merge, their single sets of twenty-three chromosomes match up to become a full set of forty-six chromosomes. The newly fertilized egg now possesses a new combination of genes that differs from both the maternal and paternal genomes (genetic diversity). The developing embryo will carry forward this new combination of genes into all of its cells.

Dominant versus recessive genes

Although many gene pairs contain identical gene sequences (homozygous gene pairs), many gene pairs do not have the exact same gene sequences (heterozygous gene pairs). In most cases, the differences are common variations found in the general population and have little or no effect on function.

In some cases, only one member of the gene pair may be expressed, effectively silencing the other member. The expressed gene is considered to be a dominant gene, whereas the gene that is not expressed is considered a recessive gene.

When two dominant genes are paired together, either one could be expressed. When a dominant gene is paired with a recessive gene, only the dominant gene will be expressed. It is only when two recessive genes are paired together that a recessive gene is expressed.

CHAPTER 25
A MARITIME MATTER

H'Ariel maintained a sense of watchfulness during her tenure as mistress of the House of H'Aleth. Due to the relative proximity of the main village and estate to H'Aleth's northern border, vigilance was essential. Although there were fewer and fewer encounters with hybrids, scouts dared not let their guard down. Bounty hunters persisted in launching raids into both Erwina and H'Aleth. Moreover, with the recent appearance of two new animal hybrids, H'Ariel asked Evard to recruit more scouts and increase the number of apprenticeships.

Yet some of H'Aleth's younger members decided that scouting was not the only adventure available. It was summertime, and several were eager to explore what lay beyond the southern coast.

A Reminder of the Past

Decades ago, Rex Cassius had built a seafaring vessel that reached H'Aleth's coastal waters, alerting the H'Aletheans to the possibility of an invasion by sea. Not long after the initial sighting, the warship floundered close to their southern shore. The ship's captain scuttled the vessel after its surviving crew came ashore. Crew members scattered and either blended into H'Aleth's territory or passed through it.

Since that time, H'Aleth's scouts maintained a close watch on their oceanfront. Strategically, H'Aletheans kept the coastal area uninhabited by humans. Except for carefully camouflaged foxholes, the H'Aletheans preserved the region for the local wildlife inhabitants, keeping it a pristine setting. Only scouts who could transform into species native to the region could enter it, thereby preventing their detection from afar. In the event of an invasion by sea, they could sound the alarm long before anyone came ashore.

Although H'Aletheans had access to the ocean on its southeast border, their territory met all of their needs, so they had little incentive to sail. Nevertheless, they did not hesitate to navigate the rivers and lakes within their territory. Most adults could operate at least one type of water vessel, and several were expert kayakers and rafters. Even at twelve years of age, children could assist in handling watercraft.

A cadre of intrepid young H'Aletheans decided it was time to explore the waters offshore. Already quite familiar with the few marine mammals that found their way into freshwater channels, including river dolphins and even the occasional bull shark, they wondered what lay beyond. Among these younger members were H'Adrianna and Eldar. Both were intrigued by the project and wanted to engage in it.

H'Adrianna was sixteen years old and entering young adulthood. Eldar, now twelve years old, already had come of age and was developing proficiency in transforming into a wolf and a fox. Both had successfully completed their swimming and diving classes at Erwina, and H'Adrianna had completed the rescue swimming course.

The two offspring descended upon their parents, citing every conceivable reason why they should join the expedition. H'Ariel suppressed the urge to say *absolutely not*. Since the project offered a unique learning opportunity, both parents approved the adventure, which would be conducted under the watchful eye of Master Stoval, the boat master.

"Be careful and use sound judgment. Do not take risks," H'Ariel urged her children. "And mind Master Stoval." As her elated offspring raced away, H'Ariel took a deep breath. Then she sent a note via courier to Master Stoval.

A New Adventure

"We have no seafaring vessels," Stoval reminded the group. "I suggest converting a barge or a riverboat into a sailboat with one or two masts and outfitting it with supplies for a week or two. Always keep the coastline within view, and use a sextant to navigate. Begin by sailing within the confines of the bay. Ocean waters are much different from those of a lake," he cautioned.

One of the young adventurers asked, "What's a sextant?"

Stoval just looked at him and then asked, "Exactly what did you learn at Erwina?"

The young man thought a moment and replied facetiously, "I learned how to swim."

Good point, thought Stoval. Any seafarer must also be a good swimmer. All of H'Aleth's students learned how to swim, row a boat, pilot a raft, and paddle a canoe or a kayak, so the prospective seafarers should have most of the skills they needed.

"Before you begin sailing upon the ocean, I suggest recruiting a few people with an aquatic mammal as their alternate species to join your ranks," Stoval advised. "You can explore the seafloor, beginning with the bay, and investigate the warship that sank off our southeast shore decades ago. You are welcome to examine any flotsam that has drifted ashore over time."

The young adventurers reviewed the reports of the vessel that had been seen off the coast. The description of the ship gave them some idea of a seafaring vessel's features. They also learned the approximate location of the sunken warship. They recruited comrades—excellent swimmers and boaters eager for an adventure—to help them search the waters and find the rest of the wreckage.

Worrisome Wreckage

Upon reaching the southeast coast, H'Adrianna transformed into a river otter and submerged in a creek. The creek in turn became a tributary of the delta that drained into the sea. Since river otters can swim in both fresh and salt water, H'Adrianna was soon in her element. Once she was in the creek, she splashed her younger brother with her tail and sped away.

There was no chance Eldar could catch her. This annoyed Eldar, who was a good swimmer for his age. *I'll get even when we're back on land*, he thought.

In the meantime, H'Adrianna delighted in romping with some river dolphins and joined them as they returned to the sea. Her comrades followed, toting an armada of rowboats, barges, and kayaks until they too reached the sea. H'Adrianna soon located the wrecked battleship. Although the ship had decayed to some degree, the skeleton of its structure remained. She guided strong swimmers to various areas of the craft to discover what the vessel had held and determine its condition.

A few days later, the adventurers returned to Stoval and gave him a detailed description of the ship's structure, its condition, and the armaments it carried. Their report augmented the observations of the ship and its sails when it was first seen long ago. From historical reports, pieces of wreckage, and now direct observation, Stoval was able to sketch plans that reflected the ship's construction. He also identified the materials used to build it. Its size, potential power, and weaponry alarmed him. Although the ship was too badly damaged to ever sail again, another one could be built with readily available materials.

Stoval's thoughts turned immediately to the Cassius Foundation. Even though there had been no sign of another warship, he was worried. *They could have built a fleet by now*, he thought worriedly, *biding their time until they are ready to strike.* He promptly took his concerns to H'Ariel and Evard.

A Maritime Defense

The sunken warship raised the specter of a possible assault from the sea, prompting H'Ariel to call a council meeting that would determine how best to secure and defend their southern coastline. Council members included Edric, Evard, Stoval, and Miriam, a marine biologist. Senior scouts in the region also attended the meeting. The discussion focused on whether or not to do more than simply maintain the current level of surveillance.

"Can you replicate this vessel and build one like it?" H'Ariel asked Stoval.

"I can," Stoval replied, "but not without cutting down many trees. We also would need much larger furnaces and forges to produce cannons and their mounts. We can make the projectiles, fuses, and gunpowder."

"I do not want to cut down a forest or create an industry primarily for the purpose of building a warship," H'Ariel asserted. She turned to Evard and asked, "How do we defend against a warship without building one?"

A moment later, he replied, "Sometimes you have to fight fire with fire."

"Which can change with the wind and wreak even more damage," Edric warned. "Perhaps we need to consider how to keep an enemy warship far enough offshore so that its cannons cannot be effective."

"There is no barrier reef," noted Miriam. "There is, however, a shelf that extends about five hundred feet. It gradually slopes downward until it drops off precipitously. The warship was found well inside the shelf break at a depth of about thirty feet of water. Given the amount of iron in its hold, I doubt it drifted anywhere."

"The range of most cannon fire is three hundred feet," advised Evard.

"At three hundred feet offshore, I estimate the depth of the water would be approximately thirty-seven feet. The ship could get another fifty feet closer to shore with a draught of thirty feet," said Stoval.

"How much damage could a barrage of cannon fire do from fifty feet ashore?"

"To us? Essentially none," replied Miriam. "To the surrounding environment and wildlife, it would be devastating."

"Including any scouts in the area," warned Edric.

"In my opinion, a preemptive strike with cannon fire would be an enormous waste of ammunition on their part," said Evard. "I would send landing parties ashore to set up a base of operations and perhaps build a pier to unload amphibious troops and matériel."

"There are all sorts of watercraft that can reach the shore," Stoval remarked. "We use most of them ourselves to cross rivers and lakes. Most shallow draft boats only need a few feet of water. Even if we get advance warning that an enemy is offshore, how can we stop an enemy force from coming ashore in small boats or barges?"

"By building a barrier reef," replied Miriam.

A New Habitat

Stoval and Miriam collaborated on what materials to use to create a barrier reef.

"Limestone would be best," explained Miriam, "but we can use other types of rocks or even create them using concrete. How do we get enough rocks to the edge of the shelf to build an effective barrier?"

Stoval offered a solution. "First, we can use the iron from the ship—at least the cannon balls, if not the cannons—to build a foundation. Then, we can use barges and boats to ferry rocks and other debris to the site. In instances where the load is very heavy, we can simply sink the vessel carrying the load." He thought for a moment. "We are going to need more boats."

"We are also going to need a way to keep the barrier intact," added Evard.

"Strong netting and embedded iron spikes will keep the rocks in place," Stoval replied.

H'Amara provided a report of the fish and other animals she had encountered on her dives. "The bull shark is the largest," she said. "So breaks in the barrier reef need to be large enough to let them traverse it and small enough to keep larger marine predators out."

"At least two of these breaks also must be large enough to allow a sailboat to pass, like the ones we use on the lakes," Stoval added.

"We should map the reef, and keep that map secured," Evard advised. "Only seafaring H'Aletheans should know the locations of the channels that will allow their boats and local marine life to navigate the reef." He thought for a moment and added, "Camouflage will be essential. The reef must be shallow enough to trap a kayak, yet still inconspicuous enough to avoid detection."

"We can camouflage the reef, especially if we use limestone as the top layer," offered Miriam. "We can plant algae and seagrasses, which will attract a wide variety of fish, coral, and other marine species. Some of them will shelter in nooks and crannies among the rocks."

Stoval took a deep breath. "Our barrier may not prove strong enough to stop a warship," he warned.

"We can only do our best," H'Ariel said. "If we can hamper at least one vessel, then perhaps others will falter as well."

Regardless of whether a warship could crash through the barrier, one entity could do so readily. The H'Aletheans remained unaware that an *Odontus pristis* patrolled the bay as well as the southeastern swamplands.

CHAPTER 26
The Scouting Bug

While H'Adrianna and Eldar were investigating a sunken warship, Edric scouted along H'Aleth's northern border. Long before he graduated from the schoolhouse, Edric had dreamed of becoming a top-notch scout. It was quite common for young adult *H. transformans* to be recruited into scouting. Edric was no exception—to the delight of Evard. Edric could transform into multiple powerful species and would blend nicely into many terrains. Last but not least, he had mastered all the skills required of a scout.

Wishful Thinking

As a youngster just learning to transform, Edric had wondered if he might achieve a level of transformation previously achieved only by females with two transforming X chromosomes. He had the genes of a Cooper's hawk and felt drawn to raptor species. *Is it because I want to fly?* he had wondered. *Do I share a kinship with them? Or is it just wishful thinking?* He studied raptors under the guidance of Erwina's master falconer to see if his sense of kinship with a Cooper's hawk would strengthen. He should be able to morph across mammalian and avian classes and become a raptor— theoretically. That begged a question. *Should I try it?* he wondered.

"No!" H'Ester advised her son emphatically. "As a young man, you are already strong and powerful. You have at your disposal three powerful alternate species—wolf, wild boar, and cougar. Do not jeopardize them and yourself to see whether or not you can transform into a bird." H'Ester still saw Rafe Cassius's twisted form in her mind's eye. "Although the power of flight offers many advantages, it is not greater than the sum of those you already possess." Even so, as a human, Edric enjoyed the enhanced visual acuity his raptor genes provided.

In theory, Edric also should be able to transform from one species directly into another species. This too had not been seen in males and was never tested. H'Ester counseled against attempting this action as well. The risk of a fatal attempt was too great.

"It is a nuisance, I know," H'Ester had acknowledged sympathetically. "Yet only females with two transforming chromosomes have been able to morph directly from one species into another. It is unknown whether or not a male with two X^T chromosomes can do the same safely. I don't want to find out through you that men cannot accomplish this feat."

Edric acquiesced to his mother's counsel and carefully followed the rules of transformation. He resumed human form before transforming from one alternate species into another. As an adult, he became quite proficient at transforming to and from human form quickly and so did not miss the ability to transform directly from one species into another.

Temperance

When H'Ariel became mistress of the House of H'Aleth, it suited Edric just fine. He preferred to be away from the hustle and bustle of village life and the administrivia of government affairs. With an inward sigh, H'Ariel cautioned her younger brother.

"You must choose your own path. Just be watchful and careful. Hybrids and hunters are not the only dangerous creatures you may encounter. Many native species are just as dangerous. Dragons are predators too and among the most deadly. You would make a fine meal."

"I am aware," Edric responded. Far from dismissing the danger, he took scouting seriously. Still, he enjoyed roaming all over H'Aleth, Erwina, and the open territories. He did not hesitate to cross into Biogenics territory, the northern mountains, and even Cassius territory . . . until he met Lilith.

Lilith tempered Edric's vagabond ways, and his scouting became more measured. As an agriculturalist, Lilith traversed fields of grass and grain all over H'Aleth and Erwina. Edric always accompanied Lilith whenever she traveled far afield and drew near to the borders. Yet whenever Lilith was safely ensconced in a secure location, Edric enjoyed scouting where few grains grew.

When Lilith became pregnant, Edric's scouting took on a grim resolve.

On Patrol

One day, while scouting as a cougar, Edric patrolled the woodlands of H'Aleth's northern border adjoining an open territory. It was early afternoon. The sun was shining with only a few fair-weather clouds, and there was a lovely breeze. Native species were out and about, and there was nothing out of the ordinary. When he wandered into an open glen, he stretched out in a sunny spot and relaxed. He even rolled around in grass interspersed with a few grains. *Lilith would scold me for crushing her wheat.*

After a while, Edric decided to stretch his legs. He headed toward a large rock formation nearby with several boulders, some of which towered over the others. *A good place to have a romp*, he decided. He ambled over to the first boulder and launched himself on top of it. He then vaulted from one boulder to another, testing his agility and his power. When he reached a convenient landing, he scanned the territory around him. It offered him a good vantage point from which to view the terrain below.

As Edric looked around, he noticed an abrupt change in the environment. Silence. No animals were moving in the forest, not even birds. Every prey species had fled the scene along with their predators. He knew immediately something was amiss—an apex predator must have entered the area. As he gazed over the landscape, searching for such a predator, he espied an enormous brown bear. It was facing away from him, crouching down, almost like a cougar or a leopard. Edric though this behavior odd for a bear.

Edric also spotted a small group of people not far away. They were walking along a well-worn path through the woodlands, heading toward the bear—completely unaware that a predator was awaiting their arrival. As Edric watched their approach, he saw the bear creeping toward the path.

Alarm bells sounded in Edric's head. *It's stalking them.* He recognized the danger immediately and bolted, leaping from one boulder to the next at breakneck speed. He knew he would never reach the people in time to prevent an attack. Yet he might still save some of them from being killed. He poured every ounce of power he had into this run—never stopping to think that a cougar was no match for a bear.

In one spectacular leap, the territory opened up before Edric. The vista was astounding, and he felt the wind on his face. Far into the distance, he pinpointed his target with precision. When he banked to acquire it, he suddenly realized he was airborne. Without intending to do so, he had transformed into a Cooper's hawk. Once again, genetic synergy supported him. It had given him the capability to transform across classes.

A series of loud, rasping calls shattered the silence. Everyone, including the bear, looked up to see the source. A Cooper's hawk rarely issued calls except during mating season. Yet this one had done so while diving toward the woods at 120 miles per hour. People and bear alike recognized that the hawk was targeting something. When the bear turned, Edric spotted two enormous canines protruding from its mouth—unmistakable evidence that it was a hybrid. None of his alternate species could battle this hybrid and survive. *But a raptor could distract it,* he surmised.

Having never transformed into a raptor of any kind, Edric was completely unpracticed in the skills that an adult hawk should possess. Yet, from his falconry training, he knew the hawk's capabilities. As Edric dove into the trees, his inexperience was evident. He lacked the well-practiced agility of a native raptor to thread through the trees. This hampered Edric's attack and slowed it considerably—to his good fortune. The bear's swipe fell short.

The travelers, still unable to see the hawk's target, finally realized that it was sounding an alarm and ran ahead, their movements drawing the bear's attention. Not for long. The hawk kept harassing it, issuing one warning call after another and constantly circling behind it. Every time the bear turned to go after its intended prey, the bird swooped in again. Infuriated, the bear rose on its hind legs to strike the hawk and put an end to its tormentor. The canopy interfered, blocking its massive paw. Frustrated, the hybrid finally gave up. Its hunt spoiled, it ambled away with one last snarl at the hawk.

Heritage

Another scout some distance away also heard the hawk's call. When she looked up, she saw a Cooper's hawk that she had not previously seen in her area. *What are you after?* she wondered as she watched the bird's steep dive into the canopy. Seconds later, she heard the cries of people shouting and their pounding footfalls. They were running toward her. She quickly readied her bow and arrow and raced to meet them. As she drew near, she could see that they were frightened. Yet she saw no attacker.

"What happened?" asked the scout.

"We saw something moving just inside the tree line," offered one traveler. "It looked like a leopard."

"I thought it looked more like a bear," offered another traveler. "It was much too large to be a leopard."

"We had better get out of here quickly," advised the scout.

After the travelers reached their destination, the scout returned to the main village. She reported the sighting of a large animal, species unknown, possibly an oversized leopard or a bear. She also apprised the wildlife specialist of the region's newest raptor. "It was quite unusual," she reported. "Its full plumage identifies it as a Cooper's hawk, and its size indicates it is female. Yet this hawk was much larger than normal. It was as big as a golden eagle."

Edric delivered his own special report privately to his sister, H'Ariel. "I caught a glimpse of an oversized bear as it ambled away. It bore canines like those of a saber-toothed tiger. Most likely, this is what the villagers saw."

"Another new animal hybrid," H'Ariel remarked. "The foundation has been very busy."

"That's not all," Edric added. "I too can become a raptor." Then he told her what actually had happened.

H'Ariel was stunned. The implications were profound. "Say nothing of this to anyone else," she insisted. "Report only that you caught a glimpse of this hybrid from far away." She had inherited her mother's intuition and caution. Although she said nothing further to Edric, she felt a sense of urgency. *If he can transform into a raptor, what else can he become?* Edric had also inherited the DNA fragment that his mother, H'Ester, had inherited from her mother, H'Eleanora.

Supplemental Notes and Citations

Morphogens

A morphogen is a biologic molecule that signals the precise formation of tissues, including when tissues are formed, where they are formed, and their pattern (Li, *et al.*, 2018; Sanger & Briscoe, 2019). They are especially active during embryogenesis (Bressloff & Kim, 2019). They can direct a cell to divide, differentiate, and migrate to a specific location. They can control growth and influence how tissues are structured. Hox genes play a major role in the development of an anterior–posterior axis (Durston, 2019; Roux & Zaffran, 2016). The Hedgehog signaling pathway is essential for embryonic patterning and development (Li, *et al.*, 2018; Wu, *et al.*, 2018).

Part V

Vengeance

CHAPTER 27
RAMPING UP

Raephela had not been idle. She had been very busy—or rather she had kept her hunters, armorists, and geneticists hopping. In addition to rebuilding her army and restoring its armaments, she focused on creating and cloning animal hybrids, terrestrial and aquatic, showing no compunctions whatsoever in cloning or genetically reengineering other species.

Raephela briefly entertained cloning some of the more powerful men in her army who could transform into apex predators. "How long would that take?" she asked Mason.

"An average of nine months to deliver a newborn baby. About twenty-two years for an adult approaching his prime," replied Mason, stone-faced. Raephela could barely tolerate a few months to clone anything.

Raephela stared intently at Mason for a moment and then waved him away, saying, "Never mind."

Of the humanoid hybrids, the serojabovid, papiopanoid, and crocutalupoid were the most successful. They were strong, relatively long-lived, and could be reproduced reliably from other mature *H. transformans* males. The serojabovid and papiopanoid were not inherently aggressive as their humanity had been preserved. They did not become violent unless they were attacked or harassed and were used primarily to augment the labor force. In contrast, the crocutalupoid was designed to hunt large prey and fight. By far the most aggressive and violent of the three humanoids, the crocutalupoid was used to attack, terrorize, and kill. Despite its origin as an *H. transformans*, little if any of its humanity remained.

Strategy

Raephela's strategy included producing enough hybrids to overwhelm her enemies. Then her army would invade and take control of a territory while her guards recaptured any surviving hybrids. Yet she knew that sheer numbers alone would not be enough. She wanted creatures like the hybrid bovi that were too big for any native animal or archer's arrow to fell. Even though the bovi could not be controlled, it could wreak havoc on anyone or anything in its path.

Also integral to her strategy, Raephela wanted to unleash new animal hybrids unknown to her enemies. Lacking prior experience with novel hybrids, her enemies would not know how to combat them. She planned to populate forests and rivers with ambush predators like the semiaquatic varan, the moresistrurus, and the ursuscro.

In addition to the hybrids the foundation already had, Raephela demanded a wider variety. "And make them more effective," she ordered.

Her geneticists immediately began developing an aquatic species to catch the unwary or ignorant by surprise. The craspedichironex [*crăs*-pĕd-ē-*cheer*-ōn-ĕx] began as a benign freshwater jellyfish. Once augmented with the venom of the deadly marine box jellyfish, it became lethal. It still looked and behaved like a common jellyfish except that it was larger than usual and had longer tentacles. Although designed to kill swimmers, it rarely attacked anyone. It simply fed on the tiny life-forms (zooplankton) that also inhabited fresh water. Unfortunately, their larger size made them readily visible in rivers, so swimmers and boaters were able to avoid contact with them.

Raephela was less than pleased with this hybrid. "Perhaps if you carry them onto the battlefield in buckets of water and heave them onto the enemy, they might actually kill someone," she mocked icily.

Mason was not quite certain how to interpret Raephela's remark until she shouted, "Get out!" Afterward, he decided to stick to mammalian and reptilian hybrids.

A Plethora of Hybrids

Raephela's geneticists quickly ramped up their efforts to create and produce more hybrids based on past successes. This tactic minimized failures associated with their trial-and-error methods and in turn increased productivity.

Illustration 23: Ovisuscrofalces

The geneticists developed the ovisuscrofalces (illustration 23), nicknamed the ovis, using the base genome of a bighorn sheep. They augmented it with the genes of a large moose for its rack, size, and power and added the genes for a wild boar's powerful shoulder and neck muscles. Along with misshapen horns, the hybrid developed a large rack of spiked horns arising from a thickened bony skull cap. At maturity, it grew to the size of a bull moose, except that it had a short, stocky neck with the neck muscles of a wild boar. Six feet tall at the shoulder and weighing almost 1,000 pounds, the ovis could easily run down anything smaller than itself. It also had the advantage of being agile in rocky terrains. With the cloven hooves of a mountain sheep, it could chase any adversary seeking shelter among the rocks. Once again, Raephela seemed unimpressed with this hybrid. Nonetheless, she approved it.

Subsequently, her geneticists developed the trialcesceramata [*trī-ăl-cēs-cĕr-ă-mă*-tă], trialces for short, using the same formula they had used for the bovi. This time the base genome was elk, augmented with an enlarged, heavily spiked rack and the spiked horn of the triceratops on its snout. Another huge animal hybrid, the trialces was considerably larger than the ovis and could sweep up and impale multiple adversaries in one strike. Although Raephela was better satisfied with this hybrid, she was annoyed that the trialces, ovis, and bovi were herbivores.

Glaring at Mason, Raephela asked sarcastically "Are you familiar with the word 'carnivore'? Do you know what that means?"

Mason gulped. "Yes, Your Majesty. We are working on two carnivorous hybrids now."

Geneticists under Rex Cassius had used the brown bear for the base genome of the ursuscro, augmenting it with the genes of a wild boar. Although still valuable as an assault weapon, it would kill any living thing in its path. So Mason decided to design a new brown bear hybrid—the ursupantheradactu [*ur*-sŭ-păn-ther-ah-*dăc*-too], which became known as the ursu. He augmented the native species with the canines and bite force of a jaguar. He could only hope that this version would be more pliable than the ursuscro. It was not.

Illustration 24: Sabrafataligrandis

Last but not least, the foundation's geneticists developed an enormous striped cougar with dramatically elongated canines on both upper (maxillary) and lower (mandibular) teeth. The mandibular canines were an unintended and most welcome outcome, likely due to the stimulation of dental stem cells. To placate Raephela, Mason added the genes of a domestic tabby cat to give the cougar a striped coat. With its enhanced size, dentition, and stripes, the cougar looked just like a saber-toothed tiger. Mason named the hybrid sabrafataligrandis (illustration 24), later called simply the sabra. *Raephela will never know the difference*, Mason thought with an inner smile.

With the addition of these new hybrids to those already available, the Cassius Foundation's armamentarium now possessed a large and varied array of animal hybrids. Yet there would be no rest for the weary. Raephela still demanded that her geneticists develop a hybrid beast similar in size and characteristics to the tyrannosaur or allosaur. Alas, the only animal model they had was the great gray dragon. Genetically engineering a dragon required dragon eggs. To Raephela's dismay, no hunter on the planet was willing to raid a dragon aery at any price.

Supplemental Notes and Citations
Cloning

Cloning is the process whereby the nucleus of a fertilized egg (a reproductive cell) is removed and replaced with the nucleus of a nonreproductive (somatic) cell (Simões & Santos, 2017). All somatic cells have a full complement of forty-six paired chromosomes. Thus, when the nucleus from one of these cells is placed into a fertilized egg, the same combination of forty-six chromosomes will direct the development of the new embryo. As a result, the animal that develops will have the same genes (genome) as the animal that donated the nucleus—effectively making a carbon copy (a clone) of the donor.

Cloning is essentially asexual reproduction. Sexual reproduction promotes genetic variability. Asexual production does not. Yet epigenetic effects can still affect gene function without changing the gene itself, and their influence can be inherited (Keefer, 2015). Even identical (monozygotic) twins do not remain genetically the same over time due to epigenetic effects.

Box jellyfish venom

Freshwater jellyfish are found worldwide (Fritz, *et al.*, 2007). Although they have a mild sting, they are not venomous. The box jellyfish is the exception. Its venom is toxic to humans and can cause blood cells to lyse (hemolysis), cardiac arrest, and respiratory failure within minutes (Brinkman & Burnell, 2007).

Smilodon fatalis (saber-toothed tiger)

A massive tiger, smilodon was a powerful carnivore thought to overpower prey as large as a bison (Brown, 2014). It weighed an estimated 800 to 900 pounds. (For comparison, a fully grown adult male lion weighs 400 to 450 pounds.) Its elongated, knifelike upper canines may have sheared through the throat, as opposed to crushing it and suffocating its prey (Brown, 2014; Figueirido, *et al.*, 2018; Manzuette, *et al.*, 2020; McHenry, *et al.*, 2007; Slater & Van Valkenburgh, 2016).

Stem cells

Stem cells are undifferentiated cells that have the ability to develop into any type of cell, as needed (Zakrzewski, *et al.*, 2019). They also have the capacity for self-renewal. Where necessary, they can replace damaged cells, thereby repairing tissues. There are different types of stem cells, some of which support embryonic development, whereas others specialize to support specific types of tissues (e.g., bone, blood, etc.) (Lou, 2015; Walmsley, *et al.*, 2016). Totipotent stem cells can differentiate and divide into any cell type. Multipotent stem cells differentiate along a specific cell line.

Dental stem cells support the development of dentition (Bansal & Jain, 2015; Friedlander, *et al.*, 2009; Thesleff, 2014; Zheng, *et al.*, 2019). Some of them have the ability to differentiate into cells that build bone (osteogenic). Growth factors influence the production and differentiation of dental stem cells. Of these, bone morphogenic proteins may be the primary regulators of tooth development (Bansal & Jain, 2015).

Thus, the notion of developing enlarged teeth in modern species is not improbable. There are approximately 300 genes that regulate tooth development. Despite the differences in size and shape, the same genes regulate tooth development across species (Thesleff, 2014).

Feline striped coats

Mutations of the taqpep gene can lead to the development of stripes, spots, and a mix of the two ("blotches") in a cat's coat (Kaelin, *et al.*, 2012; Lyons, 2012).

CHAPTER 28
Sabra

If she was to overwhelm her enemies, Raephela knew she needed not only masses of hybrids but also the element of surprise. Both H'Aleth and Biogenics could mount an effective defense, and Biogenics maintained an army. She dismissed Erwina as an effective adversary. She remained unaware that the schoolhouse trained the scouts who subsequently supported all three houses and so underestimated the strength of her enemies.

Logistics

"My enemies must not know of these new hybrids," Raephela stated emphatically. "They are to remain secret weapons to be unleashed at my command. Find a remote village where these beasts can be tested. Then report back to me on their effectiveness."

Finn was on the verge of panic. "Your Majesty," he wailed. "We don't have the means to transport hybrids weighing thousands of pounds. We can't lead or herd them anywhere. We can only provoke them to move."

"Then provoke them," replied Raephela.

Meanwhile, guards and armorists scrambled to build cages strong enough to contain the carnivorous hybrids. The ursu, the ursuscro, and the sabra required large, heavily reinforced cages. Next, the guards needed to figure out how to haul hybrids weighing 6,000 pounds over rocky terrain and through heavily forested areas to reach any villages.

Finn approached one of Raephela's structural engineers. "You must clear land and excavate roads before we can move these hybrids. Some of them weigh several tons."

"Don't take them overland," countered the engineer. "Instead, ship them downriver on a barge as far as you can, then disembark and haul or lead them overland from there."

Finn decided this was feasible with the carnivores, but not the herbivores. An herbivore would sink any barge it was on.

Wait a minute, Finn realized. *Raephela only cares about the carnivores. We probably don't need to test the herbivores at all.*

Although Finn was right, this only postponed the problem. Eventually he would have to figure out how to transport all the hybrids.

Ironically, the solution was growing right under the guards' noses. As herbivores, the ovis and the trialces grazed freely with the bovi on the fields beyond the fortress. These three species rapidly overgrazed the short scrub grass originally planted between the fortress and the forest beyond it.

To keep the hybrids fed, the guards conscripted captive family members to plant tall grasses under their watchful eyes. Even then, there was not enough grass to support adequate grazing. So forced labor cleared additional land, pushing the forest further back and making way for a road at the same time. Most of the wood from felled trees fired the furnaces that smelted iron ore for the foundation's weapons and bars for cages.

One of Raephela's hunters offered a solution for getting the massive herbivores to move voluntarily. "Cut the grass you are growing short before the animals reach it," she advised. "The remaining stalks won't be as tender or as good to eat as the grass you cut. When you want an animal to move, coax it along by offering it fresh grass to eat." The tactic worked perfectly.

Testing 1-2-3

Neither the ovis nor the trialces were tested on villagers. Given their past experience with the bovi, the guards were certain that the aforementioned hybrids would also run amok when provoked. There was no need to evaluate the effect they would have on a village. The guards had already experienced it themselves in real time.

The sabra was another matter altogether. Raephela demanded that it be unleashed on a village or an encampment in order to assess its killing quotient. *But where?* Finn wondered. When they tested the varan, it had escaped. *Who knows where it is now, or who may have seen it.*

Finn approached Raphela with his concern. "When we tested the varan in open territory, we encountered Biogenics soldiers. If we go there again, we can't be certain that we won't encounter more soldiers. They could be alerted to the new hybrid." Finn held his breath as Raphela looked directly at him.

"Good point," Raephela said, to Finn's relief. "Take the creature to one of our remotest villages and release it there."

"But it could kill our own guards in the village," said Finn with dismay.

"Or they could kill it," replied Raephela. "Find out which it is."

Overpowering

As was customary, the guards stopped feeding the sabra a week before they planned to release it. The level of effort required to transport the massive hybrid to a remote village added another two weeks. By that time, the sabra was attacking anything it could reach—and it had a long reach.

Letting the creature out of its cage was not an option. The guards knew they would have no control over it. Since they could not approach the village with any degree of stealth, Finn ordered the hybrid to be transported into the village while still in its cage.

"Here is your new hybrid," he said to his village counterpart. "I suggest you keep it well fed and in its cage until you intend to release it."

Staring at the huge sabra, his counterpart asked with great apprehension, "Why would I ever release it?"

"To let it get some exercise," replied Finn with a straight face.

His counterpart stared at him in disbelief.

Actually, Finn had no intention of leaving the sabra at the village.

He had devised a plan to test the sabra—hopefully, without putting his comrades at risk. With the successful creation of the ursu, the foundation's stock of violent, carnivorous hybrids was ample. So he brought one of the few remaining ursuscros. If Raephela found out and challenged him, he could say that the ursuscro provided a much more formidable opponent against which to test the sabra. *Too bad we can't test it against the bovi or the trialces*, he thought. *Then we would see a real battle of titans.*

"Tell your guards and the rest of the people in the village to find a safe place to hide," Finn ordered. "Not in their huts," he added emphatically. Grass-and-mud huts offered no safety.

The majority of the village's occupants climbed into trees. A few scampered behind rocks and boulders. Others climbed atop the storehouse, the only sturdy building in the village.

"Get up a tree," Finn shouted at the latter. The wooden storehouse might hold up against the sabra; however, the sabra could easily vault on top of it.

Both cages had been placed adjacent to very large trees on opposite sides of the village center. The trees were in apposition to each other, and each cage's gate faced the village center. Of necessity, long ropes were attached to two chains that would open the gates—one released the latch, and the other raised the gate. Originally, the chains had been made just long enough to reach over the top of the cages, where a guard would stand to pull up the gate. The flaw in this design was recognized when a hybrid reached through the bars and brought down a hapless guard.

When all was readied, a guard climbed onto a sturdy branch of each respective tree. From there, the guards released the latches and raised the gate of each cage. Both hybrids emerged and immediately attacked one another. The fight was fierce and savage, yet the ursuscro never stood a chance against the sabra. Once the ursuscro was overcome and killed, the hungry sabra began to feast on it. Like any native cat, it pulled off and swallowed chunks of meat while watching for prospective scavengers.

Meanwhile, several guards armed with bows and arrows stood atop the sabra's cage. They had tied ropes to their arrows. Taking careful aim, they loosed their arrows through the cage and into the ursuscro's carcass. Then they started pulling on the ropes, dragging the carcass toward the cage while they stayed close to the tree. The sabra seemed not to care as long as it could continue to feed. As the carcass inched closer to the cage, the guards scampered up the tree behind it. From there, they jostled the carcass into the cage. The sabra immediately looked up, as if scanning for scavengers trying to steal its meal. The guards froze. Cougars and tigers can climb trees.

The sabra hissed at the guards and charged the tree. A quick-witted guard yanked on what was left of the carcass. The sound drew the sabra's attention. As it saw its meal slipping away, the sabra launched into the cage to reclaim its prize. Guards promptly dropped the gate, and the latch clicked into place. "Now all we have to do is get it back to the fortress," sighed Finn.

CHAPTER 29
RESURGENCE

Recent encounters with several new animal hybrids raised the alert level for H'Aleth, Erwina, and Biogenics. Although it was possible that these hybrids had escaped accidentally from the Cassius Foundation, the allies remained convinced that the foundation was reemerging and posed an imminent threat. The hybrids heralded the foundation's potential to release massive numbers of creatures in another assault. There had been a precedent under Rafe Cassius. So, the two houses and Biogenics promptly increased their border watches and sent word to their villages to stay alert for an incursion.

Cassius was rising.

Of Wind and Water

The succession of new hybrids was not the only sign. Once again, rivers were being polluted downstream. The foundation spewed its refuse into the Taurus River and into the air. Dying vegetation, dwindling numbers of pollinators and prey species, and a souring of the air indicated that the foundation's furnaces were working hard. As the Cassius Foundation ramped up its war industry, the Pices River alerted the H'Aletheans.

Fortunately, waters of the Cassius River diluted some of the contaminants at its confluence with the Taurus. Subsequently, those contaminated waters fed the Feroxaper, which branched into the Pices and Ursus at the southwest corner of Cassius territory. The Pices flowed west by southwest across the neck of H'Aleth's Caput Canis and then continued southward past H'Aleth's main village and research center. There, sensitive noses and chemical analysis quickly detected the river's pollution.

The region around the Cassius fortress suffered the most damage. Sulfur dioxide issued from huge forges and poisoned the air whenever and wherever it combined with oxygen and nitrogen. Fresh rainwater then turned into acid rain, poisoning both the land and the waterways. Testing of explosive armaments added to the air pollution. Native species, both predator and prey, disappeared from the region. Extensive pollution of the Taurus led to the disappearance of fish and amphibian species downstream. Raptors abandoned the area as fish and waterfowl sickened and died.

Even the gray dragons avoided the area when they came down from their aeries to hunt. They knew they would find no prey there, and the stench alone was enough to keep them away. Nevertheless, they kept watch on the fortress—albeit from a distance. They knew a malevolent entity lived there.

An Unexpected Benefactor

A village woman was walking in an open meadow not far from the edge of a forest. Wild berry bushes grew there along with young saplings and multiple tree sprouts that had taken root where sunlight was plentiful. She lived in an encampment near the northern foothills, located well inside the forest—too dense for a gray dragon to enter.

The woman was gathering wild berries when she heard an animal charging through woods. As an *H. transformans*, her acute hearing could tell that it was still some distance away; however, it was moving very fast. She detected the animal's vector as the sound grew closer and discerned that it was headed in her direction. *Native or hybrid? Predator or prey fleeing a predator?* she wondered. These questions were academic. In any case, she could be in serious trouble.

There was no time for the woman to transform into her alternate species. So she immediately began running toward the tree line at an angle perpendicular to the animal's vector. If she reached the woods, she could find a tree to climb. At the same time, she called for help in the hope that other villagers or a scout would hear her. If one was nearby, he or she might arrive in time to help fend off a potential attacker. The sound of a human voice might also alert the animal and shift it away from her. She could only hope that it was not a hybrid or one of the few predators that did not fear humans. Brown bears sometimes wandered into the region looking for a meal. They were apex predators in their own right and did not fear humans.

As the sound grew nearer, the woman heard only one animal thundering through the forest, and it was quickly drawing closer. The only other sound was a strong wind blowing through the trees. Suddenly, a mammoth animal burst into view. At first glance, it looked like a deformed bighorn sheep. She was shocked to see one so far from the mountains and horrified by its appearance.

The animal was huge for a sheep—as big as a bull moose. Above its dystrophic curved horns, the hybrid had a rack of enlarged, spiked horns. The woman had no doubt it was a hybrid. It barreled through the scrub brush, tossing its head violently. When it spotted her, it turned and charged with its head down. Unable to outrun it, she dove facedown amid the shrubs and saplings abutting the forest's edge. She flattened herself as much as possible, hoping that his rack would be caught in some of the saplings, keeping her from being trampled or gored.

The creature was almost upon the woman when the thunder of hooves abruptly ceased. Amazed, the woman turned to look up. A male great gray dragon had grasped the hybrid's torso with his powerful talons and clasped its neck in his jaws (illustration 25, The Hunt). The downbeat of his powerful wings bent the saplings to the ground as he exerted the effort needed to lift a 1,000-pound hybrid off the ground and into the air. Once that was accomplished, the dragon banked away and flew off. His clan would eat well that night.

The woman had been so focused on escaping the animal charging her that she never noticed a gray dragon overhead. She knew the dragon

Illustration 25: The Hunt

could not have missed seeing her. She wondered if the dragon was simply catching prey, or if it had interceded on her behalf.

After returning to the encampment, the woman sought out a scout. She reported the incident and described the hybrid she saw. The scout immediately set off to alert other scouts, who would relay the information to H'Ariel, Evard, and Edrew. Another previously unknown animal hybrid was on the loose.

Yet the incident heralded another possibility. The allies were not alone in keeping watch. An old accord still held, forged long ago with a clan of great gray dragons.

Supplemental Notes and Citations

Acid rain

Acid rain consists of a mixture of sulfur and nitrogen which, when combined with water—rain, snow, or fog (oxygen and hydrogen)—forms sulfuric and nitric acids (Kumar, 2017; Manisalidis, *et al.*, 2020). An increase in sulfur dioxide is linked predominantly to the combustion of fossil fuels (Greenfelt, *et al.*, 2020; Manisalidis, *et al.*, 2020). Effects over time result in a widespread loss of trees, freshwater fish, and the wildlife that depend upon these resources. Air pollution, which includes a wide range of particulates as well as sulfur dioxide and nitrogen oxide, also affects human health. Air pollution can trigger or exacerbate pulmonary diseases such as asthma and emphysema, and it adversely affects mortality rates (Manisalidis, *et al.*, 2020).

CHAPTER 30
An Old Alliance

While her mate was out hunting, a dragoness was guarding the entrance to her cave, which held her nest with two precious eggs. Suddenly, a rogue male gray dragon with no clan of his own confronted her, intent on stealing her eggs. The dragoness raised an alarm as she fought with the intruder. She struggled to combat her attacker while trying not to trample the nest herself. The intruding dragon had no such compunctions. He wanted the eggs for food and had assumed that he could overpower a nesting female without too much difficulty. He was unprepared for the dragoness to bring the fight to him.

The dragoness's distressed rumbles echoed throughout her clan's territory. Hearing the alarm, a nearby female relative joined the battle. By this time, the mother was seriously wounded and pinned down by the rogue, leaving her relative to take up the fight. The angry rogue, with wounds of his own, turned on the rescuer and blanketed her in flames. The dragon knew that the entire clan had been alerted, and he needed to get away quickly. He snatched an egg in his talons and flew off. This pittance of a snack was better than none at all.

The murderer did not get far. The clan's alpha male was nearly upon him. The rogue dropped the egg as he soared away at top speed. Although the alpha could have overtaken the rogue, he had to be prudent. The murderer had broken an unspoken law in using his fire and would no doubt do so again.

So began an aerial battle of wits. The alpha would soar in close enough to evoke the rogue's fire, then dodge it. Dragon fire is not limitless. The physiologic agents that blend to create dragon fire can be exhausted. Once the rogue expended these resources, the alpha would be free to engage it.

In the savage battle that ensued, the rogue needed all of his resources, including his talons. Aerial battles at high altitudes could be deadly to both combatants. Should their talons become locked, they could crash to the ground at great speed, killing both of them. The alpha intended to drive his adversary to ground, yet the rogue would have no part of it. Whenever the alpha pressed close, the rogue turned to engage the alpha with his fire and his talons—a maneuver he used one time too many.

The alpha had learned at what point the rogue would roll over. The alpha matched his adversary's turn, diving under him at just the right moment. Powerful talons gripped the rogue's back as the alpha's powerful jaws gripped its throat (illustration 26). After a few moments in a free fall from 18,000 feet, the rogue was dead. The alpha released his grip and let the carcass crash to the ground, resuming his flight to follow it. Once on the ground, the alpha dragged the carcass to a place where he could destroy it with his fire.

The fight had traversed many miles. The alpha circled back to where he first encountered the rogue, searching for the egg. Although he scanned the area and well beyond, even his raptor-like vision failed to find the egg. It was lost.

The alpha returned to the aery of the injured dragoness. "The rogue that attacked you is dead," he rumbled, in the low frequency of dragon species. "Before we fought, the rogue dropped the egg he stole. Afterwards, I searched the entire side of the mountain and the forest below for any sign of it. I found none."

The dragoness thought it likely that her egg had smashed upon the ground. Scavengers would have descended upon it quickly and eaten the embryo within, leaving only an empty shell. Saddened yet resigned, she thanked the alpha for his efforts.

The dragoness grieved for the loss of her egg and the cousin who died coming to her aid. Still, she had one egg left, and her wounds would heal. Members of her clan would provide for her until she recovered. She and her mate were grateful for the egg they still had.

Illustration 26: Retribution

The Accord

Fortuitously, the stolen egg had fallen into a swollen mountain stream, turbulence from the stream's high flow buffering the egg's landing. Thus, its leathery shell did not break when it landed in the waters below.

The stream transported the egg with the waves jostling it. As small rivulets converged with the stream, it grew progressively larger until it became a tributary of the River Panthera. There a sharp-eyed eagle spotted it, flew down to grasp the egg with both talons, and promptly transported it to the nearest H'Aleth outpost. With a piping call, the eagle alerted human scouts, who responded quickly, taking the egg with great care. The scouts immediately recognized that it was a great gray dragon egg.

"How did it get all the way down here?" asked a surprised scout.

Once the eagle resumed human form, she described where she found it. "To reach the River Panthera, it must have fallen or rolled into a deep stream somewhere north of us. Ultimately, it was swept into the Panthera."

"We must return it to the gray dragons as soon as possible," declared Hathor, H'Aleth's lead scout at the Panthera outpost. "We have no way of knowing the egg's stage of development, and I, for one, have no idea how to raise a great gray dragon chick."

Transforming once again, the eagle flew to an outcropping high in the mountain foothills, long ago designated as one of several rendezvous points where scouts and dragons could make contact. The great gray dragons would hear her piping calls, and she would scratch the image of a dragon egg in the rock. She knew the dragons would understand. H'Aletheans had found and returned eggs in the past. Meanwhile, Hathor dispatched a second scout, who transformed into a gray wolf and raced to notify H'Ariel of their find.

H'Ariel knew exactly what to do based on the accord reached long ago with the great gray dragons. She also knew which scouts could alter the pitch of their voices to a bass or bass-baritone level to communicate with them. Several were assigned to Erwina's northeast outpost, and to H'Aleth's outposts along the northern border of Capus Canis—the outposts closest to the northern mountain ranges.

Barely a day after the egg's discovery, it was returned to its mother. The scouts met with the dragoness and her mate in a montane glade where dragons and humans had met in times past. There she reclaimed her egg, safe and sound. With a nod to the scouts, the parents flew back to their aery.

The loss of a dragon egg was extremely rare. For it to be found intact was still rarer. Thus, a rogue dragon, random chance, and a tacit understanding further strengthened an old alliance.

CHAPTER 31
Prelude to War

Once the foundation's forces had been restored and many new hybrids developed, Raephela began planning her assault against H'Aleth, Erwina, Biogenics, and ultimately Gregor. *Not only will I succeed where my grandfather failed, I will surpass his effort*, she vowed. The Cassius Foundation was ready to reassert itself.

Defeating Biogenics was Raephela's first priority. Biogenics's army and weapons of war represented the greatest threat. Although she expected H'Aleth to put up a fight, it had no weapons of war. Her superior firepower would defeat it.

Raephela disregarded Erwina. Her hunters had seen no defenses there and encountered only a few scouts. *Erwina consists of schoolteachers and pupils who are taught how to read, write, and grow crops*, she thought dismissively. Little did she know what else the faculty taught their students.

Raephela lacked the skills to map out the logistics of a battle plan, and she knew it. Her expertise lay in murdering prospective rivals. Unlike her grandfather, Rex Cassius, she had established a war council to develop strategies for conquering her enemies. She listened to her lieutenants, engineers, hunters, and guards, and then tasked the lieutenants to flesh out the tactics.

A Strategy to Defeat Biogenics

Raephela's guards had reported encountering a small Biogenics squad outside a market where they had released the new varan hybrid that escaped. Hence, she knew that Biogenics still maintained an army. Given the small number of men, she reasoned that the many years with no enemy encroachment might have induced Biogenics leadership to reduce their army's size. After all, maintaining an army with nothing to do was expensive. Nevertheless, Biogenics still maintained outposts all along its eastern border, waiting for the foundation to mount another offense.

"Biogenics keeps a close watch on its eastern border with us," reported Olsen, her chief lieutenant. "They assume any attack will come from that direction."

"Then we will not disappointment them," Raephela replied. "We will also attack them from the west. They will never see us coming."

Mason informed Raephela that the huge hybrid herbivores could not traverse any waterways where the water was too deep. "They can't swim, and they are too heavy for a barge. Both the barge and the hybrid would sink. They can forge across a river as long as their feet can reach the riverbed," he said. He thought for a minute and then added, "They should be able to cross the River Taurus anywhere the rate of flow is slow—specifically, where the river bends. From that point they could travel northward. Then we must find a way to get these animals through the northern mountains. In the meantime, the guards have trained them to be led as long as they are rewarded with fresh grasses."

To this information, Olsen added, "We can march northward along our western border. But we will need a way to cross the mountains with an army, armaments, caged hybrids, and those massive animals." Raephela promptly tasked Cole, her lead hunter, to map a route through the northern mountains by which her army could circumvent Biogenics or cut through it undetected and attack its headquarters from the west.

Cole knew the northern mountains well, including most of its inhabitants. He also recalled a wide break in Biogenics's array of outposts along its northeastern boundary. He suspected that Biogenics relied on the mountains to serve as a natural barrier between itself and Cassius territory. Yet that barrier was not impenetrable. Cole and his hunters had crossed multiple mountain passes on Mason's wild goose chases, looking for dinosaur bones.

"Only a few passes are wide enough to allow an army to pass through them, and barely," Cole told Raephela. "All of them are riddled with massive boulders and other debris. Men can climb over or walk around them. Horses can walk around but not climb over them. Cannon mounts and wagons full of armaments and other matériel will not get through," he added grimly.

Neither will the hybrid herbivores, thought Raephela. Undaunted, she turned to her engineers. "Clear the pass that Cole and Olsen think will serve as the best route through the mountains," she ordered.

"There is a narrow bend in the River Admare which points eastward," Cole continued. "The river slows at that spot. To my knowledge, there is no outpost there, and the nearest village lies farther to the north. Biogenics has a small headquarters some distance to the south. By entering Biogenics territory where the Admare bends east, you may be able to advance undetected, cross the Admare, and then march due south in open territory to reach their main headquarters."

"That would mean attacking from the north, not the west," Olsen noted.

"Many outposts guard Biogenics's western border," stated Cole. "The River Della courses along that border as well. I don't see how you can attack from the west without raising the alarm and engaging Biogenics on its western front."

Olsen turned to Raephela. "What would you have us do?" he asked.

"Plan your attack from the north," she ordered.

"Be advised," Cole added. "Once you start bringing those behemoths into Biogenics territory, all notion of stealth will be lost."

"Then we will hide them in the foothills until our armies are in place," Olsen countered. "Other beasts of burden can haul cannons on wheels." Turning to Raephela, he added, "If we begin the assault on Biogenics's southeastern front, it will draw their attention and their forces away from their northeast outposts. The distraction may help us evade detection until it is too late."

Raephela agreed. "When the time comes, I will order a diversionary force to engage Biogenics on its eastern border, where they would be expecting an assault, while the main force attacks from behind."

"I suggest your diversionary force also be your main force," Olsen advised. "Our forces will be battling an army and not scouts when we engage with Biogenics."

Raephela was well aware that it could take months—possibly a year—to engineer a route through a mountain pass. *Patience*, she counseled herself. She did not want her eagerness to undermine her goal.

A Strategy to Conquer H'Aleth

Cassius territory lay just to the north of H'Aleth territory. Given the close proximity, the majority of H'Aleth's scouts were positioned along H'Aleth's northern border. It was a long border to protect, yet H'Aleth had no army. Even so, its well-trained scouts defended it effectively.

Consistent with the plan of attack for Biogenics, Raephela also ordered her lieutenants to design a two-pronged attack against H'Aleth. The first wave would strike on H'Aleth's northern border where she knew the H'Aletheans would expect it. The attack would draw the bulk of H'Aleth's defenders and their resources to that border. Raephela surmised that an assault along the border would lead to a major battle; however, she expected the scouts to be overwhelmed eventually.

"We can conduct hit-and-run attacks at random locations along the border," Olsen suggested. "While the H'Aletheans' attention is drawn in this manner, we can attack their center of operations via the River Panthera." Raephela agreed with his proposal. When the main village came under attack, she was certain that most of H'Aleth's meager forces would be drawn to it—leaving few, if any, defenders to protect the south.

The smattering of Raephela's hunters who had slipped across H'Aleth's border unnoticed had reported a handful or no scouts along its southeastern border. So Raephela decided to resurrect her grandfather's plan with a modest modification. There would be no battleships. Instead, she would use barges to transport troops, hybrids, and weaponry along the coastline, striking H'Aleth from the rear, as her grandfather had planned—only without all the expense and grandiosity.

With H'Aleth's forces drawn to the northern border, Raephela's flotilla of barges could descend upon H'Aleth's southern coastline without meeting any resistance. Once disembarked, her army would invade H'Aleth from the south and advance to assault H'Aleth from the rear. Forced to defend themselves on two fronts, H'Aleth's scouts would be crushed in a vise.

Raephela presupposed that her incursion into the southeastern region of H'Aleth would be undetected. "They will never expect an assault by barges," she laughed. Even if her troops were spotted, it would be too late for H'Aleth to redeploy its defenses effectively.

Another lieutenant expressed a much different concern. "What about the dragons?" he asked.

"Stay away from them," retorted Raephela curtly.

"The mountains are further to the south and toward the southwest," said Cole. "If you stay away from the foothills, the dragons will probably ignore you."

Cole's reply was partly accurate. Raephela's strategists had no way of knowing that the red dragons had learned long ago to recognize H'Alethean scouts. Whereas they might not attack human strangers, they would never ignore them—especially an army of them.

A Strategy to Invade Erwina

Erwina lay to H'Aleth's west and south of Biogenics. This was perfect. Once Raephela's forces had overcome H'Aleth to the east and Biogenics to the north, her armies would simply sweep into Erwina from both directions, overwhelm the Erwinians, and occupy the territory. After all, the hunters she had sent to kidnap a paleontologist had reported no impediments or resistance.

Raephela knew that Erwina's schoolhouse served as its seat of governance. *I wonder what battle plans they draw up in that schoolhouse,* she thought mockingly. The rest of the territory seemed to be wide open, except for a few scattered villages. She knew Erwina had scouts. Those paltry forces had once tried to stop Rafe from conquering their territory. When they were being routed, a great gray dragon had appeared. *No doubt the dragon was attracted by the fighting and decided to feast on the banquet before him*, Raephela mused. *But what madness possessed my uncle to challenge the beast to single combat?*

In any case, Raephela was not about to resurrect Rafe's battle plan. It had been a disaster.

A Strategy to Invade Gregor

Raephela was well aware that nearly all, if not all, of the pedigrees and DNA from the three houses were stored at Gregor, along with other stores of DNA, probably dragon as well. Her previous attempt to gain access to those stores by subterfuge had been foiled. "No matter. This time I will take it by force," she declared. Once she had conquered H'Aleth, Erwina, and Biogenics, they would be unable to support Gregor. Raephela would be free to march on Gregor without opposition.

Claren had returned from Gregor with detailed information regarding its defenses—or rather the lack thereof. Winter appeared to be its primary and possibly only effective defense.

Since Gregor had no known defensive capability other than its location, its conquest was a foregone conclusion. With this misapprehension, Raephela assumed she could overrun Gregor and easily gain access to all of its resources. Once her geneticists had access to dragon and dinosaur DNA, her reign over all the territories and anything in between would be absolute. *Even the great gray dragons will bow to me*, she swore.

CHAPTER 32
A Change of Heart

Cole had long grown weary of trying to meet Raephela's demands. She made it quite clear that she didn't care about the risks he and his comrades had to take. She gave no thought to their welfare or survival.

At first, Raephela had paid her hunters a lucrative salary. Yet as the risks became greater, many hunters dropped out. The rest would have done so as well had Raephela not noticed the attrition. She promptly took their families hostage to staunch the loss. From that point onward, she paid the hunters just enough to provide a meager subsistence for themselves and their families. Coerced and trapped, the remaining hunters continued to accept her tasks.

An Accidental Discovery

The plan to circumvent Biogenics's borders by traversing through mountain passes meant encroaching on the hunting grounds of great gray dragons. This delicate situation was fraught with peril. Thus, Raephela sent her most experienced hunter into the northern mountains.

Cole and his men traveled northward, using dense montane forest as cover until they reached the tree line. At that point, their only option was traveling through open terrain. They weaved through narrow passageways among the rocks, choosing those paths where they could dive to the ground to avoid being picked off by a gray dragon on the hunt. They kept cold camps at night. A fire would attract unwanted attention.

One particularly cold night, a bitter wind pierced the foothills. The hunters found a niche that provided some cover and surcease from the wind. Finally, they decided to risk a small, smokeless fire. They foraged among the rocks for bits of old dried wood and dead leaves. They also collected what they thought was dried, finely shredded bark fibers.

"This should catch fire quickly," said Logan.

It did not. In fact, the substance would not burn at all even though the dried wood and leaves burned all around it.

"What is this stuff?" exclaimed O'Connor.

Curious, Cole scooped up a sample to take back to the Cassius fortress. Unbeknownst to Cole and his companions, they had stumbled upon a deposit of asbestos.

The hunters finally reached a broad canyon between two tall mountain peaks. At first it headed in a northwesterly direction before veering leftward and heading west. It was riddled with rocky debris, most of which could be tossed aside, and several small boulders that could be hauled out of the way with enough muscle. Afterward, the engineers could smooth out the canyon floor except for two enormous blocks of granite that were not going anywhere. The engineers would need to carve out a path around them.

Upon completing a visual survey of the pass, the hunters returned to the fortress where Cole gave Raephela his report. "Not far from where the River Taurus comes down from the mountains, there is a broad canyon that runs between two mountains. It should accommodate your forces once the canyon floor has been cleared. There are two enormous boulders that an earthquake might move. Your engineers will need to excavate a way around them. I do not recommend blasting them out of the way. The force of the blast will trigger landslides and probably attract the gray dragons."

"Did you encounter any dragons?" asked an anxious Navid, Raephela's chief engineer.

"We did not," Cole answered. Technically, this was true. They did not actually encounter a dragon; however, they did see them flying aloft. "There were only five of us," Cole continued, "and we kept a very low profile."

Then Cole handed the sack of black dust and fibers to Navid. The engineer looked inside and asked, "Why are you giving me this stuff?"

"It doesn't burn," replied Cole.

New and Improved

Navid was skeptical of Cole's claim. Yet when he tried to set it afire, it would not burn. *Not hot enough*, he thought. So he placed some on a cast iron platter and loaded it into the forge. It still would not catch fire, nor melt.

"Not even at temperatures that forge iron," Navid told Raephela excitedly. "I'm just not sure how we can use it. There isn't much of it."

"Give it to me," said Mason. "I know what to do with it."

It had finally dawned on Mason that genetically modifying a species to create a hybrid was not always necessary. Sometimes bigger was better. By adding somatotropin and thyroid hormone, he could make some native species larger—much larger. Simply increasing an animal's size or maximizing its existing armaments might be sufficient, and it was one thing he could accomplish quickly. Now he could use the black dust to make some of them fire resistant as well. These steps could keep him in Raephela's good graces—if she had any.

Mason was confident that his newly minted animal hybrids, enhanced with the weaponry and scutes of a triceratops, would deter or at least distract gray dragons from Raephela's forces. Once he suffused their keratin scutes with asbestos, their armor would be fire resistant. *I'd like to see one of those dragons face off with a bovi now*, he thought arrogantly.

Mason knew that the thickened scales of the obsolete lyvulseroptera had once withstood a brief strafing of fire from a red dragon. The scales on his hybrids were even thicker, and now they were fireproof. He failed to recall that the lyvulseroptera had not survived the jaws of a great gray dragon.

Raephela was pleased with the latest hybrids' embellishments and ordered Mason to create more of them. "As if I can roll them off an assembly line," Mason muttered to himself. So he tasked Cole to collect more asbestos.

"A lot more," Mason added emphatically.

Cole glared at Mason and said bluntly, "Forget it!"

"What's the problem?" asked Mason. "You were the one who brought the stuff back in the first place."

"That was an accident. We stumbled over it while trying to make our way through the mountains without being spotted by a dragon," Cole growled.

"If you stumbled over it once, you can stumble over it again," remarked Mason glibly.

When Cole looked at him with a coldly murderous expression, Mason quickly added, "Raephela wants more."

It was the last straw.

A Different Plan

With this latest assignment, Cole started mapping out various routes whereby he, his comrades, and their families could escape from Raephela. Raephela was distracted, engrossed in planning her attacks and establishing her war machine. She had pulled most of her security guards away from their usual duties to focus on her war plan. Had Cole and his men not been tasked to find more asbestos, they would have been forced to join Raephela's army. Hence, Cole accepted the task, even though it meant returning to the northern mountains.

As Raephela's lead hunter, Cole attended her strategy sessions. Consequently, he learned where and when Raephela's various contingents would be headed and how they planned to get there. With this information, coupled with his knowledge of the surrounding territories, he looked for routes to potential locations where his band and their families could disappear. This proved to be no small task.

Traveling to the north risked encountering Raephela's army. Plans were already underway to clear the mountain pass Cole had identified.

Even if they could slip past the army, the more vulnerable family members faced the risk of extreme hardship in the cold climate. Traveling to the south would take them into the open territories. Yet settling there could expose them to incursions by other hunters conducting raids to conscript new workers, and to guards dispatched to test a new hybrid. Even if they successfully passed through the open territories, they would come very close to both H'Aleth and Erwina. With Raephela vowing to conquer both of them, the refugees could encounter warfare.

Cole needed to figure out something fast. He and his men were due to move out. A delay would be noted and raise questions.

Supplemental Notes and Citations

Asbestos

Asbestos is a naturally occurring crystalline substance (silicate mineral). It is widespread and can be found in metamorphic and igneous rocks. When disturbed, it breaks down into a fine crystalline dust, which can be inhaled (Baumann, *et al.*, 2015; Pira, *et al.*, 2018). Asbestos is fire resistant. It cannot be burned or melted, even at extreme temperatures. It can only be destroyed through physical, chemical, or nuclear processes (Kusiorowski, *et al.*, 2013).

Mortar

Both mortar and cement are fire resistant up to 800°F to 1,000°F, depending upon their constituents (e.g., calcium, coal ash) (Khurram, *et al.*, 2018). Hence, bricks and mortar are often used for fireplaces and chimneys.

CHAPTER 33
The Getaway

With the foundation's mobilization of troops underway, Raephela focused her attention on getting men, hybrids, and matériel en route to their respective targets. Her flotilla of barges had already departed to H'Aleth's southeast coast. It had the greatest distance to travel.

After the barges departed, the moat was drained to allow the hybrid herbivores to cross over. The bridges over the moat had been built to carry cannons, men, and other less weighty hybrid animals. The herbivores would collapse them.

Raephela dispatched advance forces via the River Taurus to establish strategic positions within Cassius territory. There her troops would muster prior to launching their attacks. Meanwhile, the vast majority of her troops would travel overland. Hybrid herbivores would serve as draft animals for cannons and supply wagons.

A Tactical Plan

Cole knew the plans for deploying troops, hybrids, and matériel out of the fortress (illustration 27, appendix K). All of the animal cages on the north side—inside and outside the fortress—would be used to transport the hybrids. Under the supervision of guards, workers would move the cages and their occupants to the docking platform. There, they would load the cages onto barges that would ferry them to the bend in the River Taurus. At that point, the cages would be offloaded, still within Cassius territory, and transported to predetermined points of release.

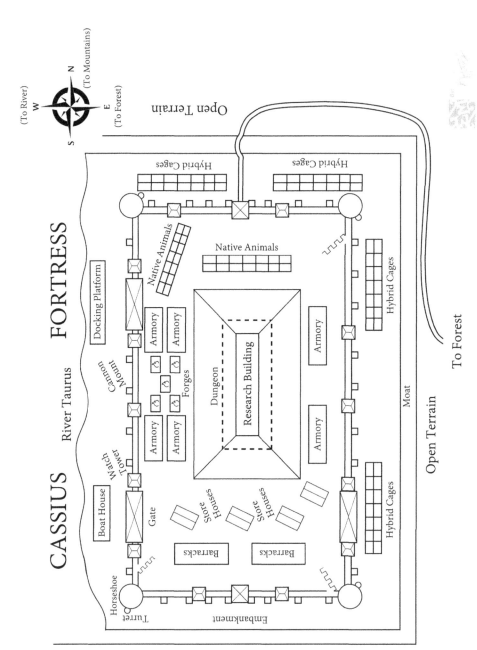

Illustration 27: Cassius Fortress

"This is a massive 'all hands on deck' effort to move men, machines, and hybrids out of the west and south gates," Cole told his colleagues. "Escaping through the north gate is our only option."

"Why not use the east gate?" asked Cooper. "It's much closer to the forest."

"To expedite troop movement, some forces may exit through the east gate," explained Cole. "Besides, we would have to get past the armories, which will be bustling with activity."

Returning to the escape plan, Cole described, "We will need to time our escape when almost all of the hybrids have been moved. As long as there are still a few cages left, the north gate will stay open. On the north side, a single guard is stationed at each of the towers from the northwest corner tower to the northeast corner tower. As soon as the hybrids on the east side and northeast corner are moved out, the guards in the northeast towers will be reassigned. This is when we make our move, escaping through the north gate at night."

"Uh, what about the guards on the northwest side?" asked Dawson.

"They will be monitoring the movement of workers as they transport the hybrids to the dock. This is where Raephela expects some workers to attempt an escape via the river. Sadly, some probably will try, only to be cut down by the tower guards."

Cole discarded the notion of entering the moat under the small bridge across from the north gate. Despite the nominal traffic, the area between the gate and bridge was still lighted to facilitate moving the hybrids. With so many family members to move, the risk of being spotted was too great.

As troops mustered and hybrids were marshaled, traffic was moving out via the west and south gates twenty-four hours a day. Cole took advantage of a new moon to lead his men and their families out of the fortress. They were taking a terrible risk as they slipped away from their quarters. Staying within the shadows, the troupe crept silently out of the research building on its north side and waited in its shadow.

As Cole had described, a single guard was stationed at the nearest watchtower. All others had been reassigned to the south and west gates through which most of Raephela's war machine was departing. With relatively little activity at the north gate, the guard had found a perch and now entertained himself watching the activities at the other gates. Cole and company heard him laugh from time to time over some observed mishap. The towers on the northwest, southwest, and southeast corners were fully lit to support mobilization. The lights of the northeast corner tower were turned inward to illuminate the armories and south gate.

Workers, most of them conscripts or hostages, had left the north gate open as they moved cages around the northwest tower to the dock. With the guard distracted, one family at a time dashed across the unlit open space between the research building and the north wall. When the opportunity came, they dashed to the moat and disappeared into it as another family sought refuge in the gate's shadow. This pattern continued until all four families reached the moat.

The moat was wide, very deep, and very dark at the bottom—especially away from the bridges. Still, crossing it without any cover risked discovery, though much less than crossing under the bridge. So, hugging the south wall of the moat, the troupe of escapees headed east. Roughly halfway between the northeast tower and the first watchtower on the east side of the fortress, they slipped out of the moat—away from the bridge, the lights, and the commotion—and disappeared into the woods.

Which Way?

Once they had moved well inside the tree line, the band of refugees headed due south. They crossed the River Taurus where it slowed as it turned to the east. At that point, they turned toward open territory. Although the Cassius Foundation had long claimed the entire region, the Cassius family never colonized it. Instead, the foundation built outposts all along its western border. One such outpost was too close to where the refugees crossed the Taurus, so they promptly headed due west. Once deep into open territory, the party had a decision to make.

Cole described their options. "We can turn south and continue to traverse the open territory between Biogenics and Cassius territories, then curve west, traveling between Biogenics's 'heel' and H'Aleth's 'dog head.' We skirt the mountains, then trek west into unknown territory. We would be traveling through montane forest all the way, which would make travel much easier for family members. Unfortunately, we will also be traveling through an active war zone."

Biogenics outposts all along its eastern border faced Cassius's outposts on the latter's western border. H'Aleth had positioned its outposts all across its northern border. In short, there were outposts everywhere. Fortunately, Cole and his men knew their locations except for those on Biogenics's western border.

"No doubt Biogenics and Cassius will be trading cannon fire," Cole added.

"What's plan B?" asked Dawson.

"Head southwest, cut across the heel of Biogenics territory, and hike through mountain passes, including mountains we have never seen," replied Cole. "We will have to cross the River Admare—a rough ride with rapids. Then we can either head west into the desert or head south toward Erwina."

"Is there a plan C?" inquired Cooper.

"Cut south through the heel," Cole answered. "There is a narrow mountain pass, which is not difficult to cross. We can skirt past the mountains to the west of Biogenics's nearest outpost. Their attention will be on the east. Raephela should be attacking them by that time. Then we can cut across the 'nose' of H'Aleth. Hopefully, most of the fighting will be well to the east of us. We can follow the River Vulpes until we reach the River Pices. Then we can ride the Pices into Erwina, but we must disembark before we reach the confluence with the Ferveo and continue on foot."

Plan C seemed to pose the least burden on family members while standing a good chance of avoiding the hostilities. Unfortunately, the hunters risked being recognized and attacked regardless of where they went. Traveling with their families might hide their true origin; however, it also exposed another logistical problem.

"Our families cannot travel through those rugged mountain passes as well as we can," Dawson commented. "They certainly can't travel as fast as we can, so it is going to be a very long journey. What about occupying some uninhabited area of Erwina and establishing a hidden settlement? The Erwinians were pretty decent to us when we went there looking for a paleontologist."

"They also escorted us out again," Logan reminded him.

"We were too close to their compound," replied Dawson.

"We might be able to pass though their southern region and get beyond it," offered Cooper.

"Has it ever been explored?" O'Connor asked.

"Not by any of us," answered Cole. "We might have to venture far into the southwest—possibly into the desert—to get away. It would be unknown territory for us. Still, it may be the lesser of the available evils."

Not long after they resumed their journey, the refugees were forced to switch to plan B and flee into Biogenics's mountains to avoid armed conflict. The hunters scouted several passes until they found ones their families could cross. These passes obliged them to head west, where they encountered the River Admare. To their relief, Biogenics believed in building bridges across its waterways—especially rivers as turbulent as the Admare.

After crossing the river, the refugees located a pass between two neighboring mountain ranges that directed them out of Biogenics territory and southwest into the foothills below. Thankfully, the foothills were sparse and relatively gentle, allowing families to weave through them while directing the refugees southward. Once beyond the foothills, Erwina's territory lay straight ahead of them.

The weary refugee party quickly crossed into Erwina at its northeast corner near the nose of Caput Canis. There the sound of cannon fire was all too close. War had reached H'Aleth's borders. Soon it would reach Erwina as well.

Part VI
Blitzkrieg

CHAPTER 34
The Rules of War

H'Aleth's scouts were prepared to face an assault from Raephela's army and a plethora of animal hybrids. H'Ariel would deploy skilled archers who rarely missed their target, and scouts whose alternate species were powerful predators. Many of her warriors were also skilled swordsmen and women.

Villagers and scouts who continued to live in the open territories offered their support as well. They were more than willing to join in the fight against the Cassius Foundation. They too had lost family and friends to the foundation. Many times, H'Aleth's scouts had stopped hunters from kidnapping them.

Early Warning Systems

Wildlife was on the move. Scouts reported an influx of nonmigratory species as well as birds migrating southward much too early for a seasonal change. All manner of animals were headed south and west—not north or east. The sudden arrival of animals bolting into Biogenics, H'Aleth, and Erwina alerted defenders that something deadly was on the move. The hasty arrival of villagers fleeing from their homes confirmed it. H'Aleth's scouts knew that the foundation's armies were headed toward them.

Given the location of H'Aleth's main village and seat of government, all nonessential personnel evacuated to villages in the south, where they settled in the underground tunnels. Each village had built a tunnel system long ago to provide shelter from severe storms and as a means of escaping dragon fire. This time, no one tried to reach Gregor. The risk of encountering a deadly enemy was too great.

H'Ariel convened her war council. Its members included Evard, Edric, her lead scouts, and representatives from Erwina, Biogenics, and the open territory.

"Our biggest concern is the cannons that Cassius may send," said Evard. "Without an effective means of neutralizing cannon fire itself, we must disable the cannoneers and their cannons so that they are rendered inoperative. Stealth is essential if we are to knock out these weapons."

"We have stationed scouts all along and across our borders," Edric reported. "Those stationed beyond our borders can camouflage themselves and give us advance warning of the enemy's approach. Once the cannons have passed by our scouts, our archers can target enemy forces."

"Cannons need not be nearby to assault our forces. They can still inflict damage from almost a mile away," Evard advised.

"Then we need to have scouts positioned at least a mile and a half away," responded Edric.

"Not necessarily," replied H'Ariel. "Those of us who can become a raptor can surveil the surrounding area from two miles away. We will see troop movements long before they arrive and can provide an early warning."

Edric and Evard glanced at each other, saying nothing. There was no point in telling H'Ariel that she should not be one of them.

"We can easily and quickly notify our scouts on both sides of the border," H'Ariel continued. "We can also notify any villages in neighboring open territories along with the Biogenics outpost to the north of us."

"Unless you get shot down," countered Edric. "The enemy has skilled archers too."

"We can provide advance warning as well," spoke a representative of the unincorporated villages. "We already post lookouts in key locations to alert nearby villages of any hunting parties in the area. None of us can become a raptor; however, we do have skilled archers who can relay a message through the air."

A representative of Biogenics also sat at the table. "We can provide a few cannons and cannoneers to support you," he proffered.

Although the H'Aletheans preferred not to use such destructive weapons, they knew that the Cassius Foundation would not hesitate to do so. Given some of the newer hybrids they had encountered, it was entirely possible that only cannon fire would stop them.

"Thank you," H'Ariel replied. "We are grateful for your support. We have one more concern. Many of the foundation's forces are conscripts—forced to fight to protect their families. If they do not, their own lives will be forfeit. Those who surrender should be held as prisoners until we can determine who they are."

Where? wondered Evard. *How many people will be needed to guard them?*

As if she could read his mind, H'Ariel added, "We have many noncombatants who want to help in our defense. They can monitor the prisoners and provide for their needs. Only a few of our security forces should be needed for this effort. I suspect many of our prisoners will be relieved to be in our hands." She was right.

So, it was settled. Where a woodland was present, archers would camouflage themselves in trees. Scouts whose alternate species could blend into the environment would be stationed in open terrain. Once alerted, they would either stay in place or move to a better vantage point from which to launch a counterattack.

Raephela's Rules of Engagement

Raephela had left her army's readiness in the hands of her lieutenants with one final directive: "Take no prisoners. Kill every enemy combatant."

"Even those who surrender?" asked Olsen, her chief lieutenant.

"Did you not hear me?" Raephela snapped.

"Yes, Your Majesty," Olsen answered. Disgusted, the lieutenant withdrew with an impassive expression.

When Olsen relayed Raephela's orders to his men, some of them took him aside.

"This order is against the rules of war. How are we going to handle this?" asked a spokesman.

Olsen had already worked out a possible solution. Anyone taking part would have to act convincingly. "We all have swords. Strike anyone trying to surrender, barely missing them. Order them to fall to the ground and play dead. Tell them to stay down until the rest of our forces have passed by and then crawl away without being seen. Take their weapons and continue going forward."

"What about the hybrids?" another member asked anxiously.

"They should have preceded us already," Olsen replied. He also considered another option that he chose not share with his comrades: defection.

CHAPTER 35
THE FIRST WAVE

Feathered sentries and arrows alike flew through the air. Raephela's armies were seen crossing into open territory all across both its western and southern borders. One branch headed toward H'Aleth, while the other marched on Biogenics. Scouts reported spotting huge armored beasts with massive horns that shredded small trees as they trampled everything in their way. They also saw beasts of burden pulling cannons mounted on wheels.

Not long afterward, an onslaught of animal hybrids followed by a contingent of armed forces stormed H'Aleth's northern border and Biogenics's southeastern border in a coordinated attack. The war had begun.

Onset of Hostilities

Raephela's first wave consisted primarily of hybrids backed up by infantry and cannons. The hybrids were released first to reveal where enemy forces were deployed and to kill as many of them as possible, thus depleting their resources. Releasing the hybrids in advance of her infantrymen was essential in keeping the hybrids from attacking her own forces. The sound of cannon fire would propel them toward her enemies.

Unlike her uncle Rafe, Raephela did not arm villagers and send them into battle. "What a colossal waste of weaponry, giving weapons to villagers who would be ineffective using them," she had told her lieutenants.

Once the first wave reduced her enemy's resistance, Raephela's guards would send in her most deadly hybrids—the sabra, the ursu, the cercopithursus, and even the ursuscro. Subsequently, the guards would release the varan and the croco to finish off any wounded lying on the ground. Aware that some of H'Aleth's people could transform into raptors, Raephela released harpyacalgryphs and lyvulfons, her top aerial predators, to counter them.

Initially, H'Aleth and Biogenics each thought the foundation had targeted its forces first. Not until later did H'Aleth and Biogenics learn that both had been attacked simultaneously.

Meanwhile, *H. sapiens* archers remained aloft in the trees, shooting as many hybrids as they could. All scouts understood that many of their purported adversaries were likely to be conscripts forced to fight or be killed by their guards, so the armed guards and animal hybrids were their primary targets. The guards were easy to identify because they all wore chain mail and carried shields and swords.

The H'Aletheans who could transform into powerful predators awaited the arrival of the enemy cannons and cannoneers. They planned to disable rather than kill the cannoneers and release the animals pulling the cannons. The sight of an apex predator would frighten the animals into running away and possibly the cannoneers too. The sounds of battle would drive the animals even farther away.

To appease her brother and her chief of security, H'Ariel decided to serve as an airborne messenger to notify combatants on and above the ground of dangers coming their way. She had rarely transformed into a peregrine falcon, preferring the strength of a great horned owl. Under present circumstances, speed was more important. The peregrine is among the smallest of raptors and a prey species for other birds of prey, yet it is also the fastest raptor. Although it prefers open spaces—prairies and grasslands—where its speed gives it an advantage, the falcon's small size also allows it to hide unnoticed in dense canopy.

Fog and Friction

Despite H'Aleth's ambush of Raephela's cannons and cannoneers, cannon fire decimated the open territory between Cassius, Biogenics, and H'Aleth. Hardly a tree, shrub, or blade of grass survived the onslaught. The few native animals that could not flee or harbor deep underground were killed.

Fluid battle lines constantly shifted. Dense smoke created by cannon fire added to the confusion. It became difficult to distinguish friend from foe or wildlife from hybrid, until practically face-to-face with one or another. Situational awareness was virtually impossible, even for a sharp-eyed falcon.

Terrified by the concussion of cannons firing one after another, many of the hybrid herbivores bolted to escape the mayhem. They stampeded, running down anything in their path, including some of Raephela's own troops. An impending disaster loomed for H'Aleth's defenders since their weaponry could not pierce the herbivores' armor. Arrows could not bring down the bovi, ovis, or the trialces (illustration 28). Only Biogenics's cannons could kill the beasts—and only then if it was a direct hit. Native species, including apex predators, could only get out of the way to avoid being trampled or gored. Ironically, the hybrid herbivores had more of an effect on the defenders than many of the earlier hybrids were having. Yet, when left alone, they did not attack.

Illustration 28: Trialces

Such was not the case for the ursu, serojalupus, sabra, and the theracapracanis. These hybrids were primed to fight. As was customary, their guards had not fed them for three or four days with the intent of adding to their savagery. This worked until the hybrid brought down a prey animal—or human—and pulled it aside. The theracapricanis would haul the carcass up a tree, feed on it, and then sit out the fight to digest its meal. By contrast, the more excitable sabra, ursu, and serojalupus would feed and then rejoin the fray. Fortuitously for the defenders, fights over ownership often took the hybrid combatants away from battle until ownership was settled and the winner had fed.

The hybrid carnivores did not know friend from foe. They recognized only rivals and prey species. Any herbivore towing a cannon mount replete with cannon and cannonballs was an easy target—or so a serojacuta envisioned. When it launched an attack on a harnessed trialces, its tusks could not penetrate the herbivore's keratin plates. Taking offense at being attacked, the trialces turned abruptly and charged the serojacuta, dragging the cannon mount behind it and tossing cannoneers and cannonballs everywhere. The serojacuta did not have keratin plates, nor did its tusks match the trialces horn or rack. The hybrid carnivore had overstepped its bounds, and it fell to the trialces.

Meanwhile, despite their size and tendency to snap at anyone and anything that came too close, the varan and the croco were being trampled. As aggressive as they were, they scrambled to get out of the morass and away from stampeding herbivores. With no body of water nearby, they were trapped on land.

An Aerial Dogfight

The peregrine falcon's sharp *kak-kak-kak* alerted the H'Aletheans, who recognized H'Ariel's alarm call. Despite atmospheric conditions, she could still see farther than any species on the ground. When her comrades saw her diving, they knew the direction of the threat. The falcon's warning gave H'Aleth's scouts enough notice to escape or prepare to engage the enemy.

Another aerial predator with equally sharp vision kept watch in the canopy—the harpyacalgryph (illustration 29). From time to time, it would glimpse the falcon weaving through the trees. At other times, the falcon would go into a short, steep dive and then bank upward sharply. As the harpy watched, it discerned a certain pattern. The falcon was clearly visible during both a dive and its subsequent rise toward the canopy where it disappeared into the foliage. The harpy repositioned itself to take advantage of the falcon's dive should it come within range. Then the harpy waited—motionless.

Its wait was rewarded. A nearby serojacuta was stalking one of H'Aleth's archers, whose attention was drawn to another hybrid charging a scout. Suddenly the falcon sounded its alarm call as it dove toward the serojacuta. The harpy immediately launched toward the falcon, which had already begun banking upward and away. In doing so, the falcon caught a glimpse of the harpy and immediately changed direction to evade its attack.

Quarters were too tight for the falcon's speed to be an advantage. It had to outmaneuver the harpy to escape. Yet the harpy was also agile. With smoke obscuring its view, the falcon had difficulty finding a space in the canopy that would be too small for the harpy to follow. H'Ariel barely dodged the swipe of a theracapracanis lounging in a tree she had targeted for safety. The swerve took her right into the path of the harpy. Just as the harpy's prize was within its reach, it suddenly wailed.

A lyvulfon (illustration 30) had launched from a shady outcrop hidden by smoke and snatched the harpy in midair. H'Ariel never knew what happened to her predator. Something had struck it. She did not linger to discover what that something was.

The Toll of Battle

The onslaught of hybrids was taking its toll. Once the sabra and ursu were released, they readily overpowered many defenders, *H. sapiens* and *H. transformans* alike. Transforming into an alternate species was of little

Illustration 29: Harpyacalgryph

Illustration 30: Lyvulfon

advantage. Most were no match for the sabra or the ursu in a fight, and many could not outrun these hybrids.

Casualties mounted, even among the Cassius guards. Many guards were lost when a hybrid turned on the nearest living thing it could reach.

Couriers who reported the battle's progress to Raephela also apprised her of the number of lost troops and hybrids. *No matter*, Raephela thought. *I have more*. Her forces had advanced successfully throughout the open territory. They were nearing Biogenics territory and encroaching on H'Aleth's border. With her army's apparent success on the battlefronts against H'Aleth's and Biogenics's forces, she felt assured that the secondary assault on H'Aleth's rear would dissolve any further resistance. She relaxed as she waited for word that her armies had crushed H'Aleth.

CHAPTER 36
A Surprise Encounter

Fully engaged on their northern border, the H'Aletheans remained unaware that another force was about to breach to the southeast. All but a few scouts had been pulled from the southern region. Those left behind watched for any enemy that might slip through H'Aleth's northern defenses. Hence, their eyes and ears were turned northward.

Dragonensis dragonis rubra

Illustration 31: Red Dragon

The red dragons (illustration 31) knew nothing of human warfare. A tacit understanding to live and let live existed between the H'Aletheans and the red dragons. The H'Aletheans had protected the dragons from hunters, egg poachers, and even animal hybrids for decades. In return, the dragons never hunted or otherwise attacked their human neighbors. They even avoided hunting their farm animals.

When a red dragon sentry observed a mass of humans coming from the sea, he thought it curious.

He observed the hybrids these humans brought in cages—some he recognized, yet many he did not. Dragons knew hybrids were violent and deadly to anything in their path, including a wayward dragon chick. So he questioned why unknown humans would bring hybrids into the territory of humans that he and his clan did know.

Recognizing the threat, the red dragon flew low overland until he spotted one of H'Aleth's scouts. After banking to turn around, he landed barely twenty feet in front of the scout. Startled by the dragon's behavior, the scout froze—half amazed and half afraid. The dragon extended an open talon toward her. The scout recalled the story of another H'Alethean who, as a lynx, had accepted a similar invitation from a red dragon. She realized that the dragon wanted to take her somewhere.

An Unexpected Ally

After catching her breath, the scout stepped forward. If the dragon had wanted to attack her, he would have done so. The dragon grasped the scout in his talon and lifted off. It was an exhilarating experience for her. To her consternation, however, the dragon took her far out over the ocean before circling back in a wide arc.

In the distance, the scout saw a long train of boats. As the dragon drew a little closer, she discerned that they were barges—some carrying humans, others carrying cages of hybrids, and some carrying armaments. The barges hugged the southeastern coastline, and the convoy appeared to be headed toward the inlet leading into the bay. *It's an invasion force*, she realized with alarm.

A lieutenant aboard one of the barges spotted the dragon and noticed it was carrying something in its talons. *Probably prey*, he assumed and dismissed the dragon when it flew away.

The red dragon turned back toward the southwest mountains where it disappeared from the invaders' view. Yet it did not take the scout into the mountains. Instead, the dragon flew his passenger well into H'Aleth's northern region, following the River Lupus until it crossed the River

Pices. Landing to the west of that juncture, the dragon released the scout at the edge of the main village and flew away. The unprecedented arrival and departure of a red dragon virtually on the village's doorstep created quite a stir.

The scout's report of what she had witnessed galvanized H'Aletheans into action. They knew they were in trouble. Hathor, one of H'Ariel's lead scouts, quickly dispatched a small contingent of scouts who were familiar with the region. Too small to withstand an invasion force, the contingent could resurrect traps that had been set long ago when a battleship appeared along the southern coast. Surprise attacks from unseen locations would disrupt and delay the enemy's advance until reinforcements could be deployed.

Invasion

Raephela's southern invasion force had successfully navigated the coastline and reached the bay. When they began advancing toward the shoreline, the more heavily laden barges—especially those carrying cannons and cannonballs—floundered on the reef and became ensnared. Lieutenants piloting other barges steered them further across the bay in an attempt to find a safe place to cross the reef. Although light craft could pass, the heavier barges still got caught.

Crews of the lighter barges, which had managed to scoot across the reef, threw ropes back to their comrades in an attempt to pull them across. Their efforts caused the barges to scrape the reef, disrupting it and strewing debris in the bay's waters. Uncommonly energetic ripples and waves coursed through the bay, traveled along a subterranean channel, and ultimately reached the lake in the southeastern swamp. This unusual disturbance drew the attention of the *Odontus pristis*.

Attracted by the possibility that prey had entered the bay's waters, the pristis dove into the lake. It swam through the underground cavern and through the channel connecting the cavern to the bay. There it found a pod of creatures milling around the reef. Some had successfully navigated the reef and moved toward shore, while others were caught on it. The pristis took full advantage of the latter's situation and promptly targeted them.

Suddenly, the massive animal rose up from the waters and attacked a barge. Grasping the barge and a few of its passengers in its jaws, the sea creature dove back into the water.

The barge had been loaded with cast-iron cannonballs and several hybrids in their cages. When the pristis attacked, it shattered not only the barge but also the cages. A cercopithursus was one of the hybrids released. Although brown bears are good swimmers in rivers and lakes, the cercopithursus was released in bay waters. It struggled against the tide and currents, which were no impediment to the pristis. As the latter seized its prey, it rolled to one side, clearly revealing the wing of a dragon as it pulled the cercopithursus under the water.

A Desperate Retreat

Terrified, those barge crews who had not yet attempted to breach the reef drew back. Those stranded on the reef struggled to follow suit—to no avail. Those who had crossed successfully tried to reach the shore as quickly as possible. Once ashore, the crews thought they had achieved some measure of safety. Yet, to their horror, the pristis also came ashore, dragging its prey. After repositioning his meal, the dragon took flight in a northeasterly direction, heading back to the swamp.

Raephela's plan for assaulting H'Aleth from the south was crumbling. Their strategy had not included dealing with a hungry dragon. Had they reached the shore with their cannons, they might well have killed it. Yet the sound of cannon fire would have alerted the H'Aletheans to their presence, costing the invaders the element of surprise.

None of the crew were willing to risk another encounter with a dragon—on land or in the bay. Those already ashore with hybrids released them to create what havoc they might. When the tide was right, the crews rowed their barges back across the reef, picking up those stranded on it.

The crewmen would leave it to their lieutenants to explain to Raephela why they had not attacked H'Aleth's southern flank.

H'Aleth's scouts, who watched everything unfold, were just as shocked as the foundation's forces to see the dragon. A scout raced back, reporting to Hathor the enemy's aborted landfall, the hybrids released, and the appearance of an entirely new species of dragon in the bay. Eventually, word of the dragon reached Miriam, H'Aleth's marine biologist, who suggested it was likely a marine dragon that may have traveled through a deep, undiscovered channel between the bay and the ocean. She was close. The subterranean channel lay between the swamp and the bay.

Some of the released hybrids promptly attacked each other. Others fled and disappeared into the southern territory. Two scouts departed to warn people living in the southernmost villages. With the red dragons already on high alert, most of the hybrids were never seen again.

CHAPTER 37
An End Run

Biogenics had been expecting another war with the Cassius Foundation ever since they met on the battlefield many years before. At that time, Biogenics had intended to let Cassius and the Erwinians exhaust their resources while battling each other. Then, Biogenics's army would intervene and overwhelm both of them. Conditions changed abruptly when a fourth party joined the battle and took command of the field along with everyone in it. At that point, Biogenics had thought it prudent to withdraw.

Biogenics was not surprised when it received word from a H'Alethean courier that the Cassius Foundation was on the march. In response to the foundation's increasing activities, Biogenics had gradually built up its army and defenses along its eastern border. A majority of its forces shored up the southern section of the eastern border to protect its research-and-development headquarters. This section extended from the foothills of the northern mountains to its "heel." Biogenics also dispatched additional troops to defend the northern section. Its leadership had not forgotten the foundation's thinly veiled attempt to overrun its marketing-and-sales division years ago.

Tributaries

Meanwhile, Raephela mustered a contingent to attack H'Aleth's and Biogenics's borders. She also dispatched expeditionary forces to attack Biogenics from the north. As planned, the second wave crossed the River

Taurus just before it bent sharply to head south. Here its flow was at its slowest and its depth relatively shallow. Some troops waded or swam across while others steered barges outfitted with wheels and loaded with supplies, equipment, and caged hybrids.

The massive herbivore hybrids could cross at this point, hauling barges loaded with cannons and cannonballs with relative ease—as long as someone lured them with fresh grass. Like other hybrids, they were kept hungry since all of the grass surrounding the fortress had been cut down to the ground.

Unconcerned about environmental conditions, the foundation knew little about tributaries, including those of the River Taurus. It had never occurred to the foundation that releasing deadly aquatic hybrids into the waterways of other territories could result in those hybrids using the tributaries to wend their way into the foundation's own rivers and streams. Hence, no one was aware that two of the foundation's semiaquatic hybrids had taken up residence along the Taurus.

Fish and wildlife that feed on fish were plentiful upstream from the fortress where the waters remained clean. Below the fortress, the river was polluted and rife with dead fish and wildlife. It was the perfect setting for a crocodylatalus, for it offered a grab-and-go smorgasbord.

Another reptilian hybrid, the varan, also found its way to the Taurus. It hunted along the river, primarily on the far side. The varan preferred fresh kills; however, it was not above scavenging for food.

Although the varan and the croco were competitors, there was just enough food and territory for each of them to occupy its respective riverbank. Imagine their delight when a migratory herd of animals—some two-legged, some four-legged—began to ford the river. Both ambush predators slipped into the water.

Missteps

Suddenly, a horrific scream pierced the air. As troops turned toward the sound, they glimpsed one of their fellows being pulled under the water as something rolled over him. Moments later, a bovi roared and bolted, kicking one leg with something hanging on to it.

Spooked by turmoil, the rest of the herd stampeded, as those members with legs in the water struggled to reach the riverbank. Shouts could be heard above the din of splashing water.

"Look out!"

"Get out of the water!"

"Get those barges across the river!"

Archers on the barges attempted a counterattack by unleashing arrows at brief flashes of their attackers. Meanwhile, the unnerved hybrids they were transporting began rattling their cages and rocking the barges carrying them. One of the barges listed too far, sending two men and a cage into the river. The two men scrambled onto the far shore. The cage and its inhabitant were lost.

Finally, men and barges reached the far shore and disembarked. The croco had already whisked its kill away and was out of the fray. The bovi eventually shook off its attacker and limped ashore with the rest of the hybrid herbivores. The varan, almost trampled by the herd, was forced to retreat—temporarily. The bovi's leg was bleeding. The varan simply followed the trail until the bovi sickened from the bite and finally fell a day later.

Raephela's expeditionary force regrouped to continue northward to the mountain pass that Cole had chosen for them and the engineers had cleared. Initially, this part of their trek was tedious—traveling through the montane forest on the east side of the mountain range. Stealth was not an issue since the mountains hid their movements from view. Or so they thought. Still, the terrain was rugged. Getting carts and mounted cannons over rocky ground and up hills often proved difficult. Chasing loose cannonballs became a frequent recreational activity.

Once they reached the pass, travel became much easier. The engineers had done their work well. There was a clear path for Raephela's forces to follow. Their efforts had aroused the interest of another species inhabiting the northern mountains.

A Silent Watch

A sentinel from Theovolan's clan of great gray dragons reported their arrival. Never before had the gray dragons seen this aspect of human behavior. Setting a watch on the workers, they waited to see what would transpire.

The engineers and their laborers never knew of the gray dragons' watch. The dragons' dark-gray coloring blended into the mountainside. They could lie along a mountain crag and appear to be part of it. From three miles away, their raptor-like vision detected humans laboring to clear the pass. Even after the engineers completed their task and departed, the dragons kept watch—waiting to see what would come of this human endeavor.

Having observed the direction from which these engineers had come and gone, Theovolan knew their origin, even before Raephela's troops reached the pass. The dragons' watch tightened when they saw a mass of humans marching through it, towing mounted cannons with them. The cannons were being drawn by enormous animals that looked familiar yet were clearly a different species.

Well acquainted with cannon fire, the dragons knew that it could kill them. Theovolan ordered his sentinels to track the army's movements in the event his clan had to defend their mountain aeries from an attack. He also sent word to neighboring clans, most of them related to his own clan, warning them of an armed force on the march.

The army took no note of the watch set on them and passed through the mountains none the wiser.

CHAPTER 38
MOVES AND COUNTERMOVES

Biogenics did not detect Cassius's forces descending from the northern mountains. Like H'Aleth, Biogenics had pulled some of its forces from its western border to augment its forces on the eastern front. Thus, Raephela's forces crossed unopposed into Biogenics territory, forded the bend in the River Admare as Cole had directed, and turned south to march on the Biogenics research-and-development headquarters.

Raephela coveted their gold mine of resources. She also bitterly resented Biogenics's rebuke of an emissary her grandfather had sent in the past. *They dared to defy him*, she fumed, promising herself that she would make them pay for their insolence.

The Hunt

Raephela's expeditionary forces moved south, confident that they would take the research-and-development center by surprise. In conjunction with the contingent attacking on their eastern border, they would crush Biogenics's forces in a vise. Following the River Admare, the expeditionary troops were positioned midway between Biogenics's east and west borders. Both the Admare and the River Della offered a buffer, should the army be discovered. Whether from the east or the west, Biogenics troops would have to cross a river to reach their opponents. Raephela's troops need not cross any more rivers to reach their target.

A romp of *dragonis fluminibus griseos* took notice. This playful, semiaquatic dragon species patrolled the River Admare and its larger tributaries. It was an extended family of griseos that included youngsters, juveniles, and adults. If parents had young chicks, aunts and uncles would stand in to supervise rowdy offspring.

The adult griseos saw the hybrids as a great opportunity to feed their families and provide additional hunting experience for their juvenile offspring. It would also be an outing for the youngsters. So they tracked Raephela's troops, staying well within the River Admare. Taking care to remain undetected, the griseos would rise up only within the crests of waves as the water spilled over rocks along the way. It would not do to spook their intended prey.

As the griseos traveled alongside Raephela's forces, they studied the different animals and their cages. The adults and juveniles were familiar with humans; however, there were many creatures previously unknown to them. They evaluated which ones might be appropriate for the juveniles—the serojacutas, lupuserojas, and serojalupuses—and which ones the adults would target. Although some hybrids were far too large even for the adults to tackle, others were quite suitable—the lupucercopiths, theracapracani, and even the sabra.

The griseos paid no attention to the paraphernalia the humans carried with them. Those items were not edible, and the griseos lacked any knowledge of cannons.

Taken by Surprise

Many hunts fail—especially when inexperienced juveniles and youngsters attempt to catch prey. Given the close proximity of their prey, this hunt stood a good chance of being successful. Their prey traveled close to the river that camouflaged the griseos. Their strategy set, some of the adults dropped back, allowing their prey to move ahead, and slipped out of the water. They would need to be airborne to attack the larger hybrids.

Meanwhile the juveniles and youngsters kept abreast, under adult supervision. The juveniles would test their skills in bringing down prey while launching directly from the river. Any prey that fell into the river the youngsters could tackle, provided the adults deemed it safe.

With the onset of the coordinated griseo attack, chaos erupted. Both the troops and the hybrids were taken by surprise. The bovi stampeded, overturning the cannon mounts they were pulling. The ovis and trialces turned to face their attackers. Yet the adults did not attack them. Thus, their cannons remained upright. The adult griseos wasted no time in tearing open the hybrid cages they targeted and dispatching each occupant. Inexperienced juveniles attempted to reach a hybrid through its cage. When that did not work, they attempted to fly away with it, cage and all. Proving to be heavier and more cumbersome than expected, many cages were dropped on the ground. Most remained intact, though some doors sprang open and released the hybrid within.

Before the lieutenants could stop their men, several had turned two cannons around and fired on the dragons. Their shots were random, poorly aimed, and completely missed their targets. Terrified by the explosions, the hybrids panicked—including the ovis and trialces, who bolted from the scene with their cannons careening behind them. The thunderous booms of the cannons and their shock waves stunned the adult and juvenile griseos. For a moment, they staggered and could not hear. Once they recovered, they dove quickly into the Admare and disappeared. The youngsters and adults that had remained underwater were spared these effects. The entire family immediately swam into the deepest channel in the Admare and headed upstream to escape. All had survived their first encounter with cannons.

The sound of cannon fire echoed through the mountain passes, alerting Biogenics to the approach of another armed force. The skeleton forces left to guard its western border mobilized to meet Raephela's contingent. It remained to be seen whose forces would be trapped in a vise.

Turnabout Is Fair Play

The griseo attack left Raephela's forces with fewer resources than they had expected to have for their assault on Biogenics. Although they had most of their cannons, some had disappeared with the hybrid herbivores. Several other hybrids had escaped when their cages were broken.

"Do we go after them?" asked one of the soldiers.

"No," his lieutenant replied, concerned that the element of surprise had been lost. "We must regroup as quickly as possible for a forced march toward the headquarters. We must arrive before Biogenics can reroute any of its troops to defend this area." Completely unaware of the outposts on Biogenics's western border, the lieutenants looked to the east for their enemy, not to the west.

The Biogenics commanders on the eastern front did not need a courier to tell them of the enemy's approach from the west. The cannon fire provided plenty of notice. Their dilemma was how to mount an effective counterattack when most of their forces were fully engaged on the eastern front. The commanders on the eastern front rerouted the platoon of soldiers they had received from the western outposts to engage the forces now descending on them from their rear.

The commander of Biogenics's western outposts dared not leave them completely unguarded. Nevertheless, she deployed a squad of soldiers to strike back at Raephela's forces.

To All Appearances

With most of the hybrids scattered, Raephela's expeditionary forces were pitted against Biogenics's meager forces now moving in on them from the east and the west. The Biogenics troops lacked cannons. Raephela's forces still had a few left, so her lieutenants felt confident that they could overwhelm both contingents sent by Biogenics. Thus, when the two adversaries clashed, Raephela's lieutenants were not surprised to see the defenders' forces fall back toward the south.

Biogenics maintained a professional army, whereas the majority of Raephela's forces were conscripts. Theoretically, the Biogenics forces should not be easily overcome. Yet they continued to fall back as Raephela's forces pushed forward. It was not long before her lieutenants could see the Biogenics research-and-development headquarters.

With their prize in sight, the lieutenants picked up the pace and advanced even more forcefully. They pushed Biogenics forces aside, driving a wedge between the eastern and western contingents and forcing them apart.

Raephela's lieutenants did not know that Biogenics had built a fortress around its headquarters—a fortress born of the threat that Rex Cassius had posed years ago. This fortress had its own contingent of armed forces, including mounted cannons.

Suddenly, cannon fire started hammering Raephela's men. Then the fortress opened up, and a fresh contingent of soldiers issued forth. Simultaneously, the eastern and western forces attacked from their positions, while another Biogenics contingent charged from the north, closing in on them from the rear. Raephela's lieutenants realized that they had been lured into a trap and were surrounded. Biogenics's apparently meager defenses were only a subterfuge.

Raephela's lieutenants immediately called for their troops to lay down their weapons, abandon their cannons, and sit on the ground. Two lieutenants walked forward, unarmed. Seeing this and the cessation of hostilities, the Biogenics troops ceased firing. One of Biogenics's captains approached the lieutenants.

"Do you surrender?" asked the captain formally.

"We do with the condition that we will be granted asylum," replied the first lieutenant.

Surprised, the captain formally asked the second lieutenant, "Do you concur?"

"I concur," answered the second lieutenant.

"Why do you seek asylum?" asked the captain.

"Our lives are forfeit," replied the first lieutenant. "We cannot go back."

The captain understood the implications. "I accept your surrender," he agreed. "For the moment, you will be our prisoners. We will get you settled once the war is over." *Assuming we win it*, he thought.

CHAPTER 39
WEARY REFUGEES

Although Biogenics had secured its western front, fierce fighting continued along all other fronts. Eowen and his scouts were guarding Erwina's northeastern border, where its territory was closest to H'Aleth. There, they would intercept any enemy force and any combatants or strangers entering Erwinian territory. With battles being waged all across the open territories, people from other regions sought refuge anywhere they could find it.

Refuge

People in the open territories suddenly found themselves caught in firefights between Biogenics and foundation forces. Per Raephela's battle strategy, a multitude of dangerous animal hybrids were released whose sole purpose was to attack whatever and whomever they encountered. Initially, anyone and anything in the open territories was at risk. After the hybrids slaughtered their way through the local inhabitants, they were expected to decimate H'Aleth's and Biogenics's forces. The hybrids, however, did not get that memo. After sating themselves, they went their own way, fleeing the sound of cannon fire. Many of them headed into Erwina (appendix L).

Meanwhile, villagers in the open territories tried to escape from the battles and the animal hybrids that beset them. Fleeing to the east was impossible without running into Raephela's forces. Likewise, fleeing north risked encountering the contingent she sent to attack Biogenics's rear flank. Those who fled south stumbled into firefights between H'Aleth's scouts and Raephela's forces. The refugees' only choice was to veer southwest and seek refuge in Erwina.

Erwinians readily accepted any refugees who reached their territory, provided they recognized them as noncombatants. Erwinians often traded with villagers living in the open territories, not only to acquire goods but also to maintain surveillance beyond Erwina's borders. Hence, the scouts knew many of the villagers who lived in the open territories and welcomed others that the villagers endorsed. In return, many capable people joined Erwina's ranks to defend its borders.

Bedraggled Refugees

Thus, Erwina's scouts were not surprised when they spotted a disheveled group of men, women, and children threading their way into Erwina territory. The men and young women seemed to be in good condition; however, the children and older women showed signs of exhaustion. Aware that subterfuge was possible, the scouts approached warily and surrounded the apparent refugees. Adults huddled around the children, shielding them. Although the enemy had used children as bait in the past, this behavior was still a good sign.

"Stand fast!" Eowen ordered. Cole recognized him immediately and knew that Eowen would do the same for him and his hunters.

Cole stepped forward and immediately pled their case. "We are fleeing the Cassius regime and have brought our families with us. We do not expect to find refuge here. We ask only for safe passage through your territory to the lands southwest of Erwina."

Eowen studied Cole for a moment. He did indeed recognize Cole. At their first encounter, Cole and his men had committed no crime other than trespassing. *They offered no resistance when escorted out of Erwina,* Eowen reflected. *Yet they might have kidnapped a paleontologist had they found one.* As for the rest of the refugees, the younger women could be hunters too, since they carried weapons. The older women and children could be hostages. Eowen had to find out before he could make a decision.

Eowen lacked the resources to escort these people anywhere or to hold them captive, so he ordered Cole and his fellow travelers to surrender their weapons. "Knives, too," he ordered, remembering their previous encounter. Eowen's men searched the men, while his two female scouts patted down the women. As they were being searched, the men and younger women were separated from the older women and children. When Eowen approached one of the children to speak with him, an older woman jumped between them.

"Get away from that child!" the woman declared angrily, aggressively barring his way. She made it crystal clear that she would engage Eowen in a heartbeat. *She may be another hunter*, he thought. He had no doubt she would fight him if he persisted.

"I mean the boy no harm," Eowen replied as he backed away. Instigating a fight between his scouts and Cole's hunters was not worth the risk. The encounter could result in fatalities on both sides.

A Surprise Attack

Suddenly, a cacophony of crashing through the forest, accompanied by snarls and growls, drew everyone's attention. As the sounds grew louder, everyone knew that something dangerous—and potentially deadly—was headed toward them. Cole and his people and Eowen and his scouts were immediately united against a common threat. The scouts promptly tossed the refugees their weapons. The old woman who had accosted Eowen helped older children to climb a nearby tree and then handed younger children up to them.

"Keep going up the tree. Get out of sight and don't move. Do not make a sound," she ordered. Then, she too climbed into the tree and disappeared.

A moment later, several hybrids burst into view—serojacutas, a serojalupus, and a theracapricanus. Some of them snapped and snarled at each other. Others seemed to be charging ahead with no particular destination in mind. Normally, they would behave as competitors and fight one another. Instead, the present assembly of hybrids had put aside their natural rivalry.

This could only mean one thing. They were fleeing from something far worse.

The defenders struck down two hybrids that appeared directly in their line of fire. To their amazement, the remaining hybrids veered away and raced right past them. Within seconds, an ursuscro (illustration 32) appeared, charging after the hybrids. It lunged at the cluster of humans. With its long reach, its claws struck down the nearest scout. Hunters and scouts loosed arrows into the beast in an attempt to bring it down. Yet the hybrid did not fall.

The ursuscro was almost on top of Dawson when a jaguar leaped from a nearby tree where it had hidden. Landing on the ursuscro's shoulders and upper back, her claws gripped the hybrid as if in a vise. With the most powerful jaws of the cat family, the jaguar sank her canines into the hybrid's head. The ursuscro roared, reared back, and tried to shake off the jaguar. It could not. Quickly, Dawson drew his sword and slashed the hybrid's throat wide open. Seconds later, it fell to the ground.

Members of both parties promptly attended to the wounded scout. Fortunately, his wounds were non-life-threatening, and he was able to travel. The jaguar promptly retreated back to the tree where she had hidden. There she resumed human form. Eowen was amazed that a powerful *H. transformans* was a member of Cole's party. This was a prize no typical bounty hunter would have protected.

Cole and Eowen glanced at each other. Both recognized a good man when they encountered one.

"If you and your party would like to remain in Erwina and help defend it, you would be welcome," Eowen offered. "But you must give up hunting other people."

"Gladly," Cole agreed.

"We would have quit working for the foundation long ago had Raephela not held our families hostage," Dawson added.

With a nod, Eowen indicated his acceptance of Cole and his fellow

Illustration 32: Ursuscro

refugees. He designated two scouts to accompany the wounded scout, along with the women and children in Cole's party, back to the compound. "They will be safe there," Eowen reassured Cole. Then Eowen uttered two short "hoos" and one long "hoooo." A great horned owl promptly responded from a nearby tree. "The owl will provide surveillance and a warning if she spots any danger."

"I would like one of my men to accompany them, in case there is another attack," Cole requested.

"Of course," Eowen replied.

A short time later, the children and the old woman descended from the same tree the jaguar had occupied. Eowen recognized her at once. *Brother! Am I glad I didn't tangle with her.*

Strategy

Shortly thereafter, Eowen and Cole conferred to discuss their strategy. Eowen knew H'Aleth's scouts were stretched thin.

"We have sent reinforcements to H'Aleth's northwest border, not only to bolster their defenses but also to intercept any enemy forces sweeping around the Caput Canis to attack us," he told Cole. "What, if anything, can you tell us of the foundation's strategy?"

Cole briefly described Raephela's plan to strike both Biogenics and H'Aleth on two fronts. "Once she has conquered them, she expects to overrun Erwina with little or no resistance."

Alarmed by the news of two more clandestine attacks on Biogenics and H'Aleth, Eowen immediately issued the alarm bark of a wolf. Moments later, a wolf, a cougar, a Cooper's hawk, and a woodland owl arrived in response. He sent the hawk and owl to Biogenics and H'Aleth headquarters, respectively, to warn them that the Cassius Foundation had planned a rear as well as a frontal assault. The wolf and cougar remained to support the newly formed company of defenders.

A moment later, a thoughtful Eowen asked, "Does she really think so little of us?" referring to Raephela's opinion of Erwina.

"Erwina's sole distinction is that you have a schoolhouse with teachers and students. What resistance could you possibly offer?" Cole answered. Cole did not mention that his own band had the same impression when they had been sent to kidnap a paleontologist. So he was surprised by the smile and soft chuckle from Eowen, who made no further comment. *There must be more to the schoolhouse than we thought*, Cole mused. Indeed, Erwina was one of the allies' best-kept secrets.

CHAPTER 40
A DOMINANT FORCE

Raephela focused her attention on two battlefronts: one along H'Aleth's northern border and the other along Biogenics's eastern border. Her forces had advanced successfully throughout the open territories and extended to H'Aleth's border. She assumed that her other forces were progressing as well. Little did she know that the rear assault on H'Aleth had dissolved. Nor was she aware that her expeditionary force making an end run around Biogenics's territory had surrendered.

A Desperate Move

With the onslaught of hybrids taking their toll on the defenders, both H'Aleth's and Biogenics's forces were being overwhelmed by the sheer volume and size of hybrids, and the number of Raephela's troops. Not even Biogenics's cannons could stop the onslaught. Many comrades and allies were lost.

As scouts, Edric and his comrades tried to push the enemy back and keep them from breaching H'Aleth's borders. To the surprise of his comrades, Edric suddenly left the battlefield and disappeared into a cluster of large boulders that had broken off from an escarpment. Moments later, his most powerful predator—the jaguar—tore into the hybrids. Aware only of Edric's wolf and fox alternate species, his compatriots could hardly believe their eyes. Yet not even the fury of a jaguar could bring down enough attackers.

When Raephela's forces released the sabra and ursu, these hybrids readily overpowered countless defenders. Even *H. transformans* were overwhelmed. Their ability to morph into another species offered little advantage unless that species could outrun the sabra and ursu.

Edric realized H'Aleth was on the verge of being overrun. Distressed at seeing so many of his comrades fall, he decided he could do more as an archer and swordsman. Desperate, he returned to the boulders to resume human form. His transformation should have occurred relatively quickly. Yet it did not. Instead, the chrysalis forming around him grew large and blended in with the other boulders. This condition persisted for hours while the battle raged. What finally awoke and arose from the chrysalis was another species altogether. The dormant DNA fragment Edric carried in his genome—the one he had inherited from his mother—had been activated. A male red dragon arose and took the field.

The sight shocked everyone. Although it was not the first time a red dragon had appeared on a field of battle, the event had happened long ago. H'Ariel knew immediately that it was her brother.

The hybrids had never seen a dragon and knew nothing of its capabilities. They saw a potential feast and did not hesitate to attack it. Edric promptly dispatched several hybrids with a blast of fire and a whip of his tail. These actions came instinctively despite his inexperience as a dragon. Yet targeting fire required practice. Edric quickly realized that his imprecise aim put allies as well as enemies in danger. In addition, he had never fledged. Taking flight also required practice, and his lack of flight experience endangered him. Even so, his attempts to lift off sent all but the hybrid herbivores tumbling.

With strength in numbers, the hybrids continued to attack him. One of Raephela's cannoneers fired his cannon at the dragon. His shot fell short and drew Edric's attention immediately. Edric responded with a blast of fire. Without knowing how to gauge its range, his blast also fell short. While Edric was engaged with hybrids and the cannoneer that had fired upon him, he failed to notice that another cannoneer had managed to position his weapon at the right angle. He fired, striking Edric's wing with a crushing blow. Although the blow was not fatal, it was devastating.

The damage rendered Edric unable to take flight or even flee while on the ground. Now the dragon was vulnerable to attack.

A Dominant Force

The sound of cannon blasts reached the northern mountains, reverberating throughout the canyons and into the aeries of the great gray dragons. This species did not flee from the sound of cannon fire. Theovolan recognized it and knew that humans were waging war once again.

He had a vested interest in the outcome of a war near his domain. Depending upon which combatant prevailed, the outcome could have significant ramifications for his clan. Whereas some humans respected the dragons' right to live, others did not. Some humans would rescue a dragon egg or chick and return it to its family, while others would try to steal them. Theovolan also knew the story of Rafe Cassius's past treachery and the old woman from H'Aleth who had once freed one of his own kind.

Thus, when Theovolan took flight, two comrades accompanied him. One of them was the proud parent of two chicks where there would have only been one had humans not found and returned a lost egg.

Upon reaching the open territories, the dragons soared high overhead. Theovolan bade his companions to remain aloft while he descended to survey the area more closely. At 8,000 feet, he could see little of the battlefield. The smoke from cannons and fires was dense. He discerned some movement but could not pinpoint any specific action. He remedied the situation by diving steeply until he was just above the range of cannon fire. Then, he strafed the scene before rapidly ascending. The resulting fifty-mile-per-hour gale-force wind blew the obscuring smoke away.

On the ground, the gust knocked down people and flipped over cannons. Defenders and attackers alike realized what had bowled them over and scrambled to regain their footing. Those who had lost weapons tried to reacquire them before hostilities resumed. Cannoneers attempted to retrieve and reset their cannons.

The H'Aletheans realized that the gray dragon was not attacking

Illustration 33: Dragon Fire

them. There had been no fire. Biogenics's forces were unsure, and Raephela's forces were certain it was an attack. The hybrids had no idea what had tossed them about—and did not care. They simply got up and looked around for something to attack. An injured red dragon became an attractive target.

When Theovolan surveyed the battlefield, he was surprised to espy a red dragon so far north. It was wounded, with one wing broken, and besieged by hybrids. Grounded by its injury, the red dragon was using his fire to drive the hybrids away; he was surrounded by attackers on all sides.

Theovolan suspected he knew the dragon's origin. Long before, one of his kinsmen had saved another red dragon embattled by deadly hybrids. Yet that dragon, a rare female *H. transformans*, had passed away. *Could this dragon be one of her descendants?* he wondered. He called his companions to strafe the battlefield again while he flew down to assist the red dragon.

All combatants on the ground saw the enormous great gray dragon when it landed in their midst. The hybrids attacking the red dragon were caught off guard. Some turned to attack the gray, while others fled. The gray easily dispatched any that stayed. Then he watched carefully to see what the humans would do.

Once again, Biogenics's forces withdrew, leaving their cannons behind. H'Aleth's scouts, still defending their border, stood fast. They knew that if they did not attack, the dragon would not attack them. Even so, they give him plenty of room.

Yet some of Raephela's forces remained undaunted. A cadre of her cannoneers hurried to reset a cannon and fire on the two dragons. In their haste, they failed to realize that the cannon's barrel had tilted too low. When they fired, the cannonball slammed into the ground yards away from the dragons, throwing up mounds of dirt and debris. This served only to draw the ire of a great gray dragon. Theovolan promptly directed his fire at the cannon as the cannoneers fled, along with the remainder of Raephela's forces (illustration 33).

Once again, a great gray dragon determined the outcome of human conflict. Gray dragons were and remained the dominant force over the land.

A Long Shadow

A cadre of scouts surrounded Edric. H'Ariel wanted to be one of them, yet she knew she could not treat his wounds. Instead, she flew at top speed to the compound at Erwina where she knew expert faculty would be available to evaluate and treat Edric. Medical staff from their infirmary could treat the rest of the wounded.

For a long while, Edric remained where he had fallen. Gradually, a chrysalis formed around him. Long hours passed while his countrymen anxiously waited to see if Edric could resume human form. The damage to his wing could interfere with the process of transformation. If the transformation was corrupted, Edric would be lost.

Early the next day, the chrysalis collapsed. Edric had resumed human form. Sadly, the injury he sustained left him with a deformity—his right shoulder, arm, and hand were contorted. Later, physicians and veterinarians at Gregor determined that they could not repair the damage. Edric's distorted right shoulder and arm were permanently frozen in that position. He would never transform again—an outcome that shadowed the fate of his maternal grandfather, who tried to force a transformation only to become trapped in it, part man, part boar.

CHAPTER 41
A Hidden Jewel

Fate spared Erwina the ravages of war. Once again, a great gray dragon had taken command of the battlefield and prevailed. All hostilities ceased, and all human forces withdrew. Surviving troops and guards who previously had not dared to leave Raephela's service fled the battlefield. Surviving hybrids scattered throughout the territories. Most of them fled southward, deep into Erwina's territory. Some headed east toward H'Aleth, while others traveled west toward Biogenics.

Gregor and Erwina dispatched medical personnel to H'Aleth, Biogenics, and the open territories to treat the wounded, including enemy combatants. Many combatants were conscripts with no loyalty or ties to the Cassius Foundation. They were more than willing to provide what little information they could about the foundation. When collated, these snippets provided valuable insights into the foundation's resources and activities.

Another Day at the Office

Meanwhile, Eowen, Cole, and their cohorts headed toward the compound. As they traveled, Eowen pointed out some of the defenses and barriers along the way. Cole then understood how Eowen's scouts knew exactly where he and his men were when they attempted to kidnap a paleontologist. Once they had stumbled over the ridge, they had all but waved a banner announcing where they were. Cole smiled and shook his head. *We had no idea . . .*

Upon arriving at the compound, Cole's men eagerly reunited with their families. Everyone had already been assigned accommodations in the guest quarters—the first step in resettlement.

"Get some rest," Eowen said to Cole. "You can have tomorrow off," he added with a grin.

"Thanks," Cole replied with a light laugh.

The next day, Eowen offered to give Cole a cook's tour of the compound. For the moment, it would be limited only to those structures that any visitor could enter. Faculty and form IV seniors remained on guard around the compound.

During the tour, everyone was alerted by something stampeding through the woods. Sensitive ears noted the vector. Whatever was coming—probably a hybrid—was headed toward the grain fields at the south end of the compound.

Apprentice scouts in that area were stationed along the hemp highway, a matrix of hemp ropes embedded throughout the tree canopy in and around the compound. They spotted an enormous, bizarre hybrid trampling across an open field, butting its head against anything that got in its way. It was a veritable battering ram, and it was headed their direction. Two designated students traversed the highway to alert faculty and those guarding the schoolhouse.

"It looks like a huge bull except that its horns are not where they should be, including a spiked horn on its snout. It also has what looks like a crown around its neck," they reported.

Eowen, Cole, and faculty members with expertise in the martial arts, swordsmanship, and archery converged on the grain fields while form IV students maintained their positions and surveillance of the perimeter. The hybrid had stopped. When the faculty drew close enough to see it, they were surprised to find it grazing peacefully on grains. Later, the refugees would identify it as a bovi.

For a while, they watched the hybrid graze. Bowen, Erwina's expert in animal husbandry, approached the hybrid gradually and carefully. When the bovi looked up at him, he froze. When the bovi continued to graze, Bowen studied the animal for a moment longer. He observed that it was eating the grass growing among the grains—not the grains. So Bowen stooped to pluck an errant patch of grass along with a few grain stalks. Stepping forward, he offered both to the hybrid. The bovi stepped forward, sniffed at the offerings, and promptly selected the grass. By now, Bowen was close enough to touch the animal. He took a deep breath and held out his hand. The bovi sniffed at it briefly, then continued munching on the grass.

When Bowen turned to his comrades, he was elated. "It's tame," he shouted excitedly. "I want to keep it."

His colleagues shook their heads. "Where?" they shouted back in unison, looking at the massive animal.

"We have some woodland glades not far from—"

Bowen's reply was abruptly interrupted when a brown bear—one of Erwina's faculty members—exploded from the tree line not far away. Charging and bellowing as he raced across the grain field, his actions clearly signaled that something deadly had entered the compound, and the bear was challenging it. Unbeknownst to anyone else, a sabra had been stalking Bowen and the bovi. The bovi reacted to the brown bear's bellows and bolted away, knocking down Bowen—thankfully, without trampling him.

Simultaneously, the rest of the faculty raced toward the bear as a massive hybrid tiger rose up and engaged it. The bear's bellows had alerted the hybrid to its attacker, so it was not caught by surprise. The ensuing violent fight pitted an eight-foot, 800-pound bear against a seven-foot, 900-pound sabra. The bear's four-inch claws were no match for the sabra's six-inch ones; however, the bear had a slightly longer reach. The two antagonists would have been evenly matched save for sabra's paired set of twelve-inch canines. If the sabra reached the bear's throat, a valuable faculty member would be lost.

Yet it was the sabra that was at hazard. Expert archers targeted its throat and chest as it grappled with the bear. Shortly thereafter, the sabra loosened its grip and fell. Several of the faculty moved in to surround the bear as it dropped down on all fours. It had many wounds, some of them deep. Fortunately, none proved to be fatal. Faculty escorted the bear to the veterinary clinic maintained at the schoolhouse. Once the bear's wounds were treated, he could resume human form and be transferred to the medical infirmary to recover.

Meanwhile, two faculty members confirmed that the sabra was dead. Veterinarians from the schoolhouse took tissue and blood samples and sent them to Gregor. Afterward, the hybrid's remains were cremated. The Erwinians were surprised to learn later that the hybrid was not a tiger.

"A cougar?!" yelled Erwina's astounded veterinarian when she reviewed the report.

A Grassy Haven

After being bowled over by the bovi, Bowen stood up. At first, he despaired of ever finding it again. Soon he spotted the giant munching on grasses at the edge of the grain field. He was tickled pink when he discovered that he could lead the bovi simply by offering it fresh grass. *What a magnificent animal*, he marveled.

A few weeks later, Bowen sighted an ovis and a trialces that had found their way into Erwina. After that, he sent out word to scouts in all the territories, asking them to notify him when they sighted one of the hybrid herbivores. All that were found were brought under Erwina's protection. Like most hybrids, their lives were short. Even so, Bowen made sure that they lived in peace amid a bounty of fresh grass.

EPILOGUE

Once again, the Cassius Foundation had underestimated the powerful alliance among the three houses and the Biogenics Corporation. Yet that alliance might have been vanquished without the intervention of two unspoken entities. The H'Aletheans had a tacit understanding with the red dragons to their south and an accord with the great gray dragons to the north. Both were pivotal in preventing the foundation from overwhelming the allies.

A New Mission

Many kinsmen and comrades had been lost in the battle against the foundation. Although the price was high, the people of H'Aleth, Erwina, and Biogenics had triumphed. This was not the case for the open territories, which took the brunt of the assault. Those regions adjacent to Cassius, H'Aleth, and Biogenics territories were devastated. Thankful for their support, the allies united once again to help the inhabitants restore their villages and reestablish commerce throughout the open territories.

Yet not everything could be restored. Knowing he could no longer transform, Edric despaired of ever scouting again. No one knew that his unknown maternal grandfather was plagued with a similar deformity, yet remained powerful until his death.

"Not so!" chided his old mentor, Master Iranapolis. "We have many sapiens scouts, and there is nothing wrong with your legs. Although you cannot draw a bow, you can still wield a sword. In calm waters, you can swim using the sidestroke or a backstroke, and you can still steer a raft or a canoe. Most importantly, you can mentor aspiring and apprentice scouts."

At first, Lilith grieved for Edric, knowing how much he had enjoyed scouring the countryside as a wolf, a cougar, or a boar. As Edric adapted to his deformity, he found that he still had all of the heightened senses his alternate species afforded. He began mentoring apprentice scouts.

Edric and Lilith spent more time together. Edric's deformity was never an impediment to romance. He and Lilith already had two children—a son, Edven, and a daughter, H'Amara—to which they added a second daughter, H'Ilythia—all *H. transformans*.

Of these three, H'Amara would harken back to her maternal grandmother (pedigree 1) and determine the foundation's ultimate fate.

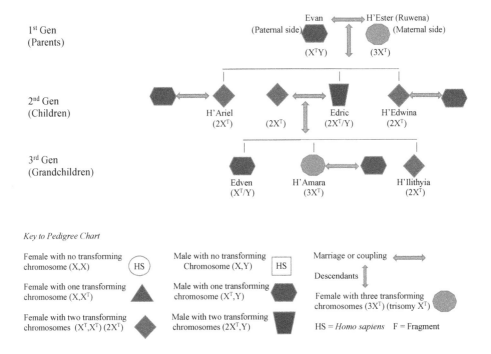

Pedigree 1: H'Ester's Descendants

A Smoldering Ember

The allies knew they had not defeated the Cassius Foundation wholly. The nidus of that organization still existed deep within its own territory. So the allies kept watch, all the while developing a strategic plan to overthrow the foundation.

In the interim, the foundation struggled to recoup and subsequently declined. Raephela's reign ended abruptly when her granddaughter, Raephedra, tired of waiting to take the reins. Mortified by her grandmother's ignominious defeat and the foundation's decrepit state, Raephedra decided that it was time for new leadership. She poisoned her grandmother, pushed her mother, Rafina, aside, and assumed control of the foundation—maintaining the family tradition.

APPENDIX A
Altered *Homo transformans*
(Hybrid Humanoids)

In an altered *Homo transformans*, the Cassius Foundation spliced the genes of one or more animal characteristics into an *H. transformans* male to augment the features already available in his alternate species. The *H. transformans* was then forced into a transformation. When the desired characteristics become apparent, the transformation was abruptly stopped (aborted). If the individual survived, the victim was trapped permanently in his transformed state, unable to transform again. The Cassius Foundation characterized the survivors as hybrid humanoids and labeled them thusly.

The Cassius Foundations selected males because of their greater muscle mass, larger bones, and greater strength. They used female *H. transformans* for breeding purposes. By convention, the names of human–animal hybrids ended in -id or -oid, which reflected the human base genome mixed with genes from one or more animal species.

Cercopithursid [*cer*-co-*pith*-ur-sid] (illustration 2, page 8)
Developed under the auspices of Rafe Cassius
Genetics: The genes of a baboon (*cercopith*-) and bear (*urs*-) were spliced into the genome of a human (-*id*), who was forced into a transformation which could not be reversed.
Description: Although the base genome was human, this hybrid had fewer human features and more bear and baboon features than the serojabovid.

Purpose: Engineered specifically for purposes of performing hard labor in Cassius villages and for serving as guards.

Crocutalupoid [*cro*-cu-ta-*lup*-oid] (illustration 12, page 58)
Developed under the auspices of Rex Cassius
Genetics: Genes of a hyena (*crocuta-*) and wolf (*lup-*) were spliced into the genome of a human (*-oid*).
Description: Although the base genome was clearly human, there were fewer human features and more hyena and wolf features.
Purpose: Engineered by Cassius specifically for purposes of hunting large prey, fighting an enemy, and guarding storehouses.

Papiopanoid [păp-ē-ō-*păn*-oid] (illustration 13, page 58)
Developed under the auspices of Rex Cassius
Genetics: The genes of a baboon (*papio*−) were spliced into the genome of a human that could transform into a chimpanzee (−*pan*).
Description: An *H. transformans* was forced to begin transformation into a chimpanzee, which was interrupted when the desired characteristics of the baboon appeared. The intent was to produce an altered transformans with the strength of a chimpanzee, the fangs of a baboon, the aggressiveness of both, and the height and dexterity of a human. The result was a transformans that could sit but not stand upright. He had long arms and hands like those of a chimpanzee, the strength of a chimpanzee, the fangs of a baboon, the ability to run almost as fast as a chimpanzee, and the aggressiveness of both the chimpanzee and the baboon.
Purpose: Engineered specifically to attack and fight.

Serojabovid [*ser*-o-ja-*bōv*-id] (illustration 3, page 8)
Developed under the auspices of Rafe Cassius
Genetics: Genes of a boar (*seroja-*) and bison (*bov-*) were spliced into the genome of a human (*-id*).
Description: An altered transformans (upright stance) approximately six

feet tall; a large build (chest, arms, legs) with a humped back; large, predominantly human head with some features of bison—especially the nose, mouth, and chin; broad, flat teeth like those of an herbivore; upwardly curved canines that extended outside of the mouth (courtesy of boar genes); vestigial (small) bison horns on either side of head; and a thick layer of body hair.

Purpose: Engineered specifically for purposes of performing hard labor in Cassius villages.

Ursoxinoid [er-*sŏx*-in-oid]

Developed under the auspices of Rex Cassius

Genetics: The genes of an ox (−*bos*) were spliced into a human that could transform into a bear (−*ursus*).

Description: An altered transformans forced to begin transformation into a bear, which was interrupted as soon as features of an ox appeared. He developed into a larger and stronger humanoid with greater strength and endurance, weighed approximately 350 pounds, and stood nearly eight feet tall. He could walk upright or on all four extremities. Additional features included a small pair of curved horns and the bony forehead of an ox.

Purpose: Engineered specifically for purposes of performing hard labor in Cassius villages, including moving large, heavy objects and hauling heavy loads of materials.

APPENDIX B
ANIMAL HYBRIDS

In animal–animal hybrids, the base genome belonged to one animal with the genes of one or more other animals added. Native animals did not have the capability to transform into another species. Consequently, animal hybrids were generated by inserting genes into a fertilized egg or a developing embryo. The names of animal–animal hybrids were composites of their species' names. The first component represented the primary species to which other species' genes were added. These naming conventions were established by the geneticists at Gregor, who named each hybrid based upon an analysis of its genome.

Aegyoptera [ā-gē-*ŏp*-tĕr-ah]
Developed under the auspices of Rafe Cassius
Genetics: Genes of a bat (*-optera*) augmented the genes of a vulture (*aegy-*).
Description: The forehead and ears of a bat with the face and beak of the vulture. Its body size was much smaller than that of a pure vulture, with smaller wings, shorter legs, and smaller claws. It had feathered wings that were scalloped and vaguely resembled bat wings. Although it survived and could fly, Cassius considered it too small to be an effective weapon.
Purpose: Serve as an aerial predator.

Bovicerahorridus [bō-vē-cĕr-ă-*hōr*-rĭ-dŭs] (Bovi) (illustration 17, page 87)
Developed under the auspices of Raephela Cassius
Genetics: The base genome of a bison (*bovi-*) was augmented with selected

genes of a triceratops (*-cerahorridus*) and somatotropin (growth hormone).

Description: A massive 12,000-pound bison with the three horns of the triceratops, a vestigial frill, and hardened keratin plates similar to the shutes of a triceratops.

Purpose: Developed to be the biologic equivalent of a Sherman tank that could run down and gore anyone or anything in its path, including a dragon.

Cercopithursus [cer-ko-*pĭth*-ur-sus] (illustration 7, page 24)
Developed under the auspices of Rafe Cassius
Genetics: The base genome of a brown bear (*-urus*) augmented with selected genes of a baboon (*cercopith-*).

Description: The shape and size of a brown bear with the face and fangs of a baboon. It had the bear's heavier lower back legs and feet; however, it had the baboon's longer, slender forearms, hands with an opposing thumb, and long, sharp claws. It weighed 800 pounds and stood eight feet tall.

Purpose: Developed to be aggressive and easily aroused.

Craspedichironex [*crăs*-pĕd-ē-*cheer*-ōn-ĕx]
Developed under the auspices of Raephela Cassius
Genetics: The base genome of a freshwater jellyfish augmented with the genes of the deadly venom of a marine box jellyfish.

Description: A freshwater jellyfish except for the long tentacles and deadly poison of the box jellyfish.

Purpose: Designed to kill H'Alethean and Erwinean swimmers who were strong enough to swim across lakes and rivers as wide as two miles.

Crocodylatalus [*Crŏ*-cō-dĭl-ă-*tăl*-ŭs] (Croco) (illustration 21, page 148)
Developed under the auspices of Raephela Cassius
Genetics: The base genome of a crocodile (*crocodyla-*) augmented with the

genes for enhanced fangs and poison of the eastern rattlesnake (-*talus*) and the addition of somatotropin.

Description: A massive adult male crocodile, twenty to twenty-two feet long from tip of nose to tip of tail, and weighing 1,800 to 2,400 pounds. It had a powerful tail that it could use as rudder or for attack and defense. Its teeth were consistent with those of a crocodile except for a pair of thick, six-inch-long fangs—one on either side of the jaw—designed to inject venom deep into another animal. It had powerful jaws with a bite force of 3,700 pounds per square inch. It could achieve speeds of fifteen to eighteen miles per hour in water, and seven to ten miles per hour on land for short bursts only.

Purpose: Apex predator that could sabotage small watercraft, including canoes, kayaks, rowboats, barges, and small sailboats, and devour anyone in them.

Harpyacalgryph [*hăr*-pē-ă-*căl*-grĭf] (illustration 29, page 226)
Developed under the auspices of Rex Cassius
Genetics: The base genome of a harpy eagle (*harpia*-) augmented with the genes of a vulture (-*grif*) and a caracal cat (-*cal*).
Description: The body of a harpy eagle with the wings of a condor, the long, tufted and tapered ears of a caracal cat, and the broad beak of a vulture, which housed the canine teeth and tongue of a caracal cat. Its larger wingspan improved its ability to soar in open space; however, it made flight more difficult when lifting off from the ground and impeded its ability to fly through forest canopy.
Purpose: Designed to be an aerial predator.

Hieractopera [*hī*-er-ac-*tŏp*-er-ah] (illustration 5, page 16)
Developed under the auspices of Raephela Cassius
Genetics: The base genome of an eagle (*hierac*-) augmented with the genes of a bat (-*topera*) and the addition of somatotropin.
Description: The head and talons of an eagle, the ears of a bat, the body of a bat with a mix of fur and feathers, and the wings of an eagle,

distorted by the fingers and thumbs of a bat. The wings were covered with bat skin bearing scattered tufts of fur and feathers. Its heavy body, dystrophic wings, and the lack of tail feathers precluded powered flight. The creature could glide, walk on the ground, and climb trees with its talons and bat thumb. An arboreal predator, it would perch in a tree, camouflaged by leaves, and launch into a dive to attack its prey from the air.

Purpose: Ambush predator.

Lupucercopith [*lu*-pu-*cer*-ko-pĭth] (illustration 22, page 151)
Developed under the auspices of Rafe Cassius
Genetics: The base genome of a wolf (*lupu-*) augmented with genes of a baboon (*-cercopith*).
Description: The body of a wolf with the long snout and fangs of a baboon; however, its fangs were much larger and longer, with the upper fangs extending well below the lower fangs. It had limited speed and agility due to deformities in its back legs. Hence, it had to get very close to its prey before launching an attack.
Purpose: An aggressive wolf–baboon hybrid developed to serve as a guard and attack in close quarters.

Lupuseroja [*loo*-pŭ-sĕr-ō-jă] (illustration 4, page 12)
Developed under the auspices of Rafe Cassius (See *Serojalupus* below)
Genetics: The base genome of a wolf (*lupus-*) augmented with the genes of a boar (*-seroja*).
Description: The body of a wolf with the snout, horns, and legs of a boar. Although designed to have the body and speed of a wolf, its shortened legs limited its stride.
Purpose: Designed to guard storerooms, silos, and armories in Cassius territory (mostly from the villagers).

Lyvulfon [lī-*vul*-fon] (illustration 30, page 226)
Developed under the auspices of Rafe Cassius

Genetics: The base genome of a lynx (*ly-*) augmented with the genes of a vulture (*-vulfon*) in an attempt to achieve a phenotype similar to that of a gryphon.

Description: Designed to be an aerial predator, its size limited its capability. The lyvulfon could only achieve speeds up to twenty-five miles per hour, and it could only sustain flight for short distances.

Purpose: In hunting for prey, the lyvulfon would have to wait in a tree or on a rocky ledge for its prey to get close enough to be snared.

Moresistrurus [*mōr*-ā-sĭs-*trū*-rŭs)] (illustration 10, page 52)

Developed under the auspices of Rex Cassius

Genetics: The base genome of a green tree python (*more-*) augmented with the genes of a pit viper (*-sistrurus*) and enhanced by growth hormone.

Description: A much larger than normal green tree python with the fangs and venom of a pit viper. It could lurk in a tree, hidden by the foliage, strike out and hold its unsuspecting prey in its coils, and inject it with venom.

Purpose: An ambush predator designed to protect territories that Rex Cassius claimed by terrorizing anyone who entered them. Rex unexpectedly lost some of his hybrids to this creation.

Ovisuscrofalces [ōv-ĭ-sŭs-crōf-ăl-cēs] (Ovis) (illustration 23, page 179)

Developed under the auspices of Raephela Cassius

Genetics: The base genome of a bighorn sheep (*ovi-*) augmented with genes of a boar (*-suscrof-*) for its powerful shoulder and neck muscles, and the genes of a moose (*-alces*) for its rack, size, and power. It size was enhanced by the addition of somatotropin.

Description: A huge 1,100-to-1,300-pound bighorn sheep about the size of a bull moose. Along with its misshapen horns, the hybrid's head had a rack of enlarged, spiked horns arising from its thickened bony skull cap. It had the powerful neck muscles of the wild boar. Although considerably smaller than the trialcesceramata, it was still six feet tall at the shoulder.

Purpose: Designed to attack, trample, and impale large animals and large groups of people.

Sabrafataligrandis [săb-ră-fă-tălē-*grăn*-dĭs] (Sabra) (illustration 24, page 180)

Developed under the auspices of Raephela Cassius

Genetics: The base genome of a cougar augmented with bone marrow stem cells, osteoblasts to increase bone size and strength, odontoblasts to increase tooth size, the taqpep gene to give the cat stripes, and somatotropin to increase overall body size and mass.

Description: Massive cougar weighing 850 to 950 pounds, with six-inch-long curved claws, and enlarged twelve-inch-long saber-toothed-tiger-like canines on both the maxilla and the mandible. The taqpep gene added stripes to the cougar's coat so it would look like a saber-toothed tiger.

Purpose: An aggressive hybrid that would prey on any species, including humans.

Serojacuta [sĕr-ō-jă-*cū*-tă] (illustration 6, page 25)

Developed under the auspices of Rex Cassius

Genetics: The base genome of a hyena (-*cuta*) augmented with the genes of a boar (*seroja*-).

Description: A shorter hyena with the stocky build of a boar, especially around its upper body and neck, which were shorter and heavier than those of a native hyena. It still had the head, jaws, and bite force (about 1,100 pounds per square inch) of the hyena, with the addition of the tusks of the boar. Its forelegs were shorter and stockier so that it no longer had the sloped back of a typical hyena. The front feet were paws, while the back feet had developed into hooves. Due to its increased size and weight, its maximum speed was reduced to twenty-five miles per hour.

Purpose: Engineered to be deadly and used as an attack or guard animal.

Serojalupus [sĕr-ō-jă-*loo*-pŭs] (illustration 8, page 39)

Developed under the auspices of Raephela Cassius, who decided to enhance the characteristics of the original lupuseroja

Genetics: The base genome of a boar (*-seroja*) augmented with the genes of a wolf (*-lupus*) and supplemented with somatotropin.

Description: Aggressive boar–wolf hybrid with the skull, tusks, snout, and stocky neck and body of a boar. It had the eyes, ears, and fangs of a wolf, a thick black coat, and the long, limber legs of the wolf. Curiously, it had the tail of a boar. Despite its large size, it could achieve a running speed of thirty-five miles per hour and leap almost six feet.

Purpose: Engineered to be an aggressive hybrid that would prey on any species, including humans.

Theracapracanis [*thĕr*-ah-căp-rah-*căn*-ĭs], plural theraparacani (illustration 9, page 45)

Developed under the auspices of Rex Cassius

Genetics: The base genome of a leopard (*-thera*) augmented with genes of a jackal (*-canis*) and an ibex (*-capra*).

Description: A large, catlike creature with the body and coat of a leopard except for the swath of black hair on it back, a gift of its jackal genes. It had the head of a jackal with two short, spiked horns—like those of a Nubian ibex, only longer and angled forward—and enlarged canines. If the creature charged in a direct attack, it would gore its opponent. It had the sure-footedness of the leopard and ibex.

Purpose: Engineered to be an aggressive hybrid that would prey on any species, including humans.

Trialcesceramata [trī-ăl-cēs-cĕr-ă-mă-tă] (Trialces) (illustration 28, page 223)

Developed under the auspices of Raephela Cassius.

Genetics: The base genome of a bull moose (*alces-*) augmented with large palmate antlers (*-mata*) and genes of a triceratops (*tri-*, *cera-*). The developing embryo and fetus were subsequently augmented with somatotropin.

Description: A massive 5,200-to-5,800-pound animal with at least ten lethal spikes on its antlers and a large spiked horn on its snout. Similar to the bovicerahorridus, thick keratin plates overlaid its hide. Like the native moose, it was easily aroused and aggressive.

Purpose: Developed to be a massive animal with lethal horns and virtually unstoppable. It was easily aroused and would attack indiscriminately.

Ursupantheradactu [*ur*-sŭ-păn-ther-ah-*dăc*-too] (Ursu)
Developed under the auspices of Raephela Cassius.

Genetics: The base genome of a bear (-*ursus*) augmented with the genes of a jaguar (-*panther*) with enlarged fangs (-*adactu*).

Description: An especially powerful hybrid with most of the characteristics of a jaguar, the size of a brown bear, and the ability to stand upright like a bear. It had the head of the jaguar with the face of a bear. Its jaw and canines were those of the jaguar, except that the upper canines were enlarged in thickness, eight inches long, and extended over the lower jaw like those of the saber-toothed tiger.

Purpose: Engineered to be an aggressive hybrid that would prey on any species, including humans.

Ursuscro [ur-*sŭs*-crō] (illustration 32, page 246)
Developed under the auspices of Rex Cassius.

Genetics: The genome of a bear (-*ursus*) augmented with the genes of a boar (-*scro*).

Description: An especially aggressive animal hybrid with the size and form of a brown bear and the snout, tusks, and disposition of a wild boar. Its upper and lower canines were enlarged. Cassius planned to use it as a weapon of war—especially against an *H. transformans* opponent whose alternate species was a bear. The architecture of its brain was distorted as a consequence of its hybridization. The hybrid eventually became deranged and uncontrollable.

Purpose: Engineered to kill anything it encountered.

Varanacrocactutus [*vār*-ăn-ah-*crŏk-ăc-too-tŭs*] (Varan) (illustration 14, page 60)

Developed under the auspices of Raephela Cassius

Genetics: Another variation on the genome of the Komodo dragon (*varan-*), it was modified by the addition of genes coding for the jaws of a crocodile (*croco-*), teeth of an alligator gar (*-actutus*), and short, spiked horns of an antelope.

Description: A 400-to-450-pound reptile with the body of the Komodo dragon, including its tough skin, embedded with bony scales which were augmented with additional keratin to harden them. It had the long, sharp, curved claws native to the Komodo; a double row of sharp, serrated teeth from the alligator gar (fish); and the bite force of a crocodile. When it reared up, the hybrid could gore its prey with its two spiked horns. Like the native Komodo dragon, it was a good swimmer.

Purpose: Engineered to be an aggressive hybrid that would prey on any species, including humans.

Varanhieracta [*var*-an-hī-ĕr-*ac*-tăh]

Developed under the auspices of Angus Cassius

Genetics: The base genome of a Komodo dragon (*varan-*) augmented with the genes of an eagle (*-hieracta*) in order to create a dragon that could fly.

Description: This creature had the head and torso of the Komodo dragon with feathers blended in among its scales, but no wings. Most importantly, all four legs had hollow bones that could not support it and shattered under its weight. It could not hunt and did not survive.

Viperoperidactyl [*vī*-per-op-erĭ-*dăc*-tyl] (illustration 11, page 52)

Developed under the auspices of Rafe Cassius

Genetics: The base genome of an arboreal lizard (*-dactyl*) augmented with genes of a viper (*viperi-*) and a bat (*-opera-*).

Description: It had physical features of a tree lizard with the tongue, fangs, and venom of a pit viper. It was designed to be a venomous lizard that could climb trees, glide between trees or to the ground, and swim. It could camouflage in trees or look like leaf debris in a stream.

Purpose: Ambush predator that killed with venom.

APPENDIX C
RESTORATION OF H'ALETH

After destroying the House of H'Aleth's main village and seat of government, the Cassius Foundation was satisfied it had conquered H'Aleth's territory. It largely ignored the southeastern and southwestern regions of both H'Aleth and Erwina. With this oversight, the H'Aletheans who had fled into the southwest mountains and desert slowly and surreptitiously slipped back into their territory. To avoid detection, they kept their villages and surrounding land looking abandoned and desolate. They did not repair their homes, reinstate industry, or tend their gardens and groves. For food sources, they relied on the grains mixed in with the grasses, and fruit from trees and gardens they had previously planted. Later, when the foundation marched on the House of Erwina, Cassius's forces had moved due west across H'Aleth toward Erwina. Cassius knew naught of the return of the H'Aletheans.

With the defeat of the Cassius Foundation and its withdrawal, the restoration of the House of H'Aleth began in earnest. Those who had fled into the southwest mountains and into the desert returned to their former villages, which had been left relatively unscathed. Lack of maintenance had permitted many of their dwellings of sod and native grasses to decline, yet buildings made from stone or wood were still intact. The H'Aletheans quickly began to restore their villages, which soon blossomed into their former state.

Both H'Aletheans and Erwinians stored matériel and other resources in caves and caverns in the event they were overrun. H'Aletheans were able to retrieve most of the items they had sequestered. Afterwards, some of these locations continued to serve as depots and places of refuge should another attack occur. Over time, however, those that were of geologic, biologic, and anthropologic significance were restored to their natural state. All traces of human habitation were removed. These places remained secluded except to those who studied them—primarily Erwina's faculty and students—and scouts who might need to shelter in them. Student field trips to these locations provided practicums in geologic and biologic sciences.

H'Aleth did not resume its role as the repository of pedigrees. It was too close to Cassius territory. Instead, the H'Aletheans sent all pedigrees to Erwina. They continued to study and record the natural history of their land and of *H. transformans*.

Erwina continued to support the schoolhouse that educated and trained youngsters from all three houses. Young adults who desired to specialize in medicine, biology, and genetics went to Gregor for advanced studies.

In the interim, gradually and cautiously, modernization moved forward in both H'Aleth and Erwina (appendix D). Yet it did so only in a few locations. Although electrical power was available, it was limited to places where its use could be hidden or disguised. It would not be wise to draw unwanted attention. Overt signs of modernization were avoided to prevent an enemy from discovering and raiding settlements.

A Harsh Lesson Learned

Finally, the H'Aletheans built a new village to replace the one that had been consumed by dragon fire. It was modeled on the village and estate that had once been H'Aleth's seat of government and housed its research facilities. This time, however, the village and estate were not left open to attack.

The debate on where to build the new village centered on the availability of a power source and geographic location—specifically, the distance from Cassius territory and from Erwina (map 2, H'Aleth). A power source was essential. There were only two rivers that had the flow rate and turbulence required to power the generators needed at the seat of government and research. The confluence of the Rivers Arcturus and Aguila, which lay to the southeast, was farther south from Cassius territory and even farther to the east away from Erwina. The relatively high flow rate of the Aguila had supported the power needs of the original village. The Arcturus had a low flow rate. Engineers agreed that the convergence would not offer any significant increase in overall flow rate. The Aquarius, into which the Aguila and Arcturus flowed, had a huge flow rate. This would be ideal. Unfortunately, both locations were deemed too far away from Erwina to provide mutual support, and the Aquarius was much too close to the coastline. The sighting of a warship off the southeast coast had not been forgotten.

The Pices, after leveling to flow westward, had a flow rate comparable to the Aguila. The Pices flow rate during descent, however, was much higher, approaching that of the Aquarius. The additional flow from the Panthera boosted the Pices's flow rate. If the new village was built above the westward bend of the Pices and south of its juncture with the Panthera, the village and research facility would have even greater power than the Aguila had originally supplied.

There was just one minor little detail to consider. Although this location was much closer to Erwina, it was also much closer to both Biogenics and Cassius territory. Still, H'Aleth, Erwina, and Biogenics had become allies after the battle with the Cassius Foundation. So H'Ester, mistress of the House of H'Aleth at that time, sent an emissary to Biogenics to consider adding a pact of mutual support among the treaty members. Should the Cassius Foundation attempt to reassert itself, it might require their combined efforts to repel it. H'Ester couldn't guarantee a great gray dragon would intercede again. The two houses and Biogenics agreed to amend the treaty to reflect mutual aid in the event of an attack by Cassius on any one of them.

With the treaty modified, a new and fortified main village and estate were built above the westward bend of the River Pices. The original village and adjoining estate were left untouched. It served as a monument to those who died defending it and a reminder of a not too distant past.

APPENDIX D
Industrial Development

After the gamma ray burst, human civilization was slow to recover initially. Post event, the primary focus was on survival and reestablishing communities. Nearly all societies were agrarian, supported by animal husbandry and the occupations associated with those activities. Gradually, communities became more organized. Basic industries such as carpentry and construction, ceramics, weaving and textiles, and blacksmithing and metalsmithing were reestablished. Wind and water mills were built, followed by granaries. During this time, a new species of human, *Homo transformans*, was recognized. The resources they could bring to bear through their alternate species did not go unnoticed.

Competition for resources led one society, the Cassius Foundation, to seek dominion over all others. At the same time, the Biogenics Corporation emerged as the foundation's chief rival and competitor. Many smaller communities were caught in the middle—especially those where *H. transformans* clustered. This led to the rise of the three related houses—H'Aleth, then Erwina, and finally Gregor—as recounted in their respective histories.

Cautious Advancement

All knowledge was not lost when a blue star exploded centuries ago. Texts of all kinds went underground with the people who carried them. When people began to reclaim the surface nearly 200 years later, they initially established an agrarian society and relied primarily on sun, wind, water, or geothermal resources for energy.

People did not dismiss other sources of energy. The H'Aletheans had discovered a huge reservoir of shale oil trapped between sedimentary layers in the southwest mountains. They tapped it sparingly and shared it with Erwina. Erwina continued to have limited supplies of coal gleaned from the northern mountains. Thus, geologists from H'Aleth and Erwina located sources of coal, tar, and shale oil. In the event another disaster drove civilization underground again, Erwina's cartographers created maps of their locations, including caches of coal hidden throughout H'Aleth and Erwina. These maps were secured in the schoolhouse at Erwina.

Similarly, the Erwinians had discovered thin veins of sodium nitrate deposits hidden within the southwest desert. When mixed with other elements under the proper conditions, it was highly explosive—a lesson learned long ago from history. This resource was also a closely guarded secret, known only to a few in H'Aleth and Erwina.

Moving Forward

Over time, human society continued to modernize. People redeveloped and restored most of the technology that had once been available to them in the nineteenth century. This included machinery driven by cranks, rods, and pistons, and small electrical grids. The latter supplied electric light to workplaces with no access to sunlight. This reduced the use of open flames and the attendant risk of fire.

Despite the availability of relatively modern technology, some societies minimized use of it to avoid detection by the Cassius Foundation. The sight, sound, and scent of technology posed the risk of discovery. Where present, generators and heavy machinery were housed in thick-walled structures built of stone or brick, or were built underground.

Despite modernization, H'Aleth and Erwina maintained many aspects of their former living conditions. Elders remembered the past all too well, and lessons learned should not be forgotten. Both H'Aleth and Erwina used electricity and machinery sparsely, primarily in research and educational settings. The majority of dwellings continued to rely on sunlight during the day and candlelight after dusk. Not even the escape tunnels had electric lights. The wiring alone would guide an enemy who had found a way into the tunnels. People avoided using any mechanization that tainted water or the air. Contaminants could be detected downstream and downwind, and could be used to track and ultimately pinpoint their origin. There was no requirement for electronic sensors. Sensitive noses of animals—whether native or an alternate species—proved to be the best monitors.

The power and energy required to support specialized instrumentation were available in very few places. The House of Gregor was the only location with an unlimited supply of geothermal energy. Hence, most advanced studies in biology, medicine, and genetics were conducted at Gregor. Gregor also served as the seat for training in these fields and in veterinary medicine.

Settlements near large rivers with turbulent flow had sufficient water power to run generators. These places were few, reinforced, and strongly defended. The Cassius Foundation had access to the River Taurus. Biogenics had access to the River Della. Both Erwina and H'Aleth had access to the River Pices. These rivers powered the one industry most critical to everyone's survival: genetics.

Weaponry

Weaponry also advanced, albeit slowly. The knowledge of how to make weapons of war had not been lost. Those schematics also were carefully preserved; however, resources were not available initially to support the manufacture of sophisticated weapons. As civilization recovered, cannons were the first artillery weapons made.

Once sufficient sources of metals were found, small numbers of rifles and pistols were handmade along with hand-casted bullets or cartridges. The latter constrained the number of guns that were made, including the hand-cranked machine gun.

Biogenics was the primary producer of armaments. Their armorists replicated a few smooth-bore muskets from historical documents. A skilled marksman could hit his or her target accurately within a range of 100 yards. At that range, a single shot was deadly. This gave the shooter an advantage others did not have—at short range. A skilled archer, however, could strike his or her target from 250 to 300 yards away.

Armaments were of little use without a sufficient supply of sodium nitrate and cartridge components. Thus, few resources were allocated to forging firearms. Although guns with ammunition were considered a far more efficient means of both offense and defense, they had one other major disadvantage—sound. Once fired, stealth was lost, especially when sensitive ears and noses and sharp eyes could quickly pinpoint the source from a long distance away. The echo of gunfire in the mountains would quickly catch the attention of a dragon.

Finally, the truce forged between the three houses and the Biogenics Corporation led to collaboration and cooperation. Biogenics ceased the manufacture of weapons of war, although all parties to the treaty agreed to keep the ones they already had in case the Cassius Foundation mounted another attack. Commerce developed as trade expanded among them. When H'Ariel assumed the duties of mistress of the House of H'Aleth, the three houses and Biogenics enjoyed a cautious prosperity, which spread to the open territories. Even so, a watch was maintained over their respective borders with Cassius territory.

APPENDIX E
H'Ester's Lineage

No one knew the complete origin of H'Ester's genotype. Many of her characteristics were not evident in her maternal lineage, which went back to Ruth, the first mistress of the House of H'Aleth (pedigree 4, H'Ester's Ancestry). H'Ester's sire was an unknown male whose donated sperm was used by the TransXformans Company. It specialized in *in vitro* fertilization that engendered offspring with desired characteristics.

Then there was the additional chromosome fragment (pedigree 5, Lineage of Fragment) revealed in H'Ester's karyotype—a single autosomal chromosome (monosomy) that was distinct from her original forty-six chromosomes. Its genes were ancient. Their ancestral lineage could be traced to the monotremes, yet they diverged from those leading to modern monotremes. The fragment's origin was unknown. It did not appear in either Ruth's or Evan's genome, so it could not have come from their line. It was first seen in H'Eleanora and subsequently inherited by H'Ester. Thus, geneticists presumed the fragment came from H'Eleanora's paternal line, whose genetic heritage was unknown.

All female *H. transformans* who possessed two transforming X chromosomes ($2X^T$) were capable of transforming across multiple classes and families within a class. Within the house of H'Aleth, all were directly descended from Ruth. Thus Ruth was designated the founder of female $2X^T$ offspring. The Cassius Foundation—and at one time the Biogenics Corporation—coveted this capability. They did not have $2X^T$ females among their own members. Thus, almost any female, including *H. sapiens*, was a prime target for bounty hunters.

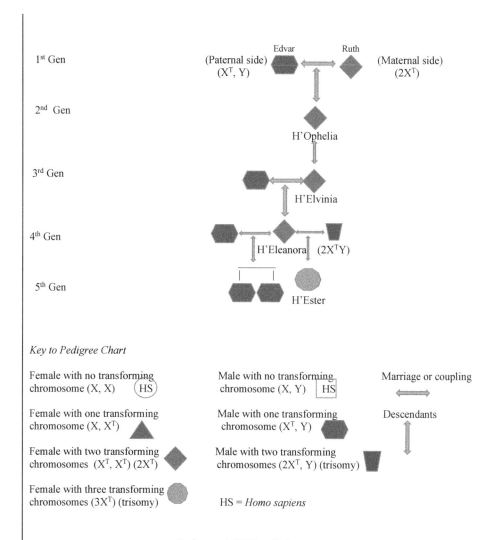

Pedigree 4: H'Ester's Ancestry

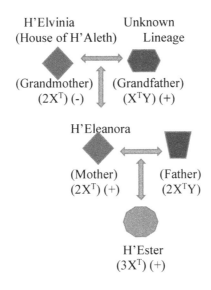

H'Elvinia   Unknown
(House of H'Aleth)   Lineage

(Grandmother)   (Grandfather)
$(2X^T)$ (-) (X^TY) (+)

H'Eleanora

(Mother)   (Father)
$(2X^T)$ (+) $(2X^TY)$

H'Ester
$(3X^T)$ (+)

Key to Pedigree Chart

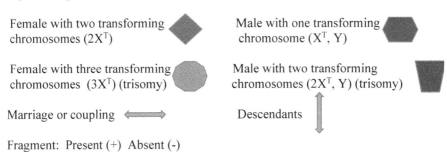

Female with two transforming chromosomes $(2X^T)$

Male with one transforming chromosome (X^T, Y)

Female with three transforming chromosomes $(3X^T)$ (trisomy)

Male with two transforming chromosomes $(2X^T, Y)$ (trisomy)

Marriage or coupling

Descendants

Fragment: Present (+) Absent (-)

Pedigree 5: Lineage of Fragment

H'Ester was the first *H. transformans* female known to have three X^T chromosomes, which amplified her capabilities. Yet, long ago, there was another female *H. transformans* with similar capabilities. Her genome was never discovered. When mortally wounded by bounty hunters, she turned her fire upon herself. Not even her ashes remained. Her origin was never discovered.

Normally, male *H. transformans* possessed one X^T, which limited their capabilities to a single class and typically to one or two species within a family. This changed with H'Ester's line. Both Edric, H'Ester's son, and later Evander, H'Ester's great-grandson, inherited $2X^T$ chromosomes from their maternal lineage. Their $2X^T$ inheritance also enhanced their capabilities and allowed them to transform across classes. This set them apart from all other *H. transformans* males. Both Edric and Evander could transform across mammalian and avian species.

Supplemental Notes and Citations

Founder

A founder is the individual in which a new characteristic is first identified. That characteristic is inherited in subsequent generations. Pedigrees are often used to trace the origin of an inherited physical trait or disposition (e.g., a familial type of cancer).

Genetic profile

An individual's genetic profile or genome is the total gene complement of that individual's genes, including specific characteristics.

Autosomal (nonreproductive) and reproductive monosomy

In monosomy, one member of a chromosome pair is missing. Most autosomal monosomies in which a *complete* chromosome is missing are lethal to the developing embryo or fetus. Any infant born with a complete autosomal monosomy dies soon after birth or in early infancy (Bunnell, *et al.*, 2017; Snyder, *et al.*, 2016). Infants with partial autosomal monosomies, in which part of a chromosome is missing [e.g., the short (p) or long (q) arm of a chromosome], may survive. Cri du chat is a partial autosomal monosomy in which the short arm of chromosome 5 (5p-) is missing.

The single exception is a missing X chromosome in a female offspring (45, XO, Turner syndrome) (figure 3) (Culen, *et al.*, 2017). This is the most common reproductive aneuploidy in female offspring. Females normally have two X chromosomes. Most but not all of the genes on the second X chromosome are inactivated, in order to be consistent with the single X chromosome present in male offspring. Thus, an embryo with only one X chromosome can survive and develop—albeit with some limitations.

Ovum

		O	XX
X	Sperm	XO (Turner's Syndrome)	XXX (Trisomy X)
Y		YO (Incompatible with life)	XXY (Kleinfelter's syndrome)

Key: X = maternal ovum
        Y = paternal sperm

Figure 3: Reproductive Aneuploidy Secondary to
Nondisjunction of the X Chromosome

Should an ovum without an X chromosome be fertilized by a sperm carrying a Y chromosome, the result—monosomy 45, YO—is incompatible with life.

Autosomal and reproductive trisomy

In trisomy, there is one additional chromosome. In autosomal trisomy, there are three chromosomes instead of two [e.g., trisomy 21 (Down's syndrome)]. This usually occurs when a paired set of chromosomes (e.g., chromosome 21) fails to separate during cellular division (nondisjunction). One cell has an extra chromosome (trisomy), while the other cell is deprived of that chromosome and is left with only one (monosomy) instead of two paired chromosomes.

In reproductive trisomy, a reproductive cell—whether it is an egg (ovum) or a sperm—should have only one half the normal complement of chromosomes—a haploid cell with twenty-three chromosomes. An ovum that has an extra X chromosome as a result of nondisjunction will have a total of twenty-four chromosomes. Its sister ovum will be missing an X chromosome and left with a total of twenty-two chromosomes.

Sex chromosome aneuploidies are not uncommon (Skuse, et al., 2018). Trisomy X (XXX) and Klinefelter's syndrome (XXY) are two sex-chromosome aneuploidies in which there is an extra X chromosome. In trisomy X, the X chromosome fails to separate properly (nondisjunction) during division of an ovum. Should the ovum (XX) be fertilized by a sperm carrying an X chromosome, the result will be a female offspring with three X chromosomes (47, XXX, trisomy X) (Tartaglia, et al., 2010; Wigby, et al., 2016). Should the ovum (XX) be fertilized by a sperm carrying a Y chromosome, the result will be a male offspring (47, XXY, Klinefelter's syndrome) (Bonomi, et al., 2017; Kanakis & Nieschlag, 2018). This is the most frequent reproductive aneuploidy in men.

These syndromes can present with a wide range of physical and mental characteristics; however, many people with trisomy XXX and XXY present without any unusual characteristics (Bonomi, et al., 2017; Kanakis & Nieschlag, 2018). Hence, these syndromes may remain undiagnosed throughout life or may be discovered only during an evaluation for infertility.

Men with Klinefelter's syndrome (XXY) produce little or no sperm and, as a result, are usually infertile (Bonomi, et al., 2017.) Male infertility also can be caused by genetic abnormalities in the X chromosome even in the absence of an extra X chromosome (Ropke & Tuttlemann, 2017).

APPENDIX F
NATIVE SPECIES

Mammals (Mammalia)

Bear, Brown (*Ursus*)—omnivore
The brown bear is the second-largest bear, reaching eight feet or more
when standing upright. It can sprint at twenty-five to thirty miles per
hour for a short distance. It has a bite force of 850 pounds per square
inch. Their preferred ranges are mountains and forests.

Boar, Wild (*Sus scrofa*)—omnivore
Male boars can weigh 300 to 500 pounds. They generally move at a
languid pace yet can be quick, reaching speeds of twenty miles per
hour. They are also good swimmers. Tusks in males range from six
inches to fifteen inches long.

Deer (*Cervidae*)—herbivore

Caribou (reindeer) (*Rangifer tarandus*) can be found in the arctic tundra
of North America and in the boreal forests of Alaska. These are large
animals. An adult male stands six to seven feet tall and weighs 350 to
400 pounds. They can run up to fifty miles per hour.

Elk (red deer) *(Cervus elaphus)* are brown to gray-colored deer with shades of red in summer and gray in the winter. They are among the largest of the deer family. The stags have branching antlers.

Mule (black-tailed) deer (*Odocoileus hemionus*) also have a reddish-brown coat in summer and gray-black coat in winter. They are larger than the white-tailed deer. The stags have antlers.

White-tailed deer (*Odocoileus virginianus*) have a reddish-brown coat in summer and gray-brown coat in winter. They are a midsized deer. The stags have antlers.

Fox (*Vulpes*)—carnivore
The coats of arctic, gray, and red foxes vary with the terrains they occupy. The arctic fox (*Vulpes lagopus*) has a white coat consistent with its tundra habitat. The gray fox (*Urocyon cinereoargenteus*) has a gray to grayish-brown color and inhabits the montane forests. The red fox (*Vulpes vulpes*) occupies southwestern regions.

Hares (*Leporid*)—herbivore
The coats of both arctic (*Lepus arcticus*) and snowshoe (*Lepus americanus*) hares are white in winter. They are easily distinguished by the long, wide back feet of the snowshoe. The arctic hare's coat turns slate blue during the summer, while the snowshoe's coat turns brown. Both are active all year. The arctic hare is the larger of the two hares. It is also the fastest, achieving speeds of about thirty-five miles per hour.

Wolves (*Canidae*)—carnivores
The gray (mountain) wolf (*Canis lupus*) is the largest species of wolf with an average weight of 80 to 100 pounds. Its bite pressure is about 400 pounds per square inch, which can crush large bones. Both the arctic and tundra wolf are subspecies of the gray wolf. They share the gray wolf's characteristics. The adult arctic wolf (*Canis lupus arctos*),

however, is all white, whereas the tundra wolf (*Canis lupus tundrarum*) is gray to black.

Cats (*Felidae*)—carnivores

Cougars (mountain lion) (*Puma concolor*) prefer to range in mountainous and lightly forested areas. Their coats are usually a variation of tan. They may have a silver to reddish hue. The cougar is the fourth-largest cat among the big cats. Adult males are about two feet tall at the shoulder, six to eight feet long, including the tail, and can weight up to 200 pounds. Females are smaller at about 120 pounds.

Although cougars are not distance runners, they can sprint up to forty or fifty miles per hour. Their bite force is 350 pounds per square inch. They have curved retractable claws and are agile climbers. They can leap upwards nearly fifteen to eighteen feet and forward twenty to forty feet, especially if running. They are also good swimmers.

Jaguars (*Panthera onca*) are smaller than lions and tigers; however, they are the largest of the panthera species, which includes the leopard. Males are larger than females and may weigh 200 to 300 pounds. They stand two to two and a half feet tall at the shoulder, and are five and a half to eight feet long, including the tail. They can run approximately thirty-five miles per hour.

Jaguars are distinguished from leopards by the dark spot within the rings of a jaguar's coat, which leopards lack. A black (melanotic) jaguar is distinguished by the color of its coat. It carries the gene for black, which is dominant. The rings and spots are still present; however, they are difficult to see even in daylight and virtually impossible to distinguish in the shade or at night.

Lynx (*Lynx canadensis*) are much smaller than their larger cousins and have carved out a niche at higher and colder latitudes. They range from Alaska to the arctic tundra.

Birds of Prey (*Avis*)

Birds of prey (raptors) are uniformly carnivores. They have large eyes with high-resolution vision that allows them see small prey from a long distance even at night, depending upon the species. They have sharp, hooked beaks and sharp, curved talons with a powerful grip. Females are larger than males

Eagles and Hawks (*Accipitridae*)

The golden eagle (*Aquila chrysaetos*) has a flight speed of twenty-eight to thirty miles per hour when soaring. It can glide up to 120 miles per hour, and its diving speed is 150 to 200 miles per hour.

The harpy eagle (*Harpia harpyja*) is the largest eagle. It can reach flight speeds of nearly fifty miles per hour. Its talons are five inches long and are among the largest and strongest of any raptor.

The Cooper's hawk *(Accipiter cooperii)* has a flight speed of twenty to fifty-five miles per hour. It is adept at flying though trees, even in a heavily wooded area.

Falcons (*Falconidae*)

The gyrfalcon (*Falco rusticolus*) is the largest member of the falcon family and lives in extreme arctic and subarctic regions. They can attain flight speeds of 130 miles per hour.

The peregrine falcon (*Falco peregrinus*) is one of the smallest raptors. Yet it is the fastest bird in flight, reaching flying speeds of about 130 to 140 miles per hour and diving speeds up to 250 miles per hour.

Owls (*Strigidae*)

These raptors are typically nocturnal with eyes designed for low light and a head rotation of over 180 degrees. They have broad wings for slow, silent flight and maneuverability.

The great horned owl (*Bubo virginianus*) is one of the largest species of owl. It occupies a wide range of terrains. Its flight speed is twenty to forty miles per hour.

The snowy owl (*Bubo scandiacus*) is also one of the largest species of owl. It occupies arctic and subarctic regions. Unlike most owls, it is active during the day. It tends to fly low to the ground, and can achieve a flight speed of about forty-five miles per hour.

The woodland (long-eared) owl (*Asio otus*) is a medium-sized bird that has a wide distribution. It prefers woodland borders.

APPENDIX G
PREDATORY THEROPOD DINOSAURS OF THE LATE JURASSIC AND CRETACEOUS PERIODS

Theropod dinosaurs (Table 1) were a clade of enormous carnivorous dinosaurs characterized by serrated teeth, large and powerful hind limbs, a long and heavy tapering tail to support an upright (bipedal) posture, and strong grasping claws on relatively small forelimbs. They lived from the late Triassic period to the end of the Cretaceous period. The largest species lived from the late Jurassic to the close of the Cretaceous. There were several families of theropods, including *Allosauridae*, *Dromaeosauridae* (small, feathered), *Tyrannosauridae*, and others.

Supplemental Notes and Citations

Theropod dinosaurs

The theropods are an enormous clade of dinosaurs within which a large number of more specific clades are housed (Hendrickx, *et al.*, 2015). These include the avian dinosaurs that evolved into modern birds, and the non-avian carnivorous dinosaurs. The non-avian dinosaurs dominated during the Jurassic and Cretaceous periods until the Cretaceous–Paleogene mass extinction event sixty-six million years ago.

Theropod Species	Length (feet)	Weight (pounds)	Skull (feet)	Distribution
Tyrannosauridae				
Tyrannosaurus rex	40	10,000–30,000	5.0 Massive	Montana, Texas, Utah, Wyoming; Alberta, Canada
Dynamoterror dynastes	30			New Mexico
Daspletosaurus horneri	30	5,000		Montana
Albertosaurus	30	3,000–5,500	3.5	Alberta, Canada
Gorgosaurus	25–30	5,000	3.3	North Carolina, Montana; Alberta, Canada
Lythronax argestes	24	5,500		Utah
Nanuqsaurus hoglundi	20–23	2,000–3500		Alaska
Teratophoneus curriei	15	1,500		Arizona
Allosauridae				
Allosaurus fragilis	28–32	5,000	3.0	Utah, Nebraska
Spinosauridae				
Spinosaurus aegyptiacus	45–60	14,000–17,000	6.0 Long, narrow	Africa

Table 1: Predatory Therapod Dinosaurs

APPENDIX H
DRAGONIDAE

Terrestrial Dragons

The great gray dragon (*Dragonis fuscus magna*) inhabited the northern and northeastern mountains and forest ranges below the frost line. It was the largest (*magna*) of the terrestrial dragon species. Its drab-gray (*fuscus*) to charcoal-colored scales blended into the granite of the northern mountains.

The red (golden) dragon (*Dragonis rubra*) inhabited the southern and southwestern mountains and forests. It was the smallest of the terrestrial dragons (exclusive of river dragons). It was named for its very colorful amber-red scales with streaks of gold on the top of its head and back.

The arctic dragon (*Dragonis arcturus alba*) inhabited the mountains in the far north bordering on the subarctic and arctic regions. It was a medium-sized dragon that was somewhat smaller than the gray. It was white except for gray coloring on top of its head, back, and wings.

Marine (Ocean) Dragons

General Characteristics
Enormous marine mammals, these animals were sleek in build for

greater speed and had large flippers to propel them through water. They did not have flukes like whales. Instead, they used their tails to propel them and as a keel. Large pectoral fins also propelled them through the water and steered changes in direction. They could achieve speeds of thirty to thirty-five miles per hour in water.

Marine dragons could hold their breath underwater for thirty to forty minutes. As mammals, they had to rise to the surface periodically to breathe. All had salivary and incendiary glands to produce fire; however, underwater, their fire had only a short range before dissipating. With the exception of the pristis, ocean-faring dragons were the only species without wings for powered flight. Nevertheless, their breaches were spectacular.

Glacialis bala was a carnivorous ocean-faring predatory species resident throughout the arctic region. They were discovered by the wildlife specialists of Gregor, who observed a large dragon in arctic waters. The bala had dark-gray coloring, an average length of fifty to sixty-five feet, and an average weight of 100 to 110 tons. They preyed on arctic fish such as cod, eelpouts, and sculpins; and mammals such as sea otters, dolphins, sea lions, seals, and occasionally polar bears. On occasion, a bala could be seen rising out of the ocean to snatch an unwary arctic tern, cormorant, and other arctic sea birds. It did not disturb boats. Nevertheless, their dietary habits served to warn those *H. transformans* whose alternate species was also a prey species.

Odontus pristis was a carnivorous, aquatic semi-marine species of predatory dragon that favored brackish waters and swamplands. The pristis had a dark bluish-black color which melded into their environment. Males weighed ten tons, females about eight. Its length was twenty-eight to thirty-six feet long. Unlike their strictly marine cousins, the pristis hunted on land as well as underwater. More terrestrial than aquatic, it adapted so that it could swim underwater as well as take flight.

Freshwater (River) Dragons

General Characteristics

Freshwater dragons included river and lake species. Just as freshwater dragons occasionally hunted on land, some terrestrial species such as the *arcturus alba* often fished in fresh or marine waters. Key differences between terrestrial and aquatic dragons were their size, preferred habitat, and coloring. Whereas arctic dragons were white with gray coloring on top, river dragons were dark except for a broad grayish-white dorsal stripe which began at the top of the head and ran to the tip of its tail. The dorsal stripe blended perfectly with the water of the rapids. The rest of the body was a dark gray or grayish blue.

River dragons were slender like the red dragon, only smaller. Nevertheless, their size limited them to deepwater rivers and lakes. They had partially webbed feet with sharp talons not only to grasp prey but also to climb up a rocky canyon wall and grip large boulders to haul themselves out of the water. Like most dragons, they had wings for powered flight. Similar to the *arcturus albus*, muscles under the skin contracted to pull scales tightly together, thereby keeping water out. Although they preferred to swim, they would become airborne if they encountered large chunks of fallen debris, waters that were too shallow, or channels through category V and VI rapids that were too narrow.

Their diet consisted primarily of fish, reptiles, and other aquatic mammals; however, they would not hesitate to take flight to catch their prey. They would also feed on hapless lifeforms that fell into the river and could not escape it.

Except when traversing rapids or hunting terrestrial species, river dragons stayed in deep water. Hence, their aquatic territory was limited by water depth. Rapids were the only place the river dragons could be spotted from land. Yet they were rarely seen—even by eagle-eyed scouts—because their movements mimicked water over rapids and their stripe blended into the crests of the waters.

Dragonensis dragonis fluminibus griseo was a subspecies of river dragon that patrolled the River Admare and ran its category V and VI rapids with aplomb at the confluence of the Admare and Lacus. This species preferred the cold waters flowing from the mountains.

The key differences between the griseo and the sitka (see below) were their range, temperature tolerance, and inclination to take flight. Although both could fly, the griseo often hunted for prey on land as well as in river waters. The sitka preferred to hunt aquatic species; however, it would not turn down a tasty morsel that came too close to the water. Both species liked to sun themselves from time to time.

Dragonensis dragonis fluminibus sitka was a subspecies of river dragon that was similar in appearance to the griseo and likely closely related to it. The sitka ranged from the confluence of the River Della through the mountain pass to just inside Erwina's northern border where they turned back. Although they preferred cold waters, they were more tolerant of warmer waters. They ranged as far south as the River Ferveo to search for food and to hone their aquatic skills by surfing the Ferveo's impressive rapids. Erwina's biologists believed that the water temperature may have been too warm for them to linger long in the Ferveo.

Supplemental Notes and Citations

Keratin

Keratin is a strong, durable protein that provides structure to tissues and is also insoluble in water (Wang, *et al.*, 2016). The top layer of the skin (*stratum corneum*) is comprised of keratinocytes, which are rich in keratin (Murphrey, *et al.*, 2019). Layers of these cells act as a barrier against the environment.

APPENDIX I
Rivers and Lakes

The major rivers and lakes found in the territories of Biogenics, Erwina, H'Aleth, and Cassius are described below. Specific characteristics of each river (table 2, table 3) and lake (table 4) are provided as well.

Biogenics Territory

The Biogenics territory was established when the Biogenetics Company merged with the Eugenics Corporation to form the Biogenics Corporation.

Located on a westward protuberance of Biogenics territory, the Lacus Antigua Mare was once a bay of an ancient sea. It became trapped by volcanic forces that created a vast plateau of basalt and volcanic ash, elevating the land. It remained an inland sea until fresh water gradually replaced the seawater. Subsequently, it became a vast, deep freshwater lake sustained by rain and heavy snow and small tributary streams. It represented an enormous source of fresh water. Thus, once it was discovered by Biogenics scouts, the company claimed the lake as part of its territory. Unbeknownst to the scouts, it also harbored an aquatic dragon, species unknown.

Located on the eastern border of Biogenics, Lacus Sitka was a natural high mountain lake, formed by a continental glacier. When the glacier retreated, the basin filled with fresh water from nearby streams, heavy rainfall, and deep snows, which continued to sustain it. Over millennia, the volcanic plain eroded, and was colonized by vegetation and finally covered by an interior spruce pine forest.

River	Length (miles)	Width (miles)	Depth (feet)	Flow Rate (CFS*)	Rapids Category
Accipitridae	115	0.125-0.50	8-12	200-300	none
Admare	1600	2-4	250-350	250,000-300,000	III-VI
Aguila	325		10-20	17,750-19,300	none
Aquarius[1]	650	6-10	200-300	300,000-950,000	II
Arctos	700	0.5-0.75	30-40	250,000-300,000 during descent 18,000-22,000 after leveling	IV-V during descent
Arcturus[1]	450		15-25	200-400	none
Cassius[1]	1350	3-5	35-45	1,300-1,700	none
Erratus	355	0.50-0.75	12-20	600-700	none
Feroxaper[2]	275	3	35-45	1100-1300	III-IV
Ferveo[3]	415	1-2	20-60	270,000-310,000 475,000 at the slip fault	III-VI
Lactus[3]	1750	3-5	350-400 1,250 at the gorge	265,000-325,000 550,000 at the gorge	I-II V-VI at the gorge
Pices[2]	1450	1-3	40-85	200,000-250,000 during descent 15,000-19,600 after leveling	none
Taurus	980	1-4	85-160	1,850,000 during descent 250,000-300,000 after leveling	II-III during descent
Tesca	370	1-2	10-20	180,500-210,000 during descent 15,000-20,000 after leveling	none

*Cubic feet per second – gradient and volume determine the rate (speed) of flow which, in turn, determines the category of rapids (if any)—the higher the flow rate, the greater the rapids.
[1]Cassius + Arcturus + Aquarius = 2450 miles.
[2]Pices + Feroxaper = 2025 miles.
[3]Lactus + Ferveo = 2065 miles.

Table 2: Major Rivers

Category	
I	Easy—low waves, gradual descent, fairly straight line, slow rate, little or no difficulty.
II	Intermediate/Moderate—regular waves, modest eddies, gradual bends in the river, somewhat steeper descent leading to a modest flow rate and modest level of difficulty.
III	Difficult—high and irregular waves, strong eddies, brisk flow rate, narrow passageways among boulders with abrupt drops into holes where flow of water blocked by a large boulder, requires skill to maneuver.
IV	Very difficult—all of the above over a much longer stretch of rapids, higher waves, greater turbulence, longer drops, steeper and narrower channels, and faster flow rates.
V	Extremely difficult and dangerous—very fast, violent waves, very steep drops eighteen to twenty-four, and very steep channels that descend rapidly.
VI	Life—threatening, nearly impossible to navigate, should be avoided, portage around rapids.

Table 3: Categories of Rapids

Lake (Lacus)	Location	Size	Depth (feet)	Other
Aequor Occulta	H'Aleth	unknown	unknown	Part of an extensive cavern system
Antigua Mare	Biogenics*	350 miles long 150 miles wide	485 average 1275 deepest	Elevation 12,455 feet
Dragona Magna	Erwina	42 miles long 30 miles wide	450 average 860 deepest	435 square miles of water, 55 square miles of islands
Litore	Gregor	180 miles long 50 miles wide	300 average 800 deepest	
Lontra	H'Aleth	17 miles long 14 miles wide	64 average 400 deepest	Dotted with several islands
Glacialis	Gregor	300 miles long 225 miles wide	1200 average 2000 deepest	Surface frozen except during arctic summer
Manatus	H'Aleth	36 miles long 28 miles wide	6 average 18 deepest	Shallow coastal lake
Pices	Erwina	20 miles long 16 miles wide	5 average 18 deepest	20 sq. miles,
Sitka	Biogenics*	30 miles long 12 miles wide	850 average 1600 deepest	Elevation 14,505 feet

*Formally Biogenetics Company and Eugenics Corporation

Table 4: Major Lakes

The River Admare, also named the River Serpentis by Eugenics, had its origin in the high mountain plateau. With its headwaters in the far north, the river had a high elevation and therefore a fast flow rate. Where the River Lacus crosses the Admare, the water was extremely turbulent. At this point, the terrain was steep and rocky, creating rapids as the two rivers separated and found their way south. The Admare continued its course due south across the Caput Canis of H'Aleth, where it was named the River Vulpes, and became a tributary of the River Pices.

The Admare was a deep river, second only to the Lacus. A species of river dragon, *Dragonensis dragonis fluminibus griseo*, patrolled the Admare and ran its category V and VI rapids with aplomb (table 2). These dragons turned back at the confluence with the Lacus. Another species of aquatic dragons claimed the Lacus River.

The River Lacus flowed southwest from the eastern border of Biogenics. Lacus Sitka was the river's source. When it reached the confluence with the River Admare, the Admare, with its faster flow rate, stole water from the Lacus. Further south, the River Della, a tributary of the Lacus, restored the waters lost to the Admare. The Lacus continued south where it carved a deep mountain gorge on its way to Erwina and was named the River Ferveo by the Erwinians. The river was about six miles wide and 400 feet deep until it reached the gorge. At that point it narrowed to about two miles wide, and its depth plummeted to over 1,200 feet.

Category V and VI rapids raged through the mountain pass. The canyon walls echoed the thunder of the river's torrent. Massive boulders littered the riverbed. They broke away from the canyon walls with recurring earthquakes. Given the river's flow rate, towering waves crashed into these rocks. Sinking gaps were left on the far side of boulders. Water flowed backward as the river refilled these gaps—essentially, flowing upstream against the current—creating even more turbulence.

The aquatic dragon *Dragonensis dragonis fluminibus sitka* ranged from the confluence of the River Della through the mountain pass to just inside Erwina's northern border where they turned back. Erwina's biologists believed that the water temperature may have been too warm to suit them. Kayakers and scouts reported rare, vague, and mostly unconfirmed sightings of sitka dragons in the River Ferveo. It is possible, however, that an adventurous adolescent had wandered south, seeking another opportunity to run category V and VI rapids.

Dragons brought their fledged chicks to Lacus Sitka for swimming and diving lessons. Hence, their subspecies name, sitka.

Erwina's Territory

Lacus Dragona Magna was a remote high mountain lake located at an altitude of 9,585 feet and surrounded by the montane forests of the western mountains. Its source was unknown due to its rugged terrain, hostile weather, and resident species of dragons—all of which precluded exploration. Mountain streams and rivers along with snow melt were probable sources.

The lake was named for the great gray dragons that inhabited the mountains. It was thought that the lake was a major source of water for them; however, this was unlikely. Many shallow lakes dotted the mountain range. At higher elevations, the mountains were always covered with snow. Great gray dragons had no difficulty reaching these altitudes.

Lacus Pices was located just southeast of the confluence of the Rivers Ferveo and Pices. It was created when a series of earthquakes caused a depression leading the River Pices to reverse flow, temporarily flooding the depression. Subsequently, its waters were maintained by rain, small streams branching from the Pices, and runoff when the Pices flooded.

Lacus Lacrima and Lacus Solea were the largest loop lakes located on either side of the River Erratus. They were formed when the Erratus changed its course over time, cutting them off. Hence, they were mostly round, relatively shallow, and about two to three miles wide. They and other, smaller loop lakes were sustained by rain and river water when the Erratus flooded. A variety of fish thrived in these lakes and served as a source of food for several prairie inhabitants, including coyotes and red-tailed hawks.

The River Ferveo was essentially a southward continuation of the River Lacus. The Ferveo, also called the Angry River, had its origins in the River Della and the River Lacus. These two rivers gathered their waters from mountain streams all across the northern mountains. Eventually, their combined flows found their way to the Ferveo. Once the Lacus exited the mountain pass between Biogenics and Erwina, it continued its rapid run as the Ferveo south into the territory claimed by Erwina.

At the Ferveo's confluence with the waters of the Pices, the Ferveo flowed over a stretch of land overlying an ancient fault line. Long ago, under stress from tectonic forces, a major earthquake caused a broad slip fault. The shift in the earth's crust created a subsidence on the far side and left a descending series of flat ledges, creating one drop after another, like a very steep staircase. Tons of rocks also fell into the subsidence. The result of all this mayhem was category IV, V, and VI rapids. The Erwinians built their largest settlement, the compound, near the southwest corner of the confluence of the Pices and Ferveo rivers. Both served as major sources of water power for the compound.

After the River Ferveo cascaded down the rapids, it forked. The right fork, the River Erratus, spilled into the southwest *prairie where it wove leisurely through prairies grasses until reaching the foothills of the southwest mountains. The left branch, a continuation of the River Ferveo,* plummeted into the southeast prairie, carving a variety of ravines and narrow canyons into the foothills around the eastern edge of the southwest mountains. There, its waters disappeared, most likely reaching a cavern system where it became an underground river.

A wide web of branches and streams from the Ferveo and the Pices supplied the prairie with sources of mountain water. Seasonal rains added to the water supply in the region. Groundwater supplied a huge aquifer that underlay the prairie.

The River Borealis, a tributary of the Pices, had its origin in the northern mountains and flowed from the north to south. Just west of its confluence with the River Pices, the River Meridio branched off the Pices to flow south where the prairie gave rise to the desert. Long ago, these two rivers were one.

When an earthquake caused a slip fault to form, the rivers' continuity was broken. Hence, they were also known collectively as the Rivers Gemini, the north and south twin rivers. The Meridio and man-made cisterns were the primary sources of water for western outposts and villages.

H'Aleth's Territory

Lacus Lontra was a natural freshwater lake located just to the west of the main village, which once hosted H'Aleth's manor and estate until all were destroyed by dragon fire. It was formed by a north–south thrust fault which created a depressed valley. Its source was the River Ursus, the first main branch off the River Pices after the latter branched from the River Feroxaper. Waters from the lake flowed into the River Rufus, which carried them through the southern grasslands and ultimately to the sea.

Lacus Aequor Occulta was located in the Caput Canis. It was a mammoth underground freshwater lake, part of an extensive complex cavern system that was fully explored. Presumably, it was fed by a branch off the River Admare, which disappeared underground and reappeared at a location due south of the cavern system. It appeared to be in line with the cavern system. It became a tributary to the Pices above the junction of the River Vulpes (Admare) with the Pices.

Lacus Manatus was located on a broad peninsula in a shallow depression east of the River Aquarius. A marine lake was left behind when the ocean's waters receded thousands of years ago. It became a freshwater lake when its water was subsequently replaced by rain, run-off, and small streams branching from the River Arcturus. Located in a somewhat swampy area, the lake supported cypress trees and manatees, for which it was named. It also harbored bass, catfish, and crappie, and hosted egrets and herons, frogs and turtles, and snakes.

The River Pices, so named by the H'Aletheans, was the right-hand branch of the Feroxaper. The Pices flowed westward, crossing the neck of the Caput Canis of H'Aleth. It continued westward across open territory into Erwina. The Rivers Lupus and Panthera, which originated in the northern mountains, converged just above the Pices. They and the River Admare were tributaries which significantly increased the volume and flow rate of the Pices as it coursed into Erwina territory. The Erwineans, in concert with their brethren in H'Aleth, kept the name Pices.

The River Aguila [*ah*-gǐ-la] was the left branch of the Feroxaper. It was renamed the Aguila by the H'Aletheans when it crossed into their territory. The Feroxaper's right branch became the River Pices.

The River Arcturus [ărk-*tour*-ŭs], so named by the H'Aletheans, was essentially an extension of the River Cassius beyond the westward branch of the River Feroxaper. Eventually, the rivers Aguila, Accipitridae, and Arcturus met to form the River Aquarius. The Aquarius flowed southeast to reach the coastline where it became a large delta as it flowed into the ocean. Upstream of the delta, several estuaries developed where smaller tributaries flowed into the Aquarius.

Strictly speaking, the rivers Accipitridae [*ak*-cǐ-*pit*-rǐ-dī], Corvus, and Strigidae [*strǐ*-gǐ-dī] were broad creeks. The Corvus branched off the Cassius past the latter's confluence with the River Taurus. The Corvus became a tributary to the River Strigidae, which was a tributary of the Aguila. The Accipitridae was the left fork of the Strigidae and was a tributary of the River Arcturus just above its confluence with the Aguila. An old woman and young child once traversed the rivers Aguila, Accipitridae, and Arcturus when they fled from the destruction of H'Aleth into Cassius territory where they disappeared.

Cassius Territory

The Cassius Foundation deliberately kept its territory secret and forbidding. Hybrid animals were released throughout the territory to feed upon any living creature, including intruders. Thus, the topography of the Cassius territory was largely unknown. This was amended somewhat when an intrepid owl first surveyed the territory to the west of the Cassius River. Later, a daring pack of wolves followed a man-made canal east of the Cassius.

The headwaters of the River Taurus originated in the northern mountains. It coursed along the western border of Cassius territory. Initially, it had a rapid flow rate, which slowed as it flowed around a wide westward bend and then turned east and leveled out on its way to its the confluence with the River Cassius. The Taurus merged briefly with the Cassius as the latter's tributary and then disengaged with the Cassius as it branched right to continue as the River Feroxaper. At the confluence, the Feroxaper bent west and left Cassius territory to enter H'Aleth's territory where it was known as the River Pices.

The Cassius fortress was built adjacent to the River Taurus. Cassius used it for both a source of power and a convenient means to dispose of waste.

The River Cassius originated in the northeast, far above Cassius territory. It was a powerful river that coursed through a central mountain range and was no doubt fed by mountain streams. After its confluence with the River Taurus, the River Feroxaper branched away and flowed southwest only to branch again. The right branch flowed due west into H'Aleth territory where it was renamed the River Arcturus.

The River Feroxaper was essentially an extension of the River Taurus after its confluence with the River Cassius. The Feroxaper had a relatively brief yet steep descent before it branched into the Rivers Pices and Aguila.

Gregor Territory

Lacus Glacialis was an enormous glacial lake that lay to the north of the mountain range in the southwest. It was fed by glacial melt and several streams and rivers that flowed from the mountains. Arctic char and smelt inhabited the lake. *Dragonis alba* visited the lake, especially when teaching their young to fish.

Lacus Litore, named for its close approximation to the eastern shoreline, may once have been the original shoreline. Gregor's geologists suspected it was cut off from the ocean by an upwelling of the earth. Snow and snow melt gradually turned it into a freshwater lake. Thus it became a source of fresh water for travelers going to and from Gregor.

Both the River Arctos and the River Tesca flowed from the mountains and emptied into the fjord. The Arctos was further west and passed through an ice field. With its origin high in the glaciers of the mountain range, it had a rapid flow rate. Thus, it cut a deep and narrow channel through the tundra and ice field. The Tesca had its origins in lower and more southerly mountains and had a leisurely flow rate. It flowed through the tundra to the innermost tip of the fjord. Both rivers hosted a variety of freshwater fish, including whitefish, salmon, grayling, and char.

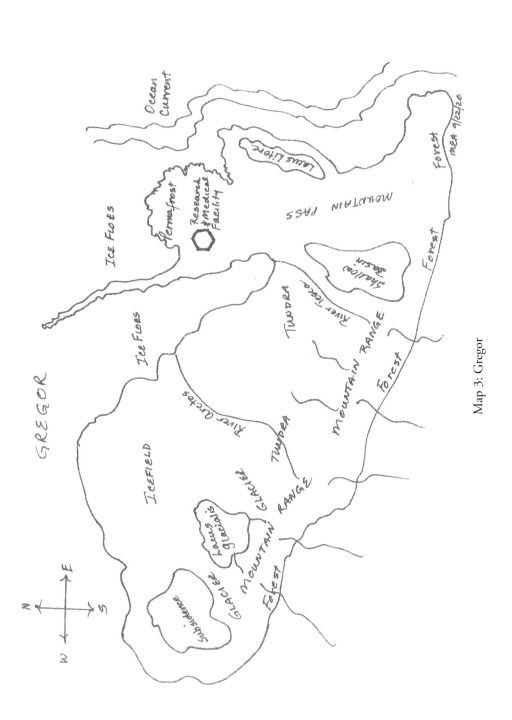

Map 3: Gregor

APPENDIX J-1
In the Far North

Gregor was remote and isolated. Its founders selected a subarctic region of tundra that would be most uninviting to an intruder (map 3, Gregor) and far removed from the hostile intentions of the Biogenics Corporation and the Cassius Foundation.

Fascination with a totally new biome spurred Gregor's biologists, geologists, and wildlife specialists to explore the surrounding territory. Some species of animals were familiar, whereas others were new, including a new species of dragon. Vegetation on the tundra was highly specialized, and there were surprising summer blooms to the south. Scientists explored the geology of the land, including two enormous lakes—the Glacialis in the west and the Litore in the east—and two major rivers—the Arctos and the Tesca.

Geography

A frigid sea lay to the north and extended to an ocean in the east. A fjord penetrated deep into the northern coastline, creating a narrow peninsula that projected into the sea. On the east side of the peninsula, a head of land bulged into the ocean, creating a bay between the land and the peninsula. Glaciers guarded the north and west until they butted up against a towering volcanic mountain range that lay to the south of Gregor. Except for the southern pass, which was open between late spring and early fall, access to Gregor was severely constrained. Even in the summer, bogs and marshes and a thousand shallow lakes dotted the tundra, waiting to trap an unwary traveler.

The vast mountain range to the south served as Gregor's southern boundary. The aeries of *Dragonensis dragonis alba* lay within their peaks. Geologists suspected that the battle between two tectonic plates continued to push the mountains upward. This activity triggered an abundance of earthquakes, most of which were deep. Gregor was built on an outcropping of land far to the north and just east of the mountains. This location buffered the effects of earthquakes.

Arctic Wildlife

Common arctic animals could be found in sparse numbers. Mammalian species included the arctic wolf, seal, snowshoe hare, and tundra vole. Avian species included the arctic tern, snowy owl, gyrfalcon, and snow bunting. The top predator was the arctic dragon, an aquatic species of mammal that hunted on land and in the sea. They made their home in the caves and caverns of the southern mountain range. In the absence of a dragon, the polar bear was the largest predator.

From time to time, the biologists would see a huge wave rise far offshore, then disappear. Certain that it was some kind of marine mammal, probably a species of whale as yet unidentified, they named it Cete. It was quite some time before they discovered it was a marine dragon, *Glacialis bala*.

Volcanism

Gregor invested considerable resources into the study of the region's geology. This was of critical importance since Gregor depended upon geothermal activity for its energy supply. Volcanism was readily apparent across the territory, both above and below the arctic ice. There were several extinct volcanoes scattered across the region and one very active one a long distance away to the north. Several small volcanic islands dotted the ocean. Gregor's geologists suspected that a massive subterranean cauldron of magma lay beneath the region. Thus, Gregor did not want for power to fuel their operations.

To the west was an enormous subsidence in the earth where mud bubbled, vents spewed acrid gases and steam into the air, and geysers shot streams of hot water upwards. The whole expanse reeked of sulfur. There was a shallow basin—almost spread out like a plain—in the southern region adjacent to the southern pass. Geologists hypothesized that it may have been an inland sea that eventually eroded into the southern pass and drained away.

Geologists, volcanologists, and oceanographers kept a close eye on the land and the sea. Should the oceanic volcano have a major eruption, it would send a massive tsunami toward the northern coastline, carrying huge ice floes with it. It would likely obliterate the peninsula that extended into the sea and slam into Gregor. Should the magma chamber to the west erupt, the lava flow might not reach Gregor; however, it could easily close the southern pass, trapping them. Hot volcanic ash would damage structures in the complex.

Paleobiology

The geologists' scrutiny of the land led to the discovery of many fossils from the Cretaceous period. During that time, Earth had a much warmer climate. Geologists found fossils of tropical plants such as ferns, insects such as bees and wasps, birds, and many species of sauropod dinosaurs. Herbivores such as the iguanodon and triceratops and carnivores such as the tyrannosaurs roamed the land. Small marsupial and placental mammals also made their appearance, as did marine reptiles such as ichthyosaurs and aerial reptiles like pterosaurs. Geologists and biologists quickly blended to become paleontologists.

Supplemental Notes and Citations

Arctic dinosaurs

During the Cretaceous period, dinosaurs inhabited a temperate environment in what is now the arctic region (Fiorillo, *et al.*, 2019; Fiorillo

& Tykoski, 2014; Gangloff, *et al.*, 2005; Godefroit, *et al.*, 2008). A wide variety of species were present, including hadrosaurs, tyrannosaurs, and other non-avian theropods.

APPENDIX J-2
Gregor's Research Facility

Fire and Ice

Initially, Gregor's founders devoted their efforts to establishing their house and building their main facility. Over several years, the Gregorians built a large, energy-efficient research center. They decided to build their facility entirely aboveground to avoid damage to the tundra and permafrost associated with excavation.

It quickly became evident that the entire region was geologically active. Tremors were common and of varying intensity. Their geologist estimated a magnitude between four and five for several tremors. So the Gregorians built their facility in sections—north wing, west wing, east wing—with flexible joints that would sway rather than crumble should an earthquake occur. They mounted their generators on anti-vibration platforms designed to buffer shifts in the ground and keep them level.

Part of the complex was honed out of glacial ice, which provided refrigeration that required no power source. They stored specimens in this section housing multiple repositories. The Arctos and Tesca, two powerful rivers in the region, were too remote to be a power source. So the facility was built near geothermal vents and powered exclusively by geothermal energy. Steam from vents powered Gregor's generators and heated the rest of the complex.

The Complex

The complex consisted mainly of a multistory building (illustration 19, page 123). The north wing bordered the botanical gardens. Classrooms and lecture halls occupied the first, second, and third floors of the northeast and northwest corners. In the middle, the rectory and the kitchen were on the first and second floor, respectively, and the archives were on the third floor. Gregor's extensive library fully occupied the fourth floor.

The west wing was devoted to quarters. Where feasible, researchers and laboratory personnel and their families quartered on the same floor as the lab where they worked. Everyone else quartered where a room was available. A block of rooms was set aside on the first floor for seasonal visitors. Each room was outfitted with a bed, a small dresser, a desk, two chairs, and a narrow armoire—reminiscent of the rooms at Erwina's schoolhouse. Families with children were allotted two rooms. All rooms had connecting doors which could be locked for privacy. There were no windows in order to achieve better insulation. Winter storms could be quite severe. Winter temperatures averaged minus twenty to minus thirty degrees and could fall to minus fifty.

The center hosted the laboratories. The first-floor laboratory was reserved for *H. sapiens*, the second floor for *H. transformans*, the third floor for hybrids—both human and animal—and the fourth floor for dragon and dinosaur studies. A special section of the fourth floor was set aside to secure the DNA of H'Ester and her descendants.

A portion of the south side was carved out for treating the sick and injured. The surgery and delivery suites were located on the first floor, an inpatient hospital was on the second floor, and outpatient clinics were on the third floor.

On the east side, the first floor served as a parlor and receiving area for travelers. Visitors could rest and have refreshments while security screened them, verifying their identity and purpose for coming to Gregor. It also had a small conference room. The second floor consisted of office space for security, and housed a weapons depot. Gregor did not forge weapons.

H'Aleth and Erwina provided supplies for an armed self-defense, if needed. Gregor's scouts were trained at Erwina and apprenticed at H'Aleth. All of them could make their own weapons. The third floor consisted of office space for administration and storage.

A segment for triage and decontamination was carved out on the south end, leading into the hospital section. A similar segment was set aside on the north end for prisoner holding cells until dangerous intruders could be escorted out of Gregor's territory—typically right before a winter storm.

The Gregorians also built a glass-enclosed two-story botanical garden to grow fruit, vegetables, herbs, and selected fruit and nut trees. It also hosted beehives and butterflies. These insects served as pollinators. The bees also provided a supply of honey. The fruit and nut trees provided branches where butterfly caterpillars could hang their chrysalises. H'Aleth's artisans crafted individual panes of thick glass, while their armorists crafted the metal structure that would host each pane. They also traveled to Gregor to help assemble the structure. The joints between each section were flexible to allow each one to move independently.

On the east end of the botanical gardens, the Gregorians built a stable to house horses, goats, chickens, and any wayward pets until they were claimed. Family pets stayed with their human companions in the west wing.

On the west end of the complex, on the other side of a covered, unheated walkway—the buffer zone—the repositories were embedded in glacial ice. They were joined by another large repository: the frozen food section. Although the walkway was protected from harsh winds and bad weather, it did not keep out the cold. Proper clothing in this area was critical. Hypothermia could develop within ten minutes at minus thirty degrees and within five minutes at minus fifty degrees.

Secure Repositories

Just before Rafe Cassius attacked the house of H'Aleth, all of H'Aleth's pedigrees and genetic records were sent to Gregor to save them and keep them out of the foundation's hands in the event H'Aleth fell. H'Aleth did indeed fall when it was consumed by dragon fire. With the subsequent threat to Erwina, the latter did the same. Thus, Gregor became the official repository of all *H. transformans* pedigrees and genomes. It was also the primary repository of all DNA samples collected, regardless of source.

Gregor had several DNA repositories based on the source of the DNA. The first main repository held human DNA. It had two directories: one for *H. sapiens* and one for *H. transformans*. H'Ester's DNA was held apart in a separate hidden repository, along with those of her descendants who also had three transforming X chromosomes. Few people knew of its existence, and only the chief geneticist and chief medical officer had access to it. The DNA housed in this repository was not available to researchers.

The second main repository contained the DNA of native plants and animals with one exception. Dragon DNA was housed in a separate restricted repository. Only the chief geneticist and chief veterinarian had access to this repository.

Gregor created a third main repository for hybrid species. It also had two DNA directories: one for altered *H. transformans*, and one for hybrid animals. Only the chief geneticist, chief medical officer, and chief veterinarian had access to these repositories.

Last but not least, Gregor established a repository for fossil DNA. Ironically, Gregor had more dinosaur DNA than dragon DNA. In addition to the fossils found in the subarctic region, fossils were abundant throughout the sandstone formations in the southwestern regions. Tar pits scattered throughout these mountains were another source. These were often discovered by accident when H'Aletheans traveled to the pits to gather the tar. Fossils could be found also in silt and clay deposits where rivers had once flowed. The H'Aletheans sent most of their fossil discoveries to Erwina for educational purposes. Erwina had an historian, who also served as an archeologist and a geologist. With Gregor's paleontologist, the three collaborated to identify many of the fossils found in caves and near archeological digs.

Most of Gregor's specimens were collected by the other two houses.

Both could conduct routine genetic testing and analysis. H'Aleth and Erwina would send the specimens to Gregor for specialized testing or to identify DNA they could not. Gregor's biologists, veterinarians, and geneticists romped through all the mysterious specimens they received from H'Aleth, Erwina, and even Biogenics.

All repositories were carefully guarded, and access was limited to a need-to-know basis. With the exception of the hidden repository, all others were available to researchers whose studies were approved by Gregor's independent review board.

Supplemental Notes and Citations

Earthquakes

Most earthquakes are caused by pressure built up along a fault line which subsequently slips (Doocy, *et al.*, 2013). They can also be caused by volcanic eruptions. People typically do not notice low-magnitude earthquakes (e.g., less than 3); however, they usually do perceive earthquakes with a magnitude of 4.5 and above. Buildings can sustain significant damage and humans suffer significant injury from earthquakes greater than 6.

APPENDIX K
THE CASSIUS FORTRESS

Angus Cassius originally built his fortress (illustration 27, page 210) to serve as his command center from which his forces would spread out and conquer other territories. He subsequently expanded its purpose to focus on the science of genetics and genetic engineering. Consequently, within the confines of the fortress, he built a large research facility for this purpose. The flow rate of the River Taurus—1,850,000 cubic feet per second during its descent—was more than enough to power the generators his geneticists demanded. They insisted that no coal-fired generators be used to power their laboratories.

The research building also housed the quarters for the Cassius family at its top and had an expansive cellar for storage. Subsequently, most of the cellar was converted into prison cells—the dungeon. Captive *H. transformans* prisoners, destined to become hybrid humanoids, were kept there.

After Raephela's edict that there would be no more hybrid humanoids, the captives were repurposed for slave labor. Yet they continued to be housed in the dungeon. Over time, the number of prisoners in each cell decreased. Guards presumed that the decline was due to illness, injury, or fatal attempts to escape. As the captives' population thinned, the guards finally moved all prisoners closer to the dungeon's entrance—for the guards' convenience.

With this change, the population of prisoners curiously stabilized. *Probably due to better conditions*, thought one guard.

Not so. As prisoners were allocated to the farthermost and darkest cell in the dungeon, some prisoners, chosen by lot, would escape through a tunnel. It had been dug long ago from the cell's back wall and reached into the forest to the east. A few prisoners would always remain behind to close its entrance and cover it with mortar. This also ensured that the cell was never left empty. The few left behind would be among those who escaped next.

When the prisoners were consolidated in cells closer to the guards' quarters, their only chance to escape was lost. The vacant cells were repurposed for storage. Over time, the tunnel fell into disrepair and degraded. Yet a remnant of it remained. Small animals such as moles, gophers, and groundhogs found it a convenient avenue for crossing the open area beyond the fortress without attracting attention. They dug a myriad of interconnecting tunnels branching off the original one, creating a vast underground network.

Prisoners were tasked to plow over the area where a garden had once flourished. Subsequently, additional armories were built there. Outdoor cages once reserved for human prisoners were used to house native animals caught by hunters. Guards moved the hybrid animal cages outside the fortress walls. Should a hybrid escape, it could not wreak havoc on the interior of the fortress.

APPENDIX L
ERWINA

Erwina had two natural barriers—the mountains to their north and the River Ferveo, which coursed north to south. The southeastern heel of the Biogenics territory and the northwestern head of H'Aleth's Caput Canis overlapped with a buffer zone of open territory between them.

The River Ferveo remained a formidable barrier to anyone who wanted to reach Erwina's main village, colloquially called "the compound." The people of H'Aleth and Erwina learned long ago not to build bridges over waterways. The Ferveo served as a natural barrier to anyone who did not know how to navigate it—or fly over it. No one was going to swim across it.

Erwina's geography and placement sheltered it from Cassius territory and the raids the foundation launched against its foes. Incursions were few, including one not long ago when hunters came looking for a paleontologist. Yet years ago, Erwina was attacked directly by Rafe Cassius after he destroyed H'Aleth's first settlement. Although Rafe was defeated, it was not through Erwina's force of arms. Erwina remained vigilant ever after. Scouts were still its sole and best defense.

Preparations

The "compound" was a village which housed Erwina's seat of government, research facilities, schoolhouse, and a wide range of other endeavors. It was secluded within a dense forest and encompassed by an artificial ridge, which served as its outer boundary line. The ridge extended well beyond the visible confines of the village.

When Headmaster Joseph sent many of Erwina's scouts to augment H'Aleth's and Biogenics's forces, the faculty remained behind to guard Erwina's borders. Most of the faculty who were experienced scouts set a guard on the northern and eastern borders. The remainder of the faculty and form IV students (ages seventeen to eighteen) guarded the inner perimeter around the compound. Form IV students who were qualified in archery and swordsmanship were issued weapons for defense only.

Form III juniors and seniors (ages fifteen to sixteen) guarded the schoolhouse. They had already attended some if not all of the classes on scouting and surveillance. Form III seniors qualified in archery were issued a bow and a sheath of arrows. All form III juniors and seniors and form IV students were issued sheathed hunting knives, primarily for utility purposes and, if necessary, for defense.

Form I, II, and III freshmen and sophomores went into the tunnels. Students were sorted into groups of eight to twelve with a designated form III sophomore as the leader.

All students were trained to avoid confrontation with an invader if at all possible. Only form IV students and faculty were allowed to confront an enemy. Sometimes the best defense is a good offense. If faculty and form IV students were overcome, form III juniors and seniors would descend into the tunnels and lead the escape from the schoolhouse. Many drills had prepared the students for such an event.

In preparation for a possible siege, the faculty and students transferred large supplies of food, water, medicine, and other necessities to bolster hidden caches of supplies already in the tunnel system. In the event the compound had to be evacuated, faculty and students had assigned tasks.

Students who were experienced equestrians assisted with the horses. Students who had completed rotations in the veterinary hospital, aviaries, and in animal husbandry assisted faculty in releasing wildlife; packing up chickens and beehives; and herding goats, sheep, cows, and other animals housed at the compound.

Students who were *H. transformans* and twelve years of age and older (form II seniors and above) could transform into their alternate species. Those who were *H. sapiens* and those who were under age eleven could not transform. A few *H. transformans* girls between eleven and twelve years of age did have the capability. Ordinarily, they were not allowed to do so because they had not yet taken the classes on transformation. Yet most parents had already taught their children about transformation in the event of an emergency. Faculty quickly gave these students a crash course in transformation.

APPENDIX M
Cast of Characters
(In alphabetical order)

Andrei, Headmaster (X^T,Y)—dual-hatted as governor of Gregor and dean of genetics studies in Gregor's doctoral program.

Barrett (X, Y)—a hunter who led an incursion to a southeastern swamp at Raephela's direction. He and his hunting party were wiped out by an *Odontus pristis.*

Bowen (X^T, Y)—Erwina's chief of animal husbandry.
Lineage: Born into the house of Erwina. Both parents were *H. transformans*, whose own parents brought them to Erwina just before the fall of H'Aleth.
Transformed within *Bovidae* family. Alternate species: Angus bull.
Biography: Specialized in animal husbandry and trained in veterinary medicine at Gregor before returning to Erwina to serve as chief.

Cassius, Angus (X^T, Y)—patriarch of the Cassius family and head of the Cassius Foundation.
Lineage: Unknown.
Transformed within *Suidae, Cervidae,* and *Bovidae* species. Alternate species: Great horned (wild) boar, elk, and bighorn sheep.
Biography: Founded one of the two largest organizations conducting research into the genetics of *H. transformans*, during the time when H'Aleth was first settled by Edvar and Ruth H'Aleth. Initially, Angus used the abilities of *H. transformans* to gain control of other companies and their resources. Subsequently, he extended his reach to encompass entire territories. Ultimately, he intended to establish himself as

absolute ruler over all territories. The Biogenics Corporation became his chief competitor and archrival.

Cassius, Raephela (X, X^T)—daughter of Rhaphedra.

Lineage: Direct descendant of Angus Cassius.

Transformed within *Suidae* and *Bovidae* species. Alternate species: wild boar.

Biography: Took control of the Cassius Foundation after the death of her uncle Rafus.

Cassius, Rafe (trisomy 2X^T, Y)—inherited leadership of the Cassius Foundation.

Lineage: Grandson of Rex Cassius and great-great-grandson of Angus Cassius.

Transformed within *Suidae, Cervidae,* and *Bovidae* species. Alternate species: Great horned (wild) boar, mule deer, and bighorn sheep.

Biography: Brother of Raphedra and Rafus, he dominated his two siblings and took control of the Cassius Foundation. His preferred alternate species was a wild boar. Originally a handsome and well-built man, he became trapped—part man, part boar—when he forced a transformation too aggressively. He survived the aborted transformation, most likely due to the second transforming X chromosome, and continued to head the foundation. The Biogenics Corporation continued to be the foundation's archrival. During the battle to invade Erwina, he challenged a great gray dragon to single combat and was killed.

Cassius, Rafina (X, X^T)—daughter of Raephela, mother of Rhaferra.

Cassius, Rafus (X^T, Y)—younger brother of Rafe, assumed control of the Cassius Foundation after the death of Rafe; subsequently relieved of his reign when murdered by his niece, Raephela.

Cassius, Rhaphedra (X, X^T)—older sister of Rafe.

Lineage: Great-great-granddaughter of Angus Cassius.

Transformed within *Suidae* and *Bovidae* species. Alternate species: wild boar.

Biography: Oppressed by her brothers, her daughter Raephela interceded, murdering her uncles and taking the reins of the Cassius Foundation.

Cassius, Rex (X^T, Y)—inherited leadership of the Cassius Foundation.

Lineage: Grandson of Angus Cassius.

Transformed within *Suidae* species.

Alternate species: Great horned (wild) boar.

Biography: Grandson of Angus Cassius, he took over the management of the Cassius Foundation after the death of his grandfather. He continued to expand the foundation's territory and resources, largely through hostile takeovers and intimidation. He pursued his grandfather's dream of absolute rule over every territory and of establishing a royal family lineage.

Claren (X, X)—a Cassius spy posing as a biologist, intent on infiltrating Gregor. She was a hunter tasked to identify Gregor's defenses and weaknesses, and to assist her co-conspirator in stealing DNA samples from Gregor's repositories.

Cole (X, Y)—an experienced lead hunter under Raephela. Raephela frequently called upon him and his band of hunters for a variety of tasks.

Cooper (X, Y)—one of Cole's hunters.

Dawson (X, Y)—one of Cole's hunters, often Cole's second in command.

Dimas, Doctor (X, Y)—one of Gregor's geneticists.

Edrew (X^T, Y)—H'Aleth's wildlife specialist and veterinarian.

Lineage: Born into the house of H'Aleth in exile. Both parents were *H. transformans*, originally from H'Aleth.

Transformed within *Felidae* family. Alternate species: lynx.

Biography: Raised in Erwina. After studying veterinarian medicine at Gregor, transferred to H'Aleth and documented native species still remaining in H'Aleth territory. As a lynx, learned to be a master of stealth and remain hidden in order to observe other species.

Edric (trisomy 2X^T, Y)—son of H'Ester and Evan.

Lineage: Born into the House of H'Aleth as it was being restored; descendant of Ruth through H'Ester.

Genealogy: He inherited a second X chromosome from H'Ester, who inherited it when her mother had an *in vitro* fertilization from an unknown male. Edric's wild boar genes originated with his mother, H'Ester, who carried the genes of a boar; however, they were never expressed in her. Since they were not previously seen in H'Ester's maternal ancestors, geneticists presumed that she inherited them from her unknown biological father. Edric also inherited avian genes from his mother.

Transformed across multiple mammalian classes, including *Canidae*, *Suidae*, *Felidae*, and *Dragonidae*; and a single avian class, *Accipitridae*. Alternate species: gray wolf, gray fox, wild boar, cougar, red dragon, Cooper's hawk.

Biography: Edric's name was derived in part from his ancestor, Edvar, who was the first master of the House of H'Aleth.

Edwin (X^T, Y)—a form III student kayaker, attacked by a varanacrocactutus while kayaking on the River Ferveo.

Eldar (X^T, Y)—son of H'Ariel, and H'Adrianna's brother.

Eowen (X^T, Y)—one of Erwina's lead scouts.

Lineage: Born into the house of Erwina; descendent of an Erwinian lineage of *H. transformans*.

Transformed within *Cervidae* family. Alternate species: mule deer.

Biography: Raised and educated at Erwina. Interned as a scout at the northeast outpost and became lead scout in the northeast region. He was one of the scouts recognized by a nearby clan of great gray dragons that lived in the neighboring northern mountain range.

Erwen, Master (X^T, Y)—faculty at Erwina's schoolhouse, Edric's mentor.

Lineage: Born into the house of Erwina; descendent of an Erwinian lineage of *H. transformans*.

Transformed within *Canidae* family. Alternate species: gray wolf.

Biography: Taught martial arts and scouting, proctored students in training to become scouts.

Evan (X^T, Y)—spouse of H'Ester, master of the House of H'Aleth.

Lineage: Born into the House of Erwina; descendent of an Erwinian lineage of *H. transformans*.

Transformed within *Canidae* family. Alternate species: red fox, gray wolf.

Biography: A skilled scout, he first met H'Ester (then known as Ruwena) on a field trip into the northeastern mountains. Later, he met her again on a scouting exercise. When he was badly injured, she stayed by his side until he recovered. Thereafter, they remained close. They finally wed after the defeat of the Cassius Foundation and oversaw the restoration of the House of H'Aleth.

Evard (X^T, Y)—chief of security under H'Ariel.

Lineage: Born into the House of H'Aleth in exile. Both parents were *H. transformans*.

Transformed within *Cervidae* family. Alternate species: elk.

Biography: Raised in Erwina and transferred to H'Aleth to assist with maintaining security when H'Aleth was an outpost populated largely by hybridized *H. transformans* who had escaped from the Cassius

Foundation. Evard had trained under Master Titus at Erwina and subsequently under Matron Kavarova at H'Aleth. He was a lead scout for many years. Upon the passing of H'Ester, Matron Kavarova returned to Erwina. H'Ariel appointed Evard to be her chief of security.

Finn (X, Y)—an experienced lead guard under Raephela.

Greyson, Doctor (X, X)—Gregor's lead geneticist for the first-floor laboratory.

H'Adrianna ($2X^T$)—daughter of H'Ariel.
Lineage: Great-granddaughter of H'Ester and direct descendent of Ruth through the maternal line.
Genealogy: She inherited a single X^T from both her mother and her father.
Transformed across multiple mammalian and avian classes, including *Canidae, Felidae, Mustelidae, Falconidae, Strigidae, Lontra*. Alternate species: gray wolf, gray fox, cougar, badger, river otter, falcon, great horned owl.

H'Ariel ($2X^T$)—mistress of the House of H'Aleth upon the death of her mother.
Lineage: Daughter of H'Ester and direct descendant of Ruth through the maternal line.
Genealogy: She inherited a single X^T from both her mother and her father.
Transformed across multiple mammalian and avian classes, including *Canidae, Felidae, Mustelidae, Falconidae, Strigidae*. Alternate species: red wolf, red fox, cougar, badger, peregrine falcon, great horned owl.
Biography: Born two years before her sister, H'Edwina, both grew up together and remained very close throughout their lives. Despite the closeness of their age, the two of them could not be confused. H'Ariel had dark, brown-black hair and amber eyes, as did her mother. H'Edwina had flaming red hair and blue eyes. Whenever a gray

and red wolf were seen together, people knew who they were. Their alternate species complemented each other and provided significant advantages when the two of them scouted together, which they often did. H'Ariel had two children, a daughter, H'Adrianna, and a son, Eldar.

H'Edwina ($2X^T$)—sister of H'Ariel and Edric.

Lineage: Daughter of H'Ester and great-great-great-granddaughter of Ruth through the maternal line.

Genealogy: She inherited two X^T chromosomes, one from each parent.

Transformed across multiple mammalian and avian classes, including *Canidae, Felidae, Lontra, Falconidae, Strigidae.* Alternate species: gray wolf, gray fox, lynx, river otter, golden eagle, long-eared owl.

Biography: See H'Ariel. Married into the house of Gregor and lived with her husband there. She would fly back to H'Aleth during the spring thaw to visit with her family for a few weeks.

Hathor (X^T,Y)—H'Aleth's lead scout at the Panthera outpost.

H'Ester (Ruwena) ($3X^T$)—mistress of the House of H'Aleth in exile and upon its restoration.

Lineage: Daughter of H'Eleanora and great-great-granddaughter of Ruth through the maternal line.

Genealogy: She inherited an autosomal $2X^T$ chromosome from an unknown male. She also inherited the chromosome fragment from her mother, H'Eleanora. As a $3X^T$, she possessed the capability to express it.

Transformed across multiple mammalian and avian classes, including *Canidae, Felidae, Accipitridae, Strigidae, Lontra, Dragonidae.* Alternate species: gray wolf, red fox, cougar, Cooper's hawk, long-eared woodland owl, river otter, red dragon.

Biography: One of two surviving descendants of Ruth through the maternal line after the destruction of H'Aleth. She became mistress of the House of H'Aleth in exile after the death of H'Ilgraith. With the support of the House of Erwina, she reestablished the House of H'Aleth. She married Evan of the house of Erwina, who then became master of the House of H'Aleth. Her daughters, H'Arianna and H'Edwina, continued the maternal lineage of Ruth. Both carried the fragment which was first found in their mother. Its genetic heritage was unknown.

Ivana (X, X^T)—Gregor's chief of security.

Iranapolis, Master (X^T,Y)—Faculty at Erwina's schoolhouse.
Lineage: Born into the house of Erwina.
Transformed within *Suidae* family. Alternate species: wild boar.
Biography: Taught wrestling, boxing, martial arts.

Joseph, Headmaster (X^T,Y)—governor of Erwina and dean of Erwina's schoolhouse.

Jozefa, Doctor (X^T,Y)—physician, northeast outpost of Erwina.
Lineage: Born into the House of Erwina; descendent of an Erwinian lineage of *H. transformans.*
Transformed across *Cervidae* species. Alternate species: white-tailed deer.
Biography: Schooled in medicine and genetics at Gregor. He specialized in the genetics of corrupted creatures and their outcomes. He often visited the northeast outpost because of the number of sightings in that region. Supervised medical students and interns rotating to Erwina.

Kaden (X^T, Y)—one of Gregor's laboratory technicians.

Karel (X^T,Y)—chief geologist at Gregor.
Transformed within *Suidae* family. Alternate species: wild boar.
Biography: Surveyed Gregor's territory and beyond. Collaborated with

volcanologists to identify the magma chamber overlying a cauldron of boiling mud and steam. He was instrumental in finding and identifying fossil remains of plants and animals from the Cretaceous period.

Kavarova, Matron ($2X^T$)—chief of security at H'Aleth upon its restoration.
Lineage: Born into the House of H'Aleth; as a descendent of Ruth, she was a sister in the House of H'Aleth until she moved to Erwina.
Transformed across *Canidae, Felidae,* and *Strigidae* families. Alternate species: mountain gray wolf, gray fox, cougar, great horned owl.
Biography: Married into the House of Erwina and moved there before the destruction of H'Aleth. She returned to H'Aleth to serve as its chief of security during H'Ester's tenure as mistress of the House of H'Aleth. Upon the death of H'Ester, she returned to Erwina and the schoolhouse where she taught surveillance techniques.

Khristina (X, X^T)—paleontologist at Gregor.
Transformed across *Bovidae* families. Alternate species: mountain goat.
Biography: Born into the house of Gregor. She often accompanied her parents, both geologists, on trips across the landscape, looking for mineral deposits and often finding dinosaur remains. She became fascinated and after advanced study in biology and genetics became Gregor's first paleontologist. She often accompanied Erwina's geologist on student field trips.

Lilith ($2X^T$)—wife of Edric.
Transformed across *Canidae* and *Felidae* families. Alternate species: malamute, lynx.
Biography: Born into the house of Erwina, attended school there, and interned as an agriculturist in H'Aleth territory where she encountered Edric.

Logan (X, Y)—one of Cole's hunters.

Merena, Madam ($2X^T$)—faculty member at Erwina's schoolhouse.
Lineage: Born into the House of Erwina; descendent of an Erwinian lineage of *H. transformans*.
Transformed across *Canidae* and *Felidae* families. Alternate species: gray fox, jaguar.
Biography: Taught swimming and diving skills.

Mason (X, Y)—chief geneticist under Raephela.

Mikalov, Master (X^T, Y)—chief geneticist at Erwina and a faculty member.
Lineage: Born into the house of Gregor and moved to Erwina; descendent of a Gregorian lineage of *H. transformans*.
Transformed within *Cervidae* family. Alternate species: caribou.
Biography: Taught genetics classes at Erwina's schoolhouse.

Miriam (X, X^T)—Erwina's marine biologist.

Morloff, Master (X^T, Y)—expert kayaker who could traverse category V rapids; instructed all students in basic kayaking, and proctored advanced students as they honed their skills.

O'Connor (X, Y)—one of Cole's hunters.

Olsen (X, Y)—Raephela's chief lieutenant and lead strategist for the war with H'Aleth and Biogenics.

Paulson (X, Y)—a Cassius geneticist sent by Raephela to infiltrate Gregor. He was tasked to acquire DNA from Gregor's repositories, preferably dragon and dinosaur DNA.

Rorik (X^T, Y)—an experienced and savvy lead agent in Gregor's security force.

Rulinda, Matron (2X^T)—chief of security at Erwina, after Matron Kavarova retired.

Lineage: Born into the house of Erwina. Her mother named her Rulinda in memory of Ruth, the first mistress of the House of H'Aleth.

Transformed across *Cervidae, Felidae,* and *Falconidae* families. Alternate species: white-tailed deer, lynx, falcon.

Biography: Also served as faculty at Erwina's schoolhouse; taught classes on security measures for young students, and proctored apprentices in security.

Ryker (X, Y)—geologist for the Cassius Foundation under Raephela.

Stoval (X, Y)—H'Aleth's chief boat master.

Theodora, Matron (2X^T)—faculty at Erwina's schoolhouse.

Lineage: Born into the house of Gregor; married into the house of Erwina.

Transformed across *Canidae, Felidae,* and *Strigidae* families. Alternate species: arctic fox, cougar, arctic owl.

Biography: Taught classes on transformation and proctored students practicing transformation.

Theovolan [thē-ō-*vō*-lăn]—alpha male of a large clan of great gray dragons.

Biography: His clan had reached an accord with the H'Aletheans to keep watch for any sign that the Cassius Foundation was rising again. They also agreed to protect their respective clan members from being killed or captured by hunters and hybrids.

Titus, Master (X^T, Y)—Erwina's chief of security.

Lineage: Born into the house of Erwina; descendent of an Erwinian lineage of *H. transformans.*

Transformed within *Canidae* family. Alternate species: gray wolf.

Biography: Taught safety measures, and surveillance and scouting with Matron Kavora.

Tyler (X, Y)—a Cassius Foundation surveyor under Raephela.

Vasgyl (X^T, Y)—one of Gregor's scouts.

Viktor (X^T, Y)—one of Gregor's geneticists.

Warren (X^T, Y)—scout, north and northeastern regions.
Lineage: Born into the house of Erwina; descendent of an Erwinian lineage of *H. transformans.*
Transformed within *Ursidae* family. Alternate species: brown bear.
Biography: Raised in Erwina and a staunch friend and ally of H'Ester and Evan.

Wes (X^T, Y)—scout and driver of the wagon transporting seven children, including H'Adrianna and Eldar, from Erwina to the main village and estate at H'Aleth.

William ("Will") (X^T, Y)—H'Ariel's spouse.
Biography: Born into the House of H'Aleth; descendent of a lineage of H'Aletheans.
Transformed within *Cervidae* family. Alternate species: red deer.

Wyatt (X^T,Y)—geologist and faculty at Erwina.
Transformed within *Cervidae* family. Alternate species: red deer (elk).
Biography: Taught geology, and collaborated with Khristina on student field trips to combine geology with paleontology.

Yana (X, X^T)—one of Gregor's geneticists.

Yelena ($2X^T$)—Gregor's chief geneticist.
Lineage: Born into the house of Gregor. Both parents were *H. transformans.*
Transformed within the *Canidae* family. Alternate species: arctic wolf, arctic fox.

Biography: Raised in Gregor by parents, both of whom were scientists. Her mother was a geneticist. Educated at Erwina, as were all children, then returned to Gregor for advanced preparation in science and genetics. Became a researcher in genetics.

ACKNOWLEDGMENTS

I wish to express my gratitude to Mrs. Suzanne Smith Sundburg, BA, Phi Beta Kappa, for her expertise as a copyeditor, to Ms. Esther Ferington for her expertise as a developmental editor, and Dr. George Crossman (posthumously) for his expertise as a line editor.

I wish to acknowledge Mr. Ross Cuippa, art director, and Mr. Carl Cleanthes, creative director, and the graphic artists and illustrators of Epic Made who provided the dramatic scenes and vivid renderings of hybrid creatures featured in the narrative.

GLOSSARY

Aneuploidy—an abnormal number of chromosomes for a given species.

Autosomes—nonreproductive chromosomes.

Blastocyst—earliest stage of embryonic development in which cells of a fertilized ovum begin to differentiate.

Chromosome—large groups or sets of genes, clustered together in a predetermined sequence, and bundled together to form a single structure that compresses DNA into a relatively small area.

Clade—a group of organisms that includes all descendants with a common ancestor (a monophyletic group), e.g., mammals, birds.

Confluence—where two or more bodies of water (e.g., rivers) meet.

Crown group—a clade that includes both living and extinct members of a group. *See also* Stem group.

Cubic feet per second (CFS)—the amount (volume) of river water that passes a given point in one second.

Deoxyribonucleic acid (DNA)—genetic material comprising gene sequences (nucleotides) supported by a sugar-and-phosphate backbone.

Drop—a steep descent in a river. Also refers to an abrupt drop in water level beyond an obstruction or barrier to the flow of water (e.g., a large boulder). *See also* Hole.

Dysplastic—abnormal configuration or shape, indicating deranged development.

Eddy—a swirl of water formed by an obstruction in a stream of water.

Extant—something that is still in existence.

Founder—the individual (or gene) in which a characteristic was first seen and which was inherited subsequently by offspring.

Gene—the basic building block of genetic matter.

Coding genes determine the physical composition of a component used in building a biologic structure (e.g., an amino acid).

Noncoding genes influence the function of other genes.

Essential—a gene that is necessary for an organism to develop, function, and survive.

Dominant—the member of a gene pair that is active (expressed) in the phenotype.

Recessive—the member of a gene pair that is not active.

Imprinted—the member of a gene pair that carries a "stamp" or a "tag" that effectively turns off that gene.

Gene expression—the physical reflection in both structure and function of an organism's genetic code (genotype).

Genetic homology—gene sequences that are conserved and reused among classes within the animal kingdom and a few even across kingdoms. The closer the degree of genetic homology between species, the more closely they are related.

Genome—the total gene complement of an individual organism.

Genotype—an individual's overall genetic composition, whether or not it is expressed as an observable characteristic.

Graben—a downward displacement of the land caused by two parallel faults, one on either side.

Heterozygous gene pair—each member of a gene pair has a variation on its genetic code.

Hole—an abrupt drop in water level caused by the diversion of water around an object obstructing its flow. To refill the gap, river water flows backward, creating turbulence.

Homozygous gene pair—both members of a gene pair have *exactly* the same genetic code.

Ledges—relatively flat slabs of rock created when layers of rocks are sheared off in an earthquake or landslide, resulting in a drop to a lower level. They are also called stair-steps or shelves.

Meiosis—the process of creating gametes (ova, sperm) wherein each gamete has only one of each chromosome for a total of twenty-three chromosomes (haploid set) instead of a set of paired chromosomes for a total of forty-six chromosomes (diploid set). This is a two-step process in which the original cell divides twice, leading to a gamete with a haploid set of chromosomes.

Mitosis—a crucial step in the process of cell division wherein certain types of nonreproductive cells replicate, effectively cloning themselves. The cell's paired chromosomes are replicated, temporarily resulting in a complement of fifty-two. The pairs are subsequently separated into two sets of forty-six chromosomes—the original set and a duplicated set. When the cell finishes dividing, the duplicated set of forty-six chromosomes has been incorporated into the new cell.

Monophyletic group—a group (-phyletic) of species with a single (mono-) common ancestor that also includes all descendants of that ancestor. *See also* Clade.

Monosomy—one member of a chromosome pair is missing.

Nondisjunction—failure of a pair of chromosomes to separate properly when a cell divides (in mitosis or meiosis), leading to an abnormal number of chromosomes (aneuploidy). The parent (dividing) cell is left with an extra chromosome (trisomy) that the daughter cell never receives and is therefore deprived of that chromosome (monosomy).

Phenotype—an individual's observable manifestations (physical characteristics) of genetic composition.

Phylogenetics—the genetic relationship of one or more groups of organisms based on genetic profiles, often comparing differences and similarities.

Point mutation—a change to a single base pair (e.g., A–T, C–G) within a DNA sequence (e.g., a gene).

Scutes—protective thickened external horny or bony plates that cover the body of an animal, especially their head, neck, and back.

Stem group—extinct members of a group that are closely related to a crown group and likely gave rise to members of the crown group. Hence, they are considered the base from which other crown groups evolved.

Tapetum lucidum—an extra layer of tissue found at the back of the eyes of nocturnal animals; reflects light so that the eyes appear to glow (eyeshine) and reflect color (e.g., red, green, blue, etc.).

Therapod—a clade of dinosaurs identified by specific physical characteristics; originally carnivorous and ultimately branched into other noncarnivorous species.

Translocation—movement of one part of a chromosome to another place on the same chromosome or to another chromosome; usually occurs as a result of a chromosome break.

Transposons (transposable elements)—sequences of DNA that can change their location within and across chromosomes.

Tributary—a stream, creek, or *river* that flows into another river or a lake.

Triceratops—family *Ceratopsidae*; herbaceous, horned dinosaurs; has a large bony frill and three horns on the skull.

Trisomy—a pair of chromosomes has an extra member [e.g., Down's syndrome (trisomy 21)].

Trisomy X—a female has three X chromosomes (XXX genotype).

Tyrannosauroids—non-avian carnivorous therapod dinosaurs of the Cretaceous period, descended from Sauropods.

Vestigial—a rudimentary remnant of a structure, not fully developed and often misshapen.

REFERENCES

Chapter 1. A New Settlement

No references.

Chapter 2. Premonitions

No references.

Chapter 3. A Wary Respite (Genome, DNA, Chromosomes)

Chen, B., Yusuf, M., Hashimoto, T., *et al.* (2017). Three-dimensional positioning and structure of chromosomes in a human prophase nucleus. *Science Advances*, 3(7), e1602231. https://doi.org/10.1126/sciadv.1602231.

Deakin, J. E., Potter, S., O'Neill, R., *et al.* (2019.) Chromosomics: Bridging the Gap between Genomes and Chromosomes. *Genes*, 10(8), 627. https://doi.org/10.3390/genes10080627.

Frixione, E., and Ruiz-Zamarripa, L. (2019.) The "scientific catastrophe" in nucleic acids research that boosted molecular biology. *The Journal of Biological Chemistry*, 294(7), 2249–2255. https://doi.org/10.1074/jbc.CL119.007397.

Minchin, S., and Lodge, J. (2019.) Understanding biochemistry: structure and function of nucleic acids. *Essays in Biochemistry*, 63(4), 433–456. https://doi.org/10.1042/EBC20180038.

Travers, A., and Muskhelishvili, G. (2015). DNA structure and function. *The FEBS journal*, 282(12), 2279–2295. https://doi.org/10.1111/febs.13307.

Zahn, L. M., Purnell, B. A., Ash, C. (2019.) The manifestation of the genome. *Science, 365(6460), 1394-1395.* doi: 10.1126/science.aaz4392.

Chapter 4. A New Lineage (Genotype/Phenotype, Homology)

Badeau, M., Lindsay, C., Blais, J., *et al.* (2017). Genomics-based non-invasive prenatal testing for detection of fetal chromosomal aneuploidy in pregnant women. *Cochrane Database Systematic Reviews*, 11(11), CD011767. https://doi.org/10.1002/14651858.CD011767.pub2.

Tschopp, P., and Tabin, C. J. (2017.) Deep homology in the age of next-generation sequencing. *Philosophical Transactions of the Royal Society B (Biological Sciences)*, 372(1713). https://doi.org/10.1098/rstb.2015.0475.

Chapter 5. Lessons Learned (Gene Synergy)

Pérez-Pérez, J. M., Candela, H., Micol, J. L. (2009.) Understanding synergy in genetic interactions. *Trends Genet*, 25(8), 368-76. doi: 10.1016/j.tig.2009.06.004.

Robson, K. J., Lehmann, D. J., Wimhurst, V. L., *et al.* (2004). Synergy between the C2 allele of transferrin and the C282Y allele of the haemochromatosis gene (HFE) as risk factors for developing Alzheimer's disease. *Journal of Medical Genetics*, 41(4), 261–265. https://doi.org/10.1136/jmg.2003.015552.

Watkinson, J., Wang, X., Zheng, T., Anastassiou, D. (2008.) Identification of gene interactions associated with disease from gene expression data using synergy networks. *BMC Systems Biology* 2, Article number: 10 (2008).

Xing, P., Chen, Y., Gao, J., Bai, L., & Yuan, Z. (2017). A fast approach to detect gene–gene synergy. *Scientific Reports*, 7(1), 16437. https://doi.org/10.1038/s41598-017-16748-w.

Chapter 6. Changing of the Guard
No references.

Chapter 7. Palace Intrigue (Aneuploidy)

No references.

Chapter 8. Branching Out (Gene Editing)

Varki, A., and Altheide, T. K. (2005). Comparing the human and chimpanzee genomes: Searching for needles in a haystack. *Genome Res,* 15, 1746–1758. doi:10.1101/gr.3737405.

Barthelemy, F., and Wein, N. (2018). Personalized gene and cell therapy for Duchenne Muscular Dystrophy. Neuromuscul Disord, pii: S0960-8966(17)31473–6. doi: 10.1016/j.nmd.2018.06.009.

Eid, A., Alshareef, S., & Mahfouz, M. M. (2018). CRISPR base editors: genome editing without double-stranded breaks. *The Biochemical Journal*, 475(11), 1955–1964. https://doi.org/10.1042/BCJ20170793.

Fry, B. G., Wroe, S., Tuuewisse, T., *et al.* (2009). A central role for venom in predation by *Varanus komodoensis* (Komodo Dragon) and the extinct giant *Varanus (Megalania) priscus. PNAS*, 106(22), 8969–8974.

Fu, B., Smith, J. D., Fuchs, R. T., *et al.* (2019). Target-dependent nickase activities of the CRISPR-Cas nucleases Cpf1 and Cas9. *Nature Microbiology*, 4(5), 888–897. https://doi.org/10.1038/s41564-019-0382-0.

Khadempar, S., Familghadakchi, S., Motlagh, R. A, *et al.* (2019). CRISPR-Cas9 in genome editing: Its function and medical applications. *J Cell Physiol*, 234(5), 5751–5761. doi:10.1002/jcp.27476.

Kim, D., Luk, K., Wolfe, S. A., Kim J. S. Evaluating and Enhancing Target Specificity of Gene-Editing Nucleases and Deaminases. (2019). *Annu Rev Biochem*, 88, 191–220. doi:10.1146/annurev-biochem-013118-111730.

Kotterman, M. A., Chalberg, T.W., Schaffer, D. V. (2015.) Viral vectors for gene therapy: Translational and clinical outlook. *Ann Rev Biomed Engin*, 17, 63–89.

Lind, A. L., Lai, Y. Y. Y., Mostovoy, Y. *et al.* (2019). Genome of the Komodo dragon reveals adaptations in the cardiovascular and chemosensory systems of monitor lizards. *Nat Ecol Evol,* 3, 1241–1252. https://doi.org/10.1038/s41559-019-0945-8.

Lundstrom, K. (2018). Viral Vectors in Gene Therapy. *Diseases (Basel, Switzerland)*, 6(2), 42. https://doi.org/10.3390/diseases6020042.

Maiuri, L., Raia, V., Kroemer, G. (2017). Strategies for the etiological therapy of cystic fibrosis. *Cell Death Differ*, 24(11), 1825–1844. doi: 10.1038/cdd.2017.126.

Nienhuis, A. W., Nathwani, A. C., Davidoff, A. M. (2017). Gene therapy for hemophilia. *Mol Ther*, 25(5), 1163–1167. doi: 10.1016/j.ymthe.2017.03.033.

Swartjes, T., Staals, R., and van der Oost, J. (2020). Editor's cut: DNA cleavage by CRISPR RNA-guided nucleases Cas9 and Cas12a. *Biochemical Society Transactions*, 48(1), 207–219. https://doi.org/10.1042/BST20190563.

VandenDriessche, T., and Chuah, M. K. (2017.) Hemophilia gene therapy: Ready for prime time? *Hum Gene Ther*, 28(11), 1013–1023. doi: 10.1089/hum.2017.116.

Chapter 9. Trials and Tribulations

No references.

Chapter 10. A New Direction

No references.

Chapter 11. An Alternate Strategy

No references.

Chapter 12. Southern Incursion (Infrared Sensory Perception, Bog Conditions)

Lynnerup, N. (2015). Bog Bodies. *Anat Rec*, 298, 1007–1012, 2015. doi.org/10.1002/ar.23138.

Roper, D. D., and Grace, M. S. (2012). Infrared sensory organs. *Cell Physiology Source Book* (Fourth Edition).

Chapter 13. Archosauria (Avian and Non-Avian Dinosaurs, Ancestral Genomes, Replicating DNA, Polymerase Chain Reaction)

Bailleul, A. M., O'Connor, J., and Schweitzer, M. H. (2019). Dinosaur paleohistology: review, trends and new avenues of investigation. *Peer J*, 7, e7764. https://doi.org/10.7717/peerj.7764.

Ghannam, M. G., Varacallo, M. Biochemistry, Polymerase Chain Reaction (PCR). In: *StatPearls*. Treasure Island (FL): StatPearls Publishing; 2020.

Griffin, D. K., Larkin, D. M., and O'Connor, R. E. (2020). Time lapse: A glimpse into prehistoric genomics. *European Journal of Medical Genetics*, 63(2), 103640. https://doi.org/10.1016/j.ejmg.2019.03.004.

Li, H., Bai, R., Zhao, Z., *et al.* (2018). Application of droplet digital PCR to detect the pathogens of infectious diseases. *Bioscience Reports*, 38(6), BSR20181170. https://doi.org/10.1042/BSR20181170.

Montanari, S. (2018). Cracking the egg: the use of modern and fossil eggs for ecological, environmental and biological interpretation. *Royal Society Open Science*, 5(6), 180006. https://doi.org/10.1098/rsos.180006.

Nicholls, H. (2005). Ancient DNA comes of age. *PLoS biology*, 3(2), e56. https://doi.org/10.1371/journal.pbio.0030056.

O'Connor, R. E., Romanov, M. N., Kiazim, L. G., *et al.* (2018). Reconstruction of the diapsid ancestral genome permits chromosome evolution tracing in avian and non-avian dinosaurs. *Nature Communications*, 9(1), 1883. https://doi.org/10.1038/s41467-018-04267-9.

Organ, C. L., Shedlock, A. M., Meade, A., *et al.* (2007.) Origin of avian genome size and structure in non-avian dinosaurs. *Nature*, 446(7132), 180–4.

Pääbo, S., Poinar, H., Serre, D., *et al.* (2004.) Genetic analyses from ancient DNA, Ann Rev Genet, 38, 645–679.

Palumbo, E., and Russo, A. (2016.) Chromosome Imbalances in Cancer: Molecular cytogenetics meets genomics. *Cytogenet Genome Res*, 150(3–4), 176–184. doi: 10.1159/000455804.

Salamon, M., Tuross, N., Arensburg, B., Weiner, S. (2005.) Relatively well preserved DNA is present in the crystal aggregates of fossil bones. *PNAS*, 102 (39), 133783–88. https://doi.org/10.1073/pnas.0503718102.

Sang, F-M., Li, X., Liu, J. (2017.) Development of Nano-Polymerase Chain Reaction and Its Application. *Chinese Journal of Analytical Chemistry*, 45(11), 1745–1753. https://doi.org/10.1016/S1872-2040(17)61051-X.

You, M., Zedong, L., Shangsheng, F., *et al.* (2020.) Ultrafast photonic PCR based on photothermal nanomaterials. *Trends in Biotechnology*, 28(6), doi: https://doi.org/10.1016/j.tibtech.2019.12.006.

Yu, M., *et al* (2017.) The principle and application of new PCR Technologies. *IOP Conf. Ser.: Earth Environ. Sci.* 100 012065. https://doi.org/10.1088/1755-1315/100/1/012065.

Chapter 14. Whither a Paleontologist (River Dynamics)

Boyer, C., Roy, A. G., Best, J. L. (2006.) Dynamics of a river channel confluence with discordant beds: Flow turbulence, bed load sediment transport, and bed morphology. *J Geophys Res*, 111, F04007. Doi: 10.1026/2005JF000458.

Chapter 15. A Chance Encounter (Theropoda, Tooth Formation, Somatotropin)

Devesa, J., Almengló, C., & Devesa, P. (2016). Multiple Effects of Growth Hormone in the Body: Is it Really the Hormone for Growth? *Clinical Medicine Insights. Endocrinology and Diabetes*, 9, 47–71. https://doi.org/10.4137/CMED.S38201.

Hendrickx, C., Hartman , S. A., Mateus, O. (2015). An Overview of Non-Avian Theropod Discoveries and Classification. *PalArch's J Vertebrate Palaeontology*, 12, 1 (2015), 1–73.

Koussoulakou, D. S., Margaritis, L. H., Koussoulakou, S. L. (2009). A curriculum vitae of teeth: Evolution, generation, regeneration. *Int J Biol Sci*, 5(3), 226-243. doi: 10.7150/ dijbs.5.226.

Lu, M., Flanagan, J. U., Langley, R. J. *et al.* (2019). Targeting growth hormone function: strategies and therapeutic applications. *Sig Transduct Target Ther*, 4, 3. https://doi.org/10.1038/s41392-019-0036-y.

Thesleff, I. (2014). Current understanding of the process of tooth formation: transfer from the laboratory to the clinic. *Australian Dent J*, 59(suppl. 1), 48–54. https://doi.org/10.1111adj.12102.

Zanno, L. E., Gillette, D. D., Albright, L. B., and Titus, A. L. (2009). A new North American therizinosaurid and the role of herbivory in "predatory" dinosaur evolution. *Proceedings. Biological Sciences*, 276(1672), 3505–3511. https://doi.org/10.1098/rspb.2009.1029.

Chapter 16. The Elusive X^T (X Chromosome, X Inactivation, Pleiotropy, Polymorphism, Epigenetics)

Balaton, B. P., Dixon-McDougall, T., Peeters, S. B., *et al.* (2018.) The eXceptional nature of the X chromosome. *Human Molecular Genetics*, 27 (R2), R242–R249. https://doi.org.10.1093/hmg/ddy148.

Disteche, C. M., and Berletch, J. B. (2015). X-chromosome inactivation and escape. *Journal of genetics*, 94(4), 591–599. https://doi.org/10.1007/s12041-015-0574-1.

Engel, N. (2015). Imprinted X chromosome inactivation offers up a double dose of epigenetics. *Proceedings of the National Academy of Sciences of the United States of America*, 112(47), 14408–14409. https://doi.org/10.1073/pnas.1520097112.

Gratten, J. and Visscher, P. M. (2016). Genetic pleiotropy in complex traits and diseases: implications for genomic medicine. *Genome*

Medicine, 8:78. doi 10.1186/s13073-016-0332-x.

Harris, C., Cloutier, M., Trotter, M, *et al.* (2019). Conversion of random X-inactivation to imprinted X-inactivation by maternal PRC2. *eLife*, 8:e44258. https://doi.org/10.7554/eLife.44258.001.

Jarrar, Y. B., and Lee, S. J. (2019). Molecular Functionality of Cytochrome P450 4 (CYP4) Genetic Polymorphisms and Their Clinical Implications. *Int J Mol Sci*, 20(17), 4274. doi: 10.3390/ijms20174274.

Jordan, D. M., Verbanck, M., Do, R. (2018). The landscape of pervasive horizontal pleiotropy in human genetic variation is driven by extreme polygenicity of human traits and diseases. http://dx.doi.org/10.2139/ssrn.3188410.

Lacal, I., and Ventura, R. (2018). Epigenetic Inheritance: Concepts, Mechanisms and Perspectives. *Front. Mol. Neurosci*, https://doi.org/10.3389/fnmol.2018.00292.

Moosavi, A., and Motevalizadeh Ardekani, A. (2016). Role of Epigenetics in Biology and Human Diseases. *Iranian Biomedical Journal*, 20(5), 246–258. https://doi.org/10.22045/ibj.2016.01.

Shvetsova, E., Sofronova, A., Monajemi, R. *et al.* (2019). Skewed X-inactivation is common in the general female population. *Eur J Hum Genet* 27, 455–465. https://doi.org/10.1038/s41431-018-0291-3.

Chapter 17. Here There and Who Knows Where (Imprinting, Ionizing Radiation, Transposons, Tracing Viral Vectors)

Blanco, Y., de Diego-Castilla, G., Viudez-Moreiras, D., *et al.* (2018). Effects of gamma and electron radiation on the structural integrity of organic molecules and macromolecular biomarkers measured by microarray immunoassays and their astrobiological implications. *Astrobiology*, 18(12). https://doi.org/10.1089/ast.2016.1645.

Bourque, G., Burns, K. H., Gehring, M., *et al.* (2018). Ten things you should know about transposable elements. *Genome Biology*, 19(1), 199. https://doi.org/10.1186/s13059-018-1577-z.

Carducci, F., Biscotti, M. A., Barucca, M., Canapa, A. (2019). Transposable elements in vertebrates: species evolution and environmental adaptation. *European Zoological J*, 86 (1), 497–503. https://doi.org/10.1080/24750263.2019.1695967.

Ferguson-Smith, A. C., and Bourc'his, D. (2018). The discovery and importance of genomic imprinting. *eLife*, 7, e42368. https://doi.org/10.7554/eLife.42368.

Garcia-Perez, J. L., Widmann, T. J., Adams, I. R. (2016). The impact of transposable elements on mammalian development. *Development*, 143: 4101–4114; doi: 10.1242/dev.132639.

Klein, S. J., and O'Neill, R. J. (2018). Transposable elements: genome innovation, chromosome diversity, and centromere conflict. *Chromosome Research,* 26(1-2), 5–23. https://doi.org/10.1007/s10577-017-9569-5.

Leopold, P. L., Ferris, B., Grinberg, I., et al. (2008). Fluorescent Virions: Dynamic Tracking of the Pathway of Adenoviral Gene Transfer Vectors in Living Cells. *Human Gene Ther*, 9(3). https://doi.org/10,1089/hum.1998.9.3-367.

Mavragani, I. V., Zacharenia, N., Spyridon, A., *et al.* (2019). Ionizing radiation and complex DNA damage: From prediction to detection challenges and biological significance. *Cancers*, 11(11), 1789. https://doi.org/10.3390/cancers11111789.

Monk, D., Mackay, D. J. G., Eggermann, T., *et al.* (2019). Genomic imprinting disorders: lessons on how genome, epigenome and environment interact. *Nat Rev Genet*, 20(4), 235–248. doi: 10.1038/s41576-018-0092-0.

Ohara, S., Sota, Y., Sato, S., Tsutsui, K. I., Iijima, T. (2017). Increased transgene expression level of rabies virus vector for transsynaptic tracing. *PLoS One*, 12(7):e0180960. doi:10.1371/journal.pone.0180960.

Platt, R. N., Vandewege, M. W., and Ray, D. A. (2018). Mammalian transposable elements and their impacts on genome evolution. *Chromosome Res* 26, 25–43. https://doi.org/10.1007/s10577-017-9570-z.

Reisz, J. A., Bansal, N., Qian, J., Zhao, W., & Furdui, C. M. (2014). Effects of ionizing radiation on biological molecules--mechanisms of damage and emerging methods of detection. *Antioxidants Redox Signaling*, 21(2), 260–292. https://doi.org/10.1089/ars.2013.5489.

Saito, Y., Kobayashi, J., Kanemaki, M. T. Komatsu, K. (2020). RIF1 controls replication initiation and homologous recombination repair in a radiation dose-dependent manner. *J Cell Science*, 133: jcs240036 doi: 10.1242/jcs.240036.

Wright, W. D., Shah, S. S., Heyer, W-D. (2018). Homologous recombination and the repair of DNA Double-Strand Breaks. *J Biol Chem*, doi: 0.1074/jbc.TM118.000372jbc.TM118.000372. https://www.jbc.org/content/early/2018/03/29/jbc.TM118.000372.full.pdf.

Yuanyuan, L., and Jinson, L. (2019). Technical advances contribute to the study of genomic imprinting. *PLoS Genetics*, https://doi.org/10.1371/journal.pgen.1008151.

Chapter 18. A New Target (mtDNA, SNP Microarrays)

Amorim, A., Fernandes, T., and Taveira, N. (2019). Mitochondrial DNA in human identification: a review. *PeerJ*, 7, e7314. https://doi.org/10.7717/peerj.7314.

Berry, N. K., Scott, R. J., Rowlings, P., Enjeti, A. (2019). Clinical Use of SNP-microarrays for the Detection of Genome-Wide Changes in Haematological Malignancies. *Crit Rev Oncol Hematol*, 142:58–67. doi: 10.1016/j.critrevonc.2019.07.016.

Bettinger, B., and Wayne, D. P. (2016). Genealogical applications for mtDNA. In: Bettinger, B.T., and Wayne, D. P., Genetic Genealogy in Practice (chapter 4). National Genealogical Society special topics series (NGS special publications no. 120).

Gao, J., Ma, L., Lei, Z., Wang, Z. (2016). Multiple detection of single nucleotide polymorphism by microarray-based resonance light scattering assay with enlarged gold nanoparticle probes. *Analyst*, 141, 1772–78.

Chapter 19. The Game's Afoot

No references.

Chapter 20. Unmasked

No references.

Chapter 21. A Grave Disappointment

Montanari, S. (2018). Cracking the egg: the use of modern and fossil eggs for ecological, environmental and biological interpretation. *Royal Society Open Science*, 5(6), 180006. https://doi.org/10.1098/rsos.180006.

Sharp, J. A., *et al.* (2011). Monotreme Reproduction and Lactation Strategy. *Encyclopedia of Dairy Sciences* (2nd edition). sciencedirect.com/topics/immunology-and-microbiology/monotreme.

Stein, K., Prondvai, E., Huang, T. *et al.* (2019). Structure and evolutionary implications of the earliest (Sinemurian, Early Jurassic) dinosaur eggs and eggshells. *Sci Rep,* 9, 4424. https://doi.org/10.1038/s41598-019-40604-8.

Chapter 22. Harbinger

No references.

Chapter 23. An Unexpected Threat

No references.

Chapter 24. A New Wrinkle (Mitosis, Meiosis, Mosaicism)

Alleva, B., and Smolikove, S. (2017). Moving and stopping: Regulation of chromosome movement to promote meiotic chromosome pairing and synapsis. *Nucleus*, 8(6), 613–624.

Campbell, I. M., Shaw, C. A., Stankiewicz, P., and Lupski, J. R. (2015). Somatic mosaicism: implications for disease and transmission genetics.

Trends in Genetics, 31(7), 382–392. https://doi.org/10.1016/j.tig.2015.03.013.

Iourov, I. Y., Vorsanova, S. G., Yurov, Y. B., & Kutsev, S. I. (2019). Ontogenetic and Pathogenetic Views on Somatic Chromosomal Mosaicism. *Genes,* 10(5), 379. https://doi.org/10.3390/genes10050379.

Ohkura, H. (2015). Meiosis: an overview of key differences from mitosis. *Cold Spring Harbor Perspectives in Biology,* 7(5), a015859. doi:10.1101/cshperspect.a015859.

Qiu, L., Ye, Z., Lin, L., *et al.* (2020). Clinical and genetic features of somatic mosaicism in facioscapulohumeral dystrophy. *J Med Genet,* pii: jmedgenet-2019-106638. doi: 10.1136/jmedgenet-2019-106638.

Wang, S., Liu, Y. Shang, Y., *et al.* (2019). Crossover Interference, Crossover Maturation and Human Aneuploidy. *Bioessays,* 41(10): e1800221.

Zickler, D., and Kleckner, N. (2015). Recombination, Pairing, and Synapsis of Homologs during Meiosis. *Cold Spring Harbor Perspectives in Biology,* 7(6), a016626. doi:10.1101/cshperspect.a016626.

Chapter 25. A Maritime Matter

No references.

Chapter 26. The Scouting Bug (Morphogens)

Bressloff, P. C., and Kim, H. (2019). Search-and-capture model of cytoneme-mediated morphogen gradient formation. *Physical Review E,* 99(5-1), 052401. https://doi.org/10.1103/PhysRevE.99.052401.

Durston A. J. (2019). What are the roles of retinoids, other morphogens, and Hox genes in setting up the vertebrate body axis? *Genesis* (New York, NY: 2000), 57(7-8), e23296. https://doi.org/10.1002/dvg.23296.

Li, P., Markson, J. S., Wang, S., *et al.* (2018). Morphogen gradient reconstitution reveals Hedgehog pathway design principles. *Science* (New York, NY), 360(6388), 543–548. https://doi.org/10.1126/science.aao0645.

Roux, M., and Zaffran, S. (2016). Hox Genes in Cardiovascular Development and Diseases. *Journal of Developmental Biology*, 4(2), 14. https://doi.org/10.3390/jdb4020014.

Sagner, A., and Briscoe, J. (2017). Morphogen interpretation: concentration, time, competence, and signaling dynamics. *Wiley Interdisciplinary Reviews. Developmental Biology*, 6(4), e271. https://doi.org/10.1002/wdev.271.

Wu, F., Zhang, Y., Sun, B., *et al.* (2017). Hedgehog Signaling: From Basic Biology to Cancer Therapy. *Cell Chemical Biology*, 24(3), 252–280. https://doi.org/10.1016/j.chembiol.2017.02.010.

Chapter 27. Ramping up (Box Jellyfish Venom, Saber-Toothed Cats, Dental Stem Cells)

Bansal, R., and Jain, A. (2015). Current overview on dental stem cells applications in regenerative dentistry. *J Natural Sci, Biol, and Med*, 6(1), 29–34. https://doi.org/10.4103/0976-9668.149074.

Brinkman, D., and Burnell, J. (2007). Identification, cloning and sequencing of two major venom proteins from the box jellyfish, *Chironex fleckeri. Toxicon*, 50, 850–860.

Brown, J. G. (2014). Jaw Function in *Smilodon fatalis*: A Reevaluation of the Canine Shear-Bite and a Proposal for a New Forelimb-Powered Class 1 Lever Model. *PLoS ONE*, 9(10): e107456. https://doi.org/10.1371/journal.pone.0107456.

Figueirido, B., Lautenschlager, S., Perex-Ramos, A., *et al.,* (2018). Distinct Predatory Behaviors in Scimitar- and Dirk-Toothed Sabertooth Cats. *Current Biology*, 28, 3260–3266. doi.org/10.1016/j.cub.2018.08.012.

Friedlander, L. T., Cullinan, M. P., Love, R. M. (2009). Dental stem cells and their potential role in apexogenesis and apexification. *International Endodontic J*, 42, 955–962.

Fritz, G. B., Schill, R. O., Pfannkuchen, M., Brummer, F. (2007.) The freshwater jellyfish Craspedacusta sowerbii Lankester, 1880

(Limnomedusa: Olindiidae) in Germany, with a brief note on its nomenclature. *J. Limnol.*, 66(1), 54–59.

Kaelin, C. B., Xu, X., Hong, L. Z., *et al.* (2012). Specifying and sustaining pigmentation patterns in domestic and wild cats. *Science* (New York, NY), 337(6101), 1536–1541. https://doi.org/10.1126/science.1220893.

Koussoulakou, D. S., Margaritis, L. H., Koussoulakou, S. L. (2009). A curriculum vitae of teeth: Evolution, generation, regeneration. *Int J Biol Sci*, 5(3), 226–243. doi: 10.7150/ dijbs.5.226.

Lou, X. (2015). Induced Pluripotent Stem Cells as a new Strategy for Osteogenesis and Bone Regeneration. *Stem Cell Rev Rep,* 11(4), 645–51.

Lyons, L. A. (2015). DNA mutations of the cat: the good, the bad and the ugly. *Journal of Feline Medicine and Surgery*, 17(3), 203–219. https://doi.org/10.1177/1098612X15571878.

Manzuette, A., Perea, D., Jones, W., *et al.* (2020). An extremely large saber-tooth cat skull from Uruguay (late Pleistocene–early Holocene, Dolores Formation): body size and paleobiological implications. *Alcheringa: Australasian J Palaeontology*, https://doi.org/10.1080/03115518.2019.1701080.

McHenry, C. R., Wroe, S., Clausen, P. D., Moreno, K., and Cunningham, E. (2007). Supermodeled sabercat, predatory behavior in *Smilodon fatalis* revealed by high-resolution 3D computer simulation. *Proceedings of the National Academy of Sciences of the United States of America*, 104(41), 16010–16015. https://doi.org/10.1073/pnas.0706086104.

Randau, M., Carbone, C., and Turvey, S. T. (2013). Canine evolution in sabretoothed carnivores: natural selection or sexual selection? *PloS one*, 8(8), e72868. https://doi.org/10.1371/journal.pone.0072868.

Simões, R., and Santos, A. R. (2017). Factors and molecules that could impact cell differentiation in the embryo generated by nuclear transfer. *Organogenesis,* 13, 156–178.

Slater, G. J., and Van Valkenburgh, B. (2016.) Long in the tooth: evolution of sabertooth cat cranial shape. *Paleobiology*, 34(3), 403–419. doi: https://doi.org/10.1666/07061.1.

Thesleff, I. (2014). Current understanding of the process of tooth formation: transfer from the laboratory to the clinic. *Australian Dent J*, 59(suppl. 1), 48–54. https://doi.org/10.1111adj.12102.

Walmsley, G. G., Ransom, R. C., Zielins, E. R., *et al.* (2016). Stem Cells in Bone Regeneration. *Stem Cell Reviews and Reports*, 12(5), 524–529. https://doi.org/10.1007/s12015-016-9665-5.

Zakrzewski, W., Dobrzyński, M., Szymonowicz, M. *et al.* (2019). Stem cells: past, present, and future. *Stem Cell Res Ther* 10, 68. https://doi.org/10.1186/s13287-019-1165-5.

Zheng, C., Chen, J., Liu, S. *et al.* (2019). Stem cell-based bone and dental regeneration: a view of microenvironmental modulation. *Int J Oral Sci* 11, 23. https://doi.org/10.1038/s41368-019-0060-3.

Chapter 28. Sabra

No references.

Chapter 29. Resurgence (Acid Rain/Air Pollution)

Grennfelt, P., Engleryd, A., Forsius, M., *et al.* (2020). Acid rain and air pollution: 50 years of progress in environmental science and policy. *Ambio*, 49, 849–864. https://doi.org/10.1007/s13280-019-01244-4.

Kumar, S. (2017). Acid RainThe Major Cause of Pollution: Its Causes, Effects. *Internat'l J Applied Chemistry*. 13(1), 53–58.

Manisalidis, I., Stavropoulou, E., Stavropoulos, A., Bezirtzoglou, E. (2020). Environmental and Health Impacts of Air Pollution: A Review. *Front. Public Health*. https://doi.org/10.3389/fpubh.2020.00014.

Chapter 30. An Old Alliance

No references.

Chapter 31. Prelude to War
No references.

Chapter 32. A Change of Heart (Asbestos)

Baumann, F., Buck, B. J., Metcalf, R. V., *et al.* (2015). The Presence of Asbestos in the Natural Environment is Likely Related to Mesothelioma in Young Individuals and Women from Southern Nevada. *J Thoracic Oncology,* 10(5), 731–737. https://doi.org/10.1097/JTO.0000000000000506.

Khurram, N., Khan, K., Saleem, M. U., *et al.* (2018). Effect of elevated temperatures on mortar with naturally occurring volcanic ash and its blend with electric arc furnace slag. *Adv Materials Sci & Engineering,* doi.org/1155/201/5324036.

Kusiorowski, R., Zaremba, T., Piotrowski, J. *et al.* (2013). Thermal decomposition of asbestos-containing materials. *J Therm Anal Calorim,* 113, 179–188. https://doi.org/10.1007/s10973-013-3038-y.

Pira, E., Donato, F., Maida, L., Discalzi, G. (2018). Exposure to asbestos: past, present and future. *J Thoracic Disease,* 10(Suppl 2), S237–S245. https://doi.org/10.21037/jtd.2017.10.126.

Chapter 33. The Getaway
No references.

Chapter 34. The Rules of War
No references.

Chapter 35. The First Wave
No references.

Chapter 36. A Surprise Encounter
No references.

Chapter 37. An End Run

Ducey, S. D., Cooper, J. S., Wadman, M. C. (2016). Case report: Bitten by a dragon. *Wilderness & Environmental Med*, 27, 291–293.

Maniscalco, K., and Edens, M. A. (2020). Human Bites. *StatPearls*. StatPearls Publishing.

Chapter 38. Moves and Countermoves

No references.

Chapter 39. Weary Refugees

No references.

Chapter 40. A Dominant Force

No references.

Chapter 41. Hidden Jewel

No references.

Epilogue

No references.

Appendix A. Altered Transformans

No references.

Appendix B. Animal Hybrids

No references.

Appendix C. Restoration of H'Aleth

No references.

Appendix D. Industrial Development

No references.

Appendix E. H'Ester's Lineage

Bonomi, M., Rochira, V., Pasquali, D., *et al.* (2017). Klinefelter syndrome (KS): genetics, clinical phenotype and hypogonadism. *J Endocrinological Investigation*, 40(2), 123–134. https://doi.org/10.1007/s40618-016-0541-6.

Bunnell, M. E., Wilkins-Haug, L., and Reiss, R. (2017). Should embryos with autosomal monosomy by preimplantation genetic testing for aneuploidy be transferred? Implications for embryo selection from a systematic literature review of autosomal monosomy survivors. *Prenatal Diagnosis*, 37(13), 1273–1280. https://doi.org/10.1002/pd.5185.

Culen, C., Ertl, D. A., Schubert, K., *et al.* (2017). Care of girls and women with Turner syndrome: beyond growth and hormones. *Endocrine Connections*, 6(4), R39–R51. doi: https://doi.org/10.1530/EC-17-0036.

Kanakis, G. A., and Nieschlag, E. (2018.) Klinefelter syndrome: more than hypogonadism. *Metabolism*, 86, 135–144. doi: 10.1016/j.metabol.2017.09.017.

Röpke, A., and Tüttelmann, F. (2017.) Mechanisms in Endocrinology: Aberrations of the X chromosome as cause of male infertility. *Eur J Endocrinol*, 177(5), R249–R259. doi: 10.1530/EJE-17-0246.

Skuse, D., Printzlau, F., Wolstencroft, J. (2018). Sex chromosome aneuploidies. *Handb Clin Neurol*, 147, 355–376. doi: 10.1016/B978-0-444-63233-3.00024-5.

Snyder, H. L., Curnow, K. J., Bhatt, S., and Bianchi, D. W. (2016). Follow-up of multiple aneuploidies and single monosomies detected by noninvasive prenatal testing: implications for management and counseling. *Prenatal Diagnosis*, 36(3), 203–209. https://doi.org/10.1002/pd.4778.

Tartaglia, N. R., Howell, S., Sutherland, A., *et al.* (2010). A review of trisomy X (47,XXX). *Orphanet J Rare Dis*, 11, 5, 8. doi: 10.1186/1750-1172-5-8.

Wigby, K., D'Epagnier, C., Howell, S., Reicks, *et al.* (2016). Expanding the phenotype of Triple X syndrome: A comparison of prenatal versus postnatal diagnosis. *Amer J Medical Genetics. Part A*, 170(11), 2870–2881. https://doi.org/10.1002/ajmg.a.37688.

Appendix F. Native Species

No references.

Appendix G. Cretaceous Predatory Dinosaurs

Hendrickx, C., Hartman , S. A., Mateus, O. (2015). An Overview of Non-Avian Theropod Discoveries and Classification. *Pal Arch's J Vertebrate Palaeontology*, 12, 1 (2015), 1–73.

Appendix H. Dragonidae.

Murphrey, M. B., Miao, J. H., Zito, P. M. (2019). Histology, Stratum Corneum. Stat Pearls [Internet]. Treasure Island (F: L) StatPearls Publishing: 2019–2019 Oct 30.

Stuart-Fox, D., Newton, E., and Clusella-Trullas, S. (2017). Thermal consequences of colour [sic] and near-infrared reflectance. *Philosophical transactions of the Royal Society of London. Series B, Biological sciences*, 372(1724), 20160345. https://doi.org/10.1098/rstb.2016.0345.

Wang, F., Zieman, A., Coulombe, P. A. (2016). Skin Keratins. *Methods Enzymol,* 568, 303–50.

Appendix I. Rivers and Lakes

No references.

Appendix J-1. In the Far North

Fiorillo, A. R., Kobayashi, Y., McCarthy, P. J., *et al.* (2019). Dinosaur ichnology and sedimentology of the Chignik Formation (Upper

Cretaceous), Aniakchak National Monument, southwestern Alaska; Further insights on habitat preferences of high-latitude hadrosaurs. *PloS ONE*, 14(10), e0223471. https://doi.org/10.1371/journal. pone.0223471.

Fiorillo, A. R., and Tykoski, R. S. (2014.) A Diminutive New Tyrannosaur from the Top of the World. *PLoS ONE*, 9(3), e91287. https://doi. org/10.1371/journal.pone.0091287.

Gangloff, R. A., Fiorillo, A. R., Norton, D. W., *et al.* (2005.) The first pachycephalosaurine (Dinosauria) from the Paleo-Arctic of Alaska and its paleogeographic implications. *J Paleontology*, 79(5), 997–1001. doi: https://doi.org/10.1666/0022-3360(2005)079[0997:TF PDFT]2.0.CO;2.

Godefroit, P., Golovneva, L., Shchepeto, S., *et al.* (2008.) The last polar dinosaurs: high diversity of latest Cretaceous arctic dinosaurs in Russia. *Naturwissenschaften,* doi: 10.1007/s00114-008-0499-0.

Appendix J-2. Gregor's Research Facility

Doocy, S., Daniels, A., Packer, C., *et al.* (2013). The human impact of earthquakes: a historical review of events 1980-2009 and systematic literature review. *PLoS currents, 5,* ecurrents.dis.67bd14fe457f1db0b 5433a8ee20fb833. https://doi.org/10.1371/currents.dis.67bd14fe45 7f1db0b5433a8ee20fb833.

Appendix K. Cassius Fortress

No references.

Appendix L. Erwina

No references.

Appendix M. Cast of Characters

No references.

Lightning Source UK Ltd.
Milton Keynes UK
UKHW040638201221
395966UK00001B/87

9 781646 634996